THE HAUNTING OF LAS LÁGRIMAS

THE HAUNTING OF LAS LÁGRIMAS

W. M. CLEESE

TITAN BOOKS

The Haunting of Las Lágrimas
Print edition ISBN: 9781789098334
E-book edition ISBN: 9781789098341

Published by Titan Books
A division of Titan Publishing Group Ltd.
144 Southwark Street, London SE1 0UP
www.titanbooks.com

First edition February 2022
10 9 8 7 6 5 4 3 2 1

A CIP catalogue record for this title is available from
the British Library.

Printed and bound by CPI Group (UK) Ltd, Croydon CR0 4YY

For Nicole

Note on the Text

The following narrative was written in October 1913 in the journal of Ursula McKinder (née Kelp). Now a forgotten figure, in the decade after the war Ursula was a widely respected gardener counting the likes of Sir Arthur William Hill, the director of Kew Gardens, among her circle.

Although the original journal has since been lost, while researching my book on the Malayan Emergency, I discovered a photostat of it in the papers of Ursula's daughter, Flores. This reproduction was most likely made in the 1950s in Singapore, where the family had relocated to avoid the bloodshed in Malay. Quite why Flores made a copy remains uncertain.

In preparing the journal for publication I was able to verify many elements of it: Ursula's passage to Argentina aboard the RMS Arlanza; her employment in Buenos Aires with the Houghton family and sudden resignation; her subsequent stay at the Hotel Bristol in Mar del Plata. I even uncovered a receipt for the latter, her accommodation coming to 336 pesos (settled by banker's draft). It is also evident that Ursula had travelled in the Pampas region. The contents of her grandfather's will were *confirmed by records held in the Cambridge offices of Cole, Cranley & White, solicitors.*

As for the disturbing events described at Las Lágrimas between 17 August and the first weeks of September 1913, I leave the reader to judge.

WMC, February 2022

The Hotel Bristol, Mar del Plata

EVERY NIGHT THE same thing happens.

I take supper in the hotel, insisting on a table in the centre of the restaurant, beneath the main chandelier, so that I am bathed in glittering light and surrounded by as many people as possible. Never did the hum of idle chatter reassure as much. I sit with my back to the windows to avoid the inky blackness of the ocean beyond. I eat only the day's catch or salad, to rest easily on my digestion, and finish with a generous glass of port wine – not to fortify but to drug me.

Then to my room where I draw a bath. The water is fiercely hot here and afterward I am left broiled and drowsy. I put on my nightclothes and sink into the sheets. They are so soft, especially with the memory of sleeping in the wilds of the Pampas still fresh in my mind. Out there, in those vast empty grasslands, the ground was hard and sodden; I had nothing but a poncho to protect me from the howling cold as I huddled, hungry and alone, in the grip of fear. Every light in the bedroom I keep switched on, something I would have once found a nonsense. Now I tremble at shadows – and what they may conceal. Finally, I swallow a sedative and close my eyes.

At first it feels as if tonight I shall be successful. My limbs relax, my breathing deepens. I slide into my private darkness and begin to drift, dimly aware of the sounds outside the window… The crash and hiss of waves against the beach, the whip of the wind through palm trees…

Then all at once I am at Las Lágrimas again – and I awaken. Thrashing and gasping and begging for deliverance.

The remembrance of that dreadful place has been with me all day: when I rise from another sleepless night, when blearily I eat breakfast, when I stroll through town. Stroll? I march, practically at a dash, around Mar del Plata, racing along the rambla to where the coastline is undeveloped, then up to the cliffs before winding back my path through grids of pretty, Alpine-fashion houses to the seafront. There have been occasions when twice I have followed this circuit. The locals are beginning to recognize me: the demented *inglesa* with her darkly ringed eyes and trailing red hair. I walk a dozen hours of the day in the vain hope I will exhaust myself sufficiently for bedtime.

I must admit that in the daylight and bracing sea air, with an abundance of people around me, I am something of my old self – albeit the numerous pleasure gardens I pass with their thoughtful planting patterns and eye-catching symmetries, gardens just now coming into bloom, gardens where once I could have idled away many happy hours, no longer captivate my interest.

Mar del Plata is a modern seaside resort growing, as high-season approaches, more clement and populated by the day. Electric-lights illuminate the streets. My hotel, the Bristol, is the best in town, plush and secure behind lock and door aplenty. Rationally, I am assured that no harm can come to me here. Yet when the memory of Las Lágrimas forces itself upon me, the terror of recent events is as immediate and blood-chilling as it was during those last days at the house. My heart hammers with such fierceness that I know I shall be awake again to witness the dawn. It has been no different these past two weeks. I came to Mar del Plata to exorcise these memories, not fall deeper under their spell.

I must do something!

On previous nights I have paced my room in a fever of agitation before, inevitably, I take myself downstairs, craving the society of others. I frequent the lobby until the small hours when all the other guests have retired and my only company is the night staff. The concierge must think I am sweet on him or, I daresay, deranged. As a young Englishwoman staying here with neither family nor husband nor any chaperone, I have raised eyebrows enough already.

I wish Grandfather were with me; never have I missed him so much. I do not need his presence, however, to be confident of what he would advise. His study was lined with the journals he had kept: leather-bound logbooks that had seen half the world, their pages distended with the salt of sea voyages and the steam of jungles more distant than ever I could imagine. Every hardship he suffered, every tropical fever and mortal threat – all those adventures that thrilled me as a child – laid to rest by writing them down. 'Ink on paper,' he would say, 'soothes the soul.'

I hear his voice now: *Write, Ursula! Write it all down, in every last detail, and it will trouble you no further.*

Can it possibly be that simple?

When I fled the house at Las Lágrimas I took only the barest of essentials. The rest – my clothes, books, gardening tools, nearly all the worldly possessions I had brought with me from Britain to Argentina – I had to abandon. I try not to think whether unseen fingers have since picked through my belongings. One thing I did slip into my pocket before I took flight was my fountain-pen, a gift from Grandfather for my twenty-first birthday, that I refused to leave. There is a stationer in the arcade by the hotel. Late this afternoon, as I returned from my long walk, I went in on the spur of the moment and purchased a pot of ink and a stiff-backed notebook bound in cloth, the self-same book I am writing these words in. I do not want to spend another night lingering in the lobby or shivering in my room purblinded by an excess of lights. I do not want a future where the thought of bed brings nothing but trepidation. I have never been prone to the nervous conditions that afflict many of my sex, like my sisters; *damn it!* say I, if I will start now. I have always understood that I am different, my temperament stronger. Indeed, I feel more possessed of myself simply in the knowledge of what I am about to undertake. I must summon all my bravery again, as I did on that final night in Las Lágrimas.

And so I shall describe the happenings of these past weeks,

setting them down as Grandfather would urge me to: in impeccable detail, as relentlessly truthful as if I were standing in court – though I am not sure all will make sense. Where the specifics are lost to me (I think, in particular, of the many ephemeral conversations) I shall capture their essence if not exactitude. I state this plainly, in advance, in order that the reader be confident that what follows is as accurate and faithful account as possible. When I am done, I pray I shall find peace anew. That it will be granted to me to lie on my crumpled bed, turn out the light-switches, and sleep. Dreamless, uninvaded sleep.

This, then, is the story I must tell. I must take myself back to Las Lágrimas. God preserve me, I must live it all once more.

A Stranger in the Garden

IT WAS THE twelfth day of August, on a dismal, chilly morning – late-winter in the southern hemisphere – when the stranger returned. Although the hour was early I was already at work in the garden, my woollen overcoat damp from the air, the tips of my fingers red and numb. To be clear, the garden was not mine. It belonged to the Houghtons, associates of my solicitor, who had lived in Buenos Aires a decade since. Their house was one of the many mansions in the Belgrano district of the city, a grand property obscured by high brick walls and mature trees, they being a rather impressive collection of jacarandas, la tipas and Japanese maples, all leafless at that time of year.

I recognized the stranger at once not least from his height. He was tall (especially for an Argentine), with a gaunt but gentlemanly face, and wearing a pigskin coat that hung down to his boots. On his head was a bowler hat. He had visited several days before and spoken with Señor Gil, our Head Gardener. It had been a brief exchange and Gil had sent the stranger packing with his usual charm. We were a garden staff of four, with myself as the most recent addition, and there was much speculation as to who this visitor might be. Gil had taken great pleasure in being tight-lipped on the subject, implying the stranger heralded important news, but offering no further insight.

The previous encounter between the two had been by appointment in Gil's hut, a building he insisted we refer to as his 'office'. That morning, however, the stranger had let himself into the garden and ambushed Gil near the iris and lupin borders. By chance I was passing nearby, my hands cupped together holding a mouse's nest. Gil often gave me jobs that brought me into contact with insects and rodents. His hope was that I would scream like an infant, but Grandfather had taught me to fear nothing, certainly not creatures smaller than my thumb! I had been clearing out pots when I found the mouse. Gil had a custom of stamping on the poor mites, so I wanted to move her to a corner of the garden where she might live unmolested. I was thus bound when I caught Gil and the stranger in conference. I was not popular amongst the staff. Any snippet of gossip I might come by would improve my standing, so I concealed myself and listened. I must confess to a certain thrill at eavesdropping, one of my uglier habits, and something Mother had often chided me for.

Gil had a spectrum of tones from the blatantly obsequious when he spoke to the Houghtons to his toad-voice for those beneath him. Presently, his parlance was at its most amphibian. '… as I told you last time, I have no interest in your offer. Now leave. I've a busy morning.'

'Imagine the opportunity,' was the stranger's reply. He had

an odd voice, commanding with a hint of the cocksure, yet a fragile quality also. 'Not a garden but an estancia. An entire estate for you to oversee.'

'Even if it weren't for the rest of it, who would want to live out there?'

'With the new rail-line to Tandil, you can make the journey in two days.'

'I don't care for trains.'

'Perhaps it's the salary?'

'Nor do I care for your money.'

My ears pricked up. Here was a detail that would startle the others when shared. Few men were more avaricious than Eduardo Gil.

'My employer is prepared to double his offer,' said the stranger.

'I have nothing else to say. I do not want your job, and I doubt you'll find any man willing to take it.'

I slipped away, my mind racing. Here was an opportunity to prove what I was capable of, to work as a proper gardener rather than a pair of 'extra hands' tolerated only because of my connection to Mr Houghton.

I hurried to the wall that bounded Calle Miñones, lowered the mouse and watched her scurry off. 'Good luck,' I wished us both. Then I straightened my overcoat and arranged my hair more tidily beneath my hat. I could never be troubled to do much with it, another misdemeanour that earned me a daily rebuke from Gil. The Houghtons' garden was designed along a grid of paths and hedges (it was, to my tastes, a little too formal). I skipped through them, positioning myself at an intersection where I knew the stranger must pass on his exit, and waited for him, pinching my cheeks to bring some colour to them. I breathed in damp lungfuls of air to steady my excitement – there was a smell of turned earth and leaf mould – and prepared what I would say. As the crunch of his footsteps on the gravel approached, I stepped out, moving deliberately so as not to waylay him. His face was a picture of annoyance and dejection.

'Señor,' I said, 'my name is Ursula Kelp. I overheard your conversation with Gil and understand you are looking to employ a gardener.'

'A Head Gardener, at an estancia in the Pampas, where I am the manager. Do you know of someone favourable?'

'I myself would like to apply for the position.'

He fixed me with his eyes and I feared he would laugh – but for a long while he said nothing. There was a hint of violet to his irises; the slightest bend to his nose. I did not shirk his gaze, Grandfather would expect nothing less, though as the seconds ticked past I had to tuck a strand of hair behind my ear by way of maintaining my composure. The stranger did not relent, as if challenging me to look away, as if he were a soul-reader. Now, of course, I wish I had – but at that moment, I had not the least intuition of the consequences.

Finally, and in a grave tone, he said, 'It is no job for a woman.'

'I have gardened all my life,' I answered him, bristling, 'and am versed in horticulture as well as any man.'

'Where are you from, Señorita? Your Spanish is good but you're no Argentine. Nor is your complexion.'

'From Britain.'

'English?'

He seemed rather emphatic on the point, which I thought a tad queer. I replied yes, from the good county of Cambridgeshire, adding, 'I can provide letters of reference should you require.'

His eyes were still set on mine, his whole bearing inanimate except for a scratching of his wrist as if some irritation troubled him there. I sensed a struggle – a calculation – going on behind his stare. 'Would you have the kindness to show me your hands?'

I have always found my hands a little on the inelegant side, not unattractive, you understand, but better buried in the soil than resting idly on my lap, manicured and adorned like my sisters'. I hesitated, then presented them, unsure what he was looking for, concerned they were either too clean or too grubby for his intended purpose.

'Do you mind?' he asked and, before I could reply, he had seized my hands, rubbing the skin to test how calloused it was. He rolled them over so my palms were facing downward and assessed the knuckles. For an alarming instant, I was convinced he planned to raise my fingers to his nose and sniff them. There was something rough in his manner as though he were examining the fetlocks of a nag at market. I freed myself from his grasp.

When next he spoke his voice was not unkind. 'Do you know Café Tortoni's?'

'Of course,' I replied.

'Meet me there this Thursday evening, six o'clock sharp.

If I haven't found someone to fill the position, you might be in luck.'

'My hours here are until six.'

'Then you will be late and I will be gone.'

With that he tipped his bowler, and strode away.

The House of Tears

FOR THE NEXT two days I could do nothing but speculate about this post. Working in the garden – digging, winter-pruning the salix and buddleia, scalding pots – my thoughts roved endlessly to it.

I had been at the Belgrano garden for six months already; I doubted I could suffer many more. The work itself was unfulfilling and made little use of my talents, and though I had discreetly looked for an alternative position, none was to be found. I was painfully lonely and found no respite in the staff that to a man – and in the garden they were all men – treated me with suspicion: because I was British; because I lived in a room in the main house, not the gardeners' block or attic; because Mrs Houghton treated me more as an equal than an employee. I am sure they thought me as a spy set amidst them. The Houghtons themselves were decent enough if not 'our kind of people', as Grandfather would say, being too interested in the price of everything and the value of nothing. Bernadice, the eldest daughter, was forever harping on over whether I had a beau back home and when I was going to get engaged; the word 'Suffrage', let alone the concept, was as profane to her as it was to my sisters. Even the garden was an object of mere show: an ornament to demonstrate their wealth, they having no true appreciation of the flowers, shrubs and trees per se. 'How can you know so much about plants?' Mrs Houghton would exclaim to me in marvel and what I thought was slight rebuke, the same rebuke I knew too well from my parents who had only ire at my wanting to garden as a profession. The one advantage of the Houghtons was they were often out of town.

If Grandfather were still alive, I would have written to him every week, unpacking my heart, and found solace in those letters. Instead, once a month I sent a brief epistle to my family, full of fallacies of how wonderful I was finding Argentina. I received no replies. To work on an estancia, where the gardens must surely be as expansive as they were grand, and achieve such through my own merits was as a dream come true. To be candid, the position of 'Head Gardener' also appealed to the vainer side of my character.

Thursday afternoon arrived. I could have asked Gil to finish early or gone to him feigning some womanly complaint but I feared he might thwart my plans. He rarely passed on an opportunity for vindictiveness toward me, especially given the Houghtons were away at the time. In the end, I simply took myself from the garden when no one was about, returned to my room, washed, changed my outfit and left bold as anything through the front door.

Dusk was already settling upon the city, the sky mauve and misty, the streetlamps fuzzing orbs. As I headed to the tram-stop the air chilled my throat. Many things had astounded me about Buenos Aires, not least how wealthy, modern and Europeanized it was. More unanticipated, however, was the weather. It had been hot and fine when first I landed but, as the year turned, the city was gripped by days of low, murky clouds. Fogs were not an irregular occurrence. These had nothing on a London particular, but were sufficient to veil the streets and cast one down. The Argentine capital certainly fell short of its name, Buenos Aires: *good airs*. I took the Number 35 tram to Avenida de Mayo and walked the final blocks through swirling vapour. It was a relief to reach the lights of Tortoni's.

Inside, chandeliers reflected off mahogany walls and smoked-glass panels, giving everything a welcoming, amber-coloured glow. It was crowded, and I felt immediately enlivened by so many people and their convivial chatter, not to mention the sweet, buttery aroma of the patisserie. The café had a reputation for the best cake, coffee and chocolate in the city – and the most condescending staff. The *maître d'hôtel* sniffed as I approached him.

'We are most busy, Señorita. You will have to wait.'

'I am meeting someone. A gentleman acquaintance. He said he would have us a table.'

'His name?'

I went to reply and it occurred to me that I had been so keyed-up by the prospect of a Head Gardenership that I had never enquired of the stranger's name nor the estancia he represented.

I foundered, at a loss as how to respond. The *maître d'* made no attempt to conceal his irritation and was about to offer some reprimand when there was a touch on my shoulder.

'*Buenas tardes*, Señorita Kelp.'

The stranger had already taken a table and, upon seeing my entrance, emerged from the depths of the café to rescue me. His countenance was still gaunt but his face was more handsome than I remembered, a rather long, Spanish face, and very smoothly shaven. I studied it until he caught me, and quickly averted my eyes. He had thick hair of the darkest hue, swept back off a high forehead.

'I'm sorry,' I said, regaining my composure. 'I forgot to ask your name.'

'Juan-Pérez Moyano.'

I offered him my hand. 'Pleased to make your acquaintance, Señor Moyano.'

He chuckled at my formality and we shook. His skin felt curiously soft to mine, as though slathering his palms in ointment was for him a daily ritual. He guided me away from the *maître d'* and in the direction of his table. 'Have you come from a funeral?' he asked with a hint of mischief.

I had worn a black, unembroidered dress and hat with no jewellery, my intention to look as serious-minded as possible. All the other women in the café were gaily attired, as bright and colourful as zinnias, and I admit to a prickle of embarrassment – one I was determined not to show. 'You should not joke about such things,' I replied tartly. I sat down before he had the chance to pull back the chair for me.

Without enquiring as to what I would prefer, he signalled

a waiter and ordered two hot chocolates. Whilst we waited for them, he began some small talk, but I wanted to know whether I had made a wasted trip or not.

'Did you find a gardener?' I asked.

'There was interest.'

'But my being offered the position is still a possibility?'

'A possibility. Yes.'

'Then you must look at these.'

I handed him my references. Moyano took them from their envelopes and read carefully before his face creased into a frown. 'These are encouraging, Señorita, but who, may I ask, is this "Deborah" Kelp?'

'Deborah was the name I grew up with. Now I prefer Ursula. It's what my grandfather called me.'

'And why did he do that?'

'Señor Moyano, are we here to discuss my name or my suitability for employment?'

He returned my references and looked at me deeply. 'Have you heard of the Estancia Las Lágrimas?'

'Should I have?'

'It was once the grandest house in all the Pampas. An estate of more than seven thousand hectares. It is where I am the general manager.'

'It doesn't sound very jolly.' Las Lágrimas, Spanish for 'the House of Tears'.

Moyano allowed me a tolerant, little smile. 'It's said that when the founder first laid eyes on that part of the Pampas he was moved to weeping by the beauty of the place. Once the house was built, people would visit from all over. It was famous for its parties, for its hunts and Christmas balls. And not least its garden. Then the owner decided to leave.'

'May I ask why?'

The waiter arrived with our order. I took a sip of chocolate. It was deliciously thick, but after a second mouthful tasted overpowering. I had not eaten since lunch, and by the time I drained the cup I experienced a certain queasiness.

'He took to God,' was Moyano's reply. 'And devoted the rest of his life to prayer. For thirty years the estancia has lain empty. Now my employer – Don Paquito Agramonte, son of the last owner, grandson of the founder – has inherited the property. He wants to return it to its former glory and live there with his family. He is keen to restore the garden to the one he remembers as a child.'

'How is it now?'

'As any garden that's been abandoned for so long: something of a wilderness. It will need work! The garden was planted in the English-style, which is why you might be an ideal candidate.'

'Are you offering me the post?'

'If I were, you do understand the remoteness of the Pampas? There are no nearby towns, nor even other houses. There are few of the modern conveniences, no telephone, only part of the property has electricity. You can get mail, but one never knows when it arrives.'

'I should be glad for the opportunity.'

He spoke his next words with feeling, almost as if hoping to dissuade me. 'I fear it might demand too much for the female constitution. It gets very lonely.'

I gave a dismissive snort and, thinking of my life at the Houghtons, replied, 'I have a tolerance for it, Señor.'

'You would have a team of gardeners working beneath you, men who may not like taking orders from a woman. They will be labourers, not horticulturists.'

'So you *are* offering me the job?'

He leant forward, not quite touching my leg beneath the table but close enough that I was aware of the movement against my dress. 'There's one thing I'm curious about, Señorita. How did you come to be in my country?'

I took care in answering for it was a matter I had no desire to discuss. 'Because of my grandfather.'

'He's with you? He will not be able to accompany you to the estancia.'

'He died. Last year.'

'Ah. I am sorry to hear that, Señorita.'

'His wish was that I make gardening my profession.'

'Surely you could have found somewhere closer to home.'

'I wanted to improve my Spanish.'

'There must be more to it than that.'

'To be entirely honest,' I replied by way of distraction, 'I was fed up with the British. We're everywhere: Africa, Asia, the Antipodes. As a nation we are drawn to exotic places; it's stifling. So to Argentina I came. Little did I know.'

Along with my dismay at the weather, another revelation had been the sheer number of British, working in the meat industry or building the railways. We even had our own daily newspaper, the *Buenos Aires Herald*. I should have foreseen it by the fact that people like the Houghtons lived here; they were beef money.

Moyano found my explanation amusing. 'Well, Señorita, you'll certainly find none of your countrymen in the Pampas.'

'Then it would seem I am a perfect match.'

'In which case it is my turn to be honest with you. I have asked every gardener in Buenos Aires to take the position at Las Lágrimas. I even took the ferry across to Montevideo to find a man there. Everyone refused me. Which is why the job is yours, should you so like it.'

It was not the most auspicious of starts, but barely twenty minutes after arriving at Tortoni's I found my signature on a contract of employment and my person outside on the pavement, lost in the fog again. If I could have overlooked my excitement, or the relish with which I would communicate to my family this promotion, I may have had pause to ask why such a prestigious job had been offered to me with such ease. Or, more importantly, why every other candidate had thought better to reject it.

Maldita *(adj.)*

IT WAS IN an altogether more aggrieved mood that I reached Constitución station the next morning. I was travelling with every item that had made its way with me to Argentina, namely three suitcases of clothes, two hatboxes, a vanity case, a chest of gardening implements and Grandfather's trunk, heavy with books and sundries. The station was cavernous and gleaming (the latest extension had been completed the year before), and reminded me of St Pancras in London. It was filled with a sense of bustle and languid, Latin urgency, the air sweetened with smuts. I found my platform, number 5, supervised the loading of my luggage, then took my seat. Señor Moyano, courtesy of Don Paquito, had provided for a first-class carriage. I settled down and waited to leave, still fuming at what had transpired earlier that day.

Moyano expected me to start forthwith at Las Lágrimas. Don Paquito and his family planned to take up residence in September. A firm of builders had been renovating the house but the garden remained 'a wild beast', as Moyano described it. He wanted a semblance of respectability to the exterior before the Don arrived. We agreed I would take the Friday morning train to arrive at the estancia by Saturday and start work on Monday, 18th August. After leaving Café Tortoni's, I returned to Belgrano and, with scarcely concealed triumph, went to see Gil in his hut. A meagre fire was burning in the stove. He told me to take a seat; I refused him.

'I wish to hand in my notice,' I declared.

'To leave when?'

'Immediately.'

Gil let out a long, condescending sigh. 'Your contract stipulates a month's forewarning, Señorita.'

Whilst Mr Houghton felt it unnecessary for me to sign a contract, Gil had been adamant, saying that exceptions could not be made otherwise it would foster resentments amongst the staff.

I decided to make plain my mind. 'Señor Gil, please, it is winter, the garden far from busy. I am sure no one, least of all you, will mourn my departure. Why not simply release me?'

'A contract is a contract, Señorita Kelp.'

'You can be reasonable, Señor, or I can speak with the master of the household.'

'You could. But you know, as well do I, that the family is away for another week. I thought you wanted to leave at once.'

'I do.'

'Have you found a new position? Or are you returning to a life of idleness?'

'You can't refuse me.'

He sucked on his teeth, a habit I found disgusting. 'Your

departure wouldn't have anything to do with Moyano sniffing roundabout?'

I felt a rush of loyalty to my new employer, equally I wanted to give away nothing. 'Who?'

Gil was not taken in by my subterfuge. This time he chuckled to himself. 'That wastrel asked every gardener from here to Uruguay to take the job. Not a single man wanted it. If you understood anything of my country, Señorita, you would be of the same mind.' Gil pondered the matter. 'If you're heading to Las Lágrimas, your notice is duly received. Good night.'

I cannot say I was sad to leave the Houghtons, for they had always reminded me too much of my own family for comfort. All the same, the next morning I left a note of farewell and genuine thanks, then went to see Gil for the final time to hand back my door-key and collect my wages for the month past. None were forthcoming.

'You are in breach of your contract,' he said, waving the agreement in my face.

'But the work I did!'

'A consideration you should have made before swanning off to the Pampas.'

Such was my zeal to start afresh, I had rather overlooked this complication, and though Gil may have been strictly correct, I nevertheless felt the hand of unfairness. 'I shall speak to Mr Houghton about this.'

'And he'll show you the exact same clause. "Should an employee leave without due notice, those earnings outstanding will be forfeit".'

Waiting for my train to depart I fought back hot, rising

tears. It was not the money, you understand, it was the principle of the matter, one that summoned memories I had tried my utmost to bury, for I felt anew the injustice of being denied what was rightfully mine through the malice of others. For several moments I was transported to the office of a Cambridge solicitor as Grandfather's will was read, my heart racing violently, until at last I made every effort to calm myself for I had no wish to make a show in public.

As it happened, only two other passengers joined me in my compartment. The first was a man of the type my sisters would describe as 'eligible'. He gave a polite nod before applying himself to his newspaper and, thankfully, paid me no heed for the rest of the journey. Shortly after, a woman of Mother's age entered. She was well outfitted with rough, veiny hands that wore fine diamonds. By her side was a cat-basket, though I saw no feline face.

At a quarter to ten, the guard blew his whistle and we began to chug away. The mistiness of the past few days had vanished overnight, the sky being a hydrangea-blue, the sun watery yet bright. The train passed through the centre of Buenos Aires, then less salubrious districts where shacks huddled either side of the line and the air had an intense, gamey tang; the skyline was dominated by the chimneys of meat-processing factories. Soon after, urban landscape surrendered to the grasslands that mark the city's limit. This was the first fringe of the Pampas. Of the region I knew little other than its vastness. It stretched from the Atlantic in the east to the foothills of the Andes in the west. The Rio Negro, the boundary between the Pampas and the land of Patagonia, was a thousand miles to the south. And in between nothing but flat, empty plains and the occasional estancia. On my map of Argentina it was drawn as a green enigma, marked with few towns and no features. The railway had braved this territory only in the last five years.

Gazing out of the window, the sun flashing into my eyes, I forgot Gil and those other, hurtful memories and instead experienced a stirring of adventure. It was not by coincidence I had come to South America: as a young man, Grandfather had travelled the continent, and to be here myself offered the solace of some connection to him, however tenuous. Perhaps, some day in the future, I would follow the route he had taken and experience in person those wonders he had related to me.

Many hours lay ahead to my station. Although the grasslands may have held the promise of adventure, after a time they did become rather monotonous. I took out my novel, *Nostromo* by Joseph Conrad (a favourite of Grandfather's, which I was dutifully ploughing through), and read. At the town of Vilela, the man opposite folded up his newspaper and disembarked. No new passenger joined the carriage. At Las Flores, I had to change trains for the branch-line to Tandil. By now it was lunchtime, and I bought some empanadas to eat whilst I waited for the connecting service. My train arrived late, and I again found myself a companion of the woman I had travelled with from Buenos Aires, the one with the cat-box. We passed a few pleasantries during which she introduced herself as Doña Ybarra. Once the train had left the station, I returned to the Conrad before feeling tired. I closed my book and napped until, some indeterminate period after, I was woken by a jolt.

The train had come to a standstill, not at a station but on a siding in the middle of nowhere. A sea of grass, rippling and swaying in the breeze, stretched as far as the eye could see out of both windows.

'Do not be troubled,' said Doña Ybarra, observing my concern. 'Delays are what we live with in the Pampas.'

'I'm meeting someone,' I replied, 'and afterward have a long journey ahead. I do not want to be late.'

'If they know the trains, they will know to wait.'

Whereupon we sat in silence except for the steady wheeze of the locomotive. The minutes passed and became a quarter, then half of an hour. I picked up *Nostromo*, but after a few pages realized I had taken in nothing of what I had read. Outside, the day began a slow but perceptible fading.

I stood up, rapping my knuckles against the window. 'How I hate dawdling,' I let forth in English. Doña Ybarra started at this outburst in a language alien to her. I apologized and translated my words.

'We'll be on our way soon,' she soothed. She was feeding her animal, dangling morsels of meat through an opening in the basket's top. 'It is only a single track ahead. Most likely we're being held for the up-train to Las Flores.'

'I hope so,' I replied, peering into her basket. I expected to see a wide-eyed, whiskered countenance. Instead, a lizard blankly returned my gaze.

'My iguana,' explained the woman.

What does one say in reply to a reptile? 'I'm sure they make loving pets.'

As if to confirm my statement she removed the beast, her

rings flashing, and held it to her cheek, making a cooing sound. 'Where are you from, Señorita?' she asked, replacing the creature in its basket.

'Britain.'

'Your Spanish is excellent.'

'My grandfather taught me. He had travelled across all the Americas.'

'And what brings you to these parts?'

'I have been offered a position, at an estancia.'

'Let me see,' she replied, animated by the prospect of a guessing-game. 'A housekeeper?'

I shook my head.

'Of course not. You are far too educated. Governess?'

'Head Gardener,' I answered, liking how it sounded for in those two words were encapsulated all my ambition and love of horticulture.

Doña Ybarra puckered her lips. 'A rather unusual choice for a lady. Which estancia?'

'Las Lágrimas.'

Her expression became more complex, her disapproval combining with dismay. 'Why would you want to go to that place? It has been deserted for years.'

'You know of it?'

'My husband and I, when we were young and recently married, were often invited there. Such lavish parties! The food and drink, the dancing through the night.' She recollected this without a flicker of enthusiasm. 'But I never liked Don Guido, the owner. You couldn't refuse his invitation, yet I never knew one more godless.'

It was a description that seemed not to tally with Moyano's. 'We are talking of the Agramonte family?' I asked.

'Guido Agramonte, yes. A wild, profane and godless man.'

'His son, Don Paquito, has taken possession of the estate, and wishes to restore it.'

'Then he is either very brave. Or a fool.'

'Why do you say these things?'

'Has no one told you about Las Lágrimas?'

'It would appear not.'

'The estancia is notorious in these parts.' She phrased her next words with care. 'It is *maldita*.'

As already noted, my Spanish is most proficient – albeit I am not wholly fluent. I still come across words I am unfamiliar with and, to that end, always keep my Tauchnitz* at hand. I flicked through the pages until I found *maldita*. It was an adjective, meaning 'cursed', and not the kind of poorly informed, heathen belief I would expect in a country as modern as Argentina. 'Doña Ybarra, you will forgive me, but my grandfather, when travelling in Peru, was put under a curse, yet little ill-fortune ever befell him. He was healthy and happy to the end, and passed away peacefully in his own bed.'

'Do not think me some superstitious old woman, Señorita. The curse of Las Lágrimas is as real as this carriage. As real as you or me. Why do you think no one has dared live there

---

* The most commonly used English–Spanish dictionary of the day. I found a well-thumbed pocket edition in the same box as the photostat of Ursula's journal, along with various other items (letters, photos, bills, etc.) from her time in South America.

for decades? You would be unwise to take it lightly. They say the dead walk the grounds of the estate.'

I was at a loss how to reply, being, at best, agnostic on such matters. I thought back to Grandfather's final day. He had died in the spring, gently squeezing my hand as I sat by his bedside. The scent of quince blossom floated in through the casement. And though I may have feared for myself and what the future might bring, from that dear, old man I felt a great peace as his grip weakened and he left me. In my naïvety, I could not imagine why the dead would wish to return.

At that moment, there was a whistle-shriek and, on the main track, a train trundled by: window after window of intermittent faces and vacant seats. As soon as it had passed, our own carriage jerked forward. 'We're on the move again,' I observed, bringing our conversation to a close. I picked up my novel and made an emphatic show of reading.

We did not exchange another word until we reached Miranda, the stop before mine. As Doña Ybarra gathered up her lizard, I bade a cheery farewell. She replied in kind and was on the point of leaving the compartment when she grasped me.

'I know you think me a dolt – but please reconsider, Señorita. Do not go to Las Lágrimas. Take the train back to Buenos Aires. Go back home to England.'

Rivacoba Makes Arrangements

THE SUN WAS beginning to set by the time the train pulled into Chapaledfú station, the sky streaked with magnolia-pink cloud. The platform was deserted and unwelcoming. Moyano, who had returned to the Pampas the same night as our interview, promised someone would be waiting for me.

'How will I recognize him?' I had asked.

'I think rather, Señorita, he will recognize you.'

As I struggled to unload my luggage, I heard a baritone voice behind me. 'Señorita Kelp, from England?'

I turned to face a gaucho of singular appearance, robust, unshaven and dressed in traditional costume: bolero hat, a damson-coloured poncho, pantaloons beneath fur *chaparejos* and boots of colt-hide; his spurs were fearsome. Later, I learnt that he was more than a simple gaucho, rather he was a *baqueano*, the name by which the guides of the Pampas call themselves, men whose endurance and topographical knowledge of the region is formidable. 'I am Rivacoba,' he growled. 'You are late.'

It was not quite the greeting I had imagined, and I found

myself replying in kind: 'Blame the Southern Railway Company, not me.'

'We cannot leave tonight.'

'Surely we can start out?'

'Look at the sun. Within the hour it will be blacker than pitch. What would be the point? I have made arrangements.'

Chapaledfú was an inconsequential farming town. If the purpose of the railway line was to advance the modern world it had so far fallen short; indeed my experience of the place was of travelling backward in time to the middle of the previous century. The town consisted of a flagstoned plaza from which led a few unpaved roads, some houses (a dozen or so of brick, the rest in timber), two or three shops, an abattoir and a smattering of agricultural buildings. There was no hotel. Instead, Rivacoba's 'arrangements' meant boarding with the station-master and his wife. They had a little cottage that adjoined the railway platform, cramped but cosy enough. To my shame, the station-master's blind mother was ejected from her room so I could sleep there. There was no sign of children. Before Rivacoba left me for the night, to lodge who knows where, he informed me of another misdemeanour: 'You have too many things.' I was handed a pair of panniers and a small trunk. 'Pack what you need in these.' I insisted that, actually, I needed everything I had brought, but was met with a gruff, unyielding response.

So it was that I spent the first hour of my stay in Chapaledfú, reducing my luggage to those items of most immediate use. My gardening clothes I must have, whilst I restricted myself to two changes for the evening; for everything else

I took my trowel, secateurs, sketchpad and, along with *Nostromo*, a small bundle of books that I deemed essential: W. Robinson's excellent volume on country-house landscapes, *Garden Design* by Madeline Ayer and a couple by my heroine, Gertrude Jekyll.

Supper was a hearty beef stew served with baked rice and a cup of red wine. Afterward, I sat by the fireplace with the old, blind mother and listened to her rambling stories, for it was her wish to impart the history of the land to which I had arrived. The wind had picked up and buffeted the cottage, causing the flames to shudder. I was glad Rivacoba insisted we not set out. The old woman spoke of the Desert Campaigns of Governor de Rosas and the native Mapuche Indians his men had massacred in order that civilization be brought to the Pampas. In turn, this had given rise to the great estancias where she found employ as a younger woman. All this was recounted with immense pride. I enquired whether she knew of Las Lágrimas. I noticed the station-master and his wife exchange a look, but the old woman claimed never to have heard of the place.

'What colour is your hair, child?' she asked later. 'They tell me the English have locks the colour of straw.'

'Some do, but mine is red.'

'Red!' This was a marvel to her; she wanted to touch it.

'Mother,' exclaimed the station-master. 'Do not trouble our guest.'

'It's no bother,' I replied, and I let her comb her gnarled fingers through my hair.

'Red as of blood?' she asked. 'Or pimientos?'

'No. Red, and gold and orange, like the leaves in autumn, my grandfather used to say.'

This description seemed to satisfy her, and after I retired to bed I was sure I could hear the old woman by the dying fire whispering to herself *like the leaves in autumn. Leaves in autumn...*

Across the Pampas

THE SUNSHINE THAT had witnessed my journey from Buenos Aires was no more when I woke the next morning. In its place low, misty clouds, the air so dank one felt it in one's joints. We set out for Las Lágrimas first thing. Even as I made sure of my breakfast, Rivacoba was knocking at the cottage door. He carried out the belongings that I had condensed into the panniers and trunk.

'What of the rest of my things?' I asked.

'They will follow.'

His response did not inspire my confidence and I wondered if I would see them again. I bade farewell to the station-master and his wife, thanking them for their hospitality and discreetly passed the former a note for five pesos, which embarrassed and pleased him in equal measure. To his blind mother I gave a small lock of my hair that earlier I had snipped off.

'May God and the Virgin protect you out there,' she said in thanks.

Rivacoba was waiting with three horses: one each for us

to ride and a third, a stocky pony, which was already loaded with my luggage. My mount was a walnut-coloured mare of about fourteen hands. I took the reins and heaved myself up on to her, not side-saddle but with my legs either side of her flanks, the way Grandfather had taught me, and which found Rivacoba's approval. The station-master waved us off. We took the horses at a walk through Chapaledfú. Few of its denizens had yet to rise. In the grey light, the place had a drear quality to it, as of a town in mourning. Perhaps in summer it was full of life and gaiety, but that August morning I was glad to be leaving. Beyond the last buildings were a score of fields, marked by fence posts, the black earth ploughed but unsown. Beyond that were the wastes. We cannot have ridden more than a quarter of an hour outside of Chapaledfú before I felt as remote as ever I have been.

Here was the Pampas proper.

At first glance the landscape was flat, the horizon a blade that separated grass from sky. On closer inspection, however, one noted slight undulations that offered the scenery a subtle rolling texture; in places it might be possible to find a sheltered spot. The one point not in contention was how endless it all seemed. It is difficult to convey to the reader just how vast the panorama was, though I imagine sailors must feel something of a like manner when far out at sea. Only two things broke the green monotony: clumps of the eponymous pampas grass (*Cortaderia selloana*) and, occasionally, small black islands of trees, or *las quintas* as the locals called these clusters. The whole day, the sky remained solid with cloud and gloom.

Having left town, we broke into a steady trot and thereafter Rivacoba alternated the pace between it and walking. No word passed between us for at least the first hour.

'Does my horse have a name?' I said by-and-by, to make conversation.

'No.'

'Then I shall call her "Dahlia". It's one of my favourite flowers.'

We continued on in silence.

A number of miles later I posed another question. 'Shall we reach the estancia tonight?'

'It's too far.'

'I am supposed to arrive to-day.'

'As you said: blame the trains.'

'I can ride faster than this,' I ventured.

'We'll work the horses soon enough. But we could gallop the whole day and still not accomplish our journey by nightfall. You must learn there are two distances in the Pampas, Señorita. Far, and farther still.' And that, pretty much, was the end of his loquaciousness.

We rode the length of the day and in that time met no other soul. That is not to say the Pampas was without life. The sky was lively with birds that flapped and darted over, some as neat as sparrows, others monstrous, and every size in between. 'What's that?' I would ask, for my knowledge of ornithology is limited. 'A viudita,' came Rivacoba's monotone reply. Or, 'Chimango.' The ground itself was more varied than first I perceived it to be. Grass, yes, an infinite quantity of it; but also speckles of tiny, white flowers; some species of wild artichoke with bluish-grey leaves; and an abundance of thistles. Most eye-catching of all was an occasional, deep-crimson flower that I took to be a miniature form of iris and that, had I been at leisure, I would have stopped to study. It grew in drifts and these appeared, from afar, not unimaginably like shoals of blood. When I quizzed my guide on them a tension hardened his features, he naming them as *las flores del diablo*. 'Why that?' I had asked.

'Because they grow only where the devil treads.'

Later, we put the horses to a canter and that sense of excitement, of adventure, which had stolen upon me when first I laid eyes on the Pampas through the train window once more enlivened my heart. I felt intoxicated with it! The untamed beauty of the wilderness quickened my blood in a manner that would have disturbed the rest of my family, for they saw staidness as a virtue, my parents expecting – insisting upon – only the most conventional of lives for me: to be untroubled by curiosity or ambition, to marry and be dutiful. In short, to be everything Grandfather had exhorted me to reach beyond, marked as he was by a disdain for convention. He would have beamed with pride that I had journeyed so far from home, and all the more so at my Head Gardenership.

As the afternoon shortened, and we were again at a plodding walk, I grew fatigued, the muscles in my thighs, shoulders and, in particular, lower back aching. I yearned for a bath and fantasized myself at Las Lágrimas deep in hot, scented water. Behind the clouds the sun began to wester, casting the landscape in progressively darker shades that only heightened the emptiness of the place. The wind picked up and an overwhelming despondency took hold of me. To travel out here by oneself, I thought, would not be my preference and I tried to imagine how men like my guide, who must ride often without companionship, sustained themselves.

When dusk closed in, Rivacoba brought us to a halt in a slight depression. 'We camp here tonight.' He had been silent for so long his voice caused me to startle. I gratefully slipped off Dahlia and left her munching on the grass.

I presumed I would have a tent or some other kind of shelter, a presumption I was promptly disabused of. Rivacoba unloaded my meagre luggage and arranged it in a semi-circle to protect us from the wind. Then he unrolled a woven-grass mat and laid it on the ground over which he placed the sheepskin from underneath my saddle. Finally, I was given a thick poncho, maroon in colour, hircine in smell – and this rude bivouac was my bed for the night!

'Is this how Don Paquito and his family travel?' I demanded as Rivacoba unlooped a faggot of sticks from the pack-pony.

'When I ride alone, I don't have a fire,' he replied, arranging the kindling on the ground. 'But Señor Moyano insisted. You are lucky.'

My good fortune extended to strips of dried beef and a tin of beans for dinner, cooked in the flames and eaten as gusts of wind snapped around us. There was also *yerba mate*, the local tea, made from the dried leaves of a species of holly plant (*Ilex paraguariensis*, if I remember). Rivacoba took its preparation seriously, boiling water, then cramming a gourd with leaves before filling it to the brim with the hot liquid.

He passed the gourd to me to drink first. I had sampled it previously in Buenos Aires and found it not to my palate. Sipping it on the Pampas it tasted as bitter as the greenest lemon, though the warming sensation that spread through my throat and chest was compensation.

Then I had buried myself inside my poncho and lain down for the night, watching the sparks from the fire whirl and dance and vanish into the darkness, a darkness so absolute it was hard to believe it real.

Next morning, I awakened stiff and damp into a half-gloom. My bladder pressed dully. The previous night I had slipped away to relieve myself. Despite the earliness of the hour, it was already too light to be afforded the same discretion. I vowed the next time I went to the lavatory it would be sitting down, enclosed by walls with a lock on the door and a chain to pull. For breakfast I had some day-old bread and a sip of coffee, mostly though I was keen to be on our way, and we broke camp as the sun began to rise. As with the previous day it was obscured by banks of thick, sullen cloud. I continued to wear the poncho in order that my body remain as snug as possible.

After what seemed like an eternity in the saddle, my spine feeling ever more brittle, I asked, 'How much longer until we are there?'

'We're making good time.' They were the first words to pass between us since leaving. 'We will arrive by afternoon.'

I entered a kind of trance, the boundless grass, the

unending sky, the regular bump of my bladder deadening my senses. The air developed an oppressiveness as if a deluge might unleash itself, albeit none came. My thoughts roved to Capitán Agramonte (for in due course I was told that the founder of the estancia, grandfather of Don Paquito, had held military rank) and the personality of a man who builds a house so far from civilization. These musings hurried my mind to my destination and I was gripped by an anxiety – one held at bay by the excitement of my new employment but now making its presence known – that I did not possess sufficient talent to take charge of the garden, I questioning why such a position had been bestowed on me in the first place. Thereafter it was, perhaps, inevitable that I thought back to the reading of Grandfather's will for as much as I had put it out of mind, in moments of lower spirit its memory intruded.

I saw again the family gathered in the solicitor's office; heard again how I had been bequeathed Grandfather's every possession, most especially the house and garden; tasted again jubilation, for in a stroke my independence had been secured. Then the solicitor had apologetically cleared his throat. There was also the matter of numerous creditors, and though the debts were not large they were beyond my means. Father could have settled them that very afternoon had he so chosen – but my pleas to him went ignored, as did those to my brothers-in-law. And so I was left to sell the property. Was ever there a more grudging, bitter transaction? For despite the considerable legacy that came to me, I would rather have lived in penury than lose the garden. Afterward

I could not bear to remain in Cambridgeshire and, when I learnt that Mother had arranged for me a possible suitor, I decided I must get as far from these people as possible, forging an opportunity for myself when the solicitor let slip he had a business acquaintance in Buenos Aires. I left for Argentina determined not to furrow the path expected of me, but one of my own self-will. If my parents had assumed their actions would force me back to their fold, I hope they felt as sorely cheated as did I.

'Riders,' said Rivacoba.

I shook myself from my reverie. 'Where?' I noted Dahlia's ears twitching.

'Ahead.'

For several moments I could determine nothing, then a group of figures materialized on the horizon. 'Who are they?'

Rivacoba seemed unconcerned. He leant forward in the saddle, scrutinizing the distance. 'Workers. From the estancia.'

'From Las Lágrimas?'

He nodded.

As they drew closer, I counted a dozen men on horseback and behind them a covered wagon. When we met, every one of us dismounted. Rivacoba moved through the party, gravely shaking hands and offering a few words; there was a murmur of chatter. No one appeared to notice me. A flask of hot water was found and a *mate* gourd circulated between the men. Whilst they drank, I stepped away from the group. The pressure on my bladder had grown steadily more discomforting. I glanced around to see if there was a clump of vegetation where I might take myself unobserved. Finding none, I walked over to the wagon, stroking the flanks of the horses as I passed them, in the hope that there might be a private spot behind. At the rear, I peered inside the cart. It was chock-full of building equipment: shovels, trowels, carpentry implements. There was a reassuring aroma of varnish and slaked lime. I could hear the men chatting but, from where I stood, was completely hidden. If I was quick, I would be able to hitch my skirts without anyone being the wiser. I seized the hem of my dress.

Something stirred in the back of the wagon. At first I thought it an animal – the work-gang's dog or some such – then I saw clearly what it was. Hidden amongst the tools, swaddled in blankets, was a young man. The cover of the wagon cast his face in shadows, a face shockingly pale, as one who has lost much blood. He was damp with sweat and shivering and, for an instant, our eyes met. There was to his countenance such a terror that my heart lost a beat. I let out an involuntary yelp, recoiling from the wagon, and almost tripped over. The man withdrew himself deeper into his blankets until I could see him no more.

Bladder forgotten, I hurried to the circle of men and made it clear to Rivacoba that I wanted to be on the move. Sensing my distemper, he agreed and presently we departed. For a while I kept glancing over my shoulder at the wagon, trying to comprehend what I had seen. Finally, I looked back and the other party was gone. The wind became squally, individual gusts rushing over us with enough force to threaten my hat. In the far distance I saw slants of falling rain, to which Rivacoba offered the assurance they would not trouble us.

He continued, 'You seem unsettled, Señorita.'

'Who were those men?'

'They have been building a new part of the estancia.'

'Did they tell you anything else?'

'Only that they're glad to be heading home.'

'There was another man,' I said, 'in the rear of the wagon. He appeared... unwell.'

'They said nothing of him, but were drinking last night, to celebrate the end of their labour.'

As an explanation it did not convince, however, I made no further comment. We continued, my distress eventually overtaken by the insistence of my bladder, and now a desire to reach my journey's end.

A league or so farther, the grass ceased and the ground became blackened and charred. Here a crop of maize had once grown, its stubble set alight after the harvest. This was common practice in the Pampas; nevertheless the scene before us suggested an act of terrible desolation, as if a retreating army had destroyed the land as it fled. 'This is the boundary of Las Lágrimas,' said Rivacoba. His face was set, the reins in his hands held tight as if he feared his animal was about to bolt. We rode through the torched landscape until gaining a track, then followed this path until what looked like a high wall blocked the way ahead. It was on an inhuman scale, running to the limit of my vision in both directions. As we approached, the air began to fill with a familiar, though seemingly impossible, sound.

'What's that noise?' It rushed and soughed in my ears. 'Is it the sea?'

For the first and only time Rivacoba's face showed a fraction of mirth. 'The Atlantico is a week's ride to the east.'

'Then what can I hear? Is it a river?'

'The trees, Señorita. The wind in the trees.'

I had been mistaken in thinking I was looking at a wall. Rather it was the beginning of a dense, dark forest. The wind skimmed the canopy and twisted through the trunks, rocking branches, shifting and shaking leaves with a sound of waves washing on a seashore – continuous, soft and deep. The likeness was uncanny. Our track led to the edge of the forest and a pair of huge, wrought-iron gates hung on two brick pillars. Atop each pillar was a massive bronze lion made virescent by the elements. There was no wall either side of the pillars, nor barrier of any other kind. This was a gate not to impede a person's entrance, but a declaration of what lay beyond.

When we reached the gate, Rivacoba drew his horse to a sharp halt. 'I have brought you here, Señorita.'

'You are coming no farther?'

'No.'

'What am I to do now?'

He tied the reins of the luggage pony to Dahlia. 'Follow the track through the trees. There are two houses on the estate. The old ruin. And the main house. Make certain you get the right one.'

'Are you sure you won't join me? To have some refreshment, or rest a while.'

'No.'

'At least allow your horse a few minutes.'

He glanced at the trees shaking in the wind. His mount was scraping at the ground, bridle clinking. 'I must be away.'

'In which case, thank you for bringing me here safely.'

'*Chau. Suerte*, Señorita Kelp.'

He turned and began trotting off.

'Wait!' I called after him. 'What about your poncho?'

'Consider it a gift,' he shouted back. 'It may keep you from harm.'

With that he spurred his horse and broke into a gallop, a solitary figure against the immense, smoke-coloured sky.

Dinner for One

ONE OF THE gates had been left open for me. I passed through it and immediately found myself deep amongst the trees. Here was a driveway, in a state of pitted disrepair, broad enough for three or four to ride abreast. It was considerably darker beneath the canopy, and the branches above had knotted together; it gave the sensation of moving through a long, shadowy vault. Although I could still hear the ocean-like wind, its roar was diminished now I was inside the forest, the sound more unsettling for it, and punctuated by the cawing of birds invisible. On the previous day, Rivacoba had mentioned that Dahlia and the pony were from the stables of the estancia. They seemed aware they were almost home and advanced at a keen rate. I held the reins tight, keeping to a cautious trot.

From the gate to the main house, as experience subsequently taught, was a distance of some two miles. It was a winding, erratic, unkept path, there being little to stimulate the eye except the tangle and weave of trees. I struggled to identify the species, noting only elms, Scotch pines and cedars amongst the many indigenous varieties of which I was not familiar.

All were ancient, at least a century old, the bark warped and cankered so that in places one had the rather unnerving impression of distorted, watchful faces. The track must have been carved through the woods so that the house could be built, sheltered in the centre. It amazed me that such a mature forest could thrive in a location as windtorn as the Pampas. I also noted that plenty of coppicing was needed and smiled: I was slipping into my role of Head Gardener with aplomb. Off the driveway were a number of paths that led to who knew where. After a good few minutes, one of these bifurcations was marked by a second gate, crowned by the same lions I had seen at the entrance, the columns thickly ivied.

I leant in close to Dahlia. 'Which way, girl?'

When she offered no indication, I headed between the two columns. I needed not ride far to realize my mistake, for the path took me to a ruined mansion. It would once have been a grand dwelling, built in a foreigner's pretence of the Georgian-style, though now had neither windows nor doors – only gaping, black cavities that revealed nothing of the interior. Much of the render had fallen off, exposing patches of brickwork that looked like ulcers. The undergrowth was sneaking up the sides of the walls, the forest inescapably reclaiming the house. The only sign of possible habitation was a washing-line, from which hung a few men's garments.

'*Hola!*' I called, dismounting. 'Is anyone there? I'm looking for the main house.'

I sensed that somebody must have heard me but no reply was forthcoming, and I had little desire to venture into the shadows of that derelict place. I thus returned to Dahlia.

Before I could mount her, the brushwood came to life, shaking and yelping, some distance away at first, then rapidly nearer.

Two German shepherds emerged and bounded toward me.

I am more than fond of dogs. Grandfather had an Irish wolfhound, called Ferryman, who I grew up with and adored, and when he died, remains the only boy ever to break my heart. To be charged at by two great beasts when I was a stranger in their territory, however, set my pulse racing. The two dogs sniffed and barked excitedly about me, then settled in expectation of a command. They were beautiful-looking animals, their coats luxuriant. I noted that the smaller of the pair had mismatched eyes, one being of pale blue, the other a mint-green.

'Do you know the way to the house?' I asked. '*A la casa?*'

As if understanding perfectly, they set off again. I mounted Dahlia and chased after them. We trotted back to the main path, following the dogs as they ran and play-snapped at each other. If I lagged behind they would slow for me. Finally, the twisting driveway came upon a straight avenue of trees. It was at least four hundred yards in length, processional in grandeur. The trees themselves (ombús, a native species, *Phytolacca dioica*), were the tallest I had seen on the estate, their trunks pleached to a crown high above. They looked more like columns from antiquity than living organisms. Riding beneath them, they invoked their desired effect: I felt as one insignificant and in awe. At the farthest end of this thoroughfare, I glimpsed a flash of sandstone, which I could only assume was the principal house of the estate.

Then, the queerest thing happened.

Three-quarters of the way along the avenue, I noticed a gap in the trees. At some point in the past, one of the ombús must have fallen down and the stump been completely removed. As I reached the void I heard – or fancied I heard – a voice on the wind. I had no doubt it was pure imagination, brought on by fatigue from the journey, but at the time it seemed real enough.

Get away from this place...

Before I could cast my gaze about to discover who might have cried these words, I left the trees and arrived at a clearing. There was an expanse of lawn, patchy in places, and rising from it a single Bismarck palm, tall and straight as a mainmast. A circular carriage-drive swept to the house. The dogs charged over the grass and I lost sight of them. As for the house itself, it was solid and the roof had a pleasing angle, even if I must confess to being a little underwhelmed. Yes, it was imposing, constructed in a faux French-château-style with turrets and any number of finials, however my expectation was for a larger edifice, something more significant. In short, a house that better reflected the size of the estate and the 'Imperial Avenue' leading toward it. Up close, I saw the walls were sprayed with lichen; there were dark blotches around the down-pipes.

I rode to the front door. Over the entrance were the words

LAS LÁGRIMAS, 1866

Now that I had gained my destination, the need to relieve myself returned with a pressing urgency. There was no one waiting to greet me. I alighted from Dahlia and seeing no obvious place to tie her and the pony, threaded their reins round a gutter-pipe, hoping the horses did not break away. It would not do to destroy the drainage as soon as I arrived. I took off Rivacoba's poncho, laying it across the saddle, put my hair into a semblance of order, and entered the house.

'*Hola, hay alguien?*' I called, expecting the rush of steps to greet me. '*Señor Moyano?*'

I was in the vestibule. Apart from the open doorway behind me there was little light. I made out a parquet floor, panelling of a similar dark material and half a dozen doors, each one of them shut. On the walls was a collection of paintings, portraits all, though it was too dim to see the details with clarity. A large fireplace had been laid but not lit.

'*Hola?*' I called anew – and listened to my voice echo forth, unanswered.

If I was vexed by the lack of welcome a more desperate urge came over me. I began opening the doors in search of a lavatory. I discovered numerous *salas* – or reception rooms – where the furniture was covered in dustsheets before a small cloakroom with toilet and washbasin revealed itself. With a gratitude verging on the comic, I sat down and finally, thankfully, passed water with a great plash against the porcelain; never was a penny more gratefully spent. Afterward, I pulled the chain – and nothing happened. I pulled again to the same effect. There was no water from the basin taps either. Unsure what to do, I undid the door and returned to the entrance hall.

Standing directly outside the lavatory, almost as if she

had been listening in, was a chit of a girl in a black dress and pinafore. My luggage from the pack-pony was heaped by her, Rivacoba's poncho draped over her arm. She dipped into an awkward curtsy, her face pale and eager, her voice dreamy and faraway. 'Señorita Kelp?'

'Yes,' I replied, glad that the dimness of the house hid the flood of colour to my face.

'I am to show you to your room.'

We walked through the vestibule, turning right into another large hallway with more doors leading off it. The years of lying unoccupied tainted the air. Halfway along was a panelled staircase, oddly proportioned, which we began to climb. I offered to help the maid with my bags but she refused all assistance, despite her appearing as one too small to manage the burden. She had the frame and limbs of a girl, though when I scrutinized her face I saw that she was older than she looked, perhaps in her twentieth year. There was an impudence to her eyes, which were large and dark-ringed, whilst her mouth was filled with an overabundance of teeth, many of them crooked. Her hair was stiff and black.

'I'm Ursula,' I said in as friendly a tone as I could muster, for the maid had a quality that precluded affability. 'What's your name?'

'Dolores,' came her breathless reply as she struggled up the stairs. (Everyone in the house called her so, though it was not until later that I gathered this was actually where she came from rather than what she was called. Dolores: a town forty miles to the north-east of the estancia. I was never party to her given name.)

The top of the first flight led to a long corridor of rooms where mine was the second on the left, at the front of the house. Dolores unlocked the door and placed my bags inside. 'Will there be anything else, Señorita?'

'Thank you, no,' I replied, absorbing my surroundings with disappointment. The curtains were open, letting in a dull light. For furniture there was a bed; an expensive-looking, albeit dated, armchair by the hearth; a miniscule desk-cum-dressing-table beneath the window; a washstand and empty bookcase. The walls were plain except for a couple of rather indifferent pictures. If not entirely cramped, it was small, certainly smaller than the room I had grown accustomed to at the Houghtons, and not my expectation for the lodgings of the Head Gardener. Was this how Señor Moyano estimated my stature? By way of compensation there was a walk-in closet and at least it appeared spotless. I had a pleasant view overlooking the front lawn, across to the avenue of ombú trees.

'One thing,' I said to Dolores. 'What time is dinner served?'

The maid had gone.

The first thing I did was test the mattress. It was lumpy but comfortable enough, especially with my back so jarred and saddle-sore. I lay down, crossing my ankles on the bed-end, and closed my eyes, thinking I would rest a moment then unpack.

When again I opened them, it was dark. I sat up, feeling grogged, unawares of having dozed off. The curtains had been drawn against the night, a candlestick and fire lit, I presumed by Dolores. It disturbed me that I had slept through this, and more so the fact that she had untied my boots and placed them in a neat pair beneath the bed. On the washstand was a basin and ewer from which I observed a shimmer of steam. After my long journey I wanted a soak before dinner, not a strip-wash. I went into the corridor and travelled its length, floorboards creaking intermittently as I stepped, to look for a bathroom. Behind every door I found only mothballed chambers until, at the far end, I came to a draughty water-closet. I reasoned the door next to it, the very last one indeed, might open to reveal a bath-tub. When I tested the handle, it was locked.

Back in my room, I washed as best I could and changed into my evening clobber, oppressed by the stillness of the house. Then I took the candlestick and went below.

'Dolores?' I called. 'Dolores?'

There was no sign of her. One of the hallway doors had been opened, light emanating from within. It was a dining room, austere and formal, dominated by a polished pearwood table and twelve high-backed, carved chairs. At one end of the table was a silver cloche beside a bowl of winter salad. I called again for Dolores; again I was greeted with silence.

Now all this was very odd, but I was too hungry to stand on ceremony. I lifted the cloche, releasing a waft of roasted meat that made me appreciate how famished I was. I served myself a plate of beef-ribs supplemented by salad, and ate. Each nick of cutlery against china sounded unnaturally loud, as did my mastication. Despite my hollow stomach, I cannot say I ate heartily for I was too self-conscious. When finished, I remained hungry but was unsure whether the food was meant solely for my consumption or if other guests were expected. Given the hush of the place it was unlikely that all the settings would be filled; nevertheless it was possible there might be other diners, and surely Señor Moyano would want supper. I did not wish to seem the glutton who had eaten all the food herself, so I left the remainder of the meat, despite wanting more, and stood up from the table. There was another door at the far end of the room that I presumed led to the servants' area. I opened it on to a narrow passage and, from there, the kitchen.

'*Hola?*' I said, growing weary of receiving no reply other than the echo of my own voice. 'Dolores? Anyone?'

The kitchen was unlit, as empty and cold as it must have been for many a year. Blue enamel saucepans hung unused. From another hook dangled a dead rabbit waiting to be skinned. Further doors led to the exterior of the house, the scullery and a small, private parlour. In the latter, I found a half-played game of solitaire, which I was careful not to disturb. I returned to the dining room with a feeling of dejection, and loitered about for another quarter-hour in the hope that someone might join me. I thought of Doña Ybarra's reminisces on the train, about the parties the house had hosted. It was hard to imagine any such jollity. More than once my eyes dwelt longingly on the beef-ribs, which glistened with juice. Doña Ybarra being on my mind brought back her warning of the estate being cursed. It was, to be sure, silliness, but with nothing except echoes for company I sensed her words stealthily taking hold of my imagination.

I made an effort to shake them off and retired to my room, where I changed for the night and slipped beneath the sheets. They were chilly and had a strong smell of mothballs. In the hearth the fire had died to a bed of embers, which cast an orange glow. From outside I heard the wind moan through the trees. More than ever, it sounded as if I were by the ocean. Beneath that strange, rushing sound I heard other unfamiliar noises: the rattle of a window casement downstairs, the creak of branches like old bones, a faint gurgle that I could not identify. Once, for the briefest moment, came the furious baying of dogs. I wondered if it could be the German shepherds I had met earlier; if so, they had been joined by a pack. And underlying all of this, the impenetrable silence of the house.

I rolled on to my side, hugging my knees tight, and waited for sleep, quite convinced I was the only human soul in all of Las Lágrimas.

A Tour of the Garden

THE CONTRAST THE next morning could not have been greater. I awakened to the sounds of life: voices calling to one another below, the clatter of cutlery, a cheerful chorus of birds. The wind had blown all night and although it had not abated it had broken up the clouds, revealing patches of wintry blue sky. Dappled sunlight streamed in through the open curtains. From the kitchen came the waft of toast and sizzling ham.

I got out of bed, scrubbed my face and put on my gardening uniform: a white blouse, navy drill-skirt and matching jacket. Once attired, I headed downstairs with a degree of self-consciousness about not having bathed properly since leaving Buenos Aires; I wished I had a bottle of perfume to dab a drop behind my ears. The hallway was brighter than it had been the day before, better revealing the portraits that had greeted me when first I entered the house. They were all heavy oils and of the same individual – Don Guido, as it turned out, father of the current Don – in a variety of different modes, costumes and improbable settings, from conquistador to romantic lover, and a man clearly not in deficit of vanity.

I found his manner to be vaguely comedic – but it was the comedy of Mr Punch, for there was a cruelty, a viciousness, to his mouth, whilst his eyes were splintered with black and bronze, his likeness seeming to confirm Doña Ybarra's claim of him as a godless man better than Moyano's assertion of piety.

Of all the portraits, the one that most caught my attention showed the subject as master gardener, looking immensely satisfied with himself, a silver trowel in one hand, a navy-blue scroll in the other tucked under his arm like a swagger-stick; for a background, there was a row of saplings, freshly staked and planted. I considered it briefly, thinking how Grandfather would have shared my scorn – and felt a familiar stab of loss. Somewhere a window was open, letting in a breeze fragrant with sweet, damp leaves and the endless miles of the Pampas. More than anything else, I suddenly wanted to be outside, drinking in fresh air.

A raised voice sounded from the dining room and, as I reached the threshold, I caught sight of Moyano. He had stood up from a half-eaten plate of eggs and was berating Dolores for some misdemeanour. Next to the towering estate manager she looked more childlike than ever. Her shoulders were stooped in shame. I did not want to add to her embarrassment by intruding and, since neither had yet to notice me, I doubled back in the direction of the breeze. I found it in the morning room, where French windows were open to a patio that led to the rear of the property. This was going to be my first sight of the house's formal garden: I felt a trill of excitement. But stepping outside, my immediate thought was,

Oh, how peculiar!

I had imagined the place in a multitude of ways, especially given Moyano's report of it being in the English-style. None of my speculations, however, prepared me for what I saw. The terrace led to a shabby knot-garden and then a wall that blocked out sight of anything else. Not the type of garden wall I was familiar with, of tidy red bricks, as we once had at home. Instead, a dry-wall of hewn black rocks, at least twenty foot in height. There was to it a 'pagan' quality, I could think of no better description. In the centre, a weather-beaten door of oak, raked with lichen, stood ajar. I walked toward it hoping to ameliorate my shock by viewing the garden beyond. As I approached, it swung shut, and from the other side I heard the retreat of loping footsteps on gravel. I went to open the door – but it was fastened tight. I pushed my weight against it then, reversing tack, tugged on the handle: neither to any avail. The door would not budge, indeed the hinges appeared solid with rust.

'You there!' I called to the person who had closed it. 'Please, can you open the door.'

The footsteps came to an immediate halt. There was silence except for the sudden angry rawk of a chimango high above. A sense came to me that whoever was on the opposite side had stopped dead as if caught in some nefarious deed. I offered what was becoming my well-worn and fruitless call in this place. '*Hola?*'

When still no reply was forthcoming I let it be known that I considered the individual most impolite, and rather irritably returned to the dining room. Upon my moving away, I heard the distinct crunch of gravel again, the steps irregular, as if the walker were lame.

Moyano was finishing his eggs as I entered. The estate manager dabbed his yolky lips with a napkin, stood and grasped my hand. He was dressed in a rather rakish suit of tobacco-coloured cloth. 'A pleasure to see you, Señorita Kelp, and my apologies if your arrival was a little subdued. We were expecting you on Saturday.'

'The train was delayed.'

'I feared you might have had second thoughts.' He offered a chair, appraising me, running his eyes over my points so that I had that feeling as when we first met of being judged like some prize-animal at a county show. His smile was benign; I hoped he was pleased with his choice. 'Until Don Paquito arrives, the staff takes Sunday off,' he continued, 'and I was attending to other business. Hence the lack of welcome. I trust you have settled in.'

'I have, thank you, though I would have liked a bath.' I sat down and he poured me coffee.

'Didn't Dolores explain? The girl is quite hopeless. There are no facilities in your part of the house. You will have to visit the new wing to bathe; your days are Wednesday and Saturday.'

'Only twice a week?' I demurred.

'There should have been hot water in your room. And I am told that you discovered the downstairs lavatory.'

I felt the colour warm my face but would not be cowed. 'I prefer a bath every day.'

'I am afraid that is not possible. All the more so when the Agramontes take residence.'

Dolores entered, carrying my breakfast, and smiled weakly at me, revealing her mouthful of crooked teeth. Whatever the cause of Moyano's reproach, it had brought a rush of tears to the girl. I thanked her for the food and ate with a sullen air, infuriated by the limited options to bathe. If Moyano was aware, he made no show of it.

When I had finished, he was keen to show me the garden. First, however, he wanted to acquaint me with Cook. We went to the kitchen which, unlike the previous night, was alive with pots bubbling and rich aromas. In the centre of the room, meat-cleaver in hand as she broke and cracked a side of beef, was a sinewy woman of considerable grace. She was what they call in this part of the world a *mestiza* – a mélange of Spanish and native blood – her skin a shade of butterscotch, her hair hidden behind a head-tie that was as bright as a parrot's plumage. Moyano introduced her as Calista who, along with her cooking duties, was to organize the household until the principal keeper arrived with the Agramontes.

'*Encantada*,' I said. 'I thought supper delicious last night.'

The cook ignored me and continued with her chopping, hands stained red.

'She's always so welcoming,' said Moyano, much surprised, as he conducted me from the kitchen. He mulled over her behaviour before adding, 'Calista is also skilled in apothecary. Should you find yourself with any ailment, you can depend on her. I often do.'

I considered those bloodied hands and how deftly she wielded the meat-cleaver and thought, on balance, I'd rather not.

Once outside, we headed toward the wall. The wind in the trees was a dull, persistent noise that did not cease for the duration of our time in the garden.

'I attempted the door earlier,' I told the estate manager. 'It wouldn't shift.'

'Don't worry yourself,' he replied. 'The door hasn't worked in an age.'

'It was open earlier. Someone went through it.'

Moyano creased his brow. 'You saw them?'

'I heard them.'

'You must be mistaken, Señorita. The door has not opened once in all the months I've been here.'

'Well, it was open this morning.'

'When the builders were at work on the new wing, they tried to release it for me. They took hammers to it, forcing-tools, chisels. In the end, they feared they would bring down the entire section before the door budged, so left it.'

I was certain of what I had seen, but chose not to pursue the matter. 'Then how does one get into the garden?'

'Let me show you.'

We kept to the perimeter of the wall until we gained a low, roughly shaped opening. 'Here the builders were able to breach the stone,' said Moyano and, bending down, he ducked inside.

I followed, stumbling, and was grateful for the hand Moyano put out to stabilize me. He held me until I was upright, letting his grip linger a fraction longer than I thought necessary.

I retrieved my hand and gazed about me. The area contained within the walls – this being the formal garden – was vast. Vast and deep with weeds. Weeds, bramble, willowherb, teasle, hawkbit, creeping cinquefoil; every undesirable one could imagine. There were nettles, and I make no exaggeration, that were ten feet high. Moyano guided me through them, parting the ways with a riding-crop like an Argentine Moses, following paths that had been hacked clear, showing me the numerous different compartment-gardens and portions therein, offering suggestions as to what I might do or things Don Paquito had requested. With each step my heart grew heavier.

Nature seemed on the point of overtaking this garden for good.

At some point the German shepherds appeared. They gambolled up to me, playing around my skirts, licking at my hands. The larger of the two stood up on its hind legs as if to embrace me and was at least an inch my taller. I eased the dog down.

'I see you've met Lola and Vasca,' chuckled Moyano.

I made a fuss of them both and, unaccustomed to such attention, they rolled over to offer me their bellies. 'They are siblings?'

'Mother and daughter. Lola, the one who wants to dance, is the pup. And you can tell Vasca from her eyes. Or hips. She had an accident, the poor beast.'

Along with Vasca's mismatched blue and green eyes, I noticed, as I had not before, that her hind legs were slightly withered and pelvis malformed, she being also the thinner and more cautious of the two dogs. It was good to see them both, though they did little to brighten my mood.

My tour of the garden continued, albeit in the hours before lunch there was not the time to venture to every corner. Often the weeds were at our chests and we both had to wade through them, arms held aloft as if crossing a river. Elsewhere, I tripped on creeping vines; thorns tugged and caught on my skirt. I found all those anxieties about the extent of my capabilities bristle anew. If a conclusion was to be made, it was that I had been mistaken in travelling here.

We arrived at a space that seemed, if it were possible, more overrun than the rest. It was broad and had along its edge yews grown so tall and wild that I had the impression of standing in an arena. Dominating the centre was an artificial, by which I mean man-made, shape hidden in its entirety by a dead Virginia creeper. 'This was once Don Paquito's favourite place in the garden,' pronounced Moyano. 'It is where he expects you to begin. For my part, it would be best if you could have the area cleared and planted by the time of his arrival. What say you, Señorita?'

'It's not what I expected,' I quietly remarked. 'It's a…' I had to reach into my pocket for my Tauchnitz to find the precise word with which to convey my despondency. '… *una selva*.' A jungle.

There was a chill to Moyano's response. 'Is it more than you are capable of, Señorita Kelp? Should I have found another gardener?'

I was tempted to tell him yes, that I would like to head back to Buenos Aires at once. I thought to what Gil had told me on the evening of my giving notice. Little wonder it was a task no one else wanted. I should not have been so hubristic in my own talents. But what alternative did I have now? I could not humiliate myself by returning to the Houghtons and begging (and I was in no doubt Gil would make me beg) for my old job. Nor could I set sail for Britain: even had I not sent my parents a defiant telegram informing them of my new position, I could never forgive them the loss of Grandfather's garden. I thought of how Mother had spoken of the suitor she found me. *I am sure he will provide you a garden, Deborah. You can tend that if you must.* As if any old replacement would pass muster.

'I feel I've been misled, Señor Moyano,' I replied at last, speaking up. 'You should have been more forthright on how overgrown the garden is.'

'This is nothing. You should have seen it before we started cutting back. At least some of the paths are passable now.'

'In which case, I am glad I did not arrive any earlier.'

He laughed at that, not with complete sincerity, and reassuringly rested his hands on my shoulders. 'You will not have to tackle your "jungle" alone,' he said. 'You have a staff, remember.'

He was trying to mollify me, though as it turned out he failed in this respect too. We broke for a spot of lunch – a creamy corn pie and boiled potatoes with a course of sardo cheese afterward – and then he gathered my so-called staff.

They were three: two native Mapuche lads and an Argentine who had grown old-fashioned side-whiskers in an attempt to conceal the worst of his complexion. The two boys –

brothers — were no older than me with hairless faces and simpleton smiles, and side by side made for rather a music-hall pairing, the one being tall and lean, the other squat and brawny. At least they were strong, and I hoped they would not lack for vigour at the task ahead. As for the other man, he introduced himself as Latigez. He wore a sheath on his thigh, prominently displayed, which safeguarded a large *facón* knife. Unlike the Mapuches, Latigez offered his hand and crushed mine when I took it. It was obvious that everything I requested of him would be ignored or dodged on principle, the principle being my womanhood and foreign birth and that I had money in the bank untouched. I also had the immediate suspicion that here was the yahoo whose footsteps I had heard earlier that morning behind the fastened door.

'Señor Latigez is also engaged in numerous tasks for me,' said Moyano. 'As well as such odd jobs around the house as they arise.'

'So in truth, all I have are two workers,' was my bitter reply. 'How can I—'

He held up his palm to quiet me. 'I am sure, Señorita, you can. When the main staff arrives with Don Paquito, there will be a dozen more. For now, I have every confidence you will get on.'

I could not determine whether the doubt I detected in his words was real, or of my own imagining.

The Trophy Room

I SPENT THE rest of the afternoon, as the wind continued to bluster, walking the garden alone, sketchbook in hand. Moyano may have given me instruction as to where my efforts should be directed, but I wanted a greater sense of the whole before setting to. An early lesson I took from Grandfather was that one must be intimate with the ground if one is going to cultivate it. A foolproof method is to plot it out. For all that the garden had grown wild, it was still possible to discern something of the intended design; I therefore positioned myself at various spots, drew what I saw, then paced out the dimensions. My goal was to create a scale diagram.

Yet as I worked, I was unable to translate what was before my eye to the page. Angles and distances morphed and distorted; my counting became erratic; more than once I failed to remember how many paces I had taken between pausing my step and putting pencil to paper. My mind felt stupid and bleary, and I was left with a gnawing frustration, like trying to piece together an intricate dream where the images, coherent and meaningful as one slept, have become intangible.

The problem was no less maddening that evening when I attempted to transfer my few sketches to best. By then night had fallen (sundown being around six o'clock) and I was in the confines of my room, having established myself at the table beneath the window with several lamps to illuminate my drawing. The air was heady with paraffin. I had suffered another of my strip-washes and changed into my house-wear; dinner would be served within the hour. As far as I could ascertain the area inside the walls of the garden was rectangular in shape, longer than it was broad as seen from the house. Yet tracing out my measurements, everything I committed to paper was misshapen and unpleasing. I grew evermore perturbed, especially as I had decided to make a gift of the plans to Don Paquito when he arrived to show my ambitions for his garden. Previously I had prided myself on my draughtsmanship; that night, I was devoid of all proficiency. My attempts were further hampered by the smallness of the table until, in a pique, I threw down my pencil and decided to search for somewhere more conducive to my task.

Downstairs, I could smell Calista at work in the kitchen. I began opening the numerous doors that led off the hallway, the gallery of portraits as my spectator. All I discovered were dark-panelled *salas* not yet ready for habitation, the furniture hidden beneath sheets. Whoever supplied the drapery for Las Lágrimas must have seen a handsome profit the year the estancia was shut down. I tried to calculate when that might have been, guessing it around the 1880s. Apart from the dining table, which I did not think proper, I came across no surface sufficiently large for my needs and was giving up hope when I opened a door to a room unlike any other. It was unlit and high-ceilinged and, when I counted the walls, octagonal in shape.

I held my lamp aloft to see better. The walls were adorned with antique maps, predominantly of Europe, but a number depicting the Levant and Africa. There were also the heads of hunting trophies – gazelles, a lion, even a crocodile, its snout projecting into the room – and, most eye-catching, a collection of white stag heads arranged in a triangular pattern that dominated a single wall, at its peak a magnificent creature with a twelve-point antler. I was both impressed and, on reflection, saddened by the display and the slaughter that necessitated it. Elsewhere, there were plaques but no actual trophy-heads. These animals, I presumed, had become mangy whilst the house stood empty and been removed. Yet another wall was dedicated to a floor-to-ceiling bookcase. I glanced at some of the titles, leather-bound volumes all, including authors Grandfather had introduced me to: Cervantes, Balzac, Gogol. There were wingback armchairs and a chaise-longue, none of the furniture being covered in dustsheets. And in the centre, a large, circular table – ideal for my needs. I felt drawn to this room, its spirit of learning and adventure, except for one aspect. It was frightfully cold, colder than the rest of an already chilly house.

I drew up a chair, opened my drawings, and attempted to fashion a plan of the garden. Once more the details ran amok when I tried to commit them to paper. And as I sketched, I became aware of a gurgling noise, indiscernibly at first, and then so that it agitated me. I stilled my pencil to concentrate on its source but failed to do so for, impossibly, it sounded beneath me, in the very fabric of the floor.

'What are you doing?'

I glanced up. 'I needed somewhere to work.'

Moyano loomed in the doorway; for how long he had been observing me I was unsure. 'Well, not in here,' he said, sharply.

I rose, gathering my materials in a rush. 'I'm sorry. I was looking for a table large enough.'

His tone softened. 'Besides, you'll catch a chill.'

'What is this room?' I asked.

'When he was a younger man, Don Guido left the estancia and went to see the world. These are the souvenirs he brought home. Better you do not come here: there are too many valuable things that you might damage.'

He escorted me to the door, closing it behind us. 'Calista tells me that dinner is almost prepared. If you need a work place, I will show you somewhere better.'

Earlier in the day I had thought Moyano a changed character to the one I met in Buenos Aires, now this thought came anew. His manner seemed ever so altered. I could not quite pin it down. Less fettered, perhaps – or more confident of himself, assured that I was his gardener and, removed from the city, there was no straightforward way in which I could leave him in the lurch.

We abandoned the Trophy Room and walked to the far end of the hallway, which was hidden by a pair of full-length, utilitarian drapes. Moyano parted the fabric to let me through. A few steps and it was as if I had entered a different time and place. The walls were pale and unadorned, the floor a navy-

and-white chequer board. The most noticeable difference was the temperature: it was comfortably warm, the type of warmth I associate with the public spaces of the very best hotels.

'The new wing,' said Moyano. He flicked on the light-switches. 'As you can see, we have electricity. This is where you'll take your baths, and' – he led me to a vacant anteroom furnished with a pair of architect's easels – 'where you can draw to your heart's content.'

'It's just what I wanted.'

'Sometimes I work here too. We can take a desk each, like clerks in an office.' My expression must have puckered, for he continued, 'Make the most of it, Señorita. When the Don and his family arrive, they'll take residence in this part of the house and the easels will be gone.'

I moved on the conversation. 'Why can't the rest of the house be so snug?'

'That would be Señor Farrido.'

'Farrido?'

'The Don's engineer. He cuts the lawns, maintains the boiler and electrics. He's very good with this modern paraphernalia, though an elusive character. You may not see much of him.' Moyano gestured for us to leave. 'For now, you are free to work here as you want. Tonight, however, I hope you'll join me for dinner.'

He led me back to the old part of the house where the drop in temperature startled. The dining room was set for two with soft candlelight, a bottle of wine and a pair of Paris goblets. It would not have looked out of place in those insipid novels my sisters read. Rather greenly, I had not considered the extent to which Moyano and I might have to spend time together alone and, as he pulled back my chair for me and then sat opposite, I felt myself more uncomfortable than I would have foreseen. His hair was tucked behind his ears and if I was struck again by how fetching he appeared, those locks were lush and raven-black, there was to his handsomeness a certain coarse-grain quality that I had not acknowledged before. That, and an odour I was unaware of in the city: a spicy, heavy scent, not unpleasant but that clung to him, as when one stands too close to a smoking bonfire, a scent impossible to rid the body of unless one's hair is washed and clothing laundered.

'Would you like wine?' he asked.

Even as I was responding in the negative, he poured us both a generous glass of red, I shamefaced that he had caught me assessing him again. He raised his goblet. 'Here's to our success at Las Lágrimas, Ursula. Together may we resurrect her.'

I struggled to recall the last occasion anyone had called me by my Christian name, even the Houghtons had referred to me as 'Miss Kelp'. Nevertheless, 'I prefer, if you will, to keep things on a more formal basis, Señor Moyano.'

He looked crestfallen. 'Of course.'

'At least… until we know each other better.'

We descended into silence as if I had given unpardonable offence, Moyano rubbing at his wrists through the cuffs of his jacket in much the same manner as when first we met (I decided it a tic of his). There are some people whose company one can share without talking and feel no strain; Moyano was not such an individual. I felt it my responsibility to speak. 'At Café Tortoni's you asked about my name.'

'Why you go by Ursula and not that of your birth. Remind me of the proper one.'

It was evident he remembered but wanted me to say it aloud. 'Deborah.'

'That's the name!' He became scornful, a retaliation for my rejection of him. 'I thought it rather affected. A girlish whimsy.'

'It was my grandfather's name for me. He used to call me his "little bear cub", and when I grew too old for that, Ursula.'

'I don't follow.'

'It's the' – I had to check my dictionary – '"diminutive" of the Latin *ursa*, or she-bear.'

'I saw a bear once, at the zoo in Buenos Aires. A terrifying animal. I hope you are not quite so fierce or,' he fixed me with a sly, teasing stare, 'that I can tame you.' He took a gulp of his wine and shouted toward the kitchen. 'Calista! Get us our dinner, will you? Señorita Kelp is starving.'

Shortly thereafter, the cook entered carrying two plates of *morcilla* sausages as an entrée, mine being served with a scowl. The sausages were good, lightly spiced with an intense, iron flavour. They were followed by feather-steak and patatas bravas. Moyano drank freely of the grape, offering me a second charge. Again I refused; again he topped me up. I continued with my best efforts to chip away at the silence.

'When exactly does Don Paquito arrive?'

'The middle of September. I trust you'll be able to make a decent start in that time.'

'From what I can tell, it's not really an English garden. Or at least what I would consider one.'

'It was the work of a famous English designer.'

'Do you know who?'

'I don't recall his name. The original plans are somewhere – when next I see them, I'll put them aside for you.'

I took a small sip of wine. 'It was a bold decision to build a house in the heart of such a forest. How did they remove all the trees?'

'By which you mean?'

'They must have been cleared to make way for the building, and then the stumps dug out. It would have taken an army of men.'

'There was not a single tree here when Guido Agramonte began construction of the house.'

'That can't be.' I wondered if he was being deliberately antagonistic. 'The woodland is at least a century old.'

'No. It was all planted after the house was finished, not more than forty years ago. I've seen the receipts for the saplings. Don Guido undertook the task himself.' My air of incredulity exasperated Moyano. 'You'll find paintings around the place that prove it,' he said. 'In fact, there's one in your bedroom.'

By the time I finished my steak, the aroma of caramel was drifting from the kitchen. I would have enjoyed pudding, but had taken my fill of Moyano's companionship. He did not stand at my leaving, simply nodded and continued with his wine. His face, his whole demeanour, looked relaxed now, one might go so far as to say sensual. I bade him goodnight and, as I walked the length of the hallway, heard him slosh the remnants of my glass into his.

In my room, I scrubbed myself vigorously with toilet-soap and flannel, and changed into my nightdress. Before taking to bed, I studied the pictures on the wall. Moyano proved himself right. There was a black-framed mezzotint of Las Lágrimas. It was dated 1869, and clearly showed the lawn and Bismarck palm, albeit at a reduced height from its current stature. There were no other trees, nor sign of any living creature. Indeed, the view of the house was from a distance to emphasize its solitary position in the bare landscape.

It was not possible. I knew for a truth that the trees surrounding the house must have stood there since before the reign of Victoria. I put such an improbable depiction down to an engraver obeying the fantasies of his employer, nothing more, and turned in for the night.

Not long after I had extinguished my lamp, whilst in the shallows of sleep, I was disturbed by a cry. For an instant I was unsure whether I had dreamt it or if it were real. I experienced a prickle of embarrassment and, if I am honest, a certain prurient fascination, for I had overheard a carnal shout, the sound of someone's muffled pleasure. Then it came again, indecipherable in its location but definitely from within the house, and I knew for a certainty I was not dreaming. But it was no shout of ecstasy, rather the cry of a child. A child tormented and in pain.

The View from the Treehouse

THE DINING TABLE was set for one the following morning.

'Did you hear anything in the night?' I enquired of Dolores as she arrived with my breakfast of maize cakes and eggs. The maid's room was on the floor above mine, in the attics; if I had heard a cry it seemed likely she too would have done so. When she shook her head, I pressed the point. 'Are there any children in the house I have not been told of?' She responded with another blank shake.

Dolores retreated toward the kitchen, then paused and timidly ventured, 'Señor Moyano says the wind can make strange sounds here. I'm sorry, Señorita, I sleep like a top. I heard nothing.'

In the garden, the day had arrived dank and overcast, and whilst the wind may have fallen, asserting itself only in sudden, sharp gusts, the trees of the parkland continued their incessant murmuring. I located the two Mapuche lads and, unsure of their capability, set them to clearing a border where I was confident they could do little damage. I demonstrated the method by which I expected them to cut back, then explained how I wanted the roots dug out to leave nothing but friable earth. Their names were Yamai (the stockier of the two) and Epulef (the more wiry). As far as I was aware both spoke Spanish, however, all my words were relayed in their native tongue from Yamai to his brother. They set to work cheerfully enough and left me with the – I admit ungenerous – impression of being rather a dim-witted pair, with their patched clothes and navvy manner.

For my own part, I was not yet ready to commence the specific assignment Moyano had requested, that portion of the garden provoking an inexplicable reluctance in me: I supposed because it made me dwell on the garden I had lost and the apprehension that its new owner would allow what had been tended with such devotion to run wild and unloved. I therefore continued my survey of the garden and was, again, daunted by the scale of what lay ahead, an undertaking that would have tested a small colony of staff. There was also the looming black wall, never more than a glance away and forever creating a mood of oppression and being shut in. In time, I must address to Don Paquito the possibility of having it dismantled.

With no one to guide me, and the paths confusing, I quickly found myself lost, a state-of-being that was to become a common occurrence during my term at Las Lágrimas. It was thus that I came to the south-west corner, a section I did not believe Moyano had shown me the previous day. I certainly did not remember a large, unmown lawn, the grass thigh-high and crowded with thistles, nor the huge cedar (*Cedrus libani*) towering above, the only tree of any proportion within the wall. Upon closer inspection, I discovered iron handrails had been fixed into the cedar's trunk. I looked upward and, through the branches, discerned a structure. For all my running wild as a girl I had not been a bold or skilled tree-climber; nevertheless, if I could scale the cedar I might be in a superior position to view the layout of the garden.

Tucking my sketchbook inside my coat, I began to climb, the handrails making my ascent one of relative ease, and I came upon a platform hidden amongst the branches. There was a trapdoor, through which I squeezed, that led to a surprisingly substantial treehouse. I assumed it had been built for Don Guido's children, quite possibly the current owner had played here as a lamb. The treehouse consisted of two rooms, one bare except for some dusty shelves, the other furnished with several tatty deckchairs and a rug in a state of decay. Greyish light seeped in from a dirty window. Some of the floorboards were rotten, and I made sure to tread with due care; that aside, the structure was sound, though would benefit from some reinforcing and a lick of paint.

The empty room led to a balcony with a wooden railing and from it a splendid panorama of the garden and surrounding parkland, or at least it could have been had so many branches not grown to obscure it. As it was, I was able to peek through the boughs to observe the scene below. My first realization was that I had climbed higher than I imagined. I spied the Mapuches, hacking away where I had left them, and nearby the house Moyano and Latigez in discussion, as thick as thieves. I expanded my outlook and was given to a shock.

From my appraisal of the garden, I had estimated the area

enclosed by black stone to be roughly rectangular in shape. I could not have been more wrong: the wall being closer to a ring, albeit a ring that had been broken and haphazardly reforged so that there were sharp lines as well as contours. Below, one had no appreciation of this. Yet it was not all disorientation. From my vantage point, I was able to discern the original layout of the garden, most notably a central avenue that led from the fastened door through that place Moyano expected me to clear and plant, and beyond my line of sight.

From behind, there came a hard, ringing clatter, as of a coin being tossed then spinning round before settling on the floor.

I was not off the truth for, when I turned, at my feet was a peso. I had missed it when first I crossed the room and, from its sudden disturbance, presumed it must have been sitting precariously on one of the shelves to be dislodged by my movements. I picked it up, the coin tarnished and icy to my touch, and considered it between my fingertips: it had been minted in 1873. From nowhere, I thought of Gil and the wages he had swindled me of, a flash of anger coursing through me before, with equal abruptness, I was my level self again, and replaced the peso on the shelf.

I took myself back to the balcony to make a sketch, leaning out against the balustrade better to see where the main avenue ended. The wood at my hip creaked perilously and, for a sickening moment, I feared it might splinter to leave me tumbling to the ground. I righted myself, then retreated to the second room where, wiping the grime from the window,

I was able to view the avenue as it continued to the far end of the wall. It was, however, what lay on the other side that most captured my attention.

Past the black henge was a meadow that ran to a great lake. The meadow itself was windswept and bare except for a monstrous clump of brambles at its near edge. Poking drunkenly through the top of the thorns was a chimney-pot.

Here seemed something to investigate further!

I climbed to ground level and struggled to find my way. Indeed, I may have lost myself entirely had it not been for Vasca loping through the undergrowth to appear at my side. I raked her fur, studying her misshapen pelvis and speculating as to what manner of accident had befallen her. Although I fussed over Vasca, and she responded with a pleasurable growl, I remained wary: regardless of her injuries she was a powerful dog and I intended to be guarded until we were more familiar. She trotted alongside me to the exit in the wall (the sole means of getting in and out as far as I was aware), then, hearing Lola bark, she bounded off.

To the north side of the house was the working area of the garden where the sheds, barns and stables were situated, as well as the accommodation for my gardening staff when they arrived. I was confident that, if I walked past these, there must be a path to the lake. A number of horses were stabled and, as I went by, I caught the walnut face of Dahlia. I stroked her flank and, the scent of Vasca still in my fingers, twinged with loneliness. I had hoped coming to Las Lágrimas might offer some companionability, but between the reticent Dolores and scowling Calista, so far my newest affiliations were of the animal kind only. I leant in close to the horse, breathing in her comforting musk.

'How have you been, girl?' I asked. She seemed pent up. 'Did you miss me?' As if in reply she bucked her head. 'Shall we ride out on the Pampas again?'

Someone hawked behind me and spat. 'Haven't you been told? You're not to leave the estate.' It was Latigez, wearing a carpenter's apron and stinking of sawdust. I do not think I have described his voice. It cracked and gurgled as though thick with catarrh, so that I wanted constantly to tell the man to clear his throat.

'I went looking for you earlier,' I answered in a brusque tone. 'To help in the garden.'

He gave my undirtied hands an accusatory glance. 'I've more important things, working for Señor Moyano. Meantime, if you're taking this nag on the Pampas, I'll be forced to tell.'

'I might possibly, on my day off.'

'You'd be a silly girl to try. These parts are only for those that knows them.'

'I am already acquainted with the Pampas and the flatness of their aspect.' I offered an uneasy tee-hee. 'So long as I don't stray too far, I doubt I could lose my way.'

'Don't laugh at me, Señorita. There's tales aplenty of those who were never seen again after setting out there.'

He had crept closer as he spoke until I could make out the individual pockmarks on his face and his greasy muttonchops offended my nose. I wanted to be free of his company with all haste. 'How do I get to the lake?' I asked.

'I wouldn't venture there either.'

'Señor Latigez, I do not want advice on where you might or might not go. I want directions to the lake.'

'There's a path behind the barns,' he replied in an unpleasant, phlegmy voice. 'Overgrown, but you'll be able to follow it.'

I parted without another word, briskly walking away.

'Don't go wandering into the trees neither!' he called after me.

To reach the border of the meadow took no more than minutes, skirting the edge of the forest as I went. The woodland had a dark and sinister quality, the higher branches clamorous with screeching birds – though their din was as nothing to the one in my heart at my exchange with Latigez. I was full of thoughts of Gil and the staff at the Houghtons and how they despised me. They might have had more reason, but I was unsure as to why the depth of animosity from Latigez. Or Calista. Was there to my personality some innate facet people found disagreeable? Did I labour under a delusion in thinking myself a kind woman, worthy of trust and always ready to 'muck in'? Arriving at the meadow, I consoled myself with thinking that perhaps it was these damnable Argentines. Such a proposition might have carried conviction if, at that equally damnable instant, my childhood had not wheedled its way into my mind.

During my early years, I had been my parents' favourite and a popular girl, counting an abundance of friends. Then, unlike my sisters, a shoot of independence sprouted in me, and I grew to be a torment to my family, culminating in the decision to send me from London to Grandfather's. What manner of twelve-year-old is so challenging that her parents cannot bear keep her at home another day? It was meant as a punishment, the presumption being that after several weeks in the countryside with an eccentric relative I barely knew and a more modest life, my lesson would be learnt. Yet its effect had been the opposite: I never returned.

In my nature, Grandfather saw something unusual, a reflection of his own unorthodoxy, something to be cherished and nurtured and, with the same love and dedication he brought to training his roses, he encouraged the freeness of my spirit – insistent that my womanhood need not curtail me as it had, to his regret, his own daughter. My mother. As the years passed I came to see my family for what they were. Prosperous and with position yes, but without ideas of their own, being so concerned as to what other people thought that they would rather me unhappy to my boots than different from them. Yet look what I had become! No other woman whose company I have kept would have taken herself to a distant land, let alone travelled to a house as remote as this, all without a male to show the way. Let them be vindictive: my parents and sisters. The staff at the Houghtons. Latigez and Calista. I did not care.

Or, at least, would not allow myself to – which, truth to tell, is not the same thing.

With this churning inside me, I had rather lost interest in my destination. Nor did the weather inspire me to dally: the sky had grown more overcast and forbidding than when I stepped out that morning; overhead there came an unexpected reverberation of thunder. I gave the half-camouflaged chimney poking through the brambles only a cursory examination, concluding that beneath the immense thicket there must be a building and that, at some point, it might be an intriguing exercise to uncover it.

As for the lake, I did not trouble myself to visit the water's edge, merely stopped when my view was clear enough. It stretched for a considerable distance before merging into a thin, green line that was the continuation of the Pampas. At the shore, a solitary figure stood gazing over its surface. I briefly took it to be Moyano, except on consideration this individual, whoever he might be, was more scraggy, his leg oddly bent. An ill-ease stirred in me, but, upon glancing again, I saw nothing other than a group of birds bobbing on the water (godwit and ibis were, I think, their species) who, for an instant, had configured to create the illusion of a man.

A wind sprung from nowhere and coldly blew off the water, right through my coat to my skin, prompting gooseflesh. There was another growl of thunder. I tried to imagine the scene in high summer, the December skies the colour of morning glory or wild geranium, the lake warm and inviting – and failed. I took no beauty from the vista, only a creeping sense of isolation.

I walked smartly back to work before it had the chance to consume me.

A Most Violent Sound

BY THE DAY's end I formulated a plan. I should concentrate on clearing and planting the area that Moyano had indicated on our tour. Simultaneously, I would set the Mapuches to cutting back the thickets either side of the central avenue, from the fastened door-in-the-wall to where I was going to toil, thus opening up the whole part of the garden nearest the house. Regardless of Moyano's insistence that the door had been sealed for an age, I was certain for a fact I had seen it ajar. If we could do so again, Don Paquito would have the pleasure of being able to stroll through the French windows of the morning room, along the avenue to his favoured spot, all the while admiring what I, as Head Gardener, had achieved. Of the coming evenings, I intended to continue with my sketches of the garden as a whole, so that I might present the Don with my proposals for the future.

Excited by my schemes I went to dinner to tell Moyano, but he was not at the table, nor did I see him for the remainder of the evening.

When I stepped out the next morning, the day was already exhausted with itself, the sky low and full of lumbering clouds streaked with darkness, an ill wind driving them forward. The two Mapuches were hacking at the undergrowth. I ordered them to follow me and, as we trod our way, I enquired after their well-being and how they had spent their night. I had no idea where on the grounds they made their home, so asked after that also. This question, as with my others, was met with suspicion, Yamai speaking in a dropped voice to Epulef and his brother shaking his head in return as if I were probing with malign intent. I received nothing but terse answers and soon gave up, needing my undivided attention to discern where the central path was. From the treehouse it appeared obvious; at ground level the skills of an archaeologist, rather than gardener, were needed as I struggled to decipher the layout from the ghosts of paths.

In the end, and fearing a forfeit of authority if I got the Mapuches lost, I used the house as my pole-star and kept us alongside the wall, aware of the deadening weight of its black, pagan stones, until we reached the fastened door. On this side, Moyano's assertion that it had not opened in years seemed entirely plausible. It was hidden beneath a curtain of tangled sprays and ivy that had not been disturbed for many a season.

Leading away from it was, at last, the central avenue. I waded through the weeds down its length toward that place Moyano had instructed me to clear – but even as we approached, the Mapuches faltered and stopped.

'We will not work here,' said Yamai.

'Why on earth not?'

For an answer, the two brothers simply trudged back whence we came.

Unwilling to enter into an argument so early in our acquaintance, I let out a sigh that made little guise of my displeasure and bent my steps after them, informing the pair that to-day, at least, they could start at that section by the door. The borders either side had all but gone back to Nature and were overrun with fearsome-looking briars. What had been a straightforward plan the previous night seemed foolhardy, even arrogant, in the face of reality and, if I am to honour my stated aim of complete verity, I must confess at that moment to some shameful part of me wondering why Moyano had trusted such an ambitious restoration to me. To a woman.

I rallied as quickly as I had been bowed and, giving a vigorous clap to claim the Mapuches' attention, explained what needed to be done. As usual, Yamai repeated my instructions. The task ahead was gargantuan, all hands were needed. So I went to find Latigez.

There was no sign of him in any of the sheds, nor at the stables, though opposite them I spied a path I had yet to explore but that must surely wind back in the direction of the house. I elected to see if I was right and whether Latigez might be found there, feeling a flutter of frustration as I went, aware of the morning ticking by and my wasting it looking for staff who really should be at my call.

I soon gained a new part of the grounds at the rear of the house and to my surprise a second walled area, this one in traditional and, let it be said, pleasing red brick. Within was an extravagant kitchen garden. It being the end of winter much of frame-yard and slips were fallow or bearing plants that would not crop for months; nevertheless a fair portion was productive and I noted beetroot, celery, seakale and carrots. This was, evidently, where the fresh vegetables that graced the dining table came from. It was also where I found Latigez, digging the ground. He was dressed in a grubby, white shirt, the collar unbuttoned. By his feet sat a trug of earthy potatoes.

I approached him stiffly. 'Señor, please, I need your help if we are to have any chance of making the garden ready for Don Paquito.'

'Not now.'

'If not now, when?'

'*Mañana.*'

I groaned. *Mañana* – 'tomorrow' – was amongst the first rejoinders one became familiar with in Argentina. Whenever it was conceivably possible, the business of to-day was put off until *mañana*. Needless to say, *mañana* never came.

In response to my groan, Latigez drove his fork into the soil and paused in his work, arching his back. 'I have to dig these for Calista.'

'And you always obey a woman's order?'

'Better that, than riling her temper.' He began a histrionic counting off of his fingers. 'Then I have more carpentry for Señor Moyano. Then I have to help Farrido with his infernal boiler. Then I have to paint the front gate.' He let forth a disgruntled expulsion of air. 'I may have an hour this afternoon.'

I was sure he was saying this simply to be rid of me; all the same I decided upon a coaxing approach, in the hope it might achieve a more felicitous result. 'That would be most helpful of you, Señor. We are trying to clear the central avenue.'

'You've a month's graft there at least.'

'Don't I know it,' I smiled. 'If only I had more workers.'

'I see your pale little paws are still clean.'

'Perhaps if you were easier to find, I should have muddied them sooner.'

He shook his head. 'And I won't work with those red-devils.'

'What devils are they?'

The sputum rattled in his throat. 'Your Mapuches,' he answered. 'Best be on guard against them, Señorita. They're lecherous beyond belief, quite unable to control their primitive urges, all the more for one so choice as yourself.'

'I'm sure you can find a spot to work alone,' I replied, flushing tremendously, and changed subject. 'Do you tend this garden as well?'

His expression made plain that he had enjoyed my blushes. 'It's Calista's. I only lend my back.' And with that, he resumed his digging.

I ambled around the rest to satisfy my curiosity. It would provide more than an abundance for the family, more even for a full contingent of guests and staff as in the house's days of old. I suspected its excess was for show, though whoever had planned its proportions, by which I meant Don Guido, saw nothing wasteful about it, nothing contemptible. A partition-wall bisected the enclosure through which an archway led to a mature orchard of apple, pear, cherry and other stoned-fruits (all in late-dormancy); peaches had been espaliered against the brickwork. The only fruit ready to pick were the oranges, which glowed brightly in the dim morning light. There also stood a considerable glasshouse.

As I stepped inside, I heard raised voices and, glancing back through the arch, I saw that Dolores, wearing a black cape over her uniform, had joined Latigez. He was stabbing his finger at her, though whether in anger or some other emotional state I could not determine. She reached for the trug of potatoes, which prompted him to wrestle it back. It was not my affair, and so I directed my attention to the interior of the glasshouse. There were neat rows of salad crops and tomato plants and, above my head, a number of contorted grape vines. One corner had been neglected, the panes occluded with mildew, and here I found a collection of cracked, ugly-looking pots seemingly dumped without regard. From within came the scuttle of rodents – which, all at once, froze.

At my rear, I sensed someone enter the glasshouse. I looked at the pane before my face and caught a dark reflection advancing toward me, the movement lolloping and awkward.

Assuming it was Dolores engaged in some prank, I turned brusquely to her and asked, 'What were you and Latigez quarrelling over?'

Through the door of the glasshouse, through the orchard and archway in the wall, I could clearly see Latigez and the maid still in argument by the potato-bed, neither paying me the least attention. Dolores managed to secure the trug and hurried away with it, Latigez jeering at her retreat. When I returned my gaze to the glass there was nothing to see but my own image, refracted and doubled in the grime. In their pots, the rodents were scuttling again.

It was rather after ten o'clock by the time I returned to my section of the garden. I had avoided walking back via the Mapuches, in part because I did not wish to be considered a fusspot overseeing their every move, but chiefly because I was keen to get going with the rough work myself. It may have rankled me to rise to Latigez's taunts, but I wanted to demonstrate I was no shirker.

As a rule, I like to garden without gloves so that I may feel the earth between my fingers, a preference that always disturbed Mother for, if it was disreputable enough that I wanted to be a gardener, actually to dirty my hands, with its connotations of the labouring class, was truly shameful. To go gloveless here was not sensible: the thorns would have cut me to ribbons. Moyano had procured me a pair of thick, sheepskin gauntlets, and I wore these to slash away at the welter. When a sufficiency had been cleared I turned over the earth with my fork, stubbing up the roots. Sometimes these proved too much and it was with a mild discontent that I realized I must depend on Yamai's brute force to complete the job. It was steady labour: foot by foot the ground revealed itself. My pile of cuttings began to heap up. In due course, these would have to be burnt – another task to consider.

I cannot say these were the happiest hours of gardening I had ever known. There was something about this spot I found disagreeable: an atmosphere, difficult to put into words, of oppression, some quality that made me feel vulnerable and not a little sad. As I dug, I pondered the kitchen garden. The disaster that had befallen this main part had not touched that place, everything there being well tended. If the kitchen garden belonged to Calista, a germ as to why the cook was so antagonistic began to form, for perhaps she feared I wanted to take its supervision from her.

At the lunch hour, Dolores arrived bearing a small hamper of bread, cured meat and a bottle of milk. She glanced nervously around her, and when I asked her to join me to chatter awhile she refused, bobbing into one of her curtsies and scurrying back inside.

After eating, my limbs in want of a stretch, I took a little exercise, following the main avenue in the direction I had not yet ventured. As I walked, a curious fluting came to my ear. It was not the call of a bird, nor the whistle of a man, rather it possessed an unworldly, choral quality. I trailed it to its source, quickly reaching the far wall, and discovered that here the dry-walling was not as solid as in other sections. There were clefts and crevices between the rocks, allowing gusts of wind to pass through them, the cause of the eerie noise.

'Music of the Pampas,' I said aloud, not entirely comforting myself.

I pressed my face to one of the chinks, feeling the cold stone against my cheek, and looked into the meadow beyond. The lake was a ponderous pewter colour and in the near-ground I clapped eyes on Vasca and Lola, tumbling around and chasing each other. I smiled as I watched them play until, unexpectedly, they froze, ears pricked. I twisted my face against the wall to see more clearly what had captured their attention, but was unable to. The dogs paused for a long, hypnotized moment – then hurtled out of view.

I returned to work. The afternoon darkened early as the

clouds sunk further still, their undersides changing from the colour of lead to sloe-black. Any lower and the estate must be plunged into fog. Despite my gauntlets, I was aware of various nicks on my arms; the muscles in my shoulders ached and my lower back felt more strained than was decent. That night I was going to have the pleasure of my first, and *decidedly overdue*, bath. My mind seized on the idea, imagining the luxuriation of hot water and being able to clean myself at last.

The next instant, my mood was elsewhere, those intermittent qualms that had troubled me since setting out for Las Lágrimas having coalesced into a most profound misgiving. I came to the realization – no, that was not forceful enough – an absolute knowledge, as sure as the knowledge one must grow old and pass on, that to restore the garden was an impossibility. I was furious that Moyano had misled me about its circumstance, furious that Grandfather had died, furious that our garden had been stolen from me when I was as content-as-ever-could-be there. These thoughts were accompanied by a deep chill, though the wind was no sharper, indeed it had dropped to a whisper.

Then came the sound.

It was violent and rhythmic, and for several moments I struggled to identify it.

Crack—

Crack—

Crack—

It was an axe being brought to bear against a tree. I was almost physically aware of steel splintering bark. The blows continued remorselessly. Someone was cutting down one of the trees in the parkland beyond. I had already identified that some coppicing was necessary; this, however, was not the sound of the surgeon cutting for the greater health of the forest. It was frenzied, as of murder. The Mapuches would not dare attempt anything of this sort and I had not seen Moyano all day, so it seemed unlikely he had chosen such a task this late. It could only be Latigez, though whether on Moyano's instructions or under his own volition I knew not. I was angry that he had accepted this chore instead of helping in the garden.

I fought to ignore the noise, concentrating my attention on my fork and attacking the roots with a fury of equal to the axe, as if I hated the very earth. The wind had returned, swirling through the trees, making it impossible to identify from where the sound originated. It continued so long that at any time I expected a cry of *timber!* – or *árbol cae!* as they say here.

Then, abruptly. It ceased.

The silence that succeeded was unmarked by bird or breeze, pervasive and mournful. And like a cloud having passed in front of the sun, my mood lightened. I was my usual self again, except exhausted – the day's exertion having plainly taken its toll. I tidied my area, gathered the cuttings into a heap and decided I had had my fill. I was counting the hours until bathtime.

As I traced my path through the garden to the tool shed, I was startled by Latigez's phlegmy voice. 'Finishing early, are we?' He was slicing away at the weeds. 'Not the best example to set, Señorita.'

I ignored his goading. 'What tree were you cutting down?'

'None. I've been here the past hour, as you told me.'

'So it was Señor Moyano?'

'He's enough with his own duties to-day.'

'Then who? They were blazing at it forever.'

A shadow passed over his face. 'I heard no tree being cut.'

'But surely…'

'No.'

I was too weary to debate the matter further, and left him to it. In the tool shed I brushed clean my fork, then sharpened and oiled my secateurs, ready for the morrow. I saw a line of axes hanging on the wall. Before I finished, I examined them briefly. They had not been touched in an age. Each head was rusty from lack of use, the chopping edge quite blunt.

The First Bath

THE NIGHT OF my first bath arrived. I ate two courses of dinner alone in that dark, austere room until Moyano bustled in replete with a bonhomie I had no energy for. A mouth-watering smell of burnt sugar, apples and spices rose from the kitchen. Once more, I had the sad realization I would deny myself pudding, for as soon as Moyano entered, I rose from the table.

'Finished so soon, Señorita?'

'It's my bath tonight.'

'We must not keep a lady from her ablutions,' he said, whether in a tone affectionate or sarcastic I could not decide. 'Has young Dolores shown you where to go?'

'I haven't seen her this evening,' I replied. The food had been waiting on the table when I came down.

He tut-tutted. 'Then it appears the duty falls upon me.'

'Do you not want to eat?'

'It can wait,' he smiled.

I said first I had to speak to Calista, and hurried to the kitchen where the smell of foaming butter and cinnamon was more intense. The range gave off a welcoming heat; copper pans glinted on hooks.

'Where's Dolores?' I asked a little breathlessly. 'I need her to show me to the bathroom.'

The cook deliberated and, for a moment, I thought my question would pass ignored. 'Señor Moyano let her the night off. It's her full-moon, the poor thing suffers.'

These were the first words I had actually exchanged with Calista. She had a bassoony voice, each word spoken slowly as if chosen with care, giving the impression of old, passed-down wisdom. Here was a woman who could make a recipe for spotted-dick sound like a verse from the Old Testament.

I decided to press this unexpected dialogue between us. 'I found the kitchen garden to-day.' As I suspected it would, the cook's face darkened. 'It is clear to me it's tended by hands that care.'

'If you want good food, you start with the soil.'

I offered my most conciliatory demeanour. 'I have more than enough to do with the main garden.'

'That's what the last one said. The next thing, he's taking mine over, telling me how to stake beans, ripping out the beetroots.'

'There was another gardener?'

'Before you. Happily, he didn't care for the place. And left.'

I spoke in soothing tones. 'Calista, on the subject of fruit and vegetables I am an ignoramus.' This was not strictly true, but it served my purpose. 'I promise you, the kitchen garden will be your domain. Yours alone.'

She gave me a long, probing stare as if to divine what lay behind my eyes, hers, as I noted, being the colour of tortoiseshell. 'It's hard to trust a lady's word when she doesn't eat puddings. Monday and yesterday you didn't want my caramel. Tonight, you seem ready to hurry off.'

'Can I assure you, it's not your desserts I find off-putting,' – I hesitated, uncertain of their relationship – 'rather the company.'

She smiled with cool approval at my candidness, revealing a gleam of white teeth, and I was sure we were going to be friends. It was a friendship I was to test sorely, but I shall come to that in its proper order. From the oven she produced an apple-turnover. 'Then eat here, with me.'

I sat at the kitchen table; the turnover was an excellent one, tasting as delicious as it smelt. I begged a second portion, less to fill myself than to confirm our new amity. When I returned to the dining room, Moyano had still to start his food and was sat away from the table smoking a panatela. I questioned him about the tree cutting and, as had Latigez, he claimed no knowledge of it.

'Are you certain,' I pressed him, 'that there are no other members of staff?'

'I should think, Señorita, that I know everyone who works under me,' he replied affably enough, though to his words there seemed a flicker of equivocation.

After I had fetched my toilet-bag and towels, Moyano conducted me into the new wing and, as he did so, I queried him about the previous Head Gardener.

'Ah. Señor Maurín. He managed a month before moving on.'

'Why did he leave?'

'I told you in Buenos Aires, this is a lonely place. Not all have the right temperament. Las Lágrimas is too remote for some, it can do things to the mind.'

'What about you, Señor?'

'I do not have the luxury of being so sensitive. Opportunity is against me. If I fail to make a success of Las Lágrimas, who knows what future there'll be for me.' He became fervid. 'Which is why everything must proceed without fault. Which is why the garden must be a triumph.'

'How long have you been at the estancia?' I asked.

He led me up a broad staircase to a corridor of rooms where came the smell of newly laid carpet, like threshed barley.

'More than a year. I helped oversee the building of this new wing. I also had a predecessor, another estate manager who had a short tenure before me. He found the house too isolated and could not bear to remain, whereas something drew me here from the start. Las Lágrimas is a place for those who have known their share of loss. I sensed that in you, Ursula, from when first we met.' Before I could protest, or rebuke him about my name, he flung open a door. 'Now here is your bathroom.'

It was generously proportioned, with space sufficient for a long, deep tub, a basinstand and rattan settee. As with all the décor in the new wing, everything was as white as a bride on her wedding day: white floor tiles, white walls, white sanitary furniture. A large mirror captured us standing side by side in the doorframe, Moyano rubbing at his wrist.

'You will be the very first person to use it,' he said

proprietarily. 'Indeed, before the family arrives, it will be for your sole use.'

'Then why can I not bathe every night?'

He took a time to configure his reply. 'The instructions of Señor Farrido, I'm afraid. He wants to break in the boiler gently, though on your allotted nights, there should be hot water aplenty.' To prove his point, he opened the tap; soon there came billows of steam.

I waited until Moyano's footsteps had receded downstairs and I was sure he was ensconced in the dining room, though that particular, smoky odour of his lingered. Then I began undressing and tied my hair in a bun. That earlier suspicion of my forearms being scratched proved correct and they stung when I slid into the water. It was the perfect temperature, hot enough to prompt a little gasp as I submerged. A sensation of bliss filled me. I lay there until the water began to lose its heat and had become greyish with dirt, then I scrubbed myself from head to toe. After five days without washing I left the bathroom as if I had been given a fresh skin. Like a snake on his honeymoon, I could almost hear Grandfather say, and chortled to myself.

I returned to the old wing, closing the light-switches as I went, leaving blackness behind me. At the dining table, Moyano was now eating his supper. I sneaked past him, past the surveillance of Don Guido's portraits and up the stairs to my poky room. Outside, the darkness was thick and I could hear the wind, which was strengthening, moan through the trees.

It was as I was folding back the sheets in preparation to get into bed when I thought I heard the creep of footsteps in the corridor. They came stealthily from the direction of the staircase, their only indication being the slightest creak of floorboards, and ended in front of my door. I waited for whomever was outside to knock, trying to imagine whatever could be wanted of me at this hour. No such knock was forthcoming, though I was sure of a person standing there in silence. Perhaps it was the estate manager, who must have after all seen me go upstairs and had some overlooked business that needed addressing; or Calista, wishing to consolidate our new friendship with the offer of a nightcap. But if it was either, why did they not simply make themselves known? I stood with the bedsheets still half-drawn back and, as I remained in that position, a peculiar agitation began to sneak through me, borne of intuition rather than reason or fact. From somewhere out on the estate the wind carried the distant howl of dogs.

Rather reluctantly, I threw on my peignoir and then reached for Rivacoba's poncho, tugging it over my head, to assure my modesty regardless of how eccentric my get-up might be – and opened the door.

'Yes?' I went to say.

The corridor was quite empty.

I craned my head in both directions and found only shadows, yet despite the evidence of my eyes I would have staked my inheritance on there being someone there.

I closed the door, turning the key and, though I do not remember making a deliberate decision to do so, from that night forth slept with my room always locked.

Beneath the Veil of Thorns

THE GLOOM OF the previous day showed no inclination of lifting the next, to which now came the additional discomfort of a bitter, nagging wind. It howled over the treetops, raw with the cold of Patagonia, Argentina's most southern province, a stretch of land, literally, at the end of the world. After all these months in South America I was still in astonishment at how far from home I had journeyed.

Until the events of the afternoon, the day proceeded much as the one before. I marshalled the Mapuches, having to repeat my prior instructions to them as if never had I issued any, then I attempted to find Latigez. Tramping around the grounds I saw not another soul, indeed it was disconcerting how rapidly one found oneself alone. No sooner were the Mapuches out of sight, than it was easy to believe the whole estancia was as deserted as it had been these past three decades. The monstrous black wall deadened all sound; the weeds grew in contempt of human intervention. Given the work that lay ahead was more onerous than anticipated, I wanted as many days as possible before Don Paquito graced us. By another measure, he could not arrive soon enough. Las Lágrimas was in need of more staff, not only to ease the burden of the garden, but to slough off the feeling that it was still dormant. I was sure to feel less unnerved when I walked around and saw other people, heard the sounds of living creatures other than the eerie shriek of chimangos.

After a fruitless twenty minutes, I gave up searching for Latigez: there was enough to do without playing hide-and-seek. I returned to my own spot in the garden and resumed my toil, the stiffness in my back from yesterday's labour taking some while to ease. Since the wind was more forceful, I was able to hear the shrill pipings and flutings caused by the chinks in the wall from this distance, the noise as of an invisible chorus whistling a diabolical tune. I soon grew to dislike it and hummed 'A British Tar', one of Grandfather's favourite melodies, to distract myself, albeit I am no admirer of Gilbert & Sullivan. I felt, too, that same oppressive atmosphere as before, a sense that my work was being scrutinized and, now and again, I glanced up as if to find someone. My mind even began to imagine Señor Moyano was hidden close by, observing me, wanting to assure himself he had not erred in his choice of Head Gardener. I remained irked by our conversation on the way to the bathroom and how easily he had read my character. Rather than my own loss, I wished I had turned his remarks in the opposite direction – and asked to know what he had been deprived of.

At midday, though given the duskiness of the sky one would scarcely know the sun was at its peak, Dolores arrived with my hamper. It was a more generous offering than yesterday's, with the bread thickly buttered, a variety of chorizos and a slice of cake. The maid looked wan, the rings beneath her eyes pronounced. As on our previous lunchtime congress, she shunned any conversation and hurried back inside.

After I had eaten, I pressed my face to one of the gaps in the Wailing Wall (for this was the name by which I came to call it: because of the evocative sounds it emitted, because of its westerly aspect – as in the Temple Wall of Jerusalem), and gazed out to find Vasca and Lola at play again. I enjoyed the brio and complete lack of self-consciousness with which they tumbled about, and tried to recall any such abandonment with my own mother as a child. In the background, the lake was ragged from the wind, flocks of birds riding upon its surface, the afternoon pierced by their occasional cries.

All at once, in a repeat of yesterday, the two German shepherds froze, as if someone had blown a whistle to capture their attention. I twisted my face against the black stone to see better. The meadow was empty. The dogs' ears pricked backward, then Lola bolted, racing to the mass of sprawling bramble, the one that had the chimney poking through the top. She sniffed vigorously along the base, before flattening her body and disappearing within. I expected her to re-emerge shortly after – but she did not. It was like watching someone dive beneath the waves: one counts the seconds until they break the surface and, when they fail to, ill-ease begins to nag at one's nerves. Vasca remained where she was, hunkered down and growling.

'Lola!' I called out, my voice light yet commanding.

I made an effort to dismiss my anxiety, aware that it was not entirely accountable. How many times must the dogs have played at this spot? Moyano had been here already a year; Lola must have vanished just-so on a hundred previous occasions without anyone troubling themselves over her. And yet... I was unable to shake off a feeling that something untoward had befallen her. What if her coat had snagged on the thorns, for they were as unforgiving as iron nails, and she was caught and bleeding?

I called to her again, counting a full sixty seconds, before I snatched up my secateurs and hurried to where the Mapuches were working.

'Bring your scythes. Come with me,' I ordered. Yamai began his translation: I cut him short. 'There's no time!'

They heard my urgency, for they followed forthwith. We raced through the garden, past the stables and to the bramble bush. Vasca had edged nearer to it, though remained at a wary distance, her body rigid, her nostrils twitching. Still there was no sign of her pup.

'Lola!' I cried. 'Lola!'

I listened for any bark or whimper that might indicate where she was and, discerning neither, began cutting back the branches of thorns at the precise point where the dog had disappeared. The Mapuches seemed hesitant to join me until I roared at them to help. We slashed and tore at the brambles, pulling them away in thick, tangled sheets. The spines were vicious, like claws, the bramble itself almost a living thing, dangerously dense. More than once I heard a tear as the material of my skirts caught. The two boys, who were not protected by gauntlets as was I, were forced to proceed with greater caution, yet even so their arms were soon bleeding.

I cut through another mass of vegetation, tossing it away, and came to a barrier of sawn logs, uniform in length, redolent of old creosote: we had cut back to whatever building lay hidden beneath the veil of thorns. I got to my knees to see if there was any gap that Lola might have squeezed herself through. At our discovery, the Mapuches exchanged hushed words in their own language. They seemed watchful and trepidatious.

'What is this place?' I asked of them.

'Tarella,' came Yamai's reply. It was a word I was unfamiliar with and, having forgotten my dictionary that day, I had to wait until the evening for the opportunity to look up its meaning. No definition was listed.

From our rear, Vasca gave a bark. She was sitting quite contentedly, her body no longer tense. At her side, head cocked at an angle, eyes bright with curiosity as to the incomprehensible ways of human behaviour, was Lola. With a laugh I ran to her and cupped her face, letting her lick my hands, even allowing her tongue to flick at my cheeks. 'You silly dog,' I chided her, feeling foolish now to have worried so.

After much fussing, during which Vasca grew jealous and I had to pet her too, the dogs trotted off and my attention returned to the building. We had made better work of uncovering it than I realized, as if the structure concealed beneath wanted to disrobe itself. That which was already exposed appeared to be in good repair, the bramble having protected it from the elements. I yanked away some more branches and revealed a section of window. Whilst the Mapuches muttered between themselves, I peered in. It was too dark to view the interior properly, though I was able to make out a sizeable room with a table and decided, pretty smartly, that if it were habitable, it might make a good place to work, certainly a step-up from my cramped bedroom or sharing easels with Moyano. I told the Mapuches to keep clearing. Now that the urgency had passed, their disinclination was more pronounced.

Gradually, we uncovered more of the structure, yet as I continued to cut, an aching disconsolation took possession of me for which I could not account. My body sagged, despair weighed behind my eyes. It was almost as if I heard a mocking whisper that a year's slog on this bramble would never see it cleared, nor any of the garden. I saw the same sentiment in my companions' faces. To ward it off I redoubled my efforts, violently slashing away, until I came to a wooden door. When I tried the handle, however, it was rusted fast and refused to yield.

Crack—

Crack—

The sound of the axe rolled out from the woodland.

'Do you hear that?' I asked the two native boys.

At first they shook their heads. I was insistent, until in the lowest murmur Yamai replied, '*Sí*, Señorita.'

'Do you know who it is?'

'No.'

'Is it Latigez? Señor Moyano?'

They laid down their scythes in union and regarded me with such gawking, imbecilic expressions that my desolation was overrun by such a vengeful irritation that I wanted to strike them both. The degree of my fury, so uncharacteristic, disturbed me.

Crack—

I struggled to control myself, and directed my words to Yamai. 'Find whoever is cutting down that tree and bring him here at once. He can help us.'

'Señorita, no.'

His adamancy drew me up short. 'Why the devil not?'

'We are forbidden to walk amongst the trees.'

'By whom?'

Yamai's expression was of alarm. He searched for a response before his usually mute brother answered in his place with a most unconvincing plea: 'Señor Moyano.'

'To hell with Moyano. I am giving you permission.'

'Our father warned us also,' added Yamai, finding his tongue. 'We are sorry, Señorita.'

After which, they bowed their heads and studied their ill-fitting boots, invincible in refusal.

'Very well,' I said sharply. 'I shall go myself, and expect you to continue here. If we can clear the rest of these brambles that, at least, will be something for the day.'

It was only as I marched off, toward one of the narrow entrances to the parkland and the dark tangle of trees beyond, that I acknowledged the true source of my exasperation. I was reluctant to venture there myself.

The Axeman

I PLUNGED INTO the twilit world of the trees. The view ahead was murky, a green that seeped into grey, patterned with shade and, beyond, darker patches still, much of the afternoon's already feeble light obscured by the canopy. All around, the wind hissed through the leaves like breakers. And somewhere, the queer rolling, echoing chop of that axe. When first I entered the woodland, it seemed evident that whoever was at work must be near at hand, but within a short space I came to understand I had been mistaken. The sound was much farther away. When I found the individual chopping at the tree, I was decided on giving them a piece of my mind.

'Should ever I find him.'

I had spoken aloud, and regretted doing so at once. My words sounded out of place, as one who talks too volubly in the hush of a cathedral.

I pressed further into the forest, following an overgrown trail that wound between the boles, stooping on occasion to avoid the lower branches. My emotions remained a muddle of despondency and inexplicable rage; I was also ashamed at my outburst against the Mapuches. And all the while, the chopping – as if its originator was insensible to fatigue, the sound playing constant tricks on me. Close enough one minute that I confidently expected to stumble across the man swinging the axe, be it Moyano or a new, undisclosed member of staff. Then the next, reverberating from the most distance edge of the parkland. I tried as best I could to chase the sound, and soon found myself without the least idea in which direction house or garden lay. I could not even retrace my steps for I had taken any number of splits in the paths, which were, in any respect, labyrinthine. What if I could not find my way back? What should happen if I was lost after dark? Would any of the staff notice my absence and trouble themselves to find me? The questions proliferated in my head, none of them comforting.

I struggled onward, in bitter disagreement with Lord Byron's line that 'There is pleasure in a pathless wood', my anxiety continuing to mount, before I emerged on to a reassuringly wide thoroughfare. It was not as broad as the 'Imperial Avenue' that I had ridden when first I arrived, nevertheless its respectable proportion suggested this was one of the main arteries through the estancia.

The sound of the axe was at once nearer again, the mystery now being why I had experienced such difficulty in locating it. Some way ahead, I spied the figure of a man working at the base of a trunk, his form dark against the fading green haze of the forest. He had not a shred of hair, making clear the outline of his skull.

I went to call out to him, to alert him to my approach.

And stopped myself. An intuition, one I could not explain, cautioned me against doing so.

The figure was attacking the tree; I could think of no better way to describe the ferocity with which he brought his axe to bear. Each blow radiated fury. He swung the axe again and drove the head so thoroughly into the wood that it lodged stuck. Needs must that he had to fight and twist to release it before raising the blade above his head in preparation to strike anew when, for the first time, he became aware of my presence.

He lowered the axe, and we appraised each other.

The light was too poor and shadowy for me to determine his features precisely. Foremost were his hands, one gripped around the shaft of the axe, the other hanging loose: they were large and coarse, the fingers gnarled at the joints, and appeared out of proportion with the rest of his body, the skin a greenish-yellow hue as of one suffering some disease. He was neither as tall as Moyano, nor short as Latigez, the most noteworthy aspect of his stature being how it emphasized his thinness. He was as a starved man and bore every trace of prolonged hardship. Could this be Farrido, the elusive boiler engineer? A ragged, black poncho hung from his shoulders, the odour of which offended my nose, it having the acrid stench of spent earth and leaves left to rot in a sack.

Now that we had seen each other, there was no reason not to address him, yet still my voice refused to come. This was absurd! I needed all the staff the estancia had to offer, especially one possessed of such fortitude.

'*Buenos días*, Señor,' I called to him, raising my hand in

vague salutation, whilst making no attempt to shorten the distance between us. For there emanated from the axeman such a sense of emotion – an emotion raw and inconsolable, yet impossible to define other than it darkened my heart – that I had no wish to intrude on it.

In response to my greeting, he lifted the hood of his poncho to cover his head, heaved the axe over his shoulder and started away from me. He had the most terrible, terrible limp, dragging his right leg behind him as if it were a dead thing.

His back to me, I found more of my voice. 'Señor, wait!' I cried. 'Please, there is a matter I wish to discuss.'

He paid no heed and continued his limping away. I became aware of the stillness around me. There was no chatter of birds; the wind had dropped to a sigh. I followed after him, reaching the tree where he had been at work, a mature tala (*Celtis tala*). There was a deep gash in it, as there was in the trunk next to it and the one after that. Indeed, all the boles about me had felt the bite of his axe – though in his work he appeared to be rather distractible, as if no sooner had he begun chopping at one than he moved on to the next.

At the base of the nearest tala an object glinted dully. I knelt to examine it and found a silver peso buried in the bark. If the axeman's intention was to free it, he had been unsuccessful, as was my own attempt to prise it loose; I might as well been trying to remove a nail hammered into timber.

I returned my attention to the axeman, hoping still to catch up with him. But when I looked up, the path was empty.

Ahead, the avenue curved through the trees and out of sight. If the axeman had continued on his way, he would have disappeared from view... excepting that the distance between where I had last spied him and that vanishing point was too great. Even discounting his injured leg, he would have needed to advance at a formidable pace. There was the possibility he had slipped off the path altogether, but the woodland either side was a great, green morass and difficult to traverse; besides, what reason would he have to do such a thing? I hurried on, convinced, as unlikely as it might be, that once I had rounded the bend, I would again observe his limping figure. When at last I made that spot, however, he was still nowhere to be seen.

The wind came back to life, chasing through the branches. Song and movement cheered the air as the birds began their preparations to nest, the hour before dusk being upon us. Although I remained baffled as to how the axeman had slipped away, my more pressing concern was now to orientate myself so that I might make my way indoors before nightfall. I marched the avenue, noting no disturbance of the path that suggested any other person had been this way and, after several minutes, understood exactly where I was in the grounds, though quite how I had managed to arrive here was a puzzle.

I was standing before the derelict mansion. It stood forlorn, dark and lifeless, yet on that first afternoon when I discovered it, I had seen signs of habitation. Was it here that the axeman dwelt? Curiosity impelled me to know. From the eaves I heard pigeons cooing.

I steeled myself, for this place was enough to give anyone the pips, and entered into a galleried hallway that was less ill-lit than I had supposed to find it, the source of its illumination being a hole in the ceiling, open to the next floor, and above that to the rafters and a jagged circle of sky. The building creaked and sighed, exhaling an odour of damp and rot mingled with the vestiges of the fire that had ravaged it. I made my transit through numerous ruined rooms, all of which were bare of furnishings and had walls of peeling black, though I could tell they had once been very fine indeed. I would have to ask Calista if she knew anything of the previous nature of this building. Thence to a dingy passageway that I followed to its far end and a door that opened on to a small parlour. Laid on the floorboards were three makeshift cots. Here it was dry and musty; I caught the tang of male sweat.

There were a number of other items that suggested this was someone's home and I deduced this must be where the Mapuches slept, though who the third bed belonged to, I could not say. Moyano's position precluded his possibility, and I snorted ironically at the prospect of Latigez bunking down with my two native charges, which led to only one conclusion. The axeman. I felt a twinge of annoyance at Moyano, for he had been untruthful to me: as I had suspected, there *was* another member of staff. I turned from the beds – and let out a cry of alarm.

Standing behind me, his face creased in curiosity at the uninvited person in his dwelling, was an aged man, the crown of his head as smooth as that of the figure I had recently seen in the woods. He had removed his stinking poncho and was dressed in shirt, waistcoat and trousers, the clothes darned many times, the fabric faded and shabby. He was barefoot and had thus nothing to conceal his toenails, which were curled and black, and quite repellent to behold.

I recovered myself and said, 'I think it rude to creep up on people.'

'And to be where you should not.'

We stood, looking as if each did not quite believe in the other. There was a familiar turn to his features. He had an etched, native face, deeply stained by a lifetime of sun and wind. If this was indeed the axeman, I was surprised that he possessed the vitality to wield an axe with such sustained exertion. I was taller than him by a margin.

'You are the English señorita?' the old man asked, his voice weak and rasping.

'My name is Ursula.'

'And I, Namuncura. My sons speak well of you.'

'You are the father of Yamai and Epulef?'

'Yes.'

'What is this place?'

'Our home.'

'And before that?'

No answer was forthcoming.

'It is not my intention to pry,' I said. 'I am simply curious.'

'Señor Moyano does not like talk of days past.'

I offered a smile. 'Then we two shall not tell him.'

At first I thought I would again be answered with silence. Then Namuncura began to speak. If secretly I hoped for a revelation I was soon disappointed, listening instead to a rambling speech, the old man occasionally falling into his native tongue. I was given to speculate whether old age had ripened his mind too much. As best as I could piece together, Namuncura had worked at the estate as a young man. The setting where he held his current audience was once used for the guests of Don Guido when every room in the main house was occupied, this during the glory period of the estancia and its infamous parties. I wondered if Doña Ybarra, the woman I had met on the train, had ever stayed in the mansion. One night, Namuncura narrated to me, a fire had broken out and consumed much of the place. In the days after, Don Guido sent his guests packing and abandoned Las Lágrimas.

'Did anyone die?' I asked.

'Some leapt from the windows and broke themselves. The wife of Don Guido suffered... how you say?' He patted his face and torso. 'Fire on her skin. But no people died.'

'What caused the blaze?'

An uncomfortable, drawn-out pause followed. 'I do not know.'

'Was it an accident? Revellers who drank too much and got carried away?'

Namuncura spoke in a husky tone. 'I am tired, Señorita. I must rest now. And you must return before night-time.'

'Of course,' I replied, sensing no more was to be learnt. 'I'm being inconsiderate. You are surely worn out after all your exertion. I would be glad if tomorrow you can join your sons in the garden. I need all the help I can.'

'I am an old man. Too old to work.'

'But earlier, with the axe. I saw you cutting the tree.'

All expression died from his face. He paled to a degree that I feared he might be in the first stages of a seizure. 'It is best you leave, Señorita.'

'If I have offended you—'

'Leave!'

I found my way out of the building, through the ruined rooms I had passed earlier, grown now full of shadows. It was only as I came to the main door that I heard the patter of Namuncura's bare feet.

'Señorita, forgive me. Please, say nothing to Señor Moyano. He is a wrathful man and has it in his will to send me and my sons away. We have no place else.'

The gloaming hour was upon the estate, the clouds having already shed what little light they had mustered through the day. As if emboldened by the dusk, the wind came in spiteful gusts, messing my hair. I hastened from the burnt-out mansion, following the route I had taken on the afternoon of my arrival, and made an effort to recall my high hopes of that first day, riding into Las Lágrimas as the Head Gardener of a great estate. It was disheartening to acknowledge how much of that enthusiasm was gone, and so soon.

Along the path, I saw the lumbering figures of Yamai and Epulef as they returned from their day's graft. We exchanged a few words and I bade them farewell for the night. Even as they passed me, I heard them whisper to each other in their native tongue. I wondered what Namuncura would tell his sons of our meeting, and the cause of his reaction at my mentioning the axeman. I remained baffled as to why this enigmatic individual had not been given to my staff. Baffled and not a little piqued, for the vigour with which he applied himself to his axe suggested he would make light work of clearing the garden.

Unbidden, the words of Doña Ybarra rose in my thoughts, for there was another possibility as to the axeman and the anaemic turn of the old Mapuche's face.

They say the dead walk the grounds of the estate.

As an explanation it did not satisfy my sense of the probable. Ghosts were for the Christmas nights and All Hallows' Eve, entertainments to be told around a crackling fire, with the lights low. I doubted very much that the axeman was some such apparition. Yet no matter how I tried to shake the notion, it lingered, perhaps because of my current situation, hurrying through the trees to beat the dusk, perhaps because of the, admittedly, inexplicable way the axeman had vanished from sight.

But no! I was not one to submit to such fancy.

I reached the Imperial Avenue, briskly walking its length past the break in the colonnade where one of the ombús was absent. Señor Moyano had been quite insistent that there were no other inhabitants on the estate, and yet, scarcely ten minutes earlier, I had engaged in conversation with Namuncura, who nobody had hinted at before. It was well within the bounds of possibility that the estate manager was being similarly disingenuous about the axeman, and wanted his presence kept a secret for reasons explicable only to himself. I made the decision to take up the subject with Moyano again that evening and, this time, refuse to let the matter rest until I had a satisfactory explanation.

The Melancholia of Sr Moyano

UPON ENTERING MY bedroom that evening, I discovered a document had been slid beneath the door. Everything was in darkness except for a fire that Dolores had lit. I applied a taper to several lamps and once there was light sufficient, retrieved the item from the floor. In my hand was a piece of canvas, folded in on itself a number of times, a faded, navy-blue colour and covered in lines of golden ink. I opened out the document until it was as wide as a copy of *The Times*, and made my best attempt to spread it across the dressing-table, the edges of the canvas flapping frustratingly over it.

A flush of anticipation filled my chest. Before me were the plans to the garden.

Poring over the details, I saw that my initial surmise – that the formal garden was intended to be rectangular in shape – had been correct. For the first time, I was able to trace its intricate system of paths and how the whole divided into a multitude of discrete parts, each of which had its own character and name. There was 'The Approach' and 'Strolling Borders' (evidently the central avenue I had observed from the treehouse), the 'Rose Garden', 'Rock & Alpine Garden', 'Evergreen', 'Golden' and 'Grey' gardens, 'Moorish Garden', the 'Picnic Lawn & Treehouse' &c. I felt a flush of pride that this was now my responsibility, and an equal measure of anxiety in my ability to restore it. At the heart of the design was the '*Jardín de tesoro*' or 'Treasure Garden', its moniker being a play on words in Spanish to mean both treasure as in the sense of jewels and one's beloved. This, you understand, was the portion of garden Don Paquito wanted me to transform first. It was marked on the document, as indeed was everything, in Spanish *and* English, a curiosity whose explanation was to be found in the signature at the bottom right corner: Sir Romero Lepping.

I was familiar with the name, if not quite as well as I should have been. As I remembered it, Sir Romero had been a garden designer, one of considerable repute, from the Victorian age, though this was the first I knew of his having travelled to, let alone taken a commission in, the Americas.*

I flipped the drawings over and found on the reverse a schema of the entire parkland, of which the formal garden was merely a detail. The house, naturally, stood at the centre and radiating from it, like the lines on a human palm, was a network of avenues. The design was devilishly clever, each of the paths leading to either the main house, to what was

---

* Sir Romero Lepping (1824–99), a British landscape designer of Italian-Jewish descent famous for his arboreta. His memoir recounts a visit to Argentina in 1870–71 where he undertook various projects in Buenos Aires, but makes no mention of Las Lágrimas.

described as *'la casa antigua'* (which I took to be the burnt-out mansion), the front gate, or doubling back on itself. It would be possible – as I had found to my experience! – to lose oneself in the parkland, only to arrive where one had started from. In all but name, I was looking at a maze.

The plan had been drafted before any planting had taken place, when Las Lágrimas stood exposed and buffeted by the winds of the Pampas. Accordingly, the blocks between the avenues were marked to be filled with trees, each one having a reference number that related to some other, missing document, one that laid out the species to be planted and the timetable for doing so. Such was the scale of the undertaking that each section of woodland had been allocated a date for the work, ranging in years from 1873 to '77. This, along with the numerals MDCCCLXX beneath Lepping's signature, would appear to confirm the improbable claim of Moyano's that the trees had been put in the ground indeed not more than four decades ago. It was not the only element to confound, for the lake was not natural either: various markings indicated how streams might be diverted for its creation. One certainly could not criticize Sir Romero, or Don Guido as his employer, for their lack of ambition, I being left to wonder how a feat of such scale had been financed, all too aware of the country-house gardens in Britain that had bankrupted their owners before they were completed.

From nowhere, a sob heaved and caught in my chest. There was so much in the drawings that provoked discussion, and it was with Grandfather I wanted to talk. An intense sensation of loss and loneliness filled me. I brushed my eyes, even though the tears that welled had not fallen, and distracted myself by attempting to follow the path I had made from the cabin to the ruined mansion. Try as I might, however, I could not determine the route I had taken that afternoon. It was thus thwarted that I became aware of something that should have been apparent from the moment of picking up the plans. I flicked them over to double-check. Neither side, not the detail nor the general layout of the parkland, showed the black stone wall encircling the formal garden.

Downstairs, the gong rang out, summoning me to dinner. I was hungry and, for once, in anticipation of seeing Moyano to confer about the many things the day had raised. By next morning, I hoped to have my mysterious axeman working alongside me and the Mapuches. But when I took my place in the dining room I found the table set only for one. Dolores entered with a steaming tureen. I devoured my soup in a manner that would have had Mother tut-tutting, and when the maid returned, asked her, 'Is Señor Moyano not joining me tonight?'

Her glance was shifty. 'He's in the other room,' she whispered.

'Tell Calista to keep back the main course until I have spoken to him.' I stood from the table.

'If I were you, Señorita, I wouldn't disturb him.'

'Why ever not?'

'Please, don't.'

I found Moyano in the octagonal Trophy Room, slumped and spent in a chair as if intoxicated. Above him were the heads of the white stags, their visages as noble as the estate manager's was presently base. I sniffed the air: it had that smoky odour his presence brought to any room, and the same subterranean chilliness from before, but I detected no alcohol.

'Señor Moyano, are you unwell?'

A single lamp illuminated the room, low on oil; it kept spitting and flickering, chasing weird shadows into the corners. The fire was unlit. In his fist he held something that he clicked together over and over, and once I caught a metallic flash, though mostly his hand was too tight for me to determine what was clasped therein. He did not bother to look at me when he replied.

'No.'

His voice sounded dead, his eyes as remote and fathomless as the trophies that decorated the walls. Dead, and also angry – though whether or not this ire was directed toward me I had no way of telling.

'I hoped we could have dinner together,' I continued. 'Perhaps a glass of your excellent wine.'

He said nothing.

'The soup is delicious, and to follow, Calista has prepared cutlets and—'

'No.'

I stood there, unsure of how to proceed, before deciding I would state my business as succinctly as possible, then take my leave. 'I discovered a building to-day, hidden beneath a thicket of brambles, near the lake. I wondered if I might use it as my study. With your permission, of course.'

'Do what you want.'

'Also, I saw a man, cutting down the trees. It would be of

a great help if I could have him in the garden, to assist with the clearing.'

'A man?'

'Yes, another member of staff,' I urged. 'One you must have overlooked in telling me about.'

He finally deemed to roll his eyes at me. 'I've told you before,' he said, with what I took as a touch of menace, 'there are no other staff.'

'I saw him clearly. Not you or Latigez or the Mapuches. Unless it was Señor Farrido. A man quite bald, with capable hands and a limp—'

Moyano leapt up so that I thought he would grab me by the throat. Instead, he stood inches from me and almost shouted into my face, I taking in the cold, iron smell of his breath. 'There is no one else! No one but us in this godforsaken hole.' His words echoed unnaturally, sucked into the walls and downward so that I imagined them reverberating beneath my feet. He was manically rubbing at his wrist.

I stepped away from him, thunderstruck.

'Do you hear me, Señorita Kelp? The subject will not be brought to me again.'

I replied levelly, albeit my heart was quivering. 'Yes.'

An agonizing silence followed. Moyano slumped backward in his chair, the melancholy emanating from him, chilly and cloying, like the fog on the night in Buenos Aires when he had offered me employment. Thinking of that interview, I was gripped by a concern that he had decided I was not worthy of the role he had bestowed on me, and I was left to wonder why I had been given the position of Head Gardener at all.

At last, I regained a little of my confidence. 'I shall leave you be, Señor Moyano,' I said, 'and hope to find you in better temper tomorrow.'

I was already departing the room, determined to enjoy, or at least finish, my repast regardless of the knot in my stomach, when he called out to me, the tone fragile and full of pleading. 'Ursula?'

Fool that I was, I returned. He stretched forth his hand for mine and, in sympathy, I reached out and almost took it.

'Yes, Señor?'

My formality killed whatever rapprochement he had in mind. 'Nothing.' His voice was of one who has given up all hope in life. Dreary and slow. 'Go back to your food.'

'I shall,' I replied. And left him to his melancholia.

Inside the Cabin

AS TO WHY Moyano was so incensed about the axeman, the answer came to me the next morning.

I had commenced work in what I now knew to be the Treasure Garden. A sallow sun tried to penetrate the heavy sky and it had turned perishingly cold, enough so that my exhalation smoked, whilst the wind tearing off the Pampas promised that the mercury was further set to drop. This barely a fortnight before spring's first day! I had been digging no more than half an hour when the urge to neglect my task stole over me: I wanted to see the cabin again, even if I could not explain this sudden compulsion. I returned to the meadow where it was evident that, although the Mapuches had continued cutting back as I went off to search the trees, they had not seen the task to its completion, for the building stood half-wreathed in coils of thorn. I set anew to their removal, and it was thus engaged that the moment of understanding visited me.

Put plainly, the axeman was not of the staff; indeed, I doubted anyone on the estancia was aware of his existence.

Perhaps he was a vagrant who had made a home of Las Lágrimas during its years of abandonment, a gaucho, possibly, whose leg was injured – hence the limp – and could no longer ride and find employ. No wonder he kept himself to himself, for fear of being banished (though in chopping trees, he would be advised to find a more discreet pastime). The only person who might know of his presence was Namuncura, which explained his anaemic turn when I had raised the issue with him, troubled that he and his sons might be evicted for offering the axeman shelter. And Moyano? He had simply demonstrated the same vexation I knew from my parents when they were ignorant of a subject but refused to admit it.

I worked alone for a spell, then went to summon Yamai and Epulef. They were reluctant to join me; I was insistent. With the three of us attacking the bramble the enterprise would be so much quicker. At some point, as we slashed away, I heard Moyano calling me, his voice in contrast to the previous night, full of boisterous verve, though remaining wary of him, I ignored his beckon. It was whilst the Mapuches and I were taking a breather, the last of the brambles offering the most arduous resistance, that I thought to try the door again.

This time, it swung open as if the handle had lain drenched in lock-oil over night.

'Shall we see inside?' I asked the Mapuches with a hint of skylarking, as if a girl who had discovered a secret den and was challenging the boys to go in first.

Epulef spoke harshly to his brother in words I could not comprehend, throwing me a glower, and walked away.

'Where is he going?' I asked.

Yamai chose his answer with care. 'Our father says we must not visit this place.'

'Why not?'

Moyano's voice cried out again, closer this time and now marked by an impatience at my lack of response. 'Señorita Kelp? Señorita?' And then, with deliberate provocation. 'Where are you, "Little Bear"?'

I did not rise to his mockery. I wanted to see inside the cabin before the estate manager learnt of my whereabouts, suspicious that he might renege on his promise of last night, and so I slipped through the door. Yamai refused to follow but stood on the threshold, peeping in. My first impression was of an echoless room more sizeable than I had imagined from without. The floor was made of brick and there was a large, roughly constructed hearth from the same black stone that encircled the garden. One might have expected the air to be cool or dank or, perhaps, sterile, but rather it was warm and frowsty, as if exhausted by the breath of many men. The light came in fragments, the sole window still partially blocked by vegetation. Although Yamai was nearby, and I took assurance from his presence, I wished he had accompanied me inside, troubled as I was by an irrational fear that the door might slam shut in the wind and trap me. That, and the sense, one I could not exactly put into words, of the cabin having been suddenly vacated upon my entrance.

There were a few pieces of furniture: a pair of old armchairs gathered by the fire, a wooden dresser and a large table where the erstwhile occupiers of the building partook in their meals. The latter I understood because the table was laid for three.

I examined the plates. They were of the finest china, the porcelain grey-spotted and chipped; hand-me-downs from the house, I surmised. A knife and fork were resting on one of the plates as if a moment before the diner had laid them down to answer the door.

A shadow sped past the window, making Yamai shout in fright. The Mapuche's cry was followed by that of a chimango.

'It's only a bird,' I said and, in setting his mind to rest, my own disquiet retreated. The table would make for a superior desk to the postage stamp I had for one in my room. I began to think that if we removed the bramble from the window and washed the panes to bring in more light, if we ventilated the place then got a fire burning and lamps lit, that the cabin would make a fine office: a place where I could hide myself away, all the more so when the rest of the staff arrived and the house was crowded. In the summer, I could perfume it with nosegays of stock and freesia.

'We should leave this place be, Señorita.'

'Why do you say that?'

His eye roved the corners. 'There are no… *las telarañas*.'

I gave a tut of irritation and flicked through my Tauchnitz. *La telaraña*. Cobweb.

That gave me pause. The cabin must have lain undisturbed for as many years as the rest of the estate. There should have been long, straggling nets of them hanging from the rafters and smothering the furniture.

I made a trifle of it. 'Then it will take less time to clean.'

'Our father tells us, do not go where spiders fear.'

With that he withdrew from the doorway, standing a good

four or five yards back, though hesitant to forsake me entirely. When I realized he intended to stay outside, I told him to finish clearing the remnants of the bramble, and returned to my inspection of the interior.

There was another door that led to a second, narrower room (the only other such in the building). It was constructed entirely of the black stone with a single, barred window high up, letting in lances of light. Three iron bedsteads, one shorter than the other two as if for parents and a child, lay overturned with neither mattress nor bedding. I righted them, the springs jangling and, when lengthways and seeing that they occupied too much space, I heaved them upright to lean against the wall so that I might pass by with greater ease. Apart from the bedsteads and a wooden chest in the corner, the room was void – and also untouched by dust or cobweb. I brushed a finger across the floor and it came away as clean as if Dolores had swept that very morning, cleaner, in fact, as I was unconvinced by the maid's application to her chores.

I turned my attention to the chest. It exhaled a sour, musty smell when I lifted the lid and was stuffed to breaking with papers, they numbering in the hundreds or, more likely, thousands. At first glance they appeared to be bills, tied in bundles with narrow purple ribbon. Before I had the opportunity better to examine them, I heard a commotion from outside: a voice raised and indignant, lambasting the unfortunate Yamai. I let the chest lid drop, and walked purposefully to the main room.

Moyano entered, cheeks flushed from the cold. His resentment was unconstrained. 'Correct me if I am wrong,

Señorita, but I employed you as my Head Gardener, not a clearer of outbuildings.'

A retort rose in my throat – when I paused. It became clear to me that I had little defence. 'You are quite right, Señor Moyano,' I said, my voice quiet and stiff.

'I am disappointed with you.'

'I don't know what came over me.'

'I will not tolerate it again. If the garden is not ready in time, I will make it my purpose that the blame rests on you.'

'It's entirely out of character, Señor, I promise.' I was as angry at myself as Moyano and sought to find a justification, however feeble, troubled that the estate manager might conclude he had made a poor choice in me, and even more so that his concern should be warranted. 'It's just that… the garden, no matter how hard we work, we make so little progress.'

'You haven't been at it a week yet.'

'It's demoralizing. To clear this place felt like an achievement.'

For a moment Moyano's expression was unreadable, then it softened. When he replied his tone was that of a father gently chiding his errant daughter, a tenderness he could never have known would raise my hackles. 'In time, we shall need to clear all these outbuildings,' he said. 'But for now, the garden must be your only consideration. We have to please Don Paquito when he arrives or we'll all be for the long ride back.'

I nodded and proffered my most contrite, doe-eyed face.

Moyano held me with a steady, compelling stare – I counted ten, eleven, twelve seconds – before he looked about himself. 'All that told, I'm sure the Don will be interested in your discovery.

I've always been too busy to give the brambles any attention. This, however, must be the original house on the estate.'

'The one built by Don Paquito's grandfather?'

'Capitán Agramonte, yes. That was in the 1830s. First there was this outpost, then the house later destroyed by fire. Until finally, the main building as it stands to-day.'

He stepped over to the window, which Yamai had, by then, cleared, and stared out at the lake, hands behind his back. 'Do you remember Café Tortoni's?' His voice was sentimental as if we were companions of old and he recalling a fond instance. 'When I told you how Las Lágrimas got its name? This is the spot Don Paquito's grandfather reached and wept for the beauty of the place; this is where he swore to build a great family home.'

I joined him at the window, he smiling at our indistinct reflections, and gazed over the water. The feeble sun of earlier had been overwhelmed by an unending mass of cloud. It was as though a blight had fallen upon Las Lágrimas, making the lake the most sombre of greys, the daylight scarcely reflecting on its surface.

'Excepting that there was no lake.'

'What do you mean?'

'I saw it on the plans you gave me. It is man-made.'

Moyano offered no reply.

By-and-by the silence, not only of the estate manager but the cabin itself, became unsettling and I felt impelled to fill it. I considered raising our contretemps from the night before but it seemed an ill-judged moment, deciding instead to pursue the issue of Sir Romero's design. 'Nor was there a wall.'

'In his final days here,' said Moyano, 'Don Guido was beset by…'

'By what?'

'The man was not well. Some of his actions were inexplicable.'

'I don't follow.'

'That's why the wall is not on the plans.' Moyano straightened his cuffs and disregarded the outlook. 'It was a long time ago, Señorita. All that matters now are the days ahead. I have great ambitions – for us both.'

Unexpectedly, alarmingly, he grasped my hands to beseech me. 'You may clear this building and use it as you wish. But I will permit it only outside of your apportioned hours.' His hands were crushing mine, the palms no longer emollient as they had been when we shook in Buenos Aires, but coarse and chapped. 'The priority must be the garden.'

He became aware of his clasp and, with a bashful apology, relinquished his grip. 'I must also,' he continued, 'apologize for my conduct last night.'

'You did rather unnerve me.'

'It was not my intention, Señorita Kelp. There are times since coming here when… when the blackest of moods possess me, almost as if something is preying on my thoughts and' – he laughed unconvincingly – 'it's as much as I can do not to dash my brains out. I trust I am forgiven.'

I offered some anodyne reply, I remember not what, and though at the time I gave his words little further attention, in the days since leaving Las Lágrimas, often have I returned to them – *possess me* – and wondered exactly what he meant.

The Cold in my Bones

FOR THE REMAINDER of the day, I drove myself and the Mapuches determinedly on, telling them we had time to make up for. They still refused to venture into the Treasure Garden, so I had them continue clearing what I now knew from Sir Romero's plans was 'The Approach', whilst I alone worked in the *Jardín de tesoro*, out of sight of the two lads, blunting my secateurs with so much cutting, digging with such fortitude as to cause my back to grumble. Thus I would banish those doubts about my abilities. Thus I would prove my worth! – to Señor Moyano as much as to myself. I suspended my exertion for barely a quarter-hour to lunch, and it was after I had eaten that the wind turned truly evil for the day.

Off the Pampas it howled, thrashing the tops of the trees, finding every breach in the black wall to cut through and torment the space within. I buttoned up my coat to my chin, wrapped my scarf around me like an old-fashioned, Victorian muffler, crammed my hat low over my ears – and still the cold pierced me. My gloves never left my hands. I hoped the vigour of my toil might ward off the worst of the gale's effect, but what little of my skin that was exposed was soon bluish and numb. I did not see Moyano for the rest of the day, and felt a certain resentment at all his hand-grasping talk of priorities set against his manner of disappearing for prolonged periods.

It was around four o'clock, the light thickening with a premature dusk, that I decided I had endured enough. I may have wanted to amend for my earlier misdemeanour but I was no martyr, and certainly not if my efforts were unwitnessed, for again the day's labour had produced only a meagre result. I resolved to work for a further ten minutes and be inside before the half-hour struck. I yearned for the warmth of the house, for, in tandem with the bone-chilling weather, the cold had crept up through the soil so that I could no more feel my feet and toes.

All at once the wind dropped, and died.

There was an eerie calm. In the instant between the two states, I was sure I had heard the crunch of footsteps on the gravel path as someone approached – or rather the tread of a boot and something dragged behind it – but now there was only silence. I experienced an unaccountable, plunging loss that caused my breath to come in shuddering gulps. To steady my lungs I inhaled – and was overwhelmed by the most glorious scent of high summer, of that moment that arrives late in the day when the heat has begun to wane and the flowers release their most heady perfumes. I smelt honeysuckle and jasmine, pelargonium and roses, such sweet roses, to my nose bourbons and damasks. Yet around me was only fetid overgrowth.

Then the wind was roaring again, the Wailing Wall singing its horrid song, and I could smell nothing but graveolent, cold air. I shook my head to clear it, as one who rises from a deep, unintended nap where a dream has invaded one's waking, and went to tell the Mapuches it was time to finish for the day.

When I reached the spot where I had left them, they were not to be found. Here was a fine blow to my conceit, for whilst I had been suffering they had decided to remove themselves indoors; clearly they were not quite as simple as I supposed them to be. I hastened to put my tools away and repaired to the inviting lights of the house, not stopping until I was inside and the door secure behind me. It rattled in its frame from the force of the gale. The fireplace in the hallway had been lit and was the only source of light, and it was in front of the blazing hearth that I positioned myself, as rigid as stone, only appreciating how cold the afternoon had made me now that I had escaped it. Uncontrollable shivers ran through me. For a short while I surveyed the portraits – the sitter as Caesar, as explorer of Africa, and always my attention captured by the master gardener, his face handsome yet curiously repelling – and noted for the first time that the blue scroll in his hand was the same as those plans Moyano had given me. Then I closed my eyes and surrendered myself to the heat.

From nearby came the rustle of material and Calista appeared holding a taper, which she applied to the lamps. She joined me by the fire.

'You're the last to finish for the day,' she said.

'I rather disappointed Señor Moyano earlier. I felt it my

duty to make amends.'

'He tells me you are working well.'

'He does? I'm sometimes left to wonder why he employed me at all.'

'That you are a fine gardener and already he could not do without you. He is nothing but compliments.'

'To you, in private,' I replied, expanding like a flower in the sun, a pride tempered by my annoyance at the same. 'To be honest, I'm not sure what to make of the man. He can be temperamental.'

'As is men's wont.'

Another shiver convulsed through me and I edged closer to the heat. 'What do you know of him?'

'Little. He gives not much away, but I have been told things.' She lowered her voice, although we were alone, and I huddled closer to her, so that I smelt the clove-and-orange of her breath, relishing our small moment of conspiracy. 'He was dismissed from his previous post.'

'For what?

'A scandal of sorts, the particulars of which I am not aware. His name was dirt, and after... he tried to take his own life.'

'Where did you hear such stories?' Like Grandfather, I have always had a suspicion for tittle-tattle.

'From Doña Javiera, my mistress. Her instruction was that I keep a watch on him.'

It took me a second or two for the full purport of this information to settle in. 'You mean Don Paquito's wife?'

Calista nodded. 'I have been in her service since I was a

child, and before that my mother was in her family's employ. When Javiera married the Don, I was retained.' She spoke in a tone I could not decipher, for her words may have contained gratitude or, as equally, the contempt of the bondwoman.

'So you were sent to spy on Señor Moyano?' I asked with a hint of indignation on his behalf.

'It was not my sole purpose.'

I waited for her to say more. For a time, no words were forthcoming and we stood together in companionable silence, watching the logs in the fire crackle. From the tail of my eye, I studied her and came to the conclusion, for which I had scant evidence, that the happiness in her life had been rationed.

When finally Calista spoke, her voice was hushed as if she had no wish to break upon the quiet of the house. 'The estancia is haunted. A curse lies upon it.'

'So said a lady on the train when I travelled here. I do not believe in such things.'

'The Don is of your opinion: my mistress more fearful. It is told that every son first born to an Agramonte will die as a child, here on the grounds. She fears for her boy.'

To me, there was something of the fairy-tale to such talk ('firstborn sons'!), but I was grateful for this intimacy and guarded my scorn with a common-sense rejoinder. 'Were it so, surely the present Don would be long dead. How could it be that he inherited the estate from his father?'

'He was the second child. His elder brother perished in an accident, the same year of the fire in the other house when his mother suffered her burns. That is why the family took flight from Las Lágrimas. Now that Don Paquito plans his return, my mistress sent me ahead to be her ears and eyes. To be watchful.'

'And what have you seen?'

Her reply was hesitant. 'Nothing.'

'Then the Doña can rest assured.'

'At least nothing worth telling.'

Whether it was worth telling or not, Calista demonstrated her reluctance to be drawn further by observing how cold I must be and helping me out of my coat. She vigorously rubbed the gooseflesh of my arms, before slipping the shawl from her own shoulders to cover mine. 'Get by the fire in your room,' she said. 'I will send Dolores with tea.'

I obediently walked up the staircase, my limbs still half-frozen, though for the first time in many a month I felt a warmth in my breast no matter how chilled the rest of my body. The brief sharing of whispers by the fire, the simple act of Calista passing me her shawl, had touched me more deeply than I cared to admit. I recalled none such at the Houghtons, having to go back to when Grandfather was alive for any like.

After changing my clothes, I positioned myself next to the fireplace, where I continued to shiver. Dolores arrived with a pot of steaming *yerba mate* and some warmed jam tarts. She was uncharacteristically garrulous, the way I remembered my sisters before they were married and Father had gentlemen guests to visit, disguising their nerves with idle prattle. Perhaps because Calista had so inclined me but I welcomed my little gas with the maid. Hovering in the background, as much as I wanted to resist it, I was also aware how much I had taken to heart the praise related to me from Moyano; I understood that I had been waiting for a word of it. And so it was as evening took hold, sitting with my stockinged toes pointed toward the fire, a cup of hot *mate* to my lips, that a sensation of contented belonging settled over me, that here, as far from home as could be imagined, I might find fulfilment and purpose at the Estancia Las Lágrimas.

Through the window, the last shreds of light had vanished from the sky; the wind howled.

Despite the cheer in my heart, the rest of my person proved harder to warm. The cold of the day had penetrated my body, making my joints and muscles ache with a rheumatic throb. I should have spent more time on my sketches for Don Paquito, but could find scant enthusiasm. Rather, the only drawing I undertook was that of my armchair closer to the fireplace. I snuggled into Calista's shawl, read a little of *Nostromo* until the revolution in Costaguana caused me to doze, and awoke still in the grip of an unshakeable coldness.

This state of frigidity persisted for the rest of the evening. I supped early and ate alone except for Dolores whose earlier affability was no more. She was agitated and wanted to serve the food as hurriedly as possible, nearly ruining the sleeve of my dress at one point with her clumsy pouring from the gravy-boat. Of Moyano, there was no sign. It was as I was speculating where he might be – where indeed he spent his many nights of absence – that a thought stole into my mind. That evening was a Friday, not a bath night, yet only a bath, the submersion of my body into steaming liquid, would banish the chill in my bones. Moyano had told me that there was a plentiful supply of hot water. How would he ever know if I took an illicit bath?

Once the idea took hold, I was unable to shake it.

After dinner I returned to my room and, stoke the fire as I might, remained stubbornly cold, waiting until I was confident that Calista and Dolores had finished for the evening. Only then did I venture downstairs. There was no sign of life, the dining room dark and empty, only the fading embers of the hallway fire casting any illumination. I moved swiftly, having already removed my shoes as to make no sound. Twice it happened that the floorboards creaked nosily beneath my feet and I froze, listening intently, hardly daring to continue. On the second occasion I chided myself. I am a grown woman, I thought, Head Gardener of Las Lágrimas no less, yet here I am, skulking around as though at boarding school after lights-out, trying to evade the housemistress.

I slipped through the drapes that led to the new wing, immediately feeling more at ease, for I doubted meeting anyone in this part of the building, and mounted the stairs. Outside, the wind was not letting up. I heard Vasca and Lola bark briefly, before they were joined by what sounded like an entire pack, so that once again I was left to wonder if there were more dogs on the estate; then all fell silent. I reached the bathroom, casually opening the door, and stepped inside. I should have noticed the sliver of electric-light at the bottom of the frame before I entered.

My breath was snatched from me.

'I'm... I'm so sorry,' I managed to blurt out, painfully aware of the colour that flamed my face.

I stood flustered and gawping, unable to tear away my appalled eyes, unsure what to do next or how to extricate myself from the situation. In the end, the best I could manage was another fumbled apology and to make as hasty an exit as possible, securing the door behind me, then running. Running all the way, back down the staircase, through the new wing to the old and up to my room, this time scarcely noticing the percussive thud of my footsteps. I did not stop until I was inside and had fastened the door behind me.

It took me several minutes to regain my pulse. The heat in my cheeks lingered.

I was furious at Moyano for having misled me, for he had been unequivocal in saying that the bathroom in the new wing was exclusively for my use until the Agramontes arrived. Yet standing there in the bath-tub, her back to me, as naked as Eve, had been Dolores, her black hair unbound and dripping wet. Her skin was pitifully white. If I had dallied, I daresay I could have counted every rib and knobbly joint of her backbone. It was not, however, her hair or spine that had so caught my attention and horrified me. Rather, the contusions running from the blades of her shoulder to her scrawny haunches: great welts, cuts and bruises, all livid and purple, as if she had been the victim of some unholy creature.

Dry Matter

OF DOLORES, AT breakfast, there was no sign.

'She forgot to fetch the eggs this morning,' said Calista in exasperated tone when I enquired to her whereabouts. It was the first instance I had known of the maid being so absent-minded.

I did not see her until after the hour of twelve when she had no excuse but to venture into the Treasure Garden to bring my hamper. To my relief, the temperature was several degrees more comfortable than the previous day, albeit a cutting, southerly wind continued to visit in intermittent squalls. A timid, dandelion sun blinked between breaks in the clouds. As happened every day, Dolores wanted to deliver her victuals and be off. That lunchtime, I did not oblige her so smart a departure. As much as it shamed me to dwell on another woman's nakedness, I was unable to shake the image of her pale, lesioned skin, nor how she had glanced over her shoulder as I intruded upon her. At first she had been startled, but as I stammered my apologies, a different expression came over her face. She seemed to gloat, to be excited in a strange and unhealthy way. Such was my embarrassment, I could not say for sure; most likely my memory was playing tricks and Dolores was as mortified as I.

'Wait,' I said as she beat a path to the house.

She skulked back, neither of us able to bring ourselves to catch the other's eye. I fumbled around as how to broach the subject, settling, as previously, on an apology. She offered me a shrug of such impudence I could only have been insulted if the circumstances had differed.

'You should have locked the door,' I said crisply.

'I wasn't expecting a visitor.'

I took a softer approach. 'Your injuries, Dolores…' I trailed off, unsure how to frame what I wanted to say.

She looked at me baffled, before understanding the nature of my reference. 'Oh, those,' she replied, in her dreamy tone, 'they don't hurt.'

'They looked very painful.'

'Not a bit.'

'How… how did you come by them?'

'I'm a clumsy thing,' was her reply after some deliberation. 'At home, *Papá* is forever scolding me for it.'

It was the least convincing explanation she could have offered, yet spoken with so little attempt at guile, that it felt churlish to challenge her. 'We can be friends, Dolores,' I said. 'You can confide in me. Someone has hurt you.'

'No.'

'Someone from the estate?'

'Honest, no.'

'Or possibly,' I ventured, 'someone who is not. A man with a limp, perhaps?'

She seemed to know who I was referring to, though her answer was curiously emphatic, as if she had been conditioned to say it. 'There is no such person.'

'Let me help you.'

Then another voice, and that familiar tang of smoke and spice. 'What are you two gossiping over?'

Moyano had appeared, a belted jacket with patch-pockets for his costume as one off to a shoot, the two German shepherds at his leg.

Dolores leant in close, and in a small, hopeless voice entreated, 'Don't tell him.' Then she turned to the estate manager and replied, 'Nothing, Señor. I was just bringing Señorita Kelp her food.' She offered us both a brisk curtsy and scuttled away.

'An odd sort of girl,' observed Moyano, once we were alone. 'Not really a domestic, she hasn't the right instruction. Calista says her ears need boxing: to buck up her ideas.'

'I do not believe that of Calista.'

'She has a cruel enough streak.' He tugged at the cuffs of his jacket to conceal his wrists. 'When the rest of the staff arrives, perhaps I'll let Dolores go. What do you think, Señorita?'

Vasca and Lola were sniffing around my lunch-hamper and, as a treat, I tossed them both a morsel of chorizo. 'I feel sorry for her.'

He seemed unmoved by my response and got down to the business that had brought him to me. 'Rain will be here tomorrow. I suggest you burn everything you've cut back.

To make what you have tidier before your day off.'

That afternoon, the Mapuches and I gathered the waste we had accumulated through the week, wheeling barrowload upon barrowload to a remote corner near the treehouse, where we pitched and mounded it into a huge pyre. I was astonished at the quantity and, even before we were finished, thought that should one of us scramble to the summit, it would be a simple jump to the top of the wall. It was a short while later when Señor Farrido, the boiler man, put in an appearance. He reeked of engine oil. It exuded from his body, his hair, even his breath, as if he swilled it by the quart, yet his clothes, especially his starched white shirt and collar, were spotless. A pair of thin wire spectacles rested on his nose. He was too portly to be mistaken for the axeman (and offer an alternative explanation to that mystery), and was quite evidently – from his blotched face and the slight slur of his speech – a drunkard. He said that he had been sent to bring us a canister of petroleum, though concerned that the assignment be too challenging for the capabilities of a mere woman and two natives, sprinkled it over the bonfire himself.

The pile caught immediately with a great whooshing roar that sent a plume of fire upward into the dimming sky. In no time it smoked and crackled, twigs popping as the resin in them expanded violently and detonated. The air had the distinctive smell of autumn, a smell that meant so many November afternoons when Grandfather would get a bonfire going, and we would feast on potatoes, wrapped in tinfoil and cooked in the hottest part, eaten slathered in butter.

Farrido surveyed his work with satisfaction, stole a swig

from his hipflask and said he must be back to the boiler.

I indicated his petrol-canister. 'Is there any more left?'

'A little,' he replied miserly. 'Not much.'

'May I take it? There is another pile, one in the meadow, that Señor Moyano requested me to burn.'

Before he conceded to hand me the canister, I suffered a bleary lecture on the risk and flammability of the fuel, and was made to swear that 'under no circumstances whatsoever' were 'the Indians' to be given charge of it. When Farrido was gone, I gave instruction to Epulef to feed the fire with the last of the garden waste, whilst Yamai was to accompany me with a barrow to the cabin. There, we collected the brambles and built a second bonfire a good distance from the building as a precaution from any sparks. Wraiths of smoke from the garden fire trailed in our direction. The wind had reduced to a breeze, the lake darkening and without undulation.

I gave Yamai the surplus petroleum and told him he could light our heap. His face became one of gratification and deep seriousness as, making sure I was stood well away, he carefully applied the vesta. The brambles, pliant with sap, wheezed and spat as the flames struggled to catch. There was nothing nostalgic to this smoke, it letting off the foulest of stenches.

'We need dry matter,' I said, and remembered the chest of old papers in the cabin.

I wheeled the barrow to the building and, offering encouragement to Yamai to follow me, stepped inside. As before, he declined. As before, I experienced the uncanny sensation of having disturbed someone upon entering, as if there might be some individual at the table who looked up in surprise at my intrusion – though the place was entirely empty. I strode to the second room where, trying the door, I found it refused to open fully. One of the bedsteads had fallen over, landing at such an angle as to block the entrance. I had to squeeze through the gap and manoeuvre the bed, the ironwork grating against the floor, this time wedging it against the wall in order there could be no risk of it toppling again. Only then did I turn my attention to the chest. Being so full, it was too heavy to drag to the front door, therefore I had to lug musty armfuls of paperwork to where Yamai waited with the handcart. After I deposited the first load, I made a cursory examination of the papers and found I had been correct in my assessment the day before: they were old bills indeed, certainly nothing anyone could miss after all these years.

Once the first barrow had been filled, we made our way back to the sputtering fire, where I told Yamai to add the papers sheaf by the sheaf in order that the flames have the best chance of taking. In the meanwhile, I revisited the cabin and, when the remainder of the bills were stacked by the door and I must wait for Yamai, I took the opportunity to study them more closely.

Each one was written in a formal copperplate on paper now yellowed and desiccated, thin as tobacco leaf, headed with the company name, BERGANZA E HIJOS.* Señor Berganza I knew to be a local nurseryman from Tandil (one of the principal towns of the Pampas, some seventy-five miles distant) who was the supplier of the estate and, as I had been

---

* Berganza & Sons.

informed by Moyano, was expected the following week with a delivery, his first in many a year. I had already given to wonder what stories he might have to tell of the estancia.

The receipts in my hand were dated 1873. I took a wad more and another, flicking through them, my interest growing, to see further dates between 1873 and '77, the self-same years as in Sir Romero's plan for the planting of the woodland. Each bill detailed the purchase of a single tree, of numerous species, invariably a three-year-old whip. Given the mass of papers, for they must have numbered in their thousands, I was – figuratively speaking – holding the parkland in my hands. And outside, Yamai was burning it! I felt a twinge of concern. I was destroying a record of the estate that perhaps should be preserved – yet here was the Mapuche returned with the empty handcart, and in the meadow behind him a pillar of flame, for the dry paper had combusted keenly.

But no, I reassured myself. If the receipts were of any value, they would not have been left to moulder in this neglected cabin.

Together we loaded the remaining bundles into the barrow and, after I had dispatched Yamai to the pyre, I searched for any last detritus that might need to be burnt. There was none, though in looking I was struck, as not before, by the little touches of comfort about the place: the curtains (though faded with age) were carefully stitched; a generous doormat insured the floor would not be muddied. Whoever its previous occupants, they must have been proud of their little home. It was as I went to close the lid of the chest that something in the bottom captured my eye. My initial instinct was to leave it be, but then I thought it would make a princely reward for Yamai and so reached in to pick it up. Between my fingers was a silver peso.

In the meadow, the brambles were blazing fiercely and the barrow sat empty. Sparks danced in the air. During my time inside the cabin, the afternoon had begun to wear into evening, the clouds now flushed mauve, the patches of sky between them gently bleeding their light. Countless birds had established themselves on the lake, which had become an immense looking-glass, the scene summoning within me all the majesty of Nature. I wanted a few minutes by myself to drink in the spectacle.

'A gift,' I said to Yamai, handing him the silver peso. 'For your hard work.'

He received it excitedly. 'You are not like Latigez, Señorita. Or Señor Moyano. You have a kindness.' His cheeks bunched into a smile of sorts before he realized what I had given him.

Immediately, he thrust it back at me.

'Oh,' I said and, swallowing the slight, made to put the coin in my pocket. Even as I did so, Yamai snatched the peso from my clasp and hurled it into the bonfire.

'You must not! Our father warns us. The silver – it brings evil.'

We stood eyeing the other, I unsure what to reply until in the end, and considering it futile to hold forth on the ills of superstition, I told him that he and his brother could finish for the day.

When I was alone, and had put aside Yamai's curious

outburst, I stood mesmerized by the fire, enjoying its heat upon my face, and watched the day as it continued its wane. The gloaming thickened around me until light and darkness were in perfect, magical balance. And then, gradually, on the water, the birds became silhouettes so that I was no longer able to determine which species was which. I inhaled to the depths of my lungs, a profound tranquillity washing through me, intoxicated by this spot. I understood why Capitán Agramonte had wanted to settle this land, even if I had to remind myself that when first he stood here, there would have been nothing but for the endless reach of the Pampas.

With a shriek and clatter of wings the birds took to the air, soaring in the opposite direction to where I stood.

I sensed the unwelcome intrusion of someone approaching and was aware of Moyano's hands coming firmly to rest on my shoulders. At first I did not know how to react, then I made up my mind that his conduct was too familiar. I shrugged him off and swung round to slang him.

I was alone in the meadow. All alone.

A creeping chill spread through my body, down from my shoulders to the small of my back. I knew for certain I had felt the touch of someone, of a man, for the hands had lacked any daintiness.

I had a sudden urge to run. To run to the house, to the company of Calista and Dolores, to the bright, electric-lights of the new wing – but my feet were rooted to the spot, my limbs utterly immobile.

Once again I heard someone approach. My blood quickened. This time, for a fact, I saw Moyano striding toward me, hands thrust in his pockets, something jangling therein as if they were full of loose change. He spoke without concern.

'I must be working you too hard, Señorita. You look pale.'

'Were you here before? Just now?'

He gave me an odd look, of the kind men reserve for the more overwrought of my sex. 'As you can see,' he said, with an uncertain laugh, 'I have only this minute arrived. I was come to tell you to burn the brambles, but you've taken it upon yourself. Good.'

'I was watching the sun set,' I replied, feeling a profound gratitude for his company, though I am sure any person would have done. I edged closer to him, close enough so that I might have brushed his sleeve, prompting Moyano to offer his arm in expectation of that possibility.

'Few things are as romantic,' he mused when I neglected to take it, 'especially by a blazing fire. Or so my wife tells me.'

'I did not know you were married.'

'With a son.'

'Where are they?' I asked, glad of such banal, domestic chat to divert me. Slowly, my heart resumed its natural beat.

'For now, in Buenos Aires. I will send for them once Don Paquito and his family are settled. I have barely seen them this past year.'

'You must miss them.'

'I fear we are becoming strangers, especially my boy.' I noticed the subtle change in his eyes, the indefinable something that lingered there, momentarily, and I felt I had looked upon something personal to himself. 'And you, Señorita. Who do you miss, apart from your grandfather?'

'No one.'

'Not your family?'

'A little of them goes a long way.'

'Is there no one special? A fiancé, an admirer?'

'None is so blessed,' I replied in a manner that made clear my feelings on any further discussion of the matter. It was enough that, over the years, I had endured numerous interrogations from my sisters and, lately, Bernadice Houghton on the subject without now submitting to my employer. To them it seemed implausible (and I suspect, 'unnatural') that a woman should not be determined to secure herself a husband, as if I were some to-be-pitied creature from a novel of Jane Austen.

'It is a common question in my country,' said Moyano, 'especially to one – if you will permit me – as striking as yourself. However, I fear I have offended you, Señorita. Think nothing of my curiosity. I will leave you to your sunset.'

I watched as he turned on his heel, knowing I should be glad to be spared any more of his obtrusive conversation, but my nerves were still keen. Try as I might, I could not shake off the feeling of those hands on my shoulders. I continued to feel their weight as if they had left an impression on me, as of cold fingers pressed into clay. The view, which moments ago had exuded such a spell, had transformed to one of hostile shadows, lonely and forlorn, all that remained of the sun being a crimson slash on the horizon. When it had faded there would be only blackness.

I shuddered and called after Moyano without humiliation, hurrying to join him so that I need not walk back alone.

A Morning at Leisure

THE PREDICTION MOYANO had made for rain proved incorrect. I awakened the next morning – my day off – to bright sunshine and immediately opened my window so that I might bathe in the light. My sleep had been restless, troubled as it was by the repeated sensation of feeling those hands, heavy and dreadful, upon my shoulders again. Three or four times I must have half-woken myself, on one occasion to hear the baying dog-pack. But, now, seeing the unblemished sky above the avenue of ombú trees, feeling the glittering sun upon my cheek, my spirits rose and I did my best to put aside the memory of the hands, eventually doing so with such success that I began to wonder if the whole episode had been brought on by too much smoke to the brain and the end of a tiring week.

I decided to go riding first thing. My preference would have been to wear something fresh; however, with my luggage still in limbo (I preferred not to consider that it had been sold to some ragman passing by Chapaledfú station), I had no choice but to continue with my gardening apparel.

It being Sunday, and the hour early, the house was quiet, as quiet as the day I arrived. Downstairs everything had a feeling of spruceness; the hearths let forth a smell of cold cinders. I found a solitary, and limited, breakfast – hard-boiled eggs in a chaffing dish, corned-beef, a caddied pot of tea – waiting for me and, whilst I chewed, I pondered the achievements of my first week. They were so unremarkable that I promptly stopped this line of thought, its effect to demoralize when the day was for enjoying.

The stables were as deserted as the house. In one pocket of my overcoat I had a hipflask of freshly brewed *yerba mate* (its taste growing on me), and in the other, Sir Romero's drawings of the estancia. Later, I wanted to revive myself through the freedom of the Pampas; for now, my wish was to explore the parkland so that I might better understand its puzzling layout. I saddled Dahlia and headed off into the trees, choosing one of the avenues that, from the plans, and if I followed its sweep far enough, should bring me to the perimeter adjoining the wastes. The woodland smelt of moss and aged bark, a breeze stirring the leaves above with the barest of murmurs, the birds hushed in their song. I kept Dahlia at a lively step whilst maintaining a tight rein; from the constant flick of her head I sensed she was eager to gallop. Through the dappled light ahead, I clapped eyes upon a familiar figure tramping toward me.

'Good morning,' I bade Dolores as we reached one another.

She was swaddled in a pelisse of the most extravagant fabric, one that if Doña Javiera were already in residence I might have suspected her of purloining, for I could not imagine how a maid might acquire such a garment. Her cheeks were flushed scarlet, as one who had been running.

I asked, 'Where have you been so early?'

'It's the Sabbath, Señorita,' came her reply, she regarding me as if I were a dullard. 'To chapel, of course. We must all say our prayers.'

I ignored the bluntness of her manner, covering my offence by a consultation of the plans; on them, no place of worship was marked. 'Which way is it?'

'Follow the avenue to its end,' she answered, tightening the pelisse about her, and hurried away with neither a farewell nor rearward glance, leaving me to speculate as to how a girl like Dolores occupied her day off.

I gave an encouraging cluck of the tongue at Dahlia and we walked on for perhaps a quarter-mile before – more abruptly than one would anticipate – the trees came to an end. I had gained the eastern margin of the parkland. There stood a rusty wire-fence, that had once kept out cattle, and was the demarcation between worked land and wild, and below it a tangle of bulrushes growing on the bank of a stream that must surely be one of the tributaries Sir Romero had redirected to feed the lake. The water ran sluggish, scummed as it was with a layer of ochre-red algae, and beyond lay the Pampas, stretching as far as the eye could reach. It was the first time I had beheld them in such radiant light, belts of grass lightening and darkening as they were chased by the breeze for, without the protection of the trees, the wind was demonstrative here. The sheer vastness of the space demanded my wonderment, and yet as much as I was stirred at the prospect of riding out there, I felt a wariness too. For all its beauty, this was a land too immense, too unpeopled to be tamed. Upon the horizon, I made out dark clouds scudding in my direction.

In this exposed spot stood the chapel, the nature of its wind-battered location meaning it was of squat, sturdy construction. The walls had been once painted a creamy-white, though the render now appeared rusted, spattered from years of algae blown off the stream. A stark iron cross stood atop the roof and directly beneath it was a foundation stone that read, 1899 – more than a decade after the estate had been abandoned. Don Guido, I supposed, must have ordered its construction after he embraced religion (though were it so, who had worshipped here?). I dismounted, securing Dahlia's reins to a branch, and was about to venture within when I paused. I had the sensation – no, certainty would be the better word – of being watched, that inescapable feeling one gets when someone is close by even if they are unobservable. I looked about me, searching the trees, and for all that I spied not a soul, the sensation lingered.

The chapel had no door, a matter of design rather than oversight, allowing the wind free passage and making the building inside clamorous with draughts and echoes. The place smelt of chalk and some other odour, like sour blossom, that seemed not right. There was an altar but neither pulpit nor a single pew, reinforcing the idea that no congregation had ever gathered here. The walls were white-washed and without decoration. In short, nothing about the chapel inspired me to loiter. Nevertheless, having made the effort to ride here, and already of the mind I was unlikely to return, I finished my inspection.

Leading off the nave was a small chamber. I glanced inside – and started. It was as severe as a prison cell, except for two objects: a lifescale depiction of Christ in his majesty, the crown of thorns piercing his wooden flesh, real nails hammered through his palms and feet; and opposite, a *prie-dieu* for an individual to kneel at and pray. I took in the effigy's wounds more closely: the globules of blood had been painted with such lurid realism that they looked as if they might roll down his cheeks at any moment. I am a product of Grandfather's staunch atheism and my parents' dutiful Anglicanism, leaving me a rather undemonstrative agnostic. The Deity I am unsure of, however, is decidedly Protestant; such gratuitous Catholic displays have always left me uneasy.

A thought came to me. The kneeling pad of the *prie-dieu* had two small impressions in the cushion: was this where Dolores had recently prayed? What if she were so indoctrinated with guilt that she was prone to self-flagellation? An unworldly child from the backwaters was bound to have grown up with all sorts of nonsense in her head. Flogging herself seemed as credible an explanation for her injuries as any. I felt a new sympathy for the maid and decided, impudent as I found her to be, that I must try harder to befriend the girl, if only to talk into her some common sense.

I was growing tired of the chapel and wanted the tonic effect of the Pampas, to feel the wind in my hair and the sunshine on my face, and so I made my way back to Dahlia. The brief period I had spent inside was sufficient that the distant clouds were rolling in, soon to obscure the sun; perhaps Moyano's forecast was correct after all, in which case I had little time to lose. Consulting Sir Romero's plan, I took the avenue that led by the shortest distance to the main gate and, with a squeeze of my heels against the horse, soon put us trotting through a tunnel of trees. Shreds of sunlight flashed through the branches that dimmed the deeper I travelled into the wood. I rounded a bend and in the middle of the path stood Namuncura, the Mapuches' father. He signalled urgently that I stop and, when I had done so, beckoned me closer, pressing a gnarled finger to his lips in order that my approach be made in stealth. I slipped off the saddle and, leading Dahlia, crept toward him. He directed my gaze into the trees – but nothing could I make out.

'What I am to see?' asked I in a dropped voice.

He shushed me, indicating with greater insistence.

My eyes struggled to penetrate the undergrowth, and I was on the point of thinking his fascination little more than senile fancy, when I caught sight of that which so captivated him.

Not twenty yards away, mostly concealed by splays of low branches, was a stag of the purest white, as of those in the Trophy Room, except alive, a thing of absolute natural beauty. The beast had been grazing, which is why I had struggled to see him, and at that moment lifted his head to stand in his full magnificence. His pelt glowed against the dimness of the wood, his head was a mitre of antlers. He looked directly at me, those black, inscrutable eyes meeting mine.

The air paused in my lungs.

I stood transfixed, experiencing a communion that nothing

in the chapel could ever have offered and, thinking of those heads in the Trophy Room, I wondered how anyone could shoot such a being. It was one of those rare subjects upon which Grandfather and I disagreed sharply. He was drawn to the hunt, less for the blood than the skill of the stalk; I always refused to take the rifle, content to disappoint him.

Then Dahlia, perhaps jealous of the other animal and my undivided attention, snorted loudly. The spell was broken. The stag took flight, bounding into the brushwood with a speed and agility that was supernatural: a streak of white, then nothing to suggest he had ever been there but swaying leaves.

Namuncura rebuked Dahlia, half in Spanish, half in his own tongue, with a comment I divined to mean horsemeat being more choice than venison.

'Where did the stag come from?' I asked when I got my breath.

'In the old times, Don Guido brought these animals. He and his friends hunted them. In packs, in the way of wolves.' He shuddered. 'Wicked men all.'

'But no one hunts them now?'

'No,' he rasped. 'There is only this one.'

'I'm glad to hear it.'

'He is rare to see.'

'Then we are blessed to-day,' I said, and remounted Dahlia.

'Where do you go, Señorita?'

'To ride, on the Pampas.'

The old man gave vent to an expression of concern. 'You must not go alone.'

'Will you come with me?' I laughed, though not mockingly.

'No.'

'Then I must ride by myself. I shall be quite fine, thank you.'
Dahlia walked on, quickly gaining speed. 'I know my way.'

In response, Namuncura called after me – though whatever
his words, they were lost to my ear, his voice being weak and
Dahlia already at a noisy clip-clop.

The Quarry & the Boy

BY THE TIME I reached the main gate, which stood wide open and newly painted by Latigez, I could feel Dahlia was keening to run and we broke the cover of the trees at no less than a canter.

Once free of the parkland we rode out into the wilds, not in the direction I had first arrived, for I had no wish to see again the charred, somewhat dispiriting maize fields but, rather, toward the west, beneath clouds that now concealed the sun and what little blue remained in the sky; bulging clouds, slaty-black with rain. I allowed the horse to take me where she desired, the Pampas extending away in every direction, beckoning us into its vastness. The wind lashed my face and tore through my hair, causing it to festoon behind me, a trail of blazing red. I gulped down lungfuls of cold air, and felt as must do a miner upon returning to the Earth's surface after a long spell below ground. I was exhilarated. Released. I pricked my heels harder against Dahlia's flanks until we were at her topmost gallop, such a rate as to summon Mother's voice into my head, warning that were I to fall at this speed I should surely break my neck. I lost all perception of time, hypnotized as I was by the drumming of Dahlia's hooves against the ground. Her occasional snorts of joy and elation were as mine.

Suddenly she veered to the left with such violence that it took all my strength, my legs clamping her sides, not to be thrown.

Dahlia came to a standstill – and not a moment too soon. Hidden by the undulations of the grass was a gigantic, yawning crater. There had been no warning signs, no indication of any type that the ground ended with such abruptness.

I alighted, and stood on the rim looking below, badly shaken. 'Gracias,' I whispered to the horse, 'mil gracias,' rubbing her flanks, which gleamed with perspiration. If she had not swerved, we would both likely have been killed. I reached for my flask of *mate* and took a long, deep drink, the hot bitterness of the tea spreading from my throat and soothing my nerves.

When, after a number of minutes, I felt sufficiently calmed, I made a closer examination of the huge cleft beneath my feet, unable to imagine what force of Nature could have caused such a calamitous gash, before the realization it was most probably man-made in origin. It had slopes of black rock, steep and sheer, and brought to mind an open-cast mining pit. I may have been close to the mark, for the black stone was the very same material as that of the wall encircling the garden. The mineral must have been quarried here, I decided, and then transported to the house. I could only marvel at the sheer physical labour of such an undertaking, one that would have made Pharaoh proud. Something else caught my attention. Against the black rock were luminous sprays of crimson: clumps of that species I had spotted on my journey to Las Lágrimas, those ones Rivacoba called 'devil-flowers', and I wanted to study better, taking them to be an iris.

The heavens had continued to darken, the air promised thunder; I could feel it in the clouds. Nevertheless, I was sure that if I was nimble, I might pick a sample of the bloom and be on my way before any rain fell.

Dahlia, wearied by her gallop, was contentedly munching on the grass: I could leave her untethered. I spied the one practical point of entry into the quarry, by way of a bluff incline, and skittered down it, safely arriving at the bottom from where the landscape of the Pampas was entirely hidden. It was like standing at the base of a pit; I could see the leaden sky, and nothing else. The crimson flower was abundant, embedded in the rocky soil and growing from many a cranny. I nipped off one to scrutinize it in detail and was gratified to find I had been correct. It was an iris, though a form I had never before encountered, its intense crimson petals cupping a heart of oxblood. Thus satisfied, I became curious at my surroundings for if this was indeed a quarry, then it was an uncommon one.

There was no sign of any mining equipment, no abandoned picks or pieces of machinery, no old, wooden structures left to the elements. In fact, there was no sign that any human hand had touched the stone in many a year. Yet this left another curiosity: if the quarry had stood exposed to the elements for so long, why was the stone so clean, so untouched by natural processes? For, irises excepted, there was no lichen, no insignificant-but-hardy weeds poking through, none of the first green signs of plant life attaching itself to the open earth to colonize it. Perhaps, I conjectured, the wind kept the stone scoured. Yet standing down here, I felt secure and sheltered from the unforgiving clime above.

There was a rumble of thunder to which Dahlia, who I could not see, whinnied.

I took this as a signal to be on my way and picked several more of the irises which, to keep safe, I pressed inside Sir Romero's plans. Dahlia whickered again. This time I thought I heard alarm.

I glanced upward. Standing on the brow of the crater, peering down at me, was a boy.

Against the greyness of the clouds, he appeared mostly in silhouette, his features obscured, yet it was enough for me to discern he must be eleven or twelve years of age and appeared half-starved. I was startled to find anyone else in such a remote a place, least of all a child, but recovered myself and raised a hand in greeting, all the while my brain providing the explanations as to why he might be here. He must be with his parents; for all I knew this was a popular spot to ride out to on a Sunday where locals took picnics. In train came contradictory thoughts of greater conviction. I was far in the Pampas, there were no locals; there was something about this place – the sterile blackness of the stone, its sapping atmosphere and loneliness – that meant no right-minded person would ever choose it as a place to lunch; that rather than a weekend jaunt, what this frail child needed was a proper feeding.

'*Hola!*' I shouted up at him.

Abruptly, the boy drew back. *Hola*, he cried in return. *Hola. Hola…* before I realized it was the echo of my own voice I was hearing, resonating off the quarry walls.

Dahlia again whinnied in fright, and I was possessed by a sudden apprehension that the boy intended to make off with her. I scrambled up the slope in a rattle of pebbles, slipping often, panicked that I might find myself stranded.

I gained the top. Over my head, the sky was like ink.

There stood Dahlia, shaking her mane and snorting in agitation, raking the ground with her hoof – but, thankfully, not stolen. A fat drop of rain landed against my cheek, one drop, no more. I spun around, searching the landscape for the boy. I could see for miles in every direction, the grass stretching flat and unbroken to the horizon. There was no sign of him. It was possible he was hiding or had fled in fear of me and that the landscape had inadvertently concealed him, and yet, as much as I tried to persuade myself, it was no use: he had simply vanished.

Unnerved, I reached again for my flask of *mate* to steady me and took a deep swig. This time there was no soothing sensation of heat. The liquid was ice cold, as foul and rank as ditch water. I retched and spat it all from my mouth.

Then, the heavens burst.

From Behind the Door

I DID NOT have a single dry thread left on me by the time I reached the stables, my hair an auburn mat lying thickly down my back. I squeezed it out as best I could, then rubbed down Dahlia, making sure she had plenty of fodder, and took myself indoors. Upon entering the house, I was struck by music, the scratchy sound of an opera recording (it was, I think, *Don Giovanni*) whose notes drifted to me from the new wing.

If this had been my own home, or even the Houghtons', a hot bath would have been the first order of my return. A concern of repeating my experience with Dolores, however, meant that henceforth I would only visit the bathroom during those hours allotted to me. So I went to my small room, towelled my hair and changed out of my sodden clothes and, with the comfort of a woollen knit cardigan over my blouse, proceeded to lunch. I sat down to a solitary plate and, having waited no more than a minute, picked it up and made my way to the kitchen in the hope of finding Calista. That afternoon, the windows dashed with rain and my thoughts still rattled by the vanishing boy, I was in no mood for the gloomy formality of the dining room, nor to eat alone.

'You should have not ridden so far,' said Calista, observing my damp hair when I found the cook in her snug, little parlour. She was at the table with a bottle and her own meal, a game of solitaire set out before her. Although no pans bubbled on the stove, from the range came a welcome, steady heat and the waft of rising teacake.

'I was soaked to the skin,' I replied.

'Then you will want a nip of this. To warm you through.' And from the bottle, which I saw as *aguardiente de caña*, a variety of local rum, she poured me a generous measure – that I knocked back in a single gulp. It was filthy strong and left a reassuring, hot glow in my gullet.

Calista raised her brows, in amusement as much as surprise, and let forth a throaty laugh.

'A trick of my grandfather's,' I said, grimacing, and let her charge me a second glass, albeit this I took my time to sip.

Luncheon was a chicken and egg pie served cold with a salad of sliced potatoes and onions drenched in oil and vinegar, and afterward, quince compote with thickly churned cream. It was a convivial affair, I daresay aided by the *aguardiente*, which Calista topped up throughout, almost as if she wanted to inebriate me. The cook spoke archly of her youth, she being born in the tropical north of Argentina and raised, as had I, by a grandparent, in her case her mother's mother. Later she shared a tale or two about the Doña who, by all accounts, sounded the most charming woman. I was looking forward to making her acquaintance, believing it possible that between us a friendship might bloom. Yet in return, Calista enquired as to little of my own life, leaving me undecided whether her attitude was one of discretion, or indifference – though, to give her the benefit of the doubt, we did indulge in a spirited digression on the Suffrage.

Toward the end of the meal, my mind drifted to the boy at the quarry. Already he seemed more a product of my imagination than an experience of the waking world.

'Calista, how old was Don Guido's son when he died?'

'Why do you ask?'

'I am curious.'

She regarded me as if aware something lay behind my words. 'Just curiosity?'

'Yes.'

'I believe he was twelve or so.'

I made no further reply, absorbing this information, wondering what difference, if any, it made to what I had seen that morning. Or fancied I had seen.

Calista corked the *aguardiente* and began to clear away our plates whilst I sat in silence – except for the execrable screeching coming from the new wing. It reminded me of Grandfather's 'Music Evenings', when the blessings of being stone-deaf were made plain.

'What is that noise?' I asked.

'Señor Moyano's gramophone.'

'He does not strike me as the type for opera.'

'Only when those black moods possess him – then we must all suffer. He will do nothing else for the rest of the day.'

'I don't suppose, if I ask, whether he'll quieten it down?'

'No.'

I pictured myself in my cramped bedroom, attempting to work on my sketches for Don Paquito or perhaps reading, growing more distracted and infuriated as the hours passed and the music tormented my ears. 'In which case, I would rather spend my afternoon in the cabin.'

'Along with spirits,' asked Calista, 'did your grandfather teach you at cards?'

'On occasion.'

'Would you like a game?'

'Yes,' I replied cautiously, for I would have been as happy to spend the coming hours left to my own devices.

'Then I will find you later,' said the cook. 'There is no one to play with here, except Señors Moyano and Latigez, and both are terrible cheats.'

The rainfall only worsened as the day wore on. It filled the gutter-pipes to overflowing until everywhere one went one heard the pour of water, as of a pitcher being emptied on to stone. I found an umbrella and, my books hidden beneath my coat, raced to the cabin, keeping under the trees to avoid the worst of the downpour. There was no such protection once I gained the meadow. Here the rain fell in sheets, driven slant by the most fierce gusts, so that the lake was scarcely visible. I completed this last leg at a sprint, battling the wind over my brolly, until with a whoop of relief I reached the cabin. Inside it was lightless and smelt as any place will do if shut up for years on end. I spent the next minute tending lamps, before bracing myself to face the elements anew and fetch some wood for the fire. A better organized woman might have thought to do this ahead. It was then that I noticed the basket by the hearth, full of well-seasoned logs. I did not recall seeing it previously, nevertheless was grateful that I need not dash outside to the woodstore. I got to my knees and built a pyramid of kindling, wishing I had kept some of the receipts from the chest, for they would have been ideal to get the fire going. As it happened, the flames took easily enough and I heaped on the logs, they releasing a spicy, heavy aroma, not unlike frankincense, and that was familiar from the smell which clung to Moyano.

The fire soon radiating its much needed heat, I sat back in satisfaction and glanced around me. On the wall opposite hung an old daguerreotype portrait, the sitters appearing to be a mother and her young son; occupants of the cabin at some earlier point, I presumed, though when I stood to examine the image, it was undated. They seemed a happy pair, rustic-faced and rather plump. I frowned to myself, troubled how I had not registered this picture before, nor the log basket, and cast my eye about in case there were other items I had missed.

At the window, there was a face staring in.

I started back, a cry escaping my mouth. When I looked again, the window was empty, as empty as it had surely been all along, for who would be standing outside on an afternoon such as this? Not Moyano absorbed in his opera or Latigez whose pleasure it had been mine not to meet these past days, not Dolores or Calista – for the face I had imagined was distinctly that of a man, the raindrops bouncing off the dome of his forehead, a large hand pressed to the pane. I had to make the conscious effort to gather my wits, compelling myself to approach the window until my nose was almost touching it. My breath misted the glass. There was no sign that any person had been there. I was regretting having partaken of so much rum.

Thus self-rebuked, I spent the next minutes rearranging the cabin better to suit my needs. I dragged the dresser to a corner where it would be out of the way, and then the table to beneath the window so that I might use it as a desk and where, on an afternoon not like to-day, the light would be superior. Once it was in place, and despite my more prudent inklings, I could not help but check the pane again. As before it was empty. What's more, my experience of seeing a face peering in was not repeated, no matter how often my eye swept in its direction until, in the end – and to put a stop to this compulsion – I made myself look at the daguerreotype each time my gaze wandered, preferring the peasant smiles of mother-and- son to rain-spattered glass. The two armchairs, already positioned by the fire, did not need shifting and were the perfect place to read and for Calista and I to play our cards, though for the latter a small table positioned between us, where we might lay our hands, would more conveniently facilitate our games. There was no such piece of furniture in the cabin until, in a flash of inspiration, I remembered the chest that had held the receipts and how it might make an impromptu substitute.

I went to the second room and found I had to force the door. Once through, and to my annoyance, I saw that the bedsteads I had moved out of the way on the previous afternoon had again fallen. With a struggle I righted them, then turned my attention to the chest. I was able to lift it up, for being empty it was now simple to manoeuvre, and lugged it into the main room toward the fireplace.

Two things happened then.

The door to the second room slammed behind me with a terrifying violence. Such was the force, it made the very walls shudder and daguerreotype jump on its hanging. At the same time, the chest in my arms, light enough for me to carry thus far, was in an instant a dead weight.

I toppled over, the trunk falling from my grasp, and watched as it landed heavily, the lid coming open. From within, releasing a mustiness as only comes from paper left to moulder for many years, spilled thousands upon thousands of yellowed bills.

Forks of pain shot up my back. I landed face first against the hard brick-floor, not daring to right myself for, so brittle did my spine feel, I feared to make the slightest movement lest it snap me in two. My breathing came in short, ragged gasps. Around me the receipts continued to flutter and spread, each one bearing the company name of BERGANZA E HIJOS and detailing a sapling bought between the years 1873 and 1877.

A scream of wind swept around the cabin, rattling the window, and died away remotely.

In the succeeding silence there came the scrape of footsteps from behind the slammed door when, for a fact, the room had been without occupant.

One, t-w-o. One, t-w-o.

Backward and forth across the floor of that empty, narrow

room. The heavy tread of a limping man. Even in my injured state, I was aware of the fine hairs on my neck standing to attention.

The steps halted. I heard a heave of effort… then the crash of metal and jangle of springs, as one of the bedsteads was thrown to the ground, with it a wave of emotion, pitching over me almost as if it were a physical entity. A wave of the most blood-curdling rage. I was gripped by terror, the agony of my spine forgotten, my respiration so loud and laboured I was convinced that whoever – *whatever* – was in that second room must surely hear me and come to investigate. The thought of that door opening was too much to bear.

There came another metallic smash as the second bedstead hit the ground. And the third.

Then the grating of iron against brick, as the three beds were dragged back to their original position.

I lay frozen on the floor, listening, waiting for what must come next.

Silence.

There was no sound but for the steady falling rain.

Calista's Remedy, Calista Speaks

FOR SOME OBSCURE reason, Gil stole into my thoughts. I pictured his loathsome, gleeful face as he waved my contract with the Houghtons at me. A murderous ire possessed my soul. I wanted this man exposed to all and sundry for what I knew him to be. A hypocrite and villain. I wanted to chant it through the boulevards of Buenos Aires, in like manner as I had wanted to the flee the solicitor's office in Cambridge and howl in the streets at my loss. I heard Father's stern tone again, almost as an echo around the cabin: *No. I will not pay these bills. It's for your own good, my girl. Nothing ever came of a garden. Your place is back home now, with us.*

Abruptly as my rancour arrived, it was spent.

My spine was too excruciating to move. Through the window, I sensed the day closing in. The fire began to die, the logs collapsing into red embers, the scent of the wood-smoke fading. I lay there, growing colder, for how long I do not know, when there came a desperate knock at the door. At once, my heart was hammering again. Then the door swung forth and Calista entered wearing a dripping cloak and bonnet, one of the German shepherds with her. The dog shook herself down, bringing the sodden chilliness of the afternoon into the cabin. Seeing me prostate on the floor, Calista rushed to my side, and I grasped hold of her, pulling her awkwardly to me, tight enough that I smelt her clovey-orangey breath; never in my life had I so yearned for the physical comfort of another. Only when I began to crush her, did she disentangle herself.

'Are you hurt?' she asked.

'My back's done for,' I sobbed in return.

'What has happened? Are you able to move?'

Lola, for now I could see which of the dogs it was, nudged my face, warming it with flicks of her tongue. I did nothing to discourage her, and indicated to Calista the source of my pain. I felt the cook's deft fingers probe the length of my backbone, pressing each vertebra until one such application caused me to hiss like a cat.

Calista spoke with reassurance: 'The Doña's mother suffered a lame back which, for all her expensive doctors, only mine could attend to. I know the remedies if you will allow me.' I did not dissuade. 'I brought these so that we might drink some more.' She placed down two glasses and the bottle of *aguardiente*. 'They will do for this.'

Calista helped to ease me out of my cardigan, then rolled up the material of my blouse, then apologetically loosened the waistband of my skirt to expose more of my spine. At some point I must have glanced at the window for, misunderstanding my trepidation, she said, 'You need not worry about your modesty, Ursula. None is abroad in this weather.'

She took one of the receipts, screwed it into a ball, and dipped it into the fire so that an edge caught.

'What are you going to do?' I asked, tremulously.

'I put the flame in the glass, the glass against your back. Don't be alarmed! It cannot burn you. When the air inside is exhausted, it will cause a suction that will free your bones.'

'Will it hurt?'

'All depends how delicate you are.'

She did as she had explained. I felt the rim of the glass pressed against my skin and a sudden, hot, skewering sensation – and nothing more. Calista repeated the treatment and, upon the second application, there was an audible snap from my spine and with it a tremendous release, to which I let forth an accompanying moan of relief.

'Where the glass touched you, you will have a fine reminder for the coming days,' said Calista, helping me to my feet. 'But no one else need see... unless you forget to lock the bathroom door.' She had spoken in jest, to lighten the mood, but I could not help think of Dolores and whether something had been let slip. The cook carefully adjusted my clothes for me. 'Now, you must keep moving. To ease the joints.'

And so, on doctor's orders, whilst Calista banked up the fire, poured us both an ample glass of the *aguardiente* and sat herself in one of the armchairs, I ranged about the room, limp and wrung-out, declining the offer of rum, for my head continued to spin from lunch. The hollow drum of rain on the roof was unabated; from far off across the Pampas came the occasional grumble of thunder. Lola had settled by the hearth, muzzle resting upon her paws, her eyes following each circuit I made.

Calista viewed the receipts strewn across the floor. 'What were you doing?'

'I wanted us a table for cards and moved the chest. I fell.'

'You should have emptied it first.'

For a long time I did not respond, concentrating instead on stiffly walking my laps, but a pressure was building in me to let forth what had happened, one that was uncontainable.

'Yesterday afternoon I burnt these papers, every last one of them. Or at least I supposed I had. Yamai did it for me, though now I must say I was not witness to the exact moment. Perhaps he failed to understand my instructions and it was something else with which he kindled the bonfire. Perhaps he thought these bills important and returned them to the chest.' None of which explained how one instant it had been effortless to lift, the next a dead weight. Nor those other things: the footsteps, the sounds of the bedsteads being moved; the very notion of them sent an icy spasm through me.

Calista sat with regal pose and took a taste of her *aguardiente*. 'I have not told this to anyone, not even my mistress.' She hesitated, and I wondered if she had changed her mind on whatever she was about to confide. 'When first I cleared the glasshouse, I found some tubs. Brutish things, full of black dirt from which grew nothing.'

'I have seen the very ones.'

'I wanted rid of them, so emptied the soil and threw the tubs on the rubbish heap. The next morning, there they were again, in the precise same spot, filled to the brim with earth. At first I believed Maurín, your predecessor, was to blame for we were already in disagreement. I did with the tubs as before and when exactly the same thing happened, confronted Maurín. He denied having touched them. I did not believe him, all the more when each morning the same continued.' She smoothed down Lola's coat. 'When finally he left us, I cleared those tubs for a last time, smashing them into crocks, and asked Señor Latigez to scatter the earth.'

To all this I had listened with a fearful interest. 'What happened?'

'Need I tell you?' She shuddered. 'I have not touched them since.'

'I thought this the very reason Doña Javiera wanted you here. Why have you not sent word to her?'

'Her husband will not abandon his plans, all his hopes and ambitions, so lightly. Not for the sake of a few tubs.'

'To which now these bills,' came my reply. Whilst making my circuits I had studiously avoided stepping on them.

'The Don is not a man to suffer trivial matters.'

'There is more,' I said. 'This very morning, I saw a boy vanish when it was not possible, and before that a limping man. An axeman. I thought him a vagrant, hiding on the estate, but heard him just now in the other room when the moment before it was quite empty.'

'You saw, you heard... but what evidence' – the word did not sound as hers, as if this was what her mistress had demanded – 'can you present?'

'Cannot Moyano speak with us? Excepting the Mapuches, he has lived here the longest of all. Surely he must have experienced whatever... haunts this place.'

'He refuses to hear such talk, thinking it but women's

chatter to seek the attention of a man. Moyano does not believe, *will* not believe.'

'Might we not at least try?'

'Speak of the matter – and he will dismiss you. Do not get on his wrong side, Ursula. He is a vindictive man. Never will I forget how Maurín bore his fury.'

I stopped my exercise at the farthest point of the cabin, as far as it was to be from the other room and not stand outside in the rain. The memory of the noises from within, my absolute dread that the door might open, remained vivid.

'What if we are in danger?' I asked.

Calista did not answer for some while. 'I do not believe we are.' She stared deeply into the burning logs. When again she spoke it was quietly, rather unwillingly. 'It is the Agramontes who need fear, not we attendants.'

Her reply did not assuage my anxiety, and I pressed the issue. 'On my journey across the Pampas, I met the builders of the new wing.'

The cook shifted uneasily in her chair. 'Yes.'

'One of their number was sick. Sick with fright, is how I would describe him.'

'Yes.'

'Might we not suffer the same?'

'He was drunk, he went outside. The others found him the next day.'

'But what happened to him?'

She regarded me with her tortoiseshell eyes. Whether she was holding back more I never discovered, for afterward she lapsed into silence. 'He took himself into the trees.'

There is one last thing I must tell of that eventful Sunday.

Grandfather's remedy for a bad back, one learnt on seaships, was of a more elementary nature than Calista's. As he grew old, and digging caused him a crook to the lumbar, he swore by it. 'Avoid the hammock, Little Bear,' he used to tell me, 'and choose the floor.'

So it was that night I made an arrangement of bolsters and blankets and lay drowsily on the floorboards of my room, my head heavy and swirling. Calista had helped me from the cabin through the rain and mulberry dusk to the house, where she prepared a supper of scrambled plover-eggs and, later, drew me a hot bath. I lay there, my mouth an inch above the surface, struggling with the fright that had affected me and, in doing so, the notion that I should leave Las Lágrimas began to take form. If I distrusted my ability to oversee such a grand garden there could, at least, be no shame in resigning for fear of an unworldly threat. Yet even as the idea took hold, the more rational part of my brain was exerting itself – that there must surely be a straightforward explanation to the strange occurrences of the day.

The heat of the water gave additional respite to my back. Afterward, Calista assisted me to my room, solicitude itself, and brought up a concoction of her own making. 'It will ease your pain,' she said as I drank the bitter-sweet linctus, 'and help you to sleep.'

The soporific soon made known its effect. Lying on the floor, the events of the day loosened themselves from my mind and, for now at least, troubled me no further. My limbs and spine grew spongy and slack, my eyelids too heavy to keep open, so that I was aware of drifting away into a deep, slumberous darkness.

It was in such a state, that I sensed someone in the corridor, feeling the slight tremor of footsteps through the floorboards as a visitor approached my door. At first I supposed it to be Calista, making sure of me one last time before retiring herself; but there came no gentle rap, no whispered enquiry. Rather, the steps halted outside my room, standing in silence, unnervingly quiet, as had happened on the night of my first bath, as if someone was listening in to determine whether or not I had fallen asleep. Dimly, I felt a stirring of unease, one I was too drugged to act upon, and which gave way to a fleeting thought about the burnt-out mansion. What if there were a fire in this house tonight? Would I be able to rouse myself sufficiently to make an escape? I remembered how Namuncura had rubbed his face to indicate the burns to Don Guido's wife.

After a lengthy pause, during which I may have fallen asleep, came the stealthy rustle of material. I heard no other sound, no creaking of wood, simply the undulation of the floorboards as whoever had been outside resumed their nocturnal journey, along the corridor to its farthest end. Had it been a different night, I would have risen to make an investigation. As it was, I descended deeper into oblivion and, with a final flutter of apprehension, knew nothing more of the day.

Gift or Warning?

THERE WAS A knocking at my door. Persistent, loud, hollow. The knocking of a person who, fearing for life, was trying to escape the corridor, pounding his fists against my door in a frantic bid to be admitted. I struggled out of sleep, wondering thickly what emergency demanded such a disturbance. Perhaps my speculation had turned prophecy and, even as I lay slumbering, the house had caught aflame and was filling with smoke...

I surfaced from the depths – not to darkness but bright daylight, one so intense as to be painful to the gaze. For a long, long moment I could not recall why I was wrapped in blankets upon the floor. Nor had I sense of the duration of my sleep: it felt like only minutes before that I had closed my eyes, whilst simultaneously, my limbs possessed the lethargy one associates with days spent laid out in a sickbed.

And still the knocking at my door!

Now that I was more in possession of myself, it sounded timid rather than desperate, a half-hearted tap-tap to rouse me. I struggled to stand and my spine gave an unforgiving creak. My joints felt rusted, my head heavy, my mouth furred. I lumbered to the door and opened it a few inches to find Dolores outside. Her eyes flicked up and down me, first in concern and then, or so my dulled brain thought, with a mocking curl to her lips.

'Calista sent me. She says Señor Moyano is looking for you.'

'What hour is it?'

'Noon.'

I experienced a lurching dismay. If there was one thing I did not want to be considered as, it was a slouch.

'Does he know I was still in bed?'

'I haven't told him.' She tried to peer past me into my room, as if expecting another person concealed behind the furniture or, more disgracefully, amongst the bedclothes. In her voice was an odd trace of satisfaction. 'Did Calista give you one of her potions?'

I nodded and asked the maid if she would fetch a glass of water whilst I dressed. Then, groggily, I tidied away the bedding and changed into my riding clobber of Sunday, the material spattered with mud, a subterfuge I hoped would convince Señor Moyano that I had been at work all morning. Dolores returned with my water and a hunk of bread, which I consumed queasily before hurrying downstairs and sneaking into the garden where I sucked in lungfuls of oxygen to clear my head. Above, the clouds were broken and drifting, exhausted by rain, the sun the same pale yellow of early helianthus.

The effect of the light and air, not to mention the briskness of my pace, was to make me feel sounder of mind than I had been the previous night, events in the cabin taking on an unreal quality. I groped around for something to settle the matter. I had drunken too freely of Calista's rum; the atmosphere of the place had been gloomy and oppressive – was it any wonder I had succumbed to the most ghoulish imaginings? Moreover, I felt I had egged on Calista. As she herself had said, what actual 'evidence' was there? It was thus I dipped through the entrance in the black wall, a measure of my good sense restored even if some part of me remained not wholly assured.

I had not penetrated far into the undergrowth when I came across the two Mapuches, conversing in underhanded tones as they laboured. Upon seeing me, they fell silent and rested on the handles of their scythes, glancing at one another, before Yamai summoned his tongue.

'It was not us, Señorita.'

I saw that they were both in a rare state. 'I'm afraid I do not understand.'

'*El Jardín de tesoro*. Yesterday we spent with our father, inside from the rain. It was not us.'

He was making no sense, and I told him so. Epulef snarled something at his brother, and they had a cross little exchange in their native language before remembering themselves.

'I cannot explain,' said Yamai. 'I must show you.'

He led me away, down the 'Strolling Borders', we taking not more than two dozen paces to become engulfed by weeds, the Mapuches having cleared but a paltry area despite their efforts of the week past. The greenery around us was alive with secret tricklings from the previous day's deluge. Ahead, Yamai slowed his pace and I saw the broad spread of his shoulders tensing. For the first time, I became aware that the parkland beyond was turbulent with bird song, an agitated, strident chatter.

Yamai halted at the edge of the brush and refused to take another step. 'It was not us,' he repeated.

I peered around him, shading my eyes from the sunlight. On Saturday, I had left the Treasure Garden mostly in a state of wilderness. That Monday afternoon it was cleared. Completely cleared and bare.

The thicket of weeds and nettles I had spent days engaged with in futile attack, had been ripped from the ground, roots and all, so that the design of the parterre was revealed as Sir Romero had intended. The borders looked as if they had been turned by a rotary tiller, the earth friable and black, whilst the paths had been refreshed with white gravel. In the centre of the garden, the shape that had formerly been hidden beneath Virginia creeper, was now exposed as a large, tiered fountain of beautiful ornamentation. Although no water cascaded down it, nor jets played, I could see that its basins were brimming from the reflection in them of the pale, blue sky. Around the perimeter, the yews were neatly clipped and gave an impression of tall, dark sentinels guarding the space.

I went to step into it. Yamai held out his hand in arrest. 'Do not walk here, Señorita.'

After a little hesitation, I pushed past, my boots making a queer crunching noise as I crossed the gravel. 'How is this possible?'

Yamai could, of course, offer no answer and stood there watching me dumbly, fretting over my every move as I paced the open paths until I became impatient of his agitation and sent him back to his brother. I trod my way from one end of the Treasure Garden to the other, once bending to rake my fingers through the clean soil – it smelt sweet and fecund – another time, picking up a piece of gravel from the path and examining it as though it were a precious stone and I a jeweller. My emotions roiled as I attempted to make sense of what I was seeing and, when I reached the far end, I did not linger but strode on to put a distance between myself and the garden, continuing into the undergrowth to the Wailing Wall, which plainted and whistled eerily. I paced beneath the black stonework, noting in one spot that the rain of yesterday had been forceful enough to wash away a small part of the foundation.

I tried to give my thoughts some order. I was in shock, without question, the sensible portion of my brain in retreat and overrun, once more, by a fear for what was not credible. It may surprise the reader to learn that also I felt cheated, for although I had gone to bed with the half-decided intention I must leave Las Lágrimas, I still considered it *my garden* to restore; I wanted it done by my sweat, my toil, the blisters on my hands, the ache in my limbs, for there is nothing so satisfying as to be weary of an evening from hard work and good air. Yet I knew this to be sentiment talking, memories of gardening with Grandfather, for I had no such satisfaction at Las Lágrimas. Here one ended the day in much the same temperament as Sisyphus concluded his.

Nevertheless, a sense of being cheated remained, its ardency not quite my natural mode.

From somewhere in the vicinity, I heard Moyano calling my name and the excited bark of Vasca and Lola. A forgotten fragment of the night came to me, when I must have woken fleetingly to hear, as on previous occasions, the baying of hounds. I made my way to the estate manager, drawn by his cries, and met him by the ornate fountain, the dogs sniffing eagerly around its base. Moyano wore an expression of elation, like a father in the presence of his newborn, and in a moment of unguarded approval he embraced me, his cheek brushing mine. With equal unguardedness, or my mind still slurred from the sleeping draught, I surrendered to his clinch for the briefest instant, before we both immediately withdrew.

'I will confess, Ursula — my apologies — Señorita, I had doubts over whether I should employ a woman. You have shown me wrong.'

I said nothing. There seemed no possible reply, for I could not come clean on the truth nor had I forgotten Calista's emphatic warning in the cabin, that to speak of powers unnatural to Moyano was to risk dismissal. For, should I resign my position, vanity dictated it be of my own decision, not because I had been sent away. I offered a weak smile of acceptance, in the hope that my reticence be considered as modesty.

Moyano seemed not to notice, for something in the fountain had caught his attention. 'The Don will be in delight!' he enthused, 'all the more if Farrido can get this working.'

He peered into the water of the lowest basin, then rolled up his sleeve, showing a muscular forearm, sleekly haired, and plunged in his hand to the depth of his elbow. 'It's cold,' he said with a sharp inhalation, retrieving an object that he held up to the sun. It caught and winked in the light.

'To add to my collection,' he said, showing me a silver peso.

'You have others?'

'They are everywhere on the estate, if you look.'

'I have seen my share, but did not know they were so readily found.'

'Don Guido was a generous host and would spread his riches as an emperor tosses roses. Gifts for his guests to find. Or at least, that's what I was told.' He dried and pocketed the coin. 'I see that you do not approve, Señorita.'

'No.'

'Of the elder Agramonte, or my taking the coins?'

'The Mapuches say they bring evil.'

'Then I must be wicked indeed,' he laughed. When I did not share his amusement he continued pointedly, 'Native superstition, and they should mind their tongues. It was only through the charity of Don Guido they were allowed to keep their home here.'

He rolled back down his sleeve. As he did so I glimpsed his wrist, that habitual spot at which he rubbed, the skin about it criss-crossed with waxen scars as if it had been slashed, so that I gave some credence to Calista's talk that he had once tried to end his life.

Prior to leaving the Treasure Garden, Moyano surveyed it one final time with deep satisfaction. The lack of any planting added to the plot's starkness. 'Calista tells me you have injured your back.'

'It's nothing.'

'I hope not. If you need anything for it, make sure that I know.' He paused, feeling me with his eyes. 'For your pains here, Señorita Kelp, I am indebted.'

The rest of the afternoon I spent in a state of turmoil, trembling in the balance as what to make of events, bolstered by Moyano's fervour, aware that in the space of a night my prospects at Las Lágrimas had been transformed. The day before, I had only disappointment and excuses to present to Don Paquito when he arrived; from to-day onward I had achieved what he had asked of me. And yet... this newly found position I owed to unseen – *unknowable* – forces whose motive I could not divine.

Had I been presented with a gift? Or, having not heeded my experiences in the cabin, a further warning?

I took myself to work alongside the Mapuches, for now that the Treasure Garden was cleared, and whilst I waited for the first plant delivery, it made sense in terms of completing my plan to help them with the Strolling Borders. They were also company, for I did not relish the prospect of working alone that day even if Epulef, suspicious at my fellowship, glanced at me continually with a chary eye.

At three o'clock, Dolores arrived with tea-things: a pot of *mate* and some *lomitos*, slices of steak served in a sweet bread roll. There was fruit-cake also and segments of orange, picked and peeled that very afternoon. To the astonishment of the Mapuches, I shared my fare with them, making us a little picnic, and afterward they seemed more settled with my oversight, at one point breaking into a native chant, slashing and digging to its rhythm. This, as much as the refreshment and weather – it remained bright all day, the wind brisk but bracing – lifted my spirits, and I hacked away at the weeds, for my back was also improved, until there was a glow to my cheeks and I felt an unexpected well-being. Thus was my mood when Vasca appeared, nudging me for attention and nosing around the freshly turned earth at my feet. It stoked my heart how the dogs would just arrive, full of curiosity and affection. At once, I made up my mind what I must do. I could make no decision as to my future at Las Lágrimas without braving the cabin again.

I encouraged the German shepherd from the garden, walking to the stables, where I searched for a length of rope, to fashion into a leash, and a brick, to use as a doorstop. Having procured both, I continued to the cabin, Vasca trotting happily by me, untroubled at being tied. The sky was paling but still light (for I do not think I could have ventured this way if dusk was seeping into the day), the only forewarning of the sunset being a few carnation-pink clouds streaking to the west. As it was, a tightness in my ribcage began to exert itself as we approached the building.

My purpose held firm.

I opened the door a sliver and peered in, catching the faintest trace of woodsmoke. All was quiet, the atmosphere inside serene. There was no sense of any presence or me having disturbed one such. I took the brick and wedged it between the door and its jamb, so that there was no possibility of the former slamming and, with Vasca on a tight lead, the rope wrapped repeatedly around my hand, we stepped inside. Everything was how Calista and I had left it the previous evening: the dresser still in the corner, the table beneath the window, the cheery mother-and-son hanging upon the wall, the two armchairs by the fireplace.

Everything, excepting the chest and spilled receipts. These were nowhere to be seen.

I strode to the second door before my nerve left me, for my heart was undeniably racing now, and flung it wide, keeping Vasca close. Here too all was peaceful, the only disturbance being that of my breath and the dog's snuffling. The bedsteads stood positioned as I had heard them done so yesterday – I shuddered at the recollection – and at the other end of the room was the chest. I opened it, the hinges giving the slightest, dry creak, and was greeted by the familiar waft of must and time. The bills had been returned, and by the neatest of hands, the sheaves tied with purple ribbon and precisely stacked, as of notes in a bank vault. I wondered what Señor Berganza would have to say regarding them (they were, after all, from his firm) and whether they might offer any explanation as to yesterday's incident, resolving to quiz the nurseryman when he visited.

Gently, I closed the lid. Vasca stared up at me with her odd-coloured eyes, the one green, the one blue, and I lavished her with strokes, feeling where her pelvis had been broken and distortedly healed. The atmosphere in the cabin remained calm, the calmness that comes after a violent storm when the thunder has spent itself.

'Come, girl,' I said. And we left.

I walked back pensively to the house, letting Vasca free as we approached the stables. The night before I was half-minded to offer my resignation. Reason endorsed it: I had been terribly afraid and do not know what evil might have befallen me if the door had swung open. It was an experience I had no desire to repeat, yet such was the tranquillity today in the cabin that already it seemed an aberration. For what exactly had I suffered? A few horrid noises, a mood of rancour; and, in the light of day, neither seemed quite so frightful as I remembered. Were these things – or indeed the cleared garden – reason enough to abandon the life I was making for myself here? Calista did not believe we were in any danger. She was a woman of perception and, those horrid pots aside, had lived on the estancia unmolested enough these past months. By remaining in post, I could also warn the Agramontes to be more vigilant than the Don's scepticism allowed.

Besides, were I to resign, where would I go? Tell me, what would I do? To find another position, one of comparable prestige, would be unlikely, and I was troubled that if my options grew evermore scant, and through no choice of my own, I might ineluctably stray back to my family and, worse still, whatever suitor Mother had procured me. I could, I suppose, set out and follow some of Grandfather's route across the continent, but in my heart I knew this was not to travel – it was to run away.

I thought of my sisters, if they had been the ones in the cabin, listening to the footsteps. They would have fled in an instant, screaming to the treetops. (I preferred to ignore the flea in my ear that said I might have done the same had not my back been injured.) To show the white feather now, to even consider having to return to my family, would be to disappoint myself most bitterly. *Deborah*, I could hear them laugh, for they only ever called me by the name of my christening. *Deborah who left us for a life as a gardener, as a working woman, and skulked back with a case of the nerves.*

Even as I imagined their voices, I felt a new resolution arise within me.

Unexpectedly, one of Grandfather's favourite expressions came to mind, his spur in time of adversity: 'Stiffen the sinews, summon up the blood!' I do not know why I had not thought of it before.

I continued on my path to the house, the late afternoon hazy, pink and golden, Vasca dancing at my heels, feeling stouter of heart and swore that, as I had set out from Britain to pursue my own path, so now must I be the mistress of my fears. I would see out my time at Las Lágrimas.

I would make a garden worthy of my talents yet.

Treasures... & a Surprise

THE REST OF that day passed with not a single occurrence beyond the humdrum, further settling my nerves. The one after, the 26th it would have been, broke with another clean, enamelled sky, the wind cold and restless, swishing through the leaves. It was in the middle of the morning when I heard a klaxon sound from the direction of the driveway. Berganza had arrived.

I had been working, alone and rosy-cheeked, to clear that wild patch between the Treasure Garden and the Wailing Wall. I drove my fork into the ground and sallied to the house, making as I went some attempt with my hair. Parked at the front were two motorlorries with canvas-covered backs. Emblazoned on the material in gold lettering, and painted also on the door of the driver's cabins, were the words, '*Lautaro Berganza e hijos, Tandil*'. A half-dozen men, dressed in black weeds, collars but no ties, had descended from the vehicles and loitered at their rear, awaiting instruction, looking not unlike a knot of burly pallbearers. Their eyes followed my approach, a mixture of curiosity and, in some, I was sure, hostility. Moyano was deep in conversation with an individual in a burgundy greatcoat that bulged around his belly. He had thick, curly hair and a bush of a beard both as black as his men's uniforms, so black as to have a suspicion of dye, for the etches around his eyes spoke a man approaching his fiftieth year.

Moyano broke away from their discussion, flicking me a rapid head-to-toe inspection to ensure I was presentable. 'This is Señorita Kelp – Ursula, though we are none of us permitted to call her so – from England. Our new Head Gardener.'

The other man snatched up my hand, pressing it to his lips, which felt fleshy and moist. '*Mucho gusto*,' he boomed. 'I am Berganza.'

In the withdrawing of my fingers, I was tactful as possible and, when I judged no one was observing, I wiped them on the back of my dress. 'Father or son?' I asked.

He puffed himself up, like a gigantic bullfrog, and hooked his thumbs under his armpits. 'What would you say?'

'Hm. Father?'

A good-natured roar of laughter. 'Son. The old buffer is fertiliser now.'

'I am sorry to hear that.'

'Don't be. He drank himself to death and near took the business with him. Though he was fortunate enough to have this account. I'm looking forward to seeing Las Lágrimas again after all these years.' He possessed one of those voices incapable of quietness, every word delivered as a bellow. 'Now, see what treasures I have brought for you, Señorita Kelp.'

He steered me to one of the lorries, its innards crammed full with plants and nursery shrubs. A proportion was bare-rooted, though the remainder sat in individual, terracotta pots: a rather needless and costly practice to my mind. I cast a wandering eye and saw oriental poppies and hedging-box for starters, nepeta, acanthus and geraniums, naming the species aloud by their scientific names (*Papaver orientale*, *Buxus sempervirens* &c). It was, truth to tell, childish, but I wanted to impress Berganza. A sweet, waxy, resinous concentration of foliage – the very scent of why I garden – enveloped me, filling my soul with such pleasure that all I could do was to stand and breathe deeply of the aroma.

Berganza watched with approval at my inhalation, if not my Latin. 'It is the salt of our lives, is it not, Señorita? You can have your fancy French perfumes, but I swear nothing in this world smells better.' He filled his own lungs and glanced over at Moyano who was peering in, as unmoved as my parents would have been. 'Only us gardeners know it.'

I asked, 'What are these plants?'

'Don Paquito ordered them.'

'They must have cost a small fortune.' And, I disapprovingly thought, explained the ostentatious use of pots.

'In the other lorry are further specimens. I have also brought you a surprise.'

At the very back, half-hidden by an ornamental bay, was my luggage from Chapaledfú, it having been railwayed to Tandil whence Berganza collected it. Dolores was summoned, keeping her eyes fixed on the ground as Berganza's men watched and whispered about her, and helped me carry the cases to my room. The maid was keen to unpack there and then, but I sent her away and returned outside to supervise the unloading of the lorries.

Those plants that were hardy enough, I had barrowed inside the garden, placed by the lee of the wall and heeled-in; those I deemed too tender to risk outside yet, I sent to the glasshouse in the kitchen garden – with Calista's consent (gracefully given). I did not allow Berganza's men admission under the glass itself, for which I daresay they judged me a martinet, but the first thing that caught my eye as I gained the entrance was that cluster of nasty black pots. I did not want them disturbed in any manner, thus I had the men carry their cargo only to the threshold, after which, no matter what the weight or dimension of plant, I struggled with it alone, my back complaining often. In short time, the glasshouse was chock-full and the panes misted with my effort. I had done well to hide my grievance upon being shown the bounty of the lorries. It was my understanding that Don Paquito would, naturally, have a hand in his garden. My strong wish, however, was that as the Head Gardener, I would be the one who decided on the specimens, who would select their type and palette; for Berganza had arrived with hundreds of plants, each of which was a choice wrested from me.

Rather than eat my hamper out of doors that day, I instead lunched with Moyano and Berganza in the dining room. The nurseryman made himself at home, demonstrating an appetite as healthy as his corpulence suggested, drinking a bottle of good red to himself – Moyano had half of a second bottle, I a single glass – and chatting boisterously throughout. There was roasted-garlic soup and a rack of beef with potatoes and carrots as supplements, and afterward *budín de pan* with a mysteriously flavoured rum sauce of which Berganza had two gluttonous portions. For my own part I ate mostly in silence and listened to, what I guessed to be, anecdotes of a perennial nature from Berganza: about life in Tandil, the business of horticulture and various local characters. The one subject I was most curious to hear him speak about, namely his family's history with Las Lágrimas, was not raised. He was a popinjay to be sure, yet I found his noisy presence reassuring, making me appreciate just how quiet and oppressive the house could be the rest of the while. Even before the pudding dishes had been cleared, he was offering a cigar-box under our noses; Moyano joined him, though myself I did not partake. The two men were soon veiled in smoke.

'I must give you a tour of the garden,' announced Moyano. 'You will not believe the miracle Señorita Kelp has accomplished these past days.'

'So long as we are quick. I swore to my men we'd be away in good time.'

'If possible' – I cleared my throat, and caught Berganza's eye – 'I would like the honour of showing our guest.'

'Of course,' was Moyano's baleful response. 'But I will accompany you.'

I got the distinct sense he did not want me left alone with the nurseryman who, fortunately, intervened. 'You and I, Juan, have had all morning to plot. Better the Head Gardener is my guide,' he said with decision. 'That was the tradition in my father's day.'

Shortly after, he rose from the table, offering me his huge, damp paw, and so the matter was laid to rest.

Berganza's Tale

HIS FIRST SHOCK was the wall.

'Begod!' he said, choking on his cigar smoke. 'Please say you are not responsible for this monstrosity.'

'I was told it was here since Don Guido's time.'

'Not at all.'

'Were you often at Las Lágrimas with your father?'

'As a boy, I was a regular visitor. There was certainly no wall. You should have seen the garden in those days, Ursula.' He had started calling me that over lunch and I had not demurred. Every time he spoke my name, Moyano's mouth would tighten.

I led him past the sealed wooden door, along the wall and so to the other entrance. Berganza squeezed himself through it, I following, and from there we plodded into the overgrowth.

'Tell me,' I said. 'What was it like then?'

'The finest garden you ever did see, running from the house to the lake and the Pampas beyond. I doubt there was a colour or shade that could not be found in the herbaceous borders. And the Perfume Garden' – he dropped his cigar, crushing it under foot, and inhaled deeply – 'I can smell it to this day. The sweet peas! The roses! Whenever Father was bound for the estate I pleaded with him to take me. In the summer, we would spend several nights, us boys allowed to sleep in the treehouse.' He was in a trance of delight. 'It was the best of treats.'

'It's hard to believe now.'

Returning from his daydream, Berganza looked about himself in disillusionment, a state that intensified the farther we walked. 'It breaks the heart,' he said, his voice for once soft. 'You are too young to appreciate it, Ursula, but here is like visiting an old flame in her widowhood, when she is worn and grey.'

As we continued, I discussed with him additional plants that I wanted to order and Berganza, after retrieving a jotter from his pocket, noted down my requests, often with a bark of approval or comments such as 'excellent choice' or 'your knowledge is impressive, Ursula'. Between us, there was much talk of annuals. We reached the newly cleared Treasure Garden, and had taken our first crunching steps upon the gravel, when a bout of agitation gripped Berganza. He froze, his face blanching, his body seeming to diminish, and twisted in the direction of the Imperial Avenue – the crowns of the ombú trees just visible from our position – as if some terrible occurrence there demanded his attention.

'Does something trouble you, Señor Berganza?'

'That sound.' His voice was a dirge.

'What sound?' I heard nothing. 'Señor?'

He made no response. There was only the wind in the trees, as of foam dragging at shingle.

'What sound?' I repeated and then, my mind in a state of uneasy speculation for the slump in Berganza's mood had a contagion to it, I ventured, 'Could it be an axe you hear, Señor? The sound of a tree being felled?'

His reply was unexpectedly stern. 'Why do you say that?'

'I only wondered, for I sometimes hear such.'

'It's nothing,' he said at last, wrapping himself in his greatcoat. His whole bearing was the picture of loss. 'My wife scolds me for drinking so much at lunchtime. I've had my fill of this place. Come, Ursula, take me back to the house.'

'There is something, first, I should like to show you.'

We made our transit to the meadow, few words passing between us. The exuberance Berganza had demonstrated at the dining table, what I took to be his natural state, had all but drained from him. His step faltered as the cabin came into view.

'Tarella's old dwelling,' said the nurseryman. 'Why on earth have you brought me here?'

'Tarella.' I was sure this was the word Yamai had spoken to me, when first we uncovered the building. 'Who is Tarella?'

'Silvio Tarella. One of your predecessors. He was the Head Gardener in the days of Don Guido. My father had many dealings with him.' He hid a belch behind his hand. 'A kind fellow. He would sneak me handfuls of cherries from the orchard.'

'I use the cabin now.'

He was much surprised. 'Not as your rooms, I hope.'

'As an office, or at least that was my intention. What I want to show you is inside.'

I opened the door and at once experienced that sensation of having disturbed someone, though the interior was vacant and dingy. Such was the intensity of the feeling that I felt a word of apology form on my lips. A glance at Berganza told me he was under a similar influence. When nothing else happened, I led him to the chest and handed him one of the bundles of receipts.

'What can you tell me of these?'

He wetted a sausage of a finger and leafed through the first dozen before, or so it seemed, he realized what I had given him. His face, already grown pale from the sound he had heard, lost yet more colour, and he thrust back the bills to me. 'Do you know what this place is?' he asked, by way of distraction.

I found his lack of candour frustrating. 'Señor Moyano,' I briskly replied, 'told me this was the first house on the estancia, the one built by Capitán Agramonte.'

'The Capitán's house was the old mansion, the one destroyed in the fire. No, this was a prison.'

I was sure I had misheard him. 'I thought you said "a prison".'

'A prison is exactly what I said. Has no one told you?' His eyes roamed fretfully and I could see that his preference would have been to leave forthwith. 'During the Desert Campaign – that is the war to wrest these lands from the natives – there was a fort here, I suppose because of the well. This building was the prison. A number of Mapuches met their last here, but chiefly it was for deserters. That is where the estancia takes its name from – Las Lágrimas.'

'Moyano claimed that when the Capitán found this spot he shed tears at its beauty.'

'I presume you know of the penalty for soldiers who refuse to fight? Their wives and mothers would come to beg clemency, only to discover how deep the Capitán's indifference, no matter what their pleas. Nor was the Capitán a man to waste powder on the condemned when starving would suffice. And so the women wept, their wails carrying far and wide, as the wind of the Pampas will do. After the war, the Capitán was given these lands for his service.'

'I would rather Moyano's story.'

'If I were you, my dear, I'd be careful of trusting too much of what Moyano has to say.'

I returned his attention to the receipts. 'As you can see, they are from your company.'

'And long before my tenure.'

'But not your father's.'

'What is it you are really asking me, Señorita?'

I spoke my case boldly. 'I believe Las Lágrimas to be cursed – haunted – and that the receipts may offer a clue as to why. I want to know if I am safe here.'

'My father spoke of ghosts,' he admonished. 'The rest is old rumours, and I am not going to fill you up with that.'

'If there are things you know, however fanciful, let me be the judge.'

He mulled over my words, chewing on his bearded lower-lip, and for an instant he appeared on the point of disclosing something – then considered better of it. 'There's nothing to tell.'

'Not even of the receipts?'

'They are the bills for the trees of the parkland,' he said.

'The ones Don Guido planted. That much I have guessed.'

'Not Don Guido! If ever there lived a man who thought it beneath himself to dirty his hands, it was he.'

'Then who?'

He angled his face away from me, his eye finding the iron bedsteads. 'That was Tarella.'

Once more he was given to silence, the vein of which I struggled to determine. Could it be fear I detected? Guilt? Or was it merely a shortcoming in his knowledge of events? I pressed him to go on.

'What do you want me to say?' he huffed. 'If Don Guido was one not to dirty his hands, he was also a man of vanity, a man who desired the esteem of others. No, not the esteem. The envy. As gardens were the fashion of his day, so he wanted his estancia to have the greatest in all the Pampas, setting a famous landscaper to create him a masterpiece—'

'Romero Lepping.'

'Lepping, yes, I had forgotten his name. It was he who designed the garden and parklands, a marvel that was justly admired, but never finished. For, to add to the Don's sins, there was a miserly streak to him – not to the hangers-on he gathered – but always those who served him.'

'He does not sound the most pleasant of men.'

'That's not the half of it. In his younger days he was not past trapping poachers or even flogging his own staff.' He mused on this. 'Some are born bad. He took Lepping's plans and dismissed him without paying his full recompense, turning instead to Tarella, his Head Gardener, to complete the work. Tarella was a man of the Pampas, a mere labourer, though one possessed of such gifts there must have been green sorcery in his fingers. As was his wont, Don Guido demanded his parkland at once, but Nature does not obey any man, no matter his riches. And so, in his impatience, the Don travelled to the Old World, leaving the enterprise to Tarella, with the expectation all would be done by his homecoming.

'Tarella had no wish to disappoint his master and undertook the planting with pride that such an auspicious task had been trusted in him. All day, every day: trees! In the howling wind and rain, on those days when the fog rolls up from the Pampas, or in midsummer when the sun is enough to burn a man's back. Year after year, though his wife begged him not to toil so. She feared the effort would do for him.'

'His wife?'

'I saw her picture in the other room.'

'The mother and child, you mean?'

Berganza nodded. 'They were a happy family, and Señora Tarella more worldly-wise than her husband. She saw how Don Guido had treated Lepping and insisted there be a contract for the work. I suspect it was she who kept these bills.' He tapped the chest with his boot. 'Each one of them a tree, all planted by Tarella's own hand.'

'This happened, what? Forty years ago,' I interjected.

'Yes.'

'You are a plantsman,' I continued. 'You must see that the trees are far older than that.'

'When first I visited the estate, this land was nothing but flatness. Within a season there were trees. By the time my voice was breaking, a forest had taken hold. I can offer you no explanation, other than to say what I speak is the truth.'

A cold, dreadful foreboding was spreading through me, as though I had swallowed a handful of ice, for an idea had insinuated itself into my mind – that if this had been Tarella's cabin, it was his ghostly, limping steps I had heard. My voice was constrained when I asked, 'And Tarella... what became of him and his family?'

Berganza phrased his answer with care. 'I am not sure anything became of them. In time, Don Guido returned from Europe, now with a Castilian beauty for a wife and a young heir. Guido was never a man of tender heart, but he doted on that boy. Later, there arrived a second son, Paquito – your employer.'

'And?'

'And that, my dear,' he earnestly said, 'is the tale told.'

I was sensible of the fact he was withholding some element, but from the set of his mouth I saw I would get nothing further from him. 'Then you do not believe in any curse?'

'A curse... or simply a coincidence. Who is to say? Don Guido's son drowned—'

'I did not know he drowned.'

'—the old mansion went up in flames. Tragedies strike all families. Years after, my brother was taken from us in a hunting accident. Even your own King's brother died!'* He spoke pointedly. 'Was he cursed too, Señorita?'

The nurseryman fell into a brown study before rousing himself and checking his pocket-watch. 'Is that really the

---

* George V (who reigned 1910–36) only ascended to the throne after the unexpected death of his elder brother, Albert, from pneumonia.

hour? I should be on my way.' He adopted a false heartiness. 'My men will be demanding extra wages.'

We left Tarella's cabin and made the house our direction. Beneath the trees all was quiet save for the irregular, whooping cry of some bird. The sense of foreboding that had seized me demanded a final question.

'Señor, what did Tarella look like?'

'It was forty years ago, Ursula.'

'You must have some memory of him.'

'He was just a man, neither short nor tall. The thickest, black hair, as I remember. Black as a raven.'

'What of his leg? Was it crippled? Did he have a limp?'

'I think I would have recalled such a detail.'

That, at least, laid to rest some of my fears.

By the time we reached the motorlorries, Berganza's men were waiting with anxious impatience. The journey back to Tandil was overnight and they wanted to be free of the estancia's land before dusk. The nurseryman said his farewells with something of his former jocund manner, though I could see it was for show. Whatever sound he had heard, and those matters of which we subsequently spoke, had left him in a state of dejection, all the natural cheer of his personality lanced. He shared a few last words with Moyano, then offered me his hand to shake.

As I took it, I leant in close and in a hushed voice asked, 'Promise me, I am safe here?'

'It all happened long ago,' was his reply. 'And none was to do with you.'

Realizing he had spoken unguardedly, and to evade further inquisition, he at once clambered into the cabin of the leading lorry and ordered the vehicles to set off. They trundled down the Imperial Avenue, leaving a stench of petroleum fumes in their wake.

'What were you saying?' asked Moyano. His voice was toneless.

I found him in the grip of one of his melancholias and answered with due caution. 'He wished me well with the garden.'

'And on your *tour*?' This last word as spiteful as any I have known.

'We mostly discussed plants. I have placed a new order. I hope it meets with your approval. Señor Berganza will be returning to deliver next month.'

'He brought with him bad tidings.'

The lorries swept round the bend and were hidden. I listened to the putter of their engines dwindle into the trees.

Moyano produced an envelope from his pocket and shook it at my face. 'News from Don Paquito.' His breath reeked of old cigars. 'He has tired of waiting in Buenos Aires and decided to take up residence earlier.'

'How much earlier?' I answered, aghast at the work still to be completed in the garden.

'He arrives next week.'

The Lights in the Trees

SLEEP VISITED ME late that night. I wish I could say it was because the unpacking of my cases took so long; in truth, my mind was too unsettled for rest. Whilst she served dinner, Dolores again offered to aid me with my luggage and exhibited such keenness that to disoblige her made me seem a spoilsport. It was also an excuse to leave the table and remove myself from Moyano's company, morose and uncommunicative as it was.

In my room, the maid wanted only to lend her hand with my clothing, removing items and draping the most decorative against her black uniform before placing them in the closet, her manner fawning and, to my way of being, somewhat discreditable. She tried on my gloves and my hats, surreptitiously at first, then bold as anything, eventually going so far as to ask if she might borrow one of my favourite puffed blouses. 'It will be far too big for you,' I replied.

My temper finally snapped when she began to pick through my undergarments. 'I can finish on my own, thank you.'

'I'm happy to help, Señorita.'

I went to the door and opened it. 'Goodnight, Dolores.'

She curtsied, but her face was crabbed as she swept past.

After I had finished with my clothes, I put my books on the shelves, proudly lining them up, and dotted those personal items and *bric-à-brac* about the room. For the first time since my arrival, the place had something of my own character about it, which only served to emphasize how unhomely the rest was. It felt more cramped than before, almost threatening claustrophobia; and old-fashioned, the furniture cumbersome, the curtain material drab, the hearthrug ever so moth-eaten. How strange, I mused, that through all my days here, it had never occurred to me how dismal the place really was. My spirits consequently diminished, I gave up on the day and retired to bed.

My spine, though much improved and not warranting another night on the floorboards, was unable to find a comfortable position, aggravated, no doubt, by having heaved so many pots around the glasshouse. Those things Berganza had told me swilled around my head. I kept making a deliberate effort to put them to aside and every time I did so, they found new and insidious ways to penetrate my thoughts. I imagined Tarella planting trees in downpours and thrashing winds…

Except it was not Tarella with his 'raven-black' hair I pictured, but the gaunt, glabrous figure of the axeman.

It was in this state of weary agitation – on the verge of sleep yet never quite crossing its threshold – that I came to fancy I heard a soft footstep come and pause outside my door, someone standing there in silence and waiting for me to fall asleep. I was unable to shake off the notion, it spreading darkly through my mind, until it was nothing less than a conviction. Previously, I had the excuse of Calista's soporific; tonight my head was clear. My heart became a beating drum, my senses alert and fearful. I tried to recollect whether I had turned the lock after Dolores left and what, exactly, my course of action should the door open.

The minutes passed. Still I remained convinced of someone outside.

In the end, it was the lack of any event that drove me from my bed. There was only one way to be sure, the alternative being a night of high alarm and no sleep. The drumbeat in my breast intensifying, I took hold of the doorknob and key with either hand, braced myself – and twisted simultaneously both.

In the corridor, all was perfectly quiet and dark.

Sheepishly, I returned to my blankets to toss to and fro. I refused to surrender to any more ghoulish speculation, instead churning over Don Paquito's premature arrival. His letter stated that he, his family and a contingent of staff would depart Buenos Aires on the morning of Sunday, 30th August to arrive for luncheon on the first day of the new month. Furthermore, he looked forward to seeing what headway had been made on the house and, most especially, the garden (not just the *Jardín de tesoro* but the entire undertaking), going so far as to mention me by name, a detail that made me sure that my progress was to come under immediate scrutiny. Given the limited time and labour I had been afforded, it seemed unreasonable for him to have too high an expectation (I hoped he had not inherited his father's impatience), however, I was wise enough to understand that reason and expectation did not always follow hand in hand. Nor, should the Don be discontented, was I convinced Moyano would defend me. I could only be grateful to those forces that had helped with the Treasure Garden... which led my thinking back to places I would rather not.

I let escape a deep sigh and rolled on to my other side. Las Lágrimas was not quite the place for a rest cure! I lit the lamp on my bedstand and reached for *Nostromo*, making headway through a dozen pages before my attention began to drift, it becoming harder to concentrate on the meaning. I closed the bookcovers and put out the lamp.

Almost at once, something lurched me back to wakefulness.

I perceived only darkness and silence, yet I was sure I had heard a noise identical to the one that had disturbed me in those first nights at Las Lágrimas. The cry of a child. Not weeping, to be clear, rather a muffled torment. If I could not be sure whether I had dreamt it, I knew for certain I was fully alert for what I heard next.

There came another cry, then the sound of a door slammed with abandon. During my restlessness, my legs had become entwined in the bedsheets and now, as I struggled from them, there came a rapid pitter-patter of footsteps from the far end of the corridor to the other, running directly past my room. Before I had time to fear, I leapt to the door and yanked it open. A faint sliver of moonlight aside, it was, as I had found a half-hour previous.

'Who's there?' I asked in a dropped voice and, when I received no reply, I called the names of the dogs in case they had found their ways indoors and were making mischief.

I heard neither snuffling nor the pant of their breath. I cannot say for certain what propelled me into the corridor, for in all wisdom I should have hidden in my room until daybreak; nevertheless I snatched up a pashmina from my newly arrived clothes and stepped out.

The air felt stirred as if indeed someone had been running and there lingered a trace of blossom, reminiscent of the one I had smelt in the chapel. I listened. From around the corners of the house came the lash of the wind, gusts moaning down the chimneys and, if I concentrated with sufficient ardour, that strange, barely perceptible gurgling that occasionally came to my ear, like the rush of water through a cavern, except not. These aside, I could determine nothing else and was on the point of returning to bed when, at the very margin of my hearing, I registered the creep of feet on floorboards.

I moved swiftly to the head of the staircase, for that was where the sound had its origin, looking both above and below. There was no figure retreating into the shadows, nor any indication that anyone had passed this way, other than that almost insensible smell of blossom. Upward led only to the attic rooms, where I might knock on Dolores' door and ask if she had been disturbed. I imagined her blinking confusedly at being roused and the little smile of scorn on her lips when she told me she had heard nothing. In truth, if someone was abroad at this hour, and with each passing moment I became less persuaded of it, there was one direction more likely to be taken.

I should have put on my slippers, for I was barefooted, I should have fetched a lamp, yet I knew that if I went back to my room my nerve would falter. It was thus I descended the stairs, pausing at the bottom to listen intently again, hoping to catch a half-stifled sob or the skitter of someone fleeing into the darkness; in short, the least of sounds that might indicate I was not alone. Hearing none, I flitted through the downstairs of the old house, checking on the rooms, peering into black recesses. All was to no avail; everything was orderly. In the Trophy Room there was a crushing chill to the air, what little light that came in through the windows glinting on the eyes of the white stags in a manner so uncanny that I almost expected them to bat their lids.

Beneath my nightdress, my skin erupted in gooseflesh and I beat a hasty retreat, deciding I should abandon my fruitless search and return upstairs to bury myself in blankets until I was warm and asleep.

I headed back toward the staircase, past the many portraits, determined to ignore their faces that seemed to stare at me and wonder why this odd *inglesa* was sneaking about so late. Through the panes of the front door, I could see the lawn and avenue of ombú trees, silver in the rays of the moon, the pleached trunks as smooth as columns of alabaster. At their base, nearby the spot where one of their number was missing, a single orb of light hung suspended at the height of a man, shockingly bright against the darkness.

A second light emerged to join the first. Then a third and a fourth, their number multiplying, like fireflies, until there were not less than a dozen.

I stepped to the front door feeling a kind of weightlessness and, although I did not dare open it, I pressed my brow to its glass so that I might better see out. The lights were old-fashioned storm-lanterns, tallow candles burning within, each one held aloft by a man. In their flicker, I glimpsed only details: a sharp nose or chin; handlebar moustaches and the wicked curl of lips; clothes of the blackest broadcloth in a style out of keeping with the present-day. More than several of the crowd were armed with carbines, whilst others carried heavy staffs. The men were reckless and rather triumphant and appeared to be conferring with each other, as if a great sport was at hand, though not a single sound emitted from their direction, for everything I was witnessing, you understand, was in absolute silence. It was this fact, as much as anything, that convinced me that these men were grown from the shadows, not real in any bodily sense – and that I was watching an echo of an event from long ago whose meaning or purpose I could not begin to comprehend. I swallowed drily and tasted a hint of something, as when one pricks a finger on a rose bush and sucks the wound clean.

Then, into that otherworldly silence, came a pleading voice. I did not know whether it was from the scene outside or within my head or even a whisper spoken behind me, for, as I heard it, I felt the slightest disturbance in the hallway. All I could be certain of were the words.

Run! Get away from this place.

The same words that I had heard on the day of my arrival. The next instant, all the lights were extinguished.

Words with Latigez

DOLORES WAS CERTAIN that she had not been disturbed in her attic room, neither by footsteps nor lights, when I questioned her at breakfast, though I was left to wonder whether something had troubled her dreams, for her eyes were ringed with shadows, seeming all the darker against the pallor of her face. Quite likely she was as worried at Don Paquito's arrival as was I, knowing she would cease to have such a primary position when the main body of staff arrived, possibly, as Moyano had hinted, that she would be dismissed altogether.

To temper my own concerns, I spent the day in a bustle of action: harrying the Mapuches to clear faster, mixing a stinking vat of blood-fish-and-bone, barrowing into position the box plants from Berganza's delivery, then raking the earth of the Treasure Garden in preparation for planting on the morrow. Whilst I toiled, I investigated my feelings on the sights and sounds that had kept me awake and took a particular pride in my conduct. For although my heart had thudded wildly, and nothing in this world would have induced me to step outside and confront the men, I had neither hollered nor taken flight – my resolve steadfast. There was in me a growing confidence that although I might experience any number of alarming and unfathomable things at Las Lágrimas, I was of sufficient bravery to face them out.

Later that afternoon, my curiosity about Tarella not fully satisfied by Berganza's account of him, I visited the burnt-out mansion to find Namuncura. He had worked on the estate during the days of Don Guido, and I wanted to quiz him further on the erstwhile Head Gardener. But, when I gained the house, not a soul was to be found there, and I returned none the wiser. That night being a Wednesday, I took a hot bath and retired early to bed, where I lay cleanly and distracted, my ears alert to the slightest suspicion of a footstep in the corridor. I had left a gap in the curtains so that if the lights returned in the trees I would be alerted to them. Before a quarter-hour had passed, however, wearied from my day's activity, I drifted away into a dreamless sleep, having been troubled by neither.

My mood and the weather were in harmony the next day, for although the sky had its share of fast and fluffy clouds, the sun had not felt so warm since my arrival, nor the day so full of promise. The wind was little and fresh and livened by bird song. Whatever irritation I held toward Don Paquito for taking a line of his own on the plants, to-day I would have the gratification of putting them into the ground – my first planting at Las Lágrimas.

I had the Mapuches fetch a barrow of manure from the stables to the Treasure Garden, and then sent them to a distant part of the garden to continue our battle against the weeds. I am sure they were disappointed, for Epulef grumbled a verse or two of his native words, but I did not trust them with the planting and, to be candid, I was selfish in wanting the enjoyment of the moment to myself. It was a moment immediately threatened when Moyano arrived to fret over the plants and where to position them and any number of other details. More than once I caught his eye upon me as though he were saying to himself, is she up to the job? Should I have trusted her with it? Nor had I forgotten his comment about my 'striking' appearance and since pondered that if I were plainer, dumpy or bespectacled, whether he would have made the same decision at Café Tortoni's. It was this, as much as my growing impatience to get cracking, that caused me to speak so sharply. 'Señor Moyano,' I said in my surest Lady Bracknell voice. 'I do not need dry-nursing! Unless *you* prefer to be the gardener and *I* manage the estate.'

He regarded me steadily and left thereafter.

Alongside his letter, Don Paquito had provided a sketch of how he wished the Treasure Garden planted, the outlines of the paths and parterres to be embossed with edges of box, in a like manner to the one Sir Romero had first envisioned and, I assumed, a facsimile of how the Don remembered the garden from his childhood.

I began with the near path, deciding I would work on the lefthand side to the distance of the fountain before beginning afresh on the right, my first task being to lay out a plumb line (for it is important with box that they are put down straight), followed by placing the plants on the gravel, at a distance of nine inches apart, ready for my trowel. Then I knelt and began to dig, a happy purpose and peace rising within me. The same sense of purpose that Grandfather had shared when first I was sent away to him and which captivated my younger self from the outset, for if gardening is anything, it is absorption and dedication – and miraculous. The eruption of colour, scent and sustenance from the simple act of pressing a seed into soil. *We two are magicians, Little Bear*, he used to say. Was it any wonder I had been so enthralled, or that in time his other beliefs, his hope that I might think without convention or restraint, took such root?

I had not long started, and was still in fond thought of Grandfather, when the sound of an axe rolled through the air.

My heart tensed… but on closer listening, it was not an axe assaulting the peace of the morning but the reverberation of a duller, more solid tool.

It was a hammer.

Further to emphasize its commonplace derivation, it was shortly superseded by sawing, the sound drifting from the south-west corner of the garden.

I have found that the tranquillity gardening brings is rarely enhanced by the din of carpentry. I worked for another ten minutes before impatience, and also inquisitiveness, got the better of me, and I trailed the noise, through those many areas where the weeds remained prodigious, to that open space that was described on the plans as the 'Picnic Lawn', though the grass remained at thigh-height, choked with horsetail and dock. In the bare portion at the base of the great cedar sat Lola, contentedly gnawing a bone, whilst resting against the trunk were several planks of timber. I spied Latigez's tool-bag and, looking upward, found the yahoo himself perched in the branches by the treehouse, a hand-saw dangling from his grip. He had been watching my approach and only averted his eyes when mine found his. From the ground I could smell the sweat of his labour and was sure he spurned toilet-soap and water deliberately to stink.

'Good morning, Señorita,' he said, making it sound anything but. 'And how are "we" to-day, Deborah?'

'How do you know that?' I felt a rush of colour to my face. 'Have you and Moyano been talking?'

He indicated my dress, and further wrong-footed me. 'I see you've taken a lesson off Dolores.'

'What do you mean?'

'Only that she's quick to her knees.' His tone was intimate and ugly, and then entirely proper as he continued, 'To say her prayers.'

I glanced down at my skirt to find two muddy patches where I had been kneeling to plant. I ignored his comment and, regaining myself, demanded how much longer he was going to be at his damnable racket.

'Till the job's done. I have important orders from Señor Moyano. They came by letter from Don Paquito himself. I am to repair the treehouse for his kids.'

'Which I suppose means I can't call upon your help any time soon.'

'If you want my advice, I'd whip your little red pals. Get their backs at it.'

'Their industry puts you to shame.'

He enjoyed my retort. 'I've a lash if you want, Señorita. I can even show you how to use it.'

I turned away from him in disgust, not least with myself in that I had risen to his taunts. As I went, I clicked my tongue to encourage Lola, for I did not want her in this detestable man's company. The German shepherd abandoned her bone and trotted after me.

'Treacherous bitch,' shouted Latigez after us, laughing unpleasantly, and at once resumed his hammering, louder than ever.

Over the Wailing Wall

THE SUNSHINE ON my face, some energetic digging and the sensation of soil between my fingers, rich and loamy, did much to expunge Latigez's beastliness as I worked through the morning, even if the row of his hammer-and-saw continued. I also had the satisfaction of – plant by plant – watching the edge of the path morph from a sharp line to one softened by the bristling verdure of the box. Lola settled close to me, lying contentedly. Every so often I would tease her by shouting '*la rata!*' and she would startle, tail athump, only for me to tickle behind her ear, after which she rested again, a brightness to her eyes. I had forgotten how companionable dogs could be and the effect on one's spirit, and vowed to spend more time with the animals, not just for my own sake but to make sure they were kept from Latigez, who I was sure could never treat them as well as I – though, admittedly, there was no evidence to the contrary.

I had already completed planting the left side of the path, up to the intersection with the fountain, and begun on the right, when footsteps on gravel foretold the arrival of Dolores with my victuals. She was excited to see Lola, clasping the hound to her, whereafter she stole a slice of meat from my hamper, rolled it thinly and placed it in her mouth as one might a cigarette. This before daintily leaning over Lola who tensed, then snatched it straight from between her lips! The maid squealed in delight.

'Shouldn't you be careful?' I said.

'Not at all,' she retorted, rolling another slice. 'It's quite safe. Epulef taught me.'

'I did not know you were acquainted with the Mapuches.'

'Only Epulef, sometimes we collect the eggs together. His brother is not so friendly,' she added, causing me to wonder if she had their names in confusion.

She let Lola snatch another morsel from her, then declared, 'One day, I will have dogs of my own, Señorita. At least three of them. Chihuahuas to sit on my lap, all dressed up with bows and rubies.'

'What day will that be?'

'When I am Doña of my own estate.'

I am afraid I laughed at her, to which she responded in an angry rush: 'I've been promised. You'll see! I'm going to be rich.'

'And who has made you this promise?'

'Rich and lazy, just like Doña Javiera.' And, so speaking, she was gone.

I ate my lunch, sharing titbits with Lola (though sensibly, from the hand), speculating as to whether there was anything more to the maid's talk than giving herself airs, for, whenever I passed time in Dolores' company, the picture of her lacerated back was never far from my mind.

When my hunger was satisfied, for the morning's graft had given me a healthy appetite, I resumed my toil, steadily making my progression toward the fountain. The day was further improved when Latigez finally ceased his carpentry. For each box plant, I would excavate a generous hole, adding a forkful of the manure and a slop of the blood-fish-and-bone I had concocted the previous day – the work may have been invigorating, but was hardly the most fragrant. Then the box went into the ground and I back-filled the hole before firming in well. For now, a gap remained between the plants, but given a few seasons they would knit together, forming a perfect, low hedge. And so I continued, through that bright afternoon – the breeze chasing clouds across a blue sky, the birds chattering – making a good going of it, until—

Out of nowhere, I was gripped by fear.

One moment I had been absorbed in my digging, the sun warm on my neck: the very next my heart was racing, my breath as ragged as if I had run a mile. I looked at Lola and found her hackles raised and lips drawn to reveal her fangs. She was staring past me into that area toward the house, where the Treasure Garden ended and the weeds remained solid and untouched by the Mapuches. I found I had not the nerve to follow her gaze. There came the sound of footsteps crunching on gravel, a solitary walker heading in my direction. The tread was too heavy for it to be Dolores returning, nor did I recognize the step as belonging to any of the male staff, yet still I called out, my voice constrained and weak.

'Señor Moyano, is that you? Señor Latigez?'

The footsteps halted.

Lola hunkered down as though readying herself to spring. A low, warning growl escaped her. The steps continued, no longer the regular, steady crunch of one foot after another, but the sound of a heavy boot landing and its pair being dragged behind. I attempted to stand up, to flee, but my legs were like things of straw. My gaze remained fixed downward on the hole I had been digging. I was clenching my trowel so tightly that my fingers burnt. Lola seemed similarly paralysed.

The steps grew unremittingly nearer. My breathing brought the acrid taste of rotting leaves to the back of my throat. I did not dare look round – but saw the silhouette of a lurching, emaciated figure steal across the patch of sunlight before me. The nape of my neck felt as if it were being scraped with hoarfrost.

The footsteps passed me by… then stopped a second time.

There was a deep, unearthly stillness, broken not even by the cry of birds, during which I found a strength of courage to cock my head. The path was empty, the gravel lying level and undisturbed with no indication that anything had been dragged across it. When the steps resumed anew it was at some distance, on the far side of the fountain, where I saw the dark, loping figure of the axeman, for although he was not carrying such a tool the wasted frame, hairless head and oversized hands could belong to no other, nor the pestilent, black poncho.

A malevolent rage emanated from him.

My heart, my lungs, my skin – all shrivelled. I experienced

a dread as I have never done, as if it were a physical force enveloping me. Crushing me.

I watched his lumbering progress, my body rooted to the spot, as he limped to the end of the Treasure Garden and into the wild patch that led to the Wailing Wall, where again he stopped. The axeman raised his fingers to his lips, as if to whistle – though no such sound came. His face remained inexact, his features too hazy and shadowed to determine. And then the most inexplicable thing of all happened.

He vanished.

It was not like watching a djinn in some clever theatrical performance where a puff of smoke disguises the actor's drop through a trapdoor. Nor did I witness his body dematerialize as such. It is difficult adequately to describe in words. One moment he was present, the next he was not, as if the blink of my eye was for him a long-drawn, lightless eternity in which he could flee from sight, yet nor was it entirely instantaneous, for there remained, however briefly, an echo or residue of his outline.

Whatever the method of his vanishing, its effect was immediate. The deathly chill left my skin; my respiration came normally again, as if choking hands had gripped my windpipe and suddenly let go. Lola was likewise released. Without pause she charged away on the axeman's trail and was shortly after swallowed by the weeds, the only sign of her advancement being how the topmost swayed in her wake. I shouted at her to stop and, when she paid no heed, chased after her, following her furious barking. I plunged into the thicket, thorns catching at my dress, nettles searing my hands, and by the time I broke through to the cleared section beyond, Lola was already at the base of the Wailing Wall.

Instinct had brought her to that spot where the rain had exposed the foundation, and she was frantically digging at it, paws flicking up dirt, getting deeper and deeper into the earth, she emitting a desperate high-pitched whining. In vain, I strove to stop her and only when it was too late realized that she had managed to burrow through. Even as I was lunging to grab hold of her, her hind legs and tail disappeared into the hole and under the black rock of the wall. I called pleadingly at her to come back, and squeezed my face to one of the gaps in the stone to see out, afraid of where her progress might take her.

Lola was already dashing across the meadow. Standing at some distance, too far for him to have travelled by the speed of his legs alone – though now motionless, as if he were hewn from oak – was the axeman.

The dog reached him.

From nowhere, he drew a whip and was transformed into a frenzy, thrashing the German shepherd with a brutality that would have made the cruellest of hearts beg mercy. Lola cowered at his feet, seemingly incapable of movement again, even as the leather left her fur criss-crossed and bleeding.

Without a second thought, or any plan as to what I might do, I began to scale the wall, using the crevices between the stones as hand- and footholds, ascending with an agility I would not have believed myself possible of. In no time, I heaved myself on to the very top from where I had a commanding panorama of the meadow, of the lake and broken sky. The landscape was empty of any living creature. Yet if I could not see her, Lola's yelp and pule resounded from every part.

I began to ease myself down the other side, the going much trickier. Almost at once, the muddy undersoles of my boots failed to make purchase. I slipped and fell, landing with such force as to knock the wind from my lungs. I struggled to my feet and ran, past Tarella's cabin, stumbling often on the uneven grass until – not far from the water's edge – I found Lola.

She was alone, painfully wounded and in a state of considerable agitation, chasing her tail, snapping and lashing out as if a swarm of invisible wasps were on the attack. Such was her violence that I was cautious in my approach.

'*Quieta, quieta*,' I said in my most coaxing tone.

Thus shushing and cooing, I was, by-and-by, able to stretch out a hand and, when I felt assured in my confidence, pull her to me, the dog surrendering to my embrace. As I continued to calm the animal, and my own pulse settled, I looked about me. There was no sign of the axeman. Yet I would not rest until both Lola and I were safe and indoors. The dog whimpered like a pup and, with horrid foreboding, I wondered where her mother was, for I had not seen Vasca all day. I got to my feet and made an encouragement for Lola to follow me from the meadow.

A hurrying cloud passed over the sun and, as I watched, the lake changed instantly to the colour of tar. Standing by the shore, his filthy, thickly knuckled fingers once again to his lips in soundless whistle, was the axeman, his rage as black as the water, the evil of his intent apparent. Here was a soul boiling with hatreds.

My heart gave a great downward lurch, then leapt into my throat.

Lola became berserk, yowling and snarling, flashing the yellow of her teeth. Confronted with such a fiercesome display, my grasp was not tenacious enough and, when she raced off, the dog's pace too powerful for me to arrest her. She hurled herself toward the spot where the moment previously the axeman had stood, but now there was only air, splashing into the water to lose her footing and be pulled under. I blundered after her and staggered myself, first to my knees and, before I had the chance to master my balance, up to my chest, for though we were at the lake's margin there seemed to be nothing below but treacherous depths.

The water was cold, as cold as embalming fluid, as if never a minute of sunlight had warmed it, and thick with tangled aquatic-weeds that roped around my legs and, combining with the weight of my skirts, dragged me down.

I floundered, struggling to keep my mouth above the brim, my hair matting around my face – yet the harder I fought the more hopeless my situation became until I sank under, my nose and mouth filling with water. And as I tried to kick myself free, my throat bursting for want of oxygen, a thought from the dark recesses asked, is this the fate that met Don Guido's son?

A hand grabbed the scruff of my dress and hauled me to the surface before I was roughly thrown on to dry ground.

'Stupid girl!'

Spluttering and sobbing, I parted my hair to see Latigez standing over me. 'Find Lola,' was all I could manage.

He waded into the water, unsheathing his *facón* knife to cut the weeds, whistling for the dog and calling her name until his voice was hoarse. A cruel wind snaked off the Pampas, causing me, in my sopping clothes, to shiver uncontrollably.

I do not know how long Latigez searched for Lola, time having become muddled, but in the end he had to concede defeat and strode back on shore.

'Take care now, Ursula,' he said with an unexpected tenderness, a touch of his hand on my shoulder. 'Are you hurt?'

I shook my head, unable to form words of reply, unable to stop convulsing.

'I heard a whistle,' he explained, 'and watched you and the dog from the treehouse. What were you thinking? I jumped straight down, over the wall.'

'Then you saw him?'

'Saw who?'

'The axeman.'

'I saw you and Lola dash to the water as if you were both gone mad and decided upon drowning yourselves.'

'No one else?'

His gruffness returned. 'No.'

'You must have.'

When I continued to protest, he grudgingly removed his jacket, malodorous with sweat and sawdust, and draped it over my trembling shoulders. 'You've had a shock,' he said, 'you're confused. There was no one in the field but you.'

'There was a man, I swear.' I wanted to weep. 'Who do you think Lola was chasing?'

'She's gone. Now we need to get you inside, before you catch your death.'

I set my face away from him to the lake, and refused to hear more, watching the last of the ripples, those last signs of Lola's struggle, as they dwindled and the surface of the water became level once more like an expanse of glass, sombre and utterly still.

Giving Notice

I LET THE water scald me, refusing the addition of any further from the cold tap, my skin scarlet in a matter of seconds. It may have been an act of practicality, to thaw my freezing self, but in greater part I understood it to be a sufferance: to assuage the horrid guilt I was feeling. And it was whilst I lay in the bath, light-headed from the heat, that the realization of what I must do became clear.

The final moments of Lola kept repeating themselves in my mind, as did a series of less heart-rending alternatives. If I had restrained her, regardless of her snapping jaws, as she bounded toward the water; if I had been faster in scaling the wall; if – and this caused me the greatest anguish – if I had put to one side my personal distaste for Latigez and left the poor dog with him, peacefully gnawing her bone beneath the treehouse. For there could be no other conclusion than Lola had perished, and that it was a consequence of my actions, however indirectly. It was in the repetition of these thoughts, and the memory of how the weeds had wound themselves around my legs as if they were a living entity bent on making an Ophelia of me, of dragging my body to the muddy bottom, that forced me to confront the reality of my situation.

Calista had been wrong. Berganza had been wrong.

Before that afternoon I had been determined to see things out at Las Lágrimas, I being convinced that whatever the disturbing, inexplicable dramas of the estate, no physical harm could befall me. Now that Lola was gone and myself nearly drowned, I knew this not to be the case. Why the axeman was the purveyor of the curse I could not answer, nor did I suppose it made much difference, for only one thing was sure.

I must act decisively!

I found Moyano in the Trophy Room, sitting in a wing-chair below the stag heads, smoking one of his panatelas, his demeanour that of a man whose satisfaction with himself knows few bounds, as if he had found a whole purse of his silver pesos. The room had its permanent chilly air, the stuffed animals ready to bear silent witness to the announcement I planned to make.

The estate manager stood the moment I entered. 'I hear you had a nasty shock at the lake.' He noted my complexion, still flushed from the bath. 'Have you considered asking Calista for one of her remedies, to ease your nerves?'

'Señor Moyano. I wish to give you my notice.'

He returned to his seat and tended his hair. I could smell that it had been freshly pomaded, even if it did not entirely hide his perpetual smoky odour. 'May I ask why?' His tone was as gelid as the room.

'I fear for my well-being.'

'Has Latigez... *upset* you in some way?'

'Why mention him?'

'Dolores complained of his behaviour once. He has the merit of being a good worker, though his conduct is not always becoming.'

'It has nothing to do with any member of staff.'

'Then what?'

'I prefer not to say.'

'Don Paquito arrives in five days.' He scratched the skin beneath his cuffs. 'I would not call it fair that my Head Gardener resigns in that interval with no word of explanation.'

'Las Lágrimas is haunted.'

There, I had said it at last, the words lingering in the space between us, never to be unspoken, his perception of me forever altered.

If previously the moods of Moyano I knew best were his charm and grating bonhomie, his bouts of melancholia, that night I was to his experience hot-bloodied ire. 'Your predecessor, Maurín, claimed likewise. Why can I not find a gardener whose mind is unfuddled by such nonsense?' Before I could form an answer he continued, practically shouting. 'Be clear, Señorita Kelp, there are no such things as ghosts.'

'What would you say if I told you I had seen one? Seen one this very afternoon.'

'Then I would say you need the asylum.'

The swift lash of his reply took me off guard, as did the depth of antipathy expressed toward me; even Gil had not resorted to such unpleasantness.

'I vow it to you, Señor Moyano, a spirit haunts the estancia that means us not well. It near cost me my life to-day. In all your time, surely you must have seen something? Something to cause the slightest doubt.' I pressed my point. 'You yourself said that strangest of moods have possessed you here.'

At that, his eyes flashed blackly.

'I have seen the ill-fortune of my life reversed,' he retorted. 'The Don will be grateful for what I have achieved; I'll not let it be ruined by the likes of you. I refuse your resignation.'

'You cannot hold me here!'

'No.' He violently stubbed out his panatela. 'Nor am I under any obligation to help you with a horse, or provisions, if you were rash enough to head off. I warn you, Señorita Kelp, do not attempt to take either – otherwise you will be a thief. Then the right to detain you will be mine.'

'So I am a prisoner?'

'You are my Head Gardener. I expect you at work first thing tomorrow. If you dislike my decision, address it to Don Paquito when he arrives.'

I stirred myself, making up my mind as soon as I departed Moyano's company: I would secret myself off the estate the next day. I hastened to my room and packed what belongings I considered essential into a small knapsack, selecting my Ayres & Lee boots (the sturdiest I possessed) and warmest clothing, rescuing Rivacoba's poncho from the wardrobe to wear atop everything else and protect me from the worst the elements might inflict, the smell that clung to it – of horse and old campfires – strangely comforting. Then I retired to bed, my plan to be astir before Calista to raid the kitchen for supplies and thence to the front gate by sun-up. I would make the journey on foot, for as much as I would have preferred to have ridden Dahlia, she was more likely to be missed, whereas with a fair chance, no one would suspect me of having left until I failed to take my place at dinner, giving me a day's start.

In taking such practical measures, and the renewal of agency I felt in my decision to leave, the day's horror began to loosen its grip. For all that, sleep did not come easily. The wind was tame in the trees, nothing more than a susurration, but it was not the elements outside that disturbed me, rather the turmoil within: the sight of the axeman, the scene with Moyano. It was in this restless state, the hour approaching midnight, that my ear made out a creak on the staircase, and thereafter I experienced that, now too familiar, sensation of someone outside my door, listening as to confirm my slumber. I held my breath, my body as still as an effigy, until I heard the sweep of material as whoever was on the other side passed by – upon which I slid out of bed. I felt a certain trepidation, a raging inquisitiveness too, but no sense of the fear that had seized me in the Treasure Garden. I opened the door a crack.

Gliding away from me was a shadowy presence holding a single candle, its feeble light dancing on the walls, so that the figure appeared to float – yet my higher senses told me I was witness to the corporeal rather than supernatural. The figure paused before a door at the far end of the corridor, tapped it noiselessly and was immediately granted admittance. At first

I thought it was the water-closet before I realized it to be the door to the right, the one that previously had been locked. The smell from within, a drowsy syrup as heady as ylang-ylang, wafted its way in my direction.

For a moment I stood, hesitant, then I crept to where the figure had entered and, standing in the pitch darkness, placed my ear against the door. It must have been thick, thicker than mine, for the noises within were barely audible. My sense was that there were at least two people, the exact purpose of their dialogue undecipherable, though I felt sure some conspiratorial negotiation was at hand. A piece of furniture was repositioned, followed by a silence of such duration that I wondered if there was some other, secret exit to the room and the occupants had slipped away by it, though as time passed there came other sounds, hushed at first but building to a crescendo: the bounce of springs, desperate pleas, a stifled shout of rapture.

I withdrew, my ear blistering.

Inexperienced as I am in such matters, I understood what I was hearing well enough, a sinful heat prickling up from my breast to stain my throat and cheeks. I hurried back toward my room, reaching near halfway along the corridor before my steps faltered. That I should not be prying was plain, and yet some reprehensible part of me was curious to hear more. To remain glued to the door was too risky, for at any instant it might be sprung open and my snooping exposed. No one, however, could query or reprimand me for using the adjoining lavatory, and so I slipped into that dark room and, full of self-remonstration, I pressed my ear against the wall.

The first thing I detected was that queer, rushing gurgle that pervaded the silences of the house. Now I gave it due consideration, I realized that it derived from the walls themselves, from the very fabric of the building. On another occasion this might have stimulated my curiosity, but for now I was more interested by what I could hear beyond. The animal urgency of a few moments previous had been replaced by a different sound, one sharp and staccato, punctuated by muffled cries, and if I could not quite place it, its rhythm brought to mind the remorseless beat of the axe in the trees. Force my ear as I might, I could not determine to whom I was listening.

I submitted to my prurience for a number of minutes longer, before remorse eventually took hold the better part of my character and commanded me back to my room. There I lit a lamp, wound my peignoir around myself and, perching on the edge of the bed, waited to confront whoever it was that sneaked nocturnally past my door. I trusted I would not have to maintain a vigil all night, for regardless of this unexpected turn, it was still my intention to rise early and abscond.

An extended period seemed to pass. Drowsiness began to lull me; it took a strong will to remain awake. Once it must have taken me, for I was started back to consciousness by the mournful howl of many dogs, though, as I shook my head and blinked, only silence filled my thoughts.

Finally, there came the quiet lifting of a latch.

In an instant I was alert, and readied myself for my night-time visitor, waiting breathlessly as the person neared, silent but for the infrequent squeak of a floorboard, until they were directly outside. Then, holding aloft my lamp in order that there was no chance to hide, I flung the door agape and stepped out into the corridor.

I do not know which of us was the more shocked. Dolores stood frozen and tremulous before me. From the light of the candle she gripped, I saw that her lips and pale face were crimson from use. Clasped against her heaving, mean breast, as if her life depended on it, was a toy llama knitted from wool.

It was the maid who moved first.

She blew out her candle and streaked away into the shadows, trailing a cloud of pungent blossom. I gave chase, but she was fleeter and more practised with the route, especially in the darkness. We raced up the staircase – one after the other – our feet percussing on the steps, to the attic rooms where she dashed through the door of her own before I could catch her. She slammed it shut, the noise reverberating through the silent house, and twisted the lock.

'Dolores! Open up at once!'

I thumped my palm against the wood, and immediately regretted my outburst. 'I am not angry with you,' I said in a more measured tone. 'I shall not tell anyone. I only want to understand.'

I heard laboured breathing and a half-suppressed giggle, as of an urchin who has evaded the constable, but no reply was forthcoming.

After a good few minutes, I had to admit that Dolores was never going to open her door whilst I remained. The maid, however, was not the only party from which an explanation could be demanded.

I stalked to the floor below, to the end of the corridor, my determination wavering only as I approached, wondering as to how I might explain my knowledge of events in the room, an entirely intimate matter, without also having to confess my eavesdropping. Might the culprit turn my prying back on me? No, my defence would be robust, my obligation to intervene entirely justified, for Dolores was impressionable and only a few years past girlhood, and I a respectable woman with no desire to be associated with such scandalous behaviour. I would discover the identity of the individual who had taken such advantage of Dolores and report him forthwith to Señor Moyano.

The door was closed but had not been locked.

I swung it open and was struck by a nasty fug laced with sweat and the tang of blossom, an odour I now understood to be as distant from spring as was possible. The window panes dripped with condensation, as did a half-consumed bottle of rum on the sill. There was no one to be found in the room. On reflection, that should not have come as a surprise, for whoever might have been with Dolores was doubtless alerted to my presence as I pursued her and had already made good his departure. In his haste, he had made not the least attempt to tidy the scene, for everything was in sordid disarray, the sheets torn from the bed, Dolores' undergarments tattered and discarded on the floor, whilst next to them lay a whip. A whip of identical kind to that which had beaten Lola, its leather flecked with blood.

Calista is Offended

DURING THE NIGHT there was a change in the weather. That foretaste of spring we had been graced with retreated, and in its stead came cool, damp, rather dreary air, felt in the bones as much as on the face, that reminded me of an English November, when the garden has been laid to bed for the year and the leaves need raking up. So it was early the next morning when I reached the main gate and looked out on to the Pampas to see a uniform sky of soot-grey clouds through which the dawn struggled to penetrate. The gates, which the last time I had passed through had been fresh from Latigez's paintbrush, were inexplicably rusted again, the metal coarse to my hand as I pushed them aside. I struck out, confident enough, cosy within Rivacoba's poncho, the knapsack on my shoulder rattling with the tinned-foods I had surreptitiously lifted from the kitchen an hour before.

However, within minutes the reality of what lay ahead – the endlessness of the landscape, the enormity of the sky, *the sheer distance I must traverse* – had brought me to the most sobering standstill.

What had seemed a rational decision the night previous, was now revealed as folly, for I had set aside such considerations as to how I might find my way – I did not even have a map! – or how challenging the journey to civilization would be. What if I became lost? Or the weather turned more wrathfully against me than the Sunday I had ridden out on Dahlia? Or if I slipped and twisted my ankle (or worse)? Any number of these could transform in a blink to mortal peril. Nor, as unlikely as it seemed, did I relish the possibility of chancing upon the quarry-boy again. Then there was Moyano: once he discovered my absence he was liable to set forth in pursuit; another scene could only antagonize our relationship further. And even if by a miracle I made my way safely to Chapaledfú, the journey by foot was bound to take longer than the four days that remained until Don Paquito arrived, when I could address him and resign in more sensible fashion.

No, to cross the Pampas represented as great, if not greater, a threat to my well-being as sitting tight, for at least on the estancia I had the security of four walls, plentiful food and the companionship of Calista. Henceforth, I would become alert to the slightest sign of any apparition and, at the first indication, immediately cut and run. If I needed any further convincing to abandon my plans, there was also the matter of Dolores. She may have been an insolent and slovenly example of my sex, but I could not abandon the girl to her tormentor: to do so would make me party to her exploitation.

I turned my back on the vastness of the Pampas and the enormous hurrying clouds above, clanged the gate closed behind me and had returned to the house before anyone was the wiser that I ever tried to leave.

I went first to the stables to find Vasca. I was aware how the dogs possessed a keen sensitivity to the ghost and, if I was to be as vigilant as I must during the next days, it was my intention to keep the German shepherd with me at all times; for her to be the canary in my coalmine, if you will (the metaphor perhaps not quite apposite, for I was determined not to lose her as I had Lola). Vasca was pleased to be fed so early, but though I fussed her, she was not her usual self, her head downcast, her mismatched eyes sad and reproachful as if she understood all too well the dreadful fate of her pup. The dog padded behind me as I wound my way inside the garden to the hole at the base of the Wailing Wall where Lola had escaped. Gravely, I filled it in, moving stones with my bare hands and packing it with dirt, until I was satisfied that it was blocked, my labour observed by a lone, ugly chimango perched above and given to the occasional, scornful rawk.

Then I progressed to the Treasure Garden to begin the day's work, my ambition to continue with the box hedge, planting that section of path as lay on the far side of the fountain. When I arrived all was serene, my tools in the exact same position where I had left them yesterday afternoon. They were damp from being outside all night and my first task was to wipe them down, then I made a rapid survey of what I had achieved the day before. Again, all was how it should be, excepting one detail. As I examined the box I had planted, I saw that the foliage facing on to the path was blackened and brittle. It reminded me of the dieback on the hedges at Grandfather's a few years before, when spring had been interrupted by a blast of winter's breath.

I commenced work, Vasca settled and content nearby, and although I remained in a sensitive state, often glancing around me, my ear keening for the first sound of footsteps, I felt in no way nervous, nor was my temper especially dampened by the gloomy clouds and dull light. Quickly, I found a rhythm and became absorbed in the planting. Only once did I startle when there came a low grumble from Vasca. She was staring intently at the fountain, her fur bristling. I readied myself for flight. The next moment, however, the animal yawned and rolled to show her belly. 'Silly dog,' I said, tickling her, but I was aware of a flood of relief.

At midday it was Calista who brought my hamper, not Dolores. She explained that the maid had taken to her sickbed, and then asked of me, 'Did you have any items from the larder?'

I replied carefully. 'Why do you say that?'

'Señor Moyano warned me to watch for you stealing food.'

I fetched my knapsack, which, since I had not returned inside the whole morning, was with me in the garden. 'I was set on leaving the estancia and needed provisions to cross the Pampas.' I unbuckled the top-flap and showed her the tins. 'You will not tell the Señor, I hope.'

She reached out, her fingers warm, and squeezed my hand. 'Your secret is safe. And I am glad that you had a change of mind. Better to face Moyano's temper than the Pampas. To have crossed them alone... I doubt it could have ended well. What on earth possessed you to undertake such a reckless thing?'

I recounted to her the events of the past day, and when I was done telling about Lola and the axeman and how Moyano rebuffed me – and feeling the solace of unburdening myself – I went on to outline how I had caught Dolores in the corridor.

The cook seemed shaken by this last revelation and that she had been unaware of such goings-on. 'Who could have corrupted her?' she asked. 'Not Señor Moyano. He may talk little of his wife and child, but is devoted to them. And Farrido has eyes only for the bottle.'

'I have my own suspicion.'

'One of the Mapuche boys? I have never trusted their race.'

'Señor Latigez.'

The colour left Calista's face except for two smudges of puce in each cheek. 'What makes you think that?' she demanded in a fury.

'Certain things he has said, certain things I have observed of him. An intuition.'

'Keep your intuitions to yourself.' She snatched back the luncheon-hamper from me. 'Dare breathe a word of this slander to Señor Moyano,' she hissed, 'and I swear, I will tell him your light fingers were in my larder.'

I thought she was going to spit at my feet. Instead, Calista stormed away without so much as a rearward glance. I called after her, imploring, doing my very best to apologize, ignorant of how I had slanged her. She would not hear me.

For the rest of the afternoon, I trusted in the absorption that hard work brings, finding myself in a state of bewilderment and disquiet at Calista's behaviour. Quite why she had taken so aggrievedly to my contention about Latigez I could not imagine, for there were grounds to my suspicions with which she might have agreed if only she had stayed to hear them. Surely she did not harbour some unrequited emotion toward the man? It was in this agitated state, digging hard even as my mind raced, that I experienced a crushing sensation of loss, one immediately taken over by the sweetness of violets and honeysuckle, that same, elusive fragrance of a garden in midsummer that I had inhaled before. An accompanying line wheedled its way into my thoughts: 'You may break, you may shatter the vase, if you will, / But the scent of the roses will hang around it still'. They were the words (from a poem of Thomas Moore's) that Grandfather had requested on his headstone, though Mother refused them and I, to my eternal shame, had been too broken-hearted to insist upon. I felt a sudden intimation of disaster, so profound I shuddered and, at the same instant, became aware that Vasca was no longer in my presence.

She was nowhere to be seen in the Treasure Garden nor, when I searched the closest patches of cleared ground, anywhere else nearby. I hurried to the wall and was relieved to find the hole I had blocked earlier remained inaccessible. I yelled out the dog's name and when she did not heel, aware that I had broken my rule of having Vasca as my admonitor, I rapidly packed up my tools. The scent of summer was no more.

It was then that she reappeared, licking my hands in a frenzy of delight as if she had been away for an age.

'What is this?' I asked as I stroked and praised her.

A collar of purple material had been tied around her neck

and into it tucked a folded paper, which I retrieved. On it was written a message in a large, rather jagged hand, like that of a disturbed child, I thought. It was unsigned:

> PLEASE. GO TO THE KITCHEN GARDEN, TO THE DOOR
> IN THE FAR WALL. THEN FOLLOW THE RIBBONS.
> VASCA KNOWS THE WAY. I NEED TO EXPLAIN ABOUT
> LAST NIGHT.

I sighed with impatience at this latest addition to my day, as much as weariness from it. Either of my sisters would have thrilled to receive such a note with its mysterious provenance, its promise of clues and revelation at the trail's end; they were forever upbraiding me for my lack of 'fun'. That afternoon, I was less inclined than usual to play, and yet I could not deny a certain intrigue, something the sender of the message was in no doubt reliant upon.

I sighed again. 'Very well, then,' I said to Vasca and, making sure that the dog remained close, I tramped off to start my treasure hunt, leaving the garden to itself and the dreary grey light.

Never an English Rose

IN THE TIME before I reached the kitchen garden, rain began to fall in a silent, penetrating mizzle. It was not long until Vasca's coat was bedewed with droplets and my poncho wet-through. More than ever, it seemed prudent not to have embarked across the Pampas.

The kitchen garden itself stood empty and rather dejected: the day's crop needing to be picked, the panes of the glasshouse opaquely reflecting the sky. I strode to the archway in the far wall and discovered, as I had been told to, a purple ribbon tied to the handle of the door, identical to the one around Vasca's neck. I pushed open the door and immediately the dog trotted through it, leading me to the boundary of the parkland where, on the lowest branch of a black acacia, there was another such strip of material. The acacia (*Acacia mearnsii*) stood at the head of a path that disappeared into the trees. I considered what to do next, absent-mindedly undoing the soggy ribbon. Despite my initial irritation, the trail of 'clues' had succeeded in arousing my curiosity, yet my legs were reluctant to carry me into the woods, recalling my previous experience of meeting the axeman.

In the end, it was the fearless Vasca who made the decision, trotting ahead as one returning along a well-remembered route, with me chasing to keep apace. Beneath the canopy at least it had the advantage of being dry, even if the light was further subdued and the shadows and gnarled boles far from welcoming. I thought of the tale Berganza had told of the trees and their planting by my forerunner, Tarella. Experience maintained it was inhuman for an individual to have created such a woodland, and I wondered, as occasionally I had done since, what had become of Tarella, for Berganza's terse elaboration when I pressed him about the gardener, his dark mutterings on departure, told of something more. Or so was my conjecture.

At intervals the path, which was well trodden, broke in two and at every bifurcation there was another purple bow to tell me which direction I should take. It was only after the third or fourth of these that I understood my error in having so thoughtlessly untied each ribbon, for, in doing so, I had forsaken my route back. Already I felt unsettlingly deep into the parkland, the gloom about me hushed and still, and I acknowledged I must depend on whoever was waiting ahead to bring me safely back. A strange foreboding was building in my chest. Luckily, there was not much farther to go.

I had passed another fork in the path when the trunks began to thin and the air to be seasoned with woodsmoke. Vasca gave a bark and gambolled onward, I following her, back into the drizzle, and to a sudden glade, at the centre of which stood a small, tidy cottage, not unlike the illustrations one sees in books of fairy tales, for it had wheel-windows and gingerbread eave-trim. From the freshness of the brick and roof tiles, I surmised it was of recent construction, whilst the garden was as yet nothing more than churned, peat-black earth. I imagined the lavender bushes, lupins and hollyhocks I would have planted if the little place were mine. Pinned to the door was the final purple ribbon.

I marched the path and knocked.

When there was no answer, I peered in through a window – from the frame came the odour of fresh creosote – and seeing no occupant, I moved to explore the rear of the cottage. The scene there was in contrast to the pleasant front: all around was the detritus of building work, whilst the treeline stood dark and much closer, ready to engulf the glade if given the chance. There was also a ramshackle outhouse that I went to investigate. Tethered up inside was the horse, Dahlia. I brought my nose to hers and raked my fingers through the coarse silk of her mane.

'I feared you might leave this morning,' said a voice behind me, 'so I brought her here.'

It was Moyano.

'I can ride other horses, you know,' came my tart reply.

Moyano continued, 'You must pardon my theatrics with Vasca and the ribbons, but we left things badly last night and I thought you would not otherwise hear me out. I'd like it if you would join me inside and we have a more civilized discussion.' When I made no reply, he added, with what I considered to be an undertow of impatience that I had not acquiesced at once,

'I wish to make amends for my conduct, Señorita.'

I gave Dahlia a final embrace and, with a measure of wariness and resignation both, let myself be escorted to the cottage door, Moyano appearing conciliatory enough. Before the estate manager allowed me entry, he pointed to my muddied boots and requested that I remove them, which I did and followed him into the warmth. The air was heavy with a familiar, spicy aroma, not unlike frankincense, that carried from the hearth.

'What is that smell?' I asked.

'Ombú wood,' was his reply. 'You must have seen the tree missing along the main avenue.'

'You cut it down?'

'It was felled in Don Guido's time and the trunk left to season. The rafters of this building were made from it; the off-cuts I burn.' He filled his lungs, savouring the scent. 'I'm rather taken by it.'

The ceiling to the cottage was lower than the exterior suggested and afforded the parlour an intimate atmosphere, one given further emphasis by the logs piled up in the grate, the drawn curtains and glowing lamps. This aside, the place had to it a feeling of being irregularly occupied. The furniture was of pine, new and functional, the walls plain and smelling of plaster similar to the new wing of the main house. There were neither rugs, nor cushions nor (curtains aside) any other soft fabrics, adding to my sense of the spartan, whilst the only objects of interest were a large, framed studio-photograph above the fireplace – and heads. The heads of deer and other wild beasts, some waiting to be attached to plaques, others trailing stuffing from their back-ends, others – most disturbingly – lacking eyes in their sockets.

'A hobby of mine,' explained Moyano. 'I am repairing these for the Trophy Room.' He received my poncho and hung it near the fire to dry, then indicated a table that was laid with a teapot, sandwiches and cakestand. 'I had Calista busy in the kitchen,' he said, drawing out a chair for me. 'I know how you English enjoy your afternoon tea.'

In a different state of mind – or, rather, should I say stomach – it would have been my preference to remain standing, to hear out the estate manager and curtly be on my way, but I had gone breakfastless that morning and Calista had confiscated my hamper; I was, in short, famished. The neat rows of sandwiches fat with chorizo; the delicate custard tarts; the sponge cake with its half-inch of cream and glistening rim of jam – all proved too tempting. I sat and ate heartily, whilst Moyano nibbled at a sandwich, tossing most of the contents to Vasca, who had taken up what seemed an habitual spot by the fireplace.

'I was wrong to lose my temper last night,' said Moyano, in a soothing tone. 'I trust that you will forgive me, Señorita. It was the anger of a man who fears his last hope might be stolen from him. Who fears for his family. But I cannot allow you to resign,' he went on fulsomely. 'Las Lágrimas needs its Head Gardener, as indeed do I.'

I made to protest; he held up his palm for silence.

'Before you speak, first, understand. I was disgraced in my last post, disgraced and dismissed and threatened that never again would I find work, not in all of Argentina, so that I saw no future for my life. Only by fluke was I offered a second chance. It has given me employment and a home – this fine, new cottage – when I had the prospect of neither.'

'Can I take it that this building explains your absences?'

'I cleared the trees myself, built it with my own hands. At first I had the help of the workers on the new wing, and of late from Latigez.'

'As a consequence, I have struggled. If the garden is as important as you say, consider the difference your efforts to it could have made.'

'I admit, I have been neglecting you, Señorita. I wanted everything ready for the day my family arrives.'

He rose from the table and retrieved the portrait above the fireplace. 'There is my reason,' he said, presenting it to me. Moyano was not in the pose. It showed a young *belleza* – if I was being ungracious, a tad too young – with a well-cut mouth and black ringlets, and a boy of around eight years, he having a similar coloured mop and his father's eyes. In its way, the picture reminded me of the daguerreotype in Tarella's cabin, though neither of the present-day sitters appeared as contented.

'Alfredo has the most terrible lung condition,' said the estate manager, the anguish evident in his voice. 'There are days when he fights to breathe.'

I was taken off guard by this confidence. 'I'm sorry to hear that.'

'He needs the good, clean air of the Pampas. If I fail here, it is he who will suffer the most. So understand my temper, Señorita. I do not want my boy to succumb.'

'Nor, Señor, do I.'

'Juan-Pérez. In my home, I insist you speak my name.'

'Of course,' I returned, after which I avoided addressing him at all. 'I appreciate your position. Truly. Nevertheless, my own remains unchanged.' I handed him back his family-pose. 'I wish to resign.'

'Because of a' – I could not determine whether his tone was infuriated or mocking – '"phantom".'

'Yes.'

'Tales are told of Las Lágrimas, mostly women's talk and whispers to scare children. But on a dark night, sitting around a camp fire and sharing stories, many is the gaucho who also will shudder. Who will search the darkness before putting his head down and then sleep ill at ease.'

'So you admit it yourself. There is a curse.'

Moyano spoke dismissively. 'It was from Don Guido that this lore began. When he left the house, he refused to pay for watchmen, and so spread rumours of ghosts and strange happenings. What simpler means to frighten off trespassers in a land so steeped in tales? Believe me, there is nothing more to it than that.'

Yet for all his emphatic denial, his voice sounded suddenly odd to my ear, that voice I have often heard in people when dismissing something not because they think it false, but because they know the opposite to be true. I was taken by the thought that Moyano was as well acquainted with the ghosts of Las Lágrimas as was I, perhaps the more so, for he had lived here the longer.

'Then explain to me what it is I have seen,' I countered. 'The axeman who took Lola. A boy at the quarry who vanished. A party of men in the trees. Men with lanterns, dressed from an age ago who were gone like that.' I clicked my fingers. 'And do not, Señor, tell me these were tricks of the light!'

'What you *alone* have seen. Not I. Or Latigez, or Señor Farrido—'

'Calista believes.'

'She has not once spoken a word of it to me.'

I was on the point of refuting him, when I buttoned my lip. Exactly what was I going to say, what other proof was I going to offer in my defence that was not a solipsism? My frustration was uprising. 'Lola was killed.'

'A dreadful accident. The dog ran wild, was caught in the weeds and drowned. Latigez told me. I have always trusted his word.'

'It was the axeman, the ghost. He lured her to the lake. I saw him quite clearly, as clear as I see you opposite me now.'

He replied kindly, as if he were speaking to an invalid. 'Have you ever considered, Señorita, that it is your mind deceiving you?'

'No.'

'That you are in the grip of an hysteria?'

'No,' I replied again, very firmly and calmly.

'I warned you, Las Lágrimas is a lonely place, and you are under a great strain with the garden. The effects of both on the nerves can be more disabling than you allow. They can take hold of you unawares. During his final days in the new wing, one of the builders lost his head – and he had the companionship of his fellows and those virtues of the masculine temperament.'

'How remiss of me, I forget I lack such an advantage.'

Moyano paid my condescension no heed. 'Once we are busy, once you have your full strength of staff, I am confident you will feel better.'

'It will alter nothing: the estate is haunted.'

'I cannot have you saying such things to the Don.'

'He must be warned.'

'I forbid it.'

'His son is in danger, I am sure of it. We all are. How can I make you believe?'

The estate manager was on the point of responding when he stilled his tongue, for some new thought seemed to have entered his mind. A clarity came to his expression, his air that of a man who has come to grasp what should have been obvious to him all along. He scratched at his wrist. 'Unless the phantom you see is but a symptom, a "manifestation", of some other emotion.'

'Meaning?'

'Doña Javiera has inclinations as yours, of ghosts and curses. I suspect the Don panders to her. It is her way – a woman's way – of arresting his…'

He did not conclude his sentence but stood away from the table, stopping by the hearth, where he returned the photograph of his family, then stabbed the fire with a poker; the flames leapt from the ombú logs, filling the room with a red flare. As they died down he ruffled Vasca and stepped deeper into the room, seeking the shadows, away from my line of sight.

I twisted around, at first thinking he had gone to fetch some object, instead he extinguished several of the lamps, one after the other, each with a short, precise blow of air until the room was but dimly lit. At the last he paused, in contemplation of who knew what, then reached for something beneath the family portrait. It was a stack of the silver pesos he was so enthused in collecting. Somehow, I had not noticed them before, nor numerous other such piles that all at once seemed to litter every nook of the cottage. Moyano appeared as a man who had submitted to some power beyond his control.

'Perhaps it is not a ghost you see,' he said, 'rather, attention you crave.'

'I do not want attention,' I replied fiercely, discomfited by the turn of events.

'So said she... once.'

'Said who?'

His reply was to allow the pesos to fall and tinkle from one palm to the other before burying the coins in his trouser pocket.

The dark, red light of the parlour pressed in on me, the heat from the fire suffocating. I felt the need to occupy my hands and enforce a calmness on myself, and so poured another cup of tea, albeit I had not the least thirst. The food I had consumed was like concrete setting hard and heavy within my stomach. Even as I raised the cup to my lips, I was aware of Moyano's stealthy approach. His voice when he spoke was suggestive, rather inquisitive; I wondered on what delivery he was bent.

'I understand how you've looked at me, Ursula. I understood from the very first, when you sought me out in the garden in Buenos Aires, and then in the café – though I fought to deny it. It was the very same look as I saw in the daughter of my previous employer.' He laid his hands on my shoulders, very softly but deliberate. 'Women have always been my devil.'

I froze, unsure of what to do.

Moyano's left hand travelled upward, finding the tender spot between my ear and throat. I felt his fingers comb through my damp hair, then tighten around the roots and gently pull back, causing my neck to arch. He leant forward so that his breath prickled against my skin, raising a tress to his nose and murmured, though such was the noisy thud-thud-thud of my heart, such my state of alarmed confusion, that I could not be sure of his words: *Many are the flowers I have enjoyed, but never an English rose*.

For another long, long moment I remained incapable of any movement, then I recoiled with such vehemence that I caused my tea to slosh over the side of the cup and splash my dress, soaking it through to the skin. I leapt away and rushed to the front door, where I pulled on my boots and began to tie the laces as fast as my trembling fingers would allow.

Mantrap

I OPENED THE front door and stepped out, readying myself to take flight back to the house.

And immediately halted.

Night was in the final stages of settling upon estate. Above the treetops, over to the west, there remained a band of sky the purple of cotinus leaves. The rest was darkness. It had stop raining, the air thickly dank to the lungs.

I hesitated, before returning my attention inside the cottage and calling Vasca. She rose lazily from her spot by the fire, stretched, but obediently came to me.

'Good girl!' I encouraged her.

Moyano blocked the German shepherd's progress. He was white-faced with indignation. 'The dog remains with me,' he said, his voice as hard and unforgiving as ever I heard it.

'You cannot expect me to go alone through the dark!' came my reply.

He ignored my appeal.

By the door was a hallstand and resting on it, next to another stack of pesos, was a battery-torch. Before Moyano had the chance to stop me, I had snatched hold of it and was hurrying through the unplanted garden of his cottage toward the trees, lighting my way with its beam. Only once did I glance over my shoulder to see what Moyano was doing; he had already closed the door.

I pelted along the path, the foliage so tangled above and around me that I could see little save for what briefly fell into the narrow, yellow blade of the torch. I swung it constantly, seeking out those last few guiding-ribbons that I had not removed from their branches. Thus the first stage of my retreat was made at a considerable pace until, inevitably, I came to a fork in the way that was without sign. I cursed my stupidity at having undone the markers. If it had been daylight still, if my mind and emotions had been more sedate, I might have recognized the direction I had taken earlier – but since neither was the case I had to trust to luck… the same again at the next divide… and the one after that, until the only thing I knew for a certainty was that I had taken a wrong turn and was lost, and so my rate slowed to a walk.

The night was hushed, nothing except a murmur of wind amongst the highest branches, whilst between the trees all was exceedingly still, no scurrying of nocturnal animals nor rustlings of any sort, as if the darkness itself was tense and in anticipation of some event. I soon learnt the different degrees of that darkness, for though some of the gnarled trunks were dimly visible, elsewhere there were black patches, like the mouths of caves, from which I shrank. And as my way grew increasingly less certain, an impulse to return to the cottage, regardless of Moyano, swept over me; yet even if

I had succumbed to it, I was no longer sure how to retrace my steps. My only hope was to continue forth and pray that I reach one of the main arteries that led to the house.

The events of the cottage churned themselves over in my mind, so that I felt a sudden, stupid want to sob. In all modesty, I am an able gardener and, in moments of stronger self-confidence, I was assured that I had been offered the Head Gardenership as a result of merit alone; other times I speculated whether it was due only to the reputation of Las Lágrimas and no other being imprudent enough to take the challenge. That night, another explanation had presented itself: Moyano's misapprehension that I was in some way infatuated with him, and that the attraction was one mutually held. I dared not think where his hand might have travelled, nor what abomination might have occurred, if I had not left the cottage forthwith, for, in that period leading to my departure, Moyano was as a different character, a man who had lain aside restraint even as the photograph of his wife looked upon us. Was the fault mine? Had I, however unintentionally, misled him in some way? Had the looks I had given him, and which he had spoken of, been full of coquettish invitation without my ever being aware?

Before I had the chance to consider the possibility, the torchlight glinted on something on the ground ahead of me. I stopped – and just in time!

Half-concealed amongst the fallen leaves, at a distance of only a pace or two more, was a mantrap.

Its jaws were prised wide open, ready to snap shut on any

unfortunate who stepped upon it; I shuddered to imagine the effect on flesh and bone. The teeth were the size of arrowheads and devilish sharp, the metal fresh from the foundry, so that the device could only have been laid recently.

I waved the torch around me as if the culprit might yet be at hand – and my heart skipped a beat. Then quickened dementedly. Every nerve in my system seemed to have woken.

Some distance ahead, the beam revealed the shadowy outline of a man blocking the path, an outline that existed at the very edge of its illumination, where light and darkness merged. If I could determine only the most abstract details of this figure, the stench assailing my nostrils – of rotting leaves and the foulest earth – was recognizable at once. So too the cascades of emotion that came upon me in a rush: of wrath and bitter outrage.

I took a step backward, away from the axeman who, though he never advanced, remained always at the periphery of the light. I withdrew further, swinging the torch behind me to illuminate my way. In the instant it was pointing in the opposite direction, I sensed a swift, furious movement coming toward me from the blackness, those knurled hands stretching out to grasp my neck and, with all alacrity, I swung the torch back to its original position – to find the axeman no nearer nor farther than before. I continued my retreat with careful steps, not removing the spotlight of the torch from the axeman, yet continually wanting to illuminate the course of my travel, for the way was uneven and I feared to trip and let the torch fly from my grasp.

I ventured another step and stumbled on a root.

My arms shot out to help me balance and, for a short second, I directed the light behind me in order that I would not slip again, catching something out of the tail of my eye. At first I could not understand what I was seeing, then it became clear with such sharpness that my senses swam and I fought not to swoon.

The whole of the ground to my rear, from the spot of my current precariousness to the limit of the torch's illumination, and I daresay beyond its range and into the inkiness thereafter, was covered in mantraps. They must have numbered in their hundreds, the ironwork glimmering clean and yellow in the light, yearning for their maiden blooding.

I shone the torch to my left and right in the hope that I might leave the pathway altogether but, even if the darkness on either side had not been so complete, the underwood was too dense and knotted to be traversed.

My heart was leaping wildly and I knew not in which direction to aim the torch. In the end I swung it back and forth – a demented, shaking pendulum – in the hope of keeping the axeman at bay, whilst also giving myself illumination sufficient that I might navigate a path through the threat on the ground. It was a route more treacherous and deadly than any I have known, my feet finding spaces between the traps that seemed scarcely large enough to accommodate my toes, for I was picking my course on the tips alone.

Step-by-step I made headway, all too aware that a single mistake would leave me peg-legged or, should I slip and fall face first, more hideously injured than the most nightmarish imaginings. My top lip was cold with sweat. I had the constant sense of those hands hovering just above my shoulders, feathering my hair.

And then, when I was weak with tension and felt I could endure no more without my heart bursting, there came a succession of sounds more horrifying than anything before.

Near my heel, I heard one of the traps activate and snap shut, so close as to feel the vibration of the gnashing metal run through my bones. There was a scream, the most frightful scream to which I have ever listened, rising from the depths of a human throat until it was high-pitched and with the uttermost strain of agony. I tasted blood and could only think that, in my shock, I had bitten my tongue (though, when later I examined my mouth I found it free of any such infliction).

No longer conscious, or caring, of the danger to my limbs, I dashed madly and in terror, driven forward by the most primal of urges to escape that dreadful sound, possessed by a blind faith that I would be spared the traps' bite, even as they snapped and clanged and sprang up around me, like so many jacks-in-a-box.

The scream was still resounding in my ears when the mantraps came to an end and the path in front was nothing more than dirt and strewn leaves. I did not break my stride but rushed on, paying no heed to my bearing, wanting only to escape the trees, to be amidst bright lights and the sanctuary of other people. I did not send the beam of the torch backward, but rather held it to the ground for fear that I would meet another tranche of wicked, metal teeth. It was thus that I did not see Moyano until he was almost upon me, we colliding into each other with such force as to cause us both to crash and fall.

He helped me to my feet. Draped over his arm was my poncho, which he claimed, in a spirit of contrition, he had been coming to return to me. Despite the events between us in the cottage, I needed desperately the contact of another human being – even this one – and though I was clear-minded enough not actually to embrace him, I nevertheless clutched hold of his sleeve, my fingers finding the warmth from his body, and gripped the material tightly.

I shone the torch into his face so that the rays came from below, making his features yellow and of long, inverted shadows. 'Did you hear it?' I demanded when at last I got my breath.

He eased me away, directing the light from his eyes.

'Did you hear it?'

Finally, and with the greatest reluctance, he answered my question, and I knew never again could he dismiss my claims as being those of a woman sliding into hysteria. 'Yes,' he admitted roughly, and shuddered. 'I heard a scream.'

Old Metal & Honeycomb

WE SET OUT from the house at earliest dawn, a party of three. The day had continued from where the previous ended, the clouds thick and dun-coloured and lying low so that the tops of the trees were shrouded in mist. Everything I touched, or that my dress brushed against, was cold and damp. 'A fine spring day we have for it,' groused Latigez from behind me. The branches above seethed and echoed with avian song, though not once did I glimpse any bird. We walked in a single file with Moyano at the lead, making first for his cottage, where he collected Vasca, and afterward searching the paths that led from the building in an attempt to retrace the course I had taken the night before. As a precaution from injurious misstep, and to save us from stumbling around in the dark, the estate manager had ruled that we wait for daybreak to begin our investigation. Not a word of conversation passed between the three of us as we followed any number of false trails.

In the end, it was Vasca's nose that led us to the object of our hunt.

We arrived at an aisle, arched with green, formed by boles

and branches, in the middle of which lay a solitary mantrap. I could not say for certain, because the night had been so thick, and my emotion so high, but I was sure it to be the very first of the traps I had come across. It was snapped shut, as I had heard it do, and trapped between its evil metal jaws was the white stag. The beast was collapsed, the rise and fall of its flanks barely observable, those legs not caught buckled and twisted away from his body at awkward angles, whilst the blood that had drained from his wound had turned a sizeable patch of earth sodden. The stag must have lain there all night. He struggled as we approached, a heart-wrenching mewl emerging from its throat, and fought to stand before his limbs gave way and he slumped to the ground.

It grieved me to look at his mangled leg. 'We must help him,' I said, anger tightening my voice that such a noble creature had been brought down in this cowardly fashion.

'There is only one thing we can do,' was Moyano's reply, he gesturing to Latigez. 'Better you do not see, Señorita.'

Latigez reached for his *facón* knife, unsheathing it with a swagger, and moved promptly to his task. Moyano took my elbow to guide me away. I shrugged him off and went and knelt by the stag, resting my hand on his ribcage, his fur velvety to the touch, sensing the final tremors of his heart through my fingertips.

'Do it quickly,' I warned Latigez.

I stared into the distance and the sifting grey of the trees. Tarella's trees. The notion streaked through my mind from nowhere, its vehemence enough to startle. Latigez positioned his blade at the animal's throat and began to saw. There was a rough, horrid sound that went on and on and I would rather not have heard, like hessian being torn, over which Moyano spoke, I assumed by way of distracting me.

'He must be from Don Guido's old herd, though I did not think any of the animals survived. Las Lágrimas was once famed for them, Señorita. Did you know that? They were the Don's great pride, he forever wanting additions to his stock. Should news reach him of an albino stag, he would pay a small fortune to have the beast brought to the estate. Then, every year, the Don selected the finest specimen for the summer hunt…'

'Please,' I told him. 'No more.'

'The chase always at night, to heighten the sport.'

'Please.'

'It was the talk of every season…'

At the periphery of my vision, I saw a creeping, glossy puddle. The white stag gave a final convulsion – and then was still. I felt a flood of grief, inexplicable in its intensity, that I checked at once, for I did not want these two men to witness any outburst or, indeed, reveal the extent of my emotion.

'What will happen to him?' I asked.

Latigez stood, fishing a rag from his pocket. 'I'm sure Señor Moyano will want the head for the Don.' He wiped clean his *facón*. 'Whilst Señora Latigez hates good meat wasted.'

Such was my abhorrence at the first half of his reply, that a moment came and went before I absorbed the revelation of the second. 'You are married to Calista?' I asked in disbelief and no small measure of revulsion.

He nodded, watching me and, as the colour crept from

my neck to my cheeks, broke out into a grin. I thought of the defamation I had made of him to his wife and muttered something feeble about being unawares. Latigez enjoyed my discomfit a while longer before saying, 'I'll fetch a barrow to take the carcass.'

I could not face walking with him, nor did I wish to remain alone in Moyano's company in that gloomy archway, so allowed Latigez a head start. As I made to follow, Moyano spoke up. 'Perhaps, Señorita, you would have the kindness to spare me a few minutes.'

I saw no reason to and strode off without reply.

'Last night was an embarrassment for us both,' he continued after me. 'I misunderstood the situation. If you will, take it as a compliment, Ursula. You are a beautiful woman—'

'I'm not beautiful.'

'And I a man missing the solace of his wife.'

His words drew me to a halt, their implication striking me forthwith, and I spun round to confront the estate manager. He had been tending the scars on his wrist.

'Dolores,' I charged him with. 'It was you with Dolores?'

'What has she to do with anything?'

'You were together, in the room along from mine. That is where you spend your nights.'

His expression showed such confusion, his whole brow knotting in befuddlement, that I immediately felt myself humiliated by the accusation; henceforth, I decided, I should have to be more circumspect where I pointed the finger.

'I am not sure what you are suggesting,' Moyano replied. 'My nights are at the cottage, finishing the work that is needed there.' He went on, 'As for my little lapse yesterday, I think it best if neither of us make any further mention of it. In particular to the Don.'

Still feeling the fool, my answer was more antagonistic than deserved to be. 'It seems there are plenty of things you do not want me to tell him.'

'Surely you cannot mean to speak of your "phantom" after this?' His boot-cap prodded the stag's body; his tone scoffed. 'There is your scream.'

'I saw your look last night. We both know what we heard.' I shuddered at the mere memory. 'It was the cry of a man, not an animal.'

'You were overwrought.'

'Your face told me everything.'

'And you told me there were other traps.' He looked about him. 'Hundreds, you claimed.'

On this, undeniably, he had a point. Whereas the previous night the path had flowed like a river of iron, that morning it lay empty in both directions, not only of mantraps but leaves or débris of any description, as if the ground had been swept clear. My eyes sought for any proof for what I was certain I had seen. Farther along, I found the impressions of my tiptoes, scattered randomly about the path where I had stepped between the lethal, metal jaws and, amongst them, a second set of tracks consisting of a single, large boot-print followed by scars of raked earth where the axeman had dragged his other foot behind.

'There!' I said victoriously. 'There is your proof.'

Whereupon, Moyano placed his own boot over the print

in the mud; it fitted perfectly. 'I would say this is the spot where we ran into each other.'

A clot of loathing lodged itself in my throat for this man and his obstinacy. 'What if the stag had been me?' I cried. 'Or you, or any of the staff? What if Don Paquito had been caught in it? How can you have permitted such a barbaric thing?'

'I did not.'

'Then how is it possible?'

Vasca was sniffing at the corpse of the stag, her tongue lolling; I drove her away.

'It must be from long ago,' conjectured Moyano. 'Like all great estancias, Las Lágrimas had its share of poachers, and Don Guido no squeamishness for such devices.'

'But the trap is brand-new!'

'I think not, Señorita.'

He steered my attention toward it, making me examine the contraption. I had paid it scant notice earlier; now, on closer acquaintance, I saw that the frame, the jaws, the teeth – all were mottled orange and brown, filthy with age.

'Well?' demanded Moyano.

I searched for a rebuttal: none was to be found. Instead, and more pathetically than I intended, I made him promise to remove the trap, and not take the stag's head for a trophy.

He replied after a time and with studied forbearance. 'I promise – *and* will accept your resignation once the Don has arrived on condition that you speak nothing of phantoms or any other business to him, or his wife.'

I thought of their son and the curse; I thought of Lola's terrible fate. 'And if I believe it my duty otherwise?'

He answered without the least intimidation, his voice sweeter than honeycomb, though to his eyes was the void gaze of his melancholic fits. They were steady on mine. 'Then I will make sure it is my business you never leave this estancia.'

He offered his hand to shake on the agreement, and I stared at it, thrust there before me, the faint, smoky smell of ombú wood emanating from him.

Here, at the Hotel Bristol, hunched over my desk, I have written without pause, never once leaving my room, nor extinguishing my blaze of lights, even during those brightest hours of the day. What few meals I have sustained myself with, I have had brought to my door and, afterward, left the half-finished plates outside in the corridor in order I be the least disturbed. There have been occasions when, so completely wearied by my undertaking, my eyelids have grown heavier than lead and slowly drooped, my whole body slumping over my journal, the ink from my pen blotting the page, and I have drifted away...

Every time, I have woken almost at once with the most violent of jerks, my heart filled with cramps, my breathing as short as if someone had been throttling me.

Those events most lately narrated, of the mantrap and discovery of the stag, occurred over the course of Friday night and the morning of Saturday, 29th August. Of the remainder of that weekend I recall little, no doubt because the tragedy and horror that occurred thereafter have obscured these more trivial days. Everyone in the house was in the grip of a torrid industry in preparation for the arrival of the Agramontes.

For my own part, I laboured in the Treasure Garden and completed all the planting, not only of the box hedges but also those areas within the parterres, a task all the more remarkable given I made sure to be finished and safely inside the house long before dusk. I was content enough with my work, even if it was very much like the artist's sketch before any oil-paint has been applied: one understood the purpose, the promise, yet came away with nothing sensual or stirring to the emotions. Elsewhere, I harried the Mapuches to work with every endeavour. More of the thickets were cleared than I had imagined us capable of, though there was time insufficient to add new plants in their place. Gravel was spread along the newly revealed paths until they were as white as bones against the black soil. The result, if at least much neater, was also perhaps a little too severe. Lest it be misunderstood that the whole garden was now in apple-pie order, there remained large swathes where the weeds were lusty and nettles continued at chest-height. Nor, despite all our efforts, did it prove possible to open the sealed door as I had planned.

To Calista, upon the self-same morning when Latigez revealed they were married, I went without delay and offered my most sincere and profuse apologies for the allegation I had levelled against her husband. She accepted my words graciously, nevertheless it saddens me to write that in those last days that we knew each other there was a certain, unspoken coolness to our interactions, something I regretted deeply and that was made no easier when over the weekend a jugged venison was served for dinner that smelt delicious but which I could not bring myself to touch. Of Dolores, she must have asked to be assigned to different duties for I scarcely saw her. If I did chance upon her, no mention was made of the night I had caught her out. As for Moyano, he joined me for dinner on Saturday night in the most genial of spirits, brimful with flattery for my horticultural skills, a strategy I saw through immediately. When he realized I was not to be taken in, he became aloof and sniping, his anger never far, an attitude that prevailed over the next days, meted out with occasional menace – to which I refused to submit.

And yet, for all that was achieved in the garden, for all that the tenor of those final few days was ordinary, albeit my relations to the other staff had been shaken up, there was in me a building dread, like a pressure in my chest. Although I experienced nothing in the garden that might frighten me, saw no dark figure, heard no ghostly sounds, nor was Vasca (who became my constant companion out of doors) in any way agitated, as I went about my digging and planting, I had an unshakeable sensation of some evil impending.

Tomorrow – or to-day, for dawn is already creeping through the window as I write – I will finish this account. My eyes are strained and gritty. My head pounds. Now I must relive the worst, the most sickening and heart-stopping, of all those things that happened to me. I shall resume on the eve of Don Paquito's arrival, the hour approaching midnight, whilst I was preparing my letter of resignation and looked out into the darkness to observe, for the second time, lights amongst the trees.

'Wrist to Elbow'

IT HAD BEEN my intention, my conceited hope, to present Don Paquito with my sketches for the garden and how I envisioned it planted, for, despite everything at Las Lágrimas, I still possessed such pride as to want him to consider me as a skilled gardener and that my resignation would be a loss. And so that night, after another meagre repast where I had declined Calista's latest offering of venison, I had settled at my equally meagre desk, stomach growling, back stiff from the day's toil, and again made my purpose those drawings I had begun some days earlier. Yet even with Sir Romero's plans as my guide, I was unable to produce draughtsmanship of the slightest competence, the attempts I made looking no better than the scrawlings of a particularly cack-handed infant. To offer these to the Don would be to embarrass myself. Every time I put nib to paper my brain grew woolly and obstructed as one experiences when trying to recall a name or specific word and it hovers beyond one's reach, until, in a huff, I abandoned the idea.

Irritably, I took the sketches and threw them on the

lowering fire, watching the paper curl and blacken and vanish into flame, tempted, for an instant, to toss Lepping's plans after them – though I resisted such vandalism.

I returned to my desk and glanced out of the window, at the front lawn and avenue of trees, both pewter-coloured under the risen moon, before I picked up my pen anew and wrote a brief letter of resignation. I made no reference to the curse, the ghost or any other of my chilling experiences, deciding such matters would be more sensitively explained in person to the Don and Doña. Once I was done I re-read my words, contemplating whether I should add a line about having given the garden my fullest attention, for I feared Moyano would insinuate otherwise, then admitted it no longer made any difference. The hopes that had first brought me to the Pampas were now done for.

I slipped the letter inside an envelope and despondently returned my gaze to the darkness outside and, in doing so, caught the ghost of my reflection in the window.

My hair hung limp and damply from washing it, for although it was not one of my prescribed nights, Moyano had given me permission to bathe – his licence delivered in the frostiest of tones – so that I might be scrubbed and fresh for the grand arrival on the morrow. I angled my chin in the glass, not to admire myself but study my face. My image stared back, sallow and drawn. There was a look in my eye that said I wanted a little joy, or, if not joy, at least to forget myself for an hour or two. I had not realized how weary I had become, not from the day's labour, which had been arduous enough, but from the duration of my stay at Las

Lágrimas: my features were pinched, my cheek bones more evident than they had been just a few weeks earlier, the skin beneath my eyes shadowed. This is what middle-age will do to me, I thought; if I tilted my head in a certain position, I glimpsed my mother looking at me.

Such maudlin reflection – especially of the most literal kind – was not the thing at bedtime and I turned from the glass. Perhaps because I was wanted to make a good impression the next day, or because Mother was on my mind, I decided to go through her nightly ritual, one I rarely troubled myself with, tugging a brush through my hair and finding some emollient to apply to my face. I had extinguished all but one of the lamps in the room and was drawing the curtains, when I looked through their gap into the night. Hovering amidst the trunks of the Imperial Avenue, in the like manner as I had observed before, was an orb of light. It was joined by a second and a third, and then a multitude emerging from the darkness. As previously, they appeared to be storm-lanterns held by men in out-dated clothes.

At once my heart began juddering in my ribcage, even though I felt quite removed and secure from the spectacle. Then came the one possible thing that had the power to over-master my fear and drive me without.

I heard Vasca barking from the very direction of the men and their lanterns, as if she were caught in their midst.

To the reader it may seem reckless but, before I had the chance to consider my actions, I sallied from my bedroom. I had fallen short in protecting Lola: it was not a dereliction I would repeat with Vasca.

The hallway below was less dark than I expected it to be, the source of its illumination being the Trophy Room, which was open and a faint glow shining hence. For the present I ignored it, bursting through the front door and winging my way across the moonlit lawn. I heard the snarl and deep-drawn howls of other dogs, a dozen or more in number, and had visions of them attacking Vasca who, with her buckled pelvis, would be no match for the pack – as neither would I. All I could pray for was to encourage the German shepherd away, and the two of us flee to the shelter of the house.

The wind whipped through the avenue of trees, heaving and booming, swaying the crowns. Beneath them, further lanterns had materialized, hanging in the darkness like balls of fluorescent mist, and I saw clearly the men with their moustaches and wicked mouths, some armed with carbines, laughing and mocking, though unlike previously I could hear the sounds of the voices, full of spiteful merriment as they were. Their attention was directed to something on the ground, close to that gap where the ombú was missing, something I could not see for the angle of my approach meant that the tree trunks denied my view. For the first time I observed that a number of the group held leashes, straining against which were the dogs I had heard, not animals of Vasca's or Lola's moderate nature, but dogs that had been starved and maltreated, whose teeth were bared and muzzles trailing slaver. They were baying viciously, frantic to be set loose.

Of Vasca I saw no sign – unless, from the outset, the only dogs I had heard were these snarling monsters.

The realization brought me to a halt. I shuddered at the

rashness of the position I found myself in, my breath ragged and escaping my lungs as vapour. None of the men seemed to have noticed me, their sole interest being whatever lay obscured in front them. Part of me yearned to see what could hold their attention so absolutely, but my greater urge was to retreat before I was discovered. A salty, coppery taste flooded my mouth, and with it a sensation of hopelessness. Then I heard a booming voice that, for an instant, I mistook as Berganza's.

Look! It's the gardener.

I tore pell-mell across the lawn in the direction I had come, back to the house, hearing the dogs bark in a frenzy and praying I had sufficient a start to outrun them, not once daring to glance over my shoulder until I crashed through the front door and slammed it shut behind me. I stood bent and gasping, lathered in a raw sweat. When eventually I peered out again, the lights were all vanished.

For how long I remained there, waiting for my heart to recover and hands to cease their trembling, I do not know. Some childish part of me wanted to find Calista and give myself to her embrace as I would Grandfather when I was a girl after a nightmare. And yet, on reflection, my fear was a curious one – it is hard exactly to describe – as if it were more than my own, like some external force bearing down upon me. Presently, however, I became aware of various knocks and thuds emanating from the Trophy Room, the sounds most definitely of commonplace origin. As I had observed in my earlier dash past, the door to the room had been left open, a light shining from within, and now I skulked toward it, the painted-eyes of Don Guido, disagreeable and vaguely ridiculous, seeking me out.

Inside the Trophy Room, I was met by the familiar chill. There was no person present, though a lamp had been left burning. My eyes roamed past the maps and jutting stag heads, to the bookcase. A panel of the shelving stood ajar, revealing, as never before, it to be a false-front concealing a secret doorway. It was from here the sounds were coming. I stole a look inside and discovered a low, narrow compartment quite without attribute except for an opening in the ground from which peeked the top rungs of a ladder. The glow of another lantern came from the depths and, as I crouched by the hole, I saw Latigez below, lugging about pieces of old junk. I had mostly avoided him these past days, for if Calista had been magnanimous about my misguided charge, I doubted her husband's attitude would be of similar generosity.

'What on earth are you doing?' I demanded.

He looked up, apparently wholly unsurprised to see me. 'You're about late again, Deborah.' His voice crackled with catarrh.

'Why do you call me that?'

'It's your name, isn't it?'

He went back to his work.

'Well?' I asked a second time. 'Are you going to tell me?'

'Come down and see for yourself.'

Although I was unsure if his words contained an element of malice, there was most obviously a hint of challenge, the way Gil used to speak when offering an unwelcome enterprise and daring me to tackle it. It was that, as much as my inquisitiveness about this hidden room, which convinced me to clamber down the ladder, descending no more than a dozen rungs before, once again, the ground was beneath my feet. A subterranean coldness struck me. I found myself stooped in a tight chamber of black, oozing walls, its only feature being a brick cylinder rising from the ground, seven or eight courses in height and of similar diameter. Heavy boards had been laid across its mouth, capping it, and stacked atop them were any number of incongruent objects: broken pieces of lumber, lead piping, even a hunk of the black stone from which the garden wall was built. Latigez was adding to these items, building a bizarre, underground pyre. There was a mouldering, dank smell to the air.

'A charming spot you have found,' I said. 'What is this place?'

'The old well,' replied Latigez. 'When Capitán Agramonte first settled this land, it was from here the water was taken for the gaol.' He shifted one of the boards. 'See for yourself.'

A moist wind drove into my eyes. There was a sharp drop that ended in a channel of dark, fast-flowing water, the undulations of its surface catching the light from Latigez's lamp – rather less a well, than an aperture over a river. The rushing, gurgling water reverberated nosily into the brickwork and, I daresay, the very foundations of the house, thence the walls, so that it must be heard faintly throughout the old section of the building.

I replaced the board. 'None of which explains what you are doing.'

His sigh was as weary as it was histrionic. 'My last

instruction for the day. To make sure the well was blocked, to make sure there was no chance, *what-so-ever*, anyone might fall down it.'

Hitherto, I had surmised that the son of Don Guido – that is to say the deceased brother of the current Don – had perished in the lake, now the pieces clicked into place.

'This is where the boy drowned.'

Latigez grunted an affirmative. 'When the builders were at work on the new wing, word was sent to make a false wall to hide this space. Orders from Don Paquito. We did a good job, you'd never know the well was here. Then tonight, Señor Moyano comes to me in an agitation, fearing of the so-called curse and worried that the Don's kid might find his way here. He tells me to weigh it down so that the devil himself couldn't fight his way out. Gives me silver for my troubles.'

He retrieved a peso from his pocket to show me, and with it the anger broke in him, his tone becoming livid, the look in his eye threatening. 'You've a tongue on you, girl, and an evil one at that. First, all that slander you gave Calista. Now those ideas you've put in Señor Moyano's head, with your gup of phantasms and the sort.'

'The family should be warned.'

'You frighten the Doña back to Buenos Aires, and Calista and me will be on the dungheap. You'll ruin Moyano too. He's told me, quite plain, if it goes wrong here he'll kill himself, like he tried before. When his wife cleared out.'

'She left him?'

'Didn't you know? It was after that business at his last job with the daughter-of-the-house,' he leered, seeming familiar with the details and relishing them. 'His wife washed her hands of him and took off. Stole his lad too.'

'He told me none of this.'

'That's why he built his cottage,' he answered. 'To show he'd turned a new leaf. To win them over.'

'Be it so, must the Agramontes suffer for the errors of Moyano's life?'

Latigez snatched up my forearm, squeezing hard on the bone. 'Have you seen the scars on his wrist?' I struggled to pull away. He dragged me closer, so I saw the spittle on his lips; my stomach convulsed at the thought of that mouth on Calista. 'He'll do it this time for sure. What's he got to live for if he can't get his son back?' His fingers tightened around me. 'I told him, the advice of a friend – you never go cross-wise. You have to cut wrist to elbow.'

I wrested myself free, wanting more than anything to be away from him and this dreadful chamber, and began to ascend the ladder.

'Think on that, Señorita,' he shouted after me, his words echoing horribly, 'before you go blurting to the Don and wreck a man's life. Wrist to elbow, so the surgeon can't sew you back up.'

The Arrival of Don Paquito

'YOU WILL HAVE to change your clothes,' said Moyano brusquely upon finding me the next day.

That morning I had woken from a sleep troubled by the happenings of the night and omens I could not recall, leaving me unrefreshed and on edge. It was in such a state that I had put on a loden-green dress, having pressed the garment myself, finishing my habiliment with the matching hat, my hair neatly arranged, and boots polished by Yamai; I had thought myself more than presentable.

'Whatever is wrong with them?' I asked.

'I expect the female staff to be dressed in white for the arrival of the Don.'

The estate manager himself was not in his workaday garb but a sombre morning-suit with tails, his collar boiled and starched. I wondered how a man of his ilk had faced the humiliation of his wife leaving and taking his son from him, his erratic conduct perhaps more explicable because of it – even if it changed little in my own attitude toward him. For a moment or two I challenged his instruction, explaining that I intended to spend the first hours of the morning on the final tidying of the garden and that in white I was destined to make a mess of myself, yet Moyano was insistent that I change, continuing at me until I came to the conclusion this could only be a futile argument. And so I had returned to my room; and so I had dressed in white; and so within the hour I found myself with a greenish smudge upon my sleeve and splatters of dark earth along my hem. I tried to clean them off which, inevitably, led me to discolouring the material further.

'How does it look?' I asked Yamai.

His cheeks reddened at my question, and he struggled to find an answer that he hoped would not offend before alighting on the response, 'It is not your wedding dress, Señorita.'

We were working alone in the garden, his brother, being nimbler of foot, having been stationed at the main gate to dash back and inform Moyano on the first sight of the Don's cavalcade. Together, Yamai and I picked celery, onions and beetroot from the kitchen garden for that night's inaugural dinner, then, in the main garden, raked over those sections of earth that had most recently been cleared, picking at any newly pushed-through weeds.

As I toiled, an anticipatory tension lay heavily upon me, for although I had yet to meet my employer, I feared for his well-being and that of his family. I kept Vasca (who I learnt had spent the night securely indoors at Moyano's cottage) close by at all times. Once again it had turned much colder and a dark mantle of rainless cloud looked to be settling over the estate for the day. The wind snapped constantly, carrying upon it the cries of birds, melodious one moment, harsh and sawing the next.

It was gone eleven-and-a-quarter when the summons came for me to return to the house. I made for the scullery, where I left Vasca, then went smartly to the front door to see the first wagon draw up. It belonged to a vinter in Tandil, whose draymen were already unloading case upon case of the finest wines, and wore the same expression that I had seen amongst those of Berganza: a grim set to the jaw, a look of curiosity and misgiving. That they had visited Las Lágrimas would be a tale to tell their wives or share amongst friends over a *mate* gourd – but they would be glad soon to be leaving. Moyano directed them to the house's cellar and, when they were done, signed for the account.

By the time the drays headed off, the first of the Don's party was arriving. There came a procession of more carts, drawn by weary horses, containing furniture and luggage, and victuals enough for an army, and eventually the staff. They were not the type of person I had been given to expect, being instead rather an uncouth-looking crew, who appeared ill at ease in their new uniforms. Whilst Moyano took charge of the chattels, it was left to Calista, acting as the housekeeper, to greet and organize the servants, assigning them to different parts of the building, though for all her long service in the Agramonte household she was acquainted with but a few of the new arrivals, passing the barest number of words with them, the exception being a stout, tremulous member of our sex whom she knew better. I watched from a distance as Calista spoke to the woman, the cook's welcoming smile

morph, over the course of a minute, to a knotted frown and
then grimace.

'What did she say?' I asked, when Calista returned to
my side.

'The Don was not able to hire the staff he needed. Stories
of the place dissuaded too many. Nor will Señora Paredes,
who keeps the house in Buenos Aires, be joining us. We are
going to be short-handed, and those we do have look a…'

'A rum bunch?'

'I daresay.'

'What of gardening staff?'

'You have none.'

I would have been indignant, if I was not for leaving.

Whilst the procession of people and moveables continued,
and Moyano ordered the Mapuches to make themselves
scarce, we of the original staff were made to wait at the front
door, us women in white (Calista and Dolores had remained
spotless, making me yet more self-conscious of my slightly
soiled appearance), Latigez and Señor Farrido in black, the
latter wan and at intervals mopping his forehead, suggesting
he was sober and suffering for it. He kept trying to pester
Dolores into conversation, leaving the maid flurried and ready
to volunteer for the least errand, going so far as to enquire
if I had any task for her. Now that I knew her secret, one
would have expected her to be shamefaced in my presence.
Instead, she was innocence itself, leading me to suspect that,
whoever her co-conspirator, the maid had been offered
some reward to behave thus and ensure her character was
beyond reproach.

I soon grew irritable of such pointless waiting. 'Must we dawdle so?' I complained to Moyano.

'We are to wait for the Don,' he had snapped. 'Not the other way round.'

And so the minutes added up to twenty, then thirty, forty and fifty, until we reached almost an hour of tarrying, and though I grew bored, I could not shake the sensation of the woodland that ringed the house growing darker and creeping invisibly closer. The wind continued to whip and blast; often I had to steady my hat.

Finally, there came a distant putt-putt-putt of motor engines.

I felt the rate of my heart double. Would the curse strike at once, as I feared possible? Would the axeman materialize and step into the car's path, forcing the Don to swerve and collide into one of the immense trunks of the Imperial Avenue, concertinaing the vehicle and throwing his son clear – and to his death?

The car came into view through the trees, followed closely by a pantec* laden, as I was shortly to discover, with family heirlooms and treasure. Moyano shooed us into line, alternating between male and female members of staff, with me at the far end, so that I could not help but think we resembled the keyboard of some oversized piano.

'Be courteous and polite,' Moyano warned us. 'There must be no speaking unless something is asked of you. Do you hear me, Señorita Kelp?'

---

* Pantechnicon: a large motorised-van for transporting furniture.

Don Paquito's motorcar was the largest, the most beautiful I had ever seen, its coachwork in a peacock-blue. It completed two fast loops of the driveway, its horn parping, and came to a halt outside the door. The hood of the vehicle was fastened down and on the backseat I saw a woman, who I presumed to be Doña Javiera, her sable hair lending emphasis to the pallor and strain of her face, her arms wrapped around a boy and a girl sitting on either side of her. I took the driver, for there were no other passengers, to be Don Paquito himself. As the pantec pulled up at the rear of his vehicle, he stood from the wheel, slid back his driving-goggles and, placing a gauntleted-hand on each hip, surveyed his estancia. Coiled around his neck was a silk scarf of ivory thread.

He inhaled deeply through his nose. Contentedly. 'I remember that sound as if it were yesterday.' I was sure he glanced at me as he said in addition, 'Just like the ocean.' His voice was patrician if not quite as deep and resonant as one would have imagined.

Agramonte jumped down off the running-board and, with a curious skip, moved to the rear door, which he opened for his family. The boy, I estimated him to be twelve or so, eagerly clambered out followed by his sister, who was no older than her tenth year. As the Don offered his hand to his wife, helping her out, I heard him say loud enough for us all, 'There, are you happier now? No misfortune has struck us! I can only say again, my love, we shall all be safe here.'

I have often wondered since on those words – and how profound, how painful, must his regret have been at such confident a proclamation.

Moyano stepped forward and shook the hand of his employer, which was taken, or so I thought, with rather less enthusiasm by the Don. There were no more handshakes as the estate manager introduced the rest of us, each member of staff dipping their head in respectful submission, excepting for Dolores who dropped into one of her curtsies. The Doña pressed her cheek briefly against Calista's as they passed, then patted her on the elbow as one might an old pet. When he reached me at the end of the line, Moyano spoke tensely, 'And this is your Head Gardener. The English woman we have discussed: Señorita Kelp.'

To the surprise of everyone, none more so than myself, the Don seized my hand and pumped it heartily, his grip a little spongey. From the portraits of his father, I recognized his features, the cruel twist to the mouth, the black-and-bronze eyes, though neither were as pronounced or callous. The nose he must have inherited from his mother's side, it being more aquiline, and lending him a somewhat bookish countenance. His hair was dark, greying about the ears, and worn with an immaculate part that hours of motoring seemed not to have ruffled. He took in all of my person without once lifting his gaze from my eyes, an assessment that left me impelled to say something, for which the only words I could find were to apologize for the state of my dress.

'When I was a boy,' he replied in good, treacly-accented English, 'my father used to tell me, never trust an honest judge, a pious priest. Nor a clean gardener.'

'I did not know you spoke English.'

'And French. Some Italian and Arabic too,' he said, without boasting; yet nor was he entirely modest. He expected me to be impressed by his linguistic facilities, and was elated when I let my admiration be known.

'How is it that you speak so many languages?'

'After the "events" here of my youth, Father would not have me on the estate. Would not have me in Argentina. The poor man feared for my well-being.' All this was spoken in a tone that suggested it was a course of action that Don Paquito had not taken with much seriousness. 'So I was sent off to Europe, until I was of age. I would like it, Señorita, if we can speak often in English, in order that I may improve.'

Given I had no intention of remaining, I was unsure how to answer and simply offered a yes.

None of this exchange, you understand, was intelligible to anyone but us. I noticed Moyano's expression of alarm, as if he feared those few words I had uttered were nothing but the frankest talk of ghosts and the estate manager's less gentlemanly conduct. For the Doña's part, a little jealous scowl stole across her features, which she made every endeavour to conceal.

The son stepped forward to me. He had the sable hair of his mother with the same slight curl to it, his cheeks dotted with freckles. 'Good morning, Señorita,' he chimed in clumsy English. 'My name is León Agramonte.'

'And a boy who speaks as well as his father.'

He showed no sign of having comprehended a word of my reply, and held out his hand to shake. I took it and, delighted I had fallen into his trap, he crunched it as hard as he was able, digging his uncut nails into the flesh of my palm. Don Paquito, observing his son, let out a laugh, thinking it an amusing game, and made no intervention, leaving it for me to extricate my hand.

That was the end of our audience.

After the long burden of expectation, of all my days at Las Lágrimas leading to this single hour, it had proved to be something of a non-event. The Agramontes seemed as amicable and self-involved, as entitled, as any family of the upper classes – they could have been neighbours of my parents or the Houghtons, albeit with their own forest – no sense of doom or tragedy hung about them. Nor had the curse struck as I was sure it must. I shall confess to feeling unsure of myself and not a tiny bit foolish; perhaps Señor Moyano had been the more level-headed of us all along. And yet that low stir of foreboding that I had woken with and been my companion for the day, the recent terrors I had lived through, had not abandoned me. The great expanse of trees that surrounded us on all sides remained as dark and threatening, and I retained the sensation of someone lurking in them, watching the family, watching us all.

And waiting.

Doña Javiera clasped the hands of her children and as she led them inside the house, I chanced to look in her direction. She was smiling for her husband, but I saw that her jaw was clenched and, from the tension behind that smile, I was convinced she felt exactly as did I.

Around noon, a maid, one of those newly arrived, fetched me my hamper. She was crop-full of chatter, though it was a loquaciousness I did not reciprocate, finding her as I did somewhat coarse, and after she was gone I made sure that she had pilfered none of my luncheon.

By-and-by, another maid, yet another unfamiliar face, wound her way to the garden with the message I had been summoned to Doña Javiera's rooms. I followed the maid to the house, wondering, if the opportunity presented itself, whether this was a time to warn the Doña of the danger to her son. As if anticipating this possibility, I found Moyano waiting by the kitchen door. He gave no acknowledgement of my presence, though at the moment I passed by him he spoke in a voice low and minatory: 'I warn you, Señorita.'

Having removed my boots, I let the maid escort me to the new wing, across the chequer-board floor, up two flights of stairs to a part of the house I had never visited. Now that the family had taken residence, Farrido's boiler was at work all the more vigorously, the air warmer than for my liking. The maid entered one of the rooms whilst I was obliged to wait by the closed door. On the other side I caught the burble of voices and then, for an extended period, nothing, so that I found myself uncertain as what to do. Was I to knock, or wait to be called?

'Enter!' The Doña's voice was kittenish and staccato.

I did as requested and found myself in a suite of sumptuously appointed rooms. There was no sign of the maid who had brought me. I had the impression of luxury and taste, of shimmering silks, crepes threaded with gold, ostrich-feather fans. The furniture was expensive and of ebony; scattered on the floor, Oriental mats of a most iridescent weave. A hoard of trunks and cases, which presuming they were full must contain more clothes than I had owned during the span of my life, stood waiting to be unpacked. In closer relation to the Doña than earlier, I saw that her face had the perfect proportions of a porcelain doll, even if her chin was perhaps a little too pointed and, from the slight pucker of her mouth, I understood the tension of her arrival remained. Her eyes were the darkest brown flecked with a sparkle of gems so that one wanted constantly to look at and admire her. I felt an immediate desire to be her friend, albeit there was a quality to her attire, something louche, that I could not entirely approve of. She had changed into a flowing dress, velvet and wine-coloured, one side having fallen free, exposing her shoulder of which she was either not aware or cared less.

'I hope that you have settled in well,' I said freely. 'How are the children finding their new home?'

Her response was to thrust an empty vase at me. 'Explain.'

'I beg your pardon?'

'Look at it. Look at them all!' She swept an arm in consternation at the numerous vases about the room. 'Every one empty. The same in the hallway. And downstairs. At home in Buenos Aires I always have fresh flowers. *Every day*.'

At first I thought it some joke, the humour of which I did not quite appreciate, before I realized she was in earnest. 'We... that is, I... haven't grown any yet.'

'You are Head Gardener. Flowers are your responsibility.'

I stumbled for an answer. 'There has been no chance to

establish a cuttings border. It's not even the season.'

She made straight toward me, putting her face close to mine, and for one mad instant I was convinced she was going to strike me or, worse, kiss me on the lips. 'I expect flowers!'

A short time later, and more stunned than I would think possible from such a succinct interview, I found myself retreating along the corridor. There was a clatter of steps from the staircase and the son appeared, hurtling in my direction and calling excitedly: *Mamá! Mamá!*

'Look, Señorita, what I found,' he cried. 'Two of them!' He flashed the silver pesos in his little hand.

I murmured something in reply and continued away from him, my only wish to be outside with Vasca again. From a room on the other side of the corridor a maid looked out and, when she spied me, darted back in.

Blood on my Clothes

IT WAS IN the bitterest of terms that I relayed my encounter with the Doña to Calista as, later in the day, she went about preparing dinner. The cook had several new girls to help her, albeit that they seemed rather hapless, clumsy creatures, and she was somewhat distracted as we conversed. The kitchen swirled with rich aromas of beef, broth and bread.

'Do not judge her too harshly,' replied Calista. 'She is a fine lady, made anxious by this place. Her mood is all fear for her son – and you have borne the brunt.'

'I was planning to tell her what I have seen.'

'You must,' implored Calista. 'Before it is too late.'

But I was aggrieved at my treatment and so felt entirely justified in lacking either goodwill or sympathy toward the lady of the house. My experience with her had furthered my resolve to leave Las Lágrimas.

It was not my only reason to be discontented that evening. Now that the family had arrived, I was to be exiled from the dining room and henceforth eat my meals with the rest of the staff. For those more junior members that meant the long table in the kitchen; for myself, Señor Jalón (he being Don Paquito's valet) and the maid who had fetched me to the Doña, we were given the table in Calista's parlour. Whereas the meal I had previously taken there was of a welcome intimacy, sitting with these strangers felt cramped. Jalón, who had served as a corporal in the Paraguayan army, possessed a heavy, drooping moustache, the lower bristles of which dripped as he ate his soup, so that I could not bear to look in his direction.

It was whilst I was in this moment of pique-and-potage that there came from the kitchen a terrible commotion. Vasca was barking outside the door, I heard a number of the maids cry out in distress, and then a voice of anguish and desperation called my name. I rushed through to the other room and found Epulef, gasping as one who has run far and fast, his shirt sleeves bloodied.

'Señorita, come quick!'

'What has happened?'

He did not offer a reply, but stumbled back into the night.

Alarmed as I was, I sought the first lamp my hand found, then, pausing to untie Vasca, I followed Epulef from the house, struggling to keep pace with him as we raced through the kitchen garden and into the woodland beyond. A biting wind gusted through the canopy, causing it to shake and shriek, so that the trees themselves seemed alive as with unholy voices that sang only one thing: this was not a night to be abroad.

'What emergency is this?' I asked of the Mapuche as we plunged deeper into the darkness. Vasca bounded by my side.

He hurried on madly and without explanation until we

came to a most dreadful scene. We had reached that place where the white stag had breathed its last. The flame of my lamp struggled in the wind, shedding only a scant light, though I saw the details plainly enough. Yamai was on his knees and weeping. Beneath him, deathly pale, sprawled and broken as the deer had been, lay his father, his right leg caught in a mantrap. It was an ancient, rusted device and the teeth had snapped shut deeply through his shin bone. Whether in pain or shock, Namuncura had collapsed unconscious on his side, his trouser-legs and moccasins drenched in blood.

'Have you tried to spring the trap?' I asked.

'We do not know how,' came Yamai's reply.

In the sputtering light my eyes strained to examine the device, searching for a release mechanism and, when none was to be found, I realized that the only chance we had to free the old Mapuche was to prise the jaws open by brute strength. Whilst Epulef looked on, Yamai and I struggled to force the metal wide. It was soon apparent, however, that without an implement of some description it was a hopeless endeavour and that, in all likelihood, it would end with us injuring ourselves rather than Namuncura being freed. Vasca crouched nearby, a low, anxious whimper emerging from her.

'Get back to the house,' I ordered Epulef. 'Find Señors Moyano and Latigez. Tell them I have been injured and need their help.'

Epulef's face burnt with indignation. 'You are not hurt.'

'Tell them it's me or they will not come at all. Latigez must bring his tool-bag. Go now!'

Namuncura was senseless. I told Yamai to remove his

jacket and drape it over his father to keep his body warm. For myself, I had left the house in such a panic that there had been no time to take my own coat, otherwise I would have rolled it into a pillow to place under the elderly man's head to make him as comfortable as I might. I shivered in the wind. 'What happened to him?' I asked.

'He was not at home when we arrived from work. Sometimes he forgets himself and goes walking. Later we heard his scream and ran to find him.' Yamai was also trembling, from cold or worry or both, his eyes shooting in every direction. 'Will he die?'

'He has lost some blood, but I do not think so.'

We waited for Epulef to return, it taking far, far longer than it should have done to retrace his steps to the house, rouse the others and make their way back. I began to fear some accident had befallen him. Might he also be caught in a mantrap? I felt a spurt of rage toward Moyano who, despite my protestations, had not removed the device. But no, if Epulef had met a similar fate we must surely have heard his own scream.

The lantern I had taken from the kitchen had been far from full and, as we crouched there, the minutes stretching by, the flame began to gutter in the dregs of the oil, causing the small pool of light we were sat in to flicker. I pulled Vasca closer, comforted by the fact that, although she continued to whimper, she had not adopted her raised-hackles position that presaged a supernatural arrival. The old Mapuche stirred, his eyes bulging whitely as he came to and appreciated his surroundings. He scrabbled in the dirt, as if to trying to escape some unseen horror, causing the teeth embedded in his leg to bite deeper and for him to yell out. Yamai reached for his father, mumbling words of comfort in their native language. Namuncura looked from his son to me, and spoke in a rasping, stricken whisper.

'I heard him, Señorita.'

'Heard who?'

'He called from all round. *Namuncura... help me... Namuncura, por favor...*'

My pulse quickened, for there was only one who would want to lure the old Mapuche to this particular location. 'It was the axeman calling you?'

'Not him. He does not speak.'

'Then who?'

'Tarella,' sobbed the old man.

'You mean the gardener, from long ago?'

'Yes.'

There came a gust so startling, so violent, that it rushed through the tunnel of trees where we huddled, like the howl of some ferocious, starved beast. This was an ill time – and an even iller setting – to question Namuncura as I had wanted to; nevertheless, I had to ask, 'Do you know what happened to Tarella?'

'He was a good man.'

'But what became of him?'

'His wife died.'

'Here?' I answered, wishing he would make more sense. 'On the estate?'

'Far away, in the big city. There was a fire.'

'And Tarella?' I urged.

'He cursed this land.'

'Because of his wife?'

'Don Guido he… I do not know the word.' He murmured something in his alien tongue to Yamai.

'Tricked,' said his son.

'Yes,' continued the old man painfully, and I saw in the waning light that his lips were darkened with blood. 'The Don tricked Tarella.'

'By what means?'

'He did not pay – but had him whipped. We workers were made to watch. And so Tarella came back. For the trees. After that, I did not see. I only heard.'

'Heard what?'

'His suffering…'

Even as he spoke these words, the last of the lamp-oil exhausted itself, the flame turning a dirty yellow, shrinking and then dying, leaving the wick to glow briefly before it too was no more and we found ourselves in a pit-like darkness. I felt a well of hopelessness, and there we remained in shivering silence, all of us too disturbed to talk, until Vasca roused herself and began to bark into the surrounding blackness. My heart stood still within me for, at a distance through the trees, I saw a light, swaying at the height of a man. It was joined by a second and a third, converging swiftly on our spot.

Namuncura clawed at me, begging that I find the means to release him. 'I should not have talked of Don Guido.' He spoke wildly and in terror. 'I have raised him and his men, as in days of old.'

Short of abandoning the old Mapuche, there was nothing

to be done and, even if I had been of a mind to flee into the brushwood, I preferred to meet my fate in the company of other, living beings. I pressed close to Yamai, knowing his strength would be of no use to us, and together we shielded his maimed father as best we could, whereafter I must have squeezed my eyes shut, for I was not aware of the final approach of the lights, only a crashing sound as they neared, and the clink-and-jangle of metal.

'Here's a cosy little scene.'

Latigez's face leered from the darkness, his muttonchops cast in the dazzle of his lantern, the pockmarks of his skin made to look theatrical, as if they had been applied with a paintbrush. Next to him were Epulef and Moyano, the one also holding a lantern, the other his torch. The estate manager was in a state of ire and directed it to Latigez.

'I told you to do away with the trap!'

'I did, Señor. I swear it. And searched for the others as you asked, though I couldn't find a single one.'

'Then how do you explain this? Consider the consequences if it had been the Don, or his children—'

'Now is not the time,' I cried, the equal of Moyano's anger. 'We must release Namuncura.'

Slung over Latigez's shoulder, source of the jangling sound, was a bag of implements from which he removed a forcing-tool and, kneeling on the ground, positioned it between the jaws of the trap.

'This will hurt,' he said, with not the slightest sympathy, and began to jerk the rod.

Namuncura clutched his sons' hands as, inchmeal, the

device was prised open, he stifling a scream as the teeth pulled from his bone, and once more slumping into the relief of unconsciousness as the pain became too intense.

As soon as he was free, I examined the wound, a spasm of nausea contracting my gullet. 'He will need a doctor.'

'Likely an amputation,' interjected Latigez, and he let the empty jaws snap back.

The countenances of the two Mapuches, already ashen, became paler still.

'Do not listen to him,' I said, 'he cannot help his ignorance.'

Moyano observed the scene, his expression one caught between dismay, irritation and the plain desire to want all the trouble of it gone. 'We have carbolic for the wound and Calista will be able to concoct something for the pain, but there is no doctor.'

'What if it had been the Don?' I posed to him. 'What if any of the family took badly ill, what would they do?'

'Set out at once for Tandil, by motorcar.'

'Then they must do the same for Namuncura.'

'They will not.'

'He is an old man, he deserves more than to be left. The wound' – I spoke softly, so as to not alarm further his sons – 'may become gangrenous.'

'Consider it from the Don's position. The Mapuche is nothing more than a labourer, one who no longer works at that. The Don will not bloody his car for him. It will ruin the leatherwork.'

'I do not believe Don Paquito to be so cold-hearted. Let me speak to him.'

Moyano held me in an unshrinking gaze. 'One thing is for certain,' he said at last, the wind messing at his hair, 'he cannot remain out here. None of us can. We must get him to the old mansion.'

I moved to help the Mapuches carry their father – but Moyano intervened.

'You have done more than your duties require already this night, Señorita. Let Latigez escort you back to the house. I'll take care of this business from now.'

I was reluctant to abandon the old man, suspicious as I was of Moyano, and before leaving I made sure to check upon, and reassure, Namuncura one final time. As my fingers stroked at his cheek, he woke suddenly – making me flinch – and uttered a babble of mostly incoherent thanks before his eyes became clear and he beckoned me close to him, as if he had a confession to whisper, so close that I needed to lean my ear over his lips to hear his words. 'Stay in the house,' he rasped in the most ominous of tones. 'Do not go into the trees.'

The old Mapuche was borne away by his sons, Moyano at their rear. As I made in the opposite direction, the estate manager called after me.

'Be certain, Señorita Kelp, that none of the family sees you as you are.'

I glanced down at myself and the white of my dress, the get-up that Moyano had insisted I wear that morning. It was patterned in gory handmarks.

'Do not trouble yourself,' said Latigez, as I exclaimed in horror. 'Calista has a talent for laundering the blood from clothes.'

The Garden & the Ghost

OF THE MAPUCHES, all three were gone before dawn the next day, Moyano, as he later informed me, having made discreet arrangements for a cart to take them away. Whether the old man was seen by a doctor, why both his sons chose to abandon their home and leave with him – what became of them after – I cannot say. I never saw or heard of them again.

An hour or so after they must have left, I was awakened by a scratching sound from my door. I had once more slept disturbedly, from troubling over Namuncura's claims and obscure nightmares of gnashing teeth, but also, having grown accustomed to the silences of the house, because it was now full of unfamiliar noises. There were extra maids in the attics above; Señor Jalón had taken a room along the corridor – and throughout the night I had been aware of various coughs and snores, creaking floorboards and the giggling of girls. After yearning for more souls to fill the place, the reality had proved somewhat less consoling. I rose wearily and with bagged eyes to find a note had been posted under the door. It was from Don Paquito, notifying me that he wished to visit the garden that morning to see my progress and I was to meet him by the door-in-the-wall. Nine o'clock sharp.

When the appointed hour arrived, I found him and León, the son, already waiting, Vasca sat rather primly to one side. The Don was dressed in a worsted suit of the best quality, the cloth coloured as is the plumage of a pheasant, the trousers tucked into well-made riding boots; the child wore the costume of a pirate, his outfit completed with tricorn hat, eye-patch and toy cutlass. There was a sneer to the boy's expression as I approached, and he loudly announced, '*Papá* has a surprise for me!' As for myself, I had rubbed a spot of rouge into my cheeks to give myself some colour, its effect only to make me look the worse.

The Don was rattling the handle of the door, and then proceeded to aim an ineffectual kick at the wood. 'It won't budge.' His mood seemed more fractious than the day before, and I was left to speculate whether I was not the only one to have experienced a bad night's sleep.

'The door does not open,' I explained.

He stood away from it, defeated. 'Well, I expect it repaired this very morning. I'd have thought you or Moyano would have already seen to it. And whose idea was this wall?'

'Señor Moyano tells me your father had it built.'

'Nonsense! There was no such thing when I was a child. It will have to come down: the whole point is the view to the lake.'

I walked the Don and his son along the perimeter of the stonework to the usable entrance, Vasca trailing us, her nose a constant distraction as she sniffed out crevices in the black henge so that now and again I had to call for the dog to keep up, after which she would excitedly dash ahead until the next curious scent caught her. There was sunshine anew, pale and primrosy, for a boisterous wind had blown all night, cutting to strips the clouds and leaving what remained scattered and hurrying across the sky. In my pocket was my letter of resignation. I intended this tour to be my last official duty and, once I had completed it, would make formal my desire to leave Las Lágrimas. My second imperative, whether to speak of the curse and warn the family of all I had seen, I would leave upon the reaction to my epistle.

We reached the gap in the wall, the boy charging through it, and then his father. I was on the point of ducking after them and calling for Vasca to follow when, with a catch of my heart, I saw that the dog had frozen, every hair on her body standing on end, a low whine escaping her throat.

'Come on, girl!' I encouraged her with a lightness I did not feel.

She refused my call, taking, instead, a step backward. And then another, her lips curling to reveal fangs.

'Leave the dog,' said Don Paquito from the other side of the wall. 'The blasted animal kept me awake last night with her yowling. Her and her mates.'

I hesitated, unsure as to what I should do, a quiet, prudent voice in my head urging me to run – but with the Don impatient to see what I had achieved, and his son playing and careless, I felt a sudden embarrassment – an awkwardness – at the thought of disobliging the man who was, after all, still my employer.

And so, for the sake of decorum, I joined them.

The Don's temper improved as we explored that part-tended, part-still-wild space within the enclosure. He was possessed of a respectable, if *Gardeners'-Chronicle*-type knowledge of plants, going so far as to suggest certain species for various spots, even if most of my choices would have been different (and, let it be said, more apposite for the conditions). All the same, I found myself imbibing his enthusiasm, not least because he was so approving of what I had accomplished and, as we pressed deeper, I began to make our amble a tad more theatrical, deliberately choosing paths to reveal some small portion that had been cleared or an unexpected detail, and deciding I should keep the Treasure Garden for my finale. As we walked, the boy skipping ahead and slicing at the weed tops with his pirate's cutlass, the Don conversed in both Spanish and English, dependent on how his vocabulary served him, so that sometimes a sentence would begin in one language and end in another, the effect somewhat disconcerting. Every section of the garden, even if it remained obscured by weeds, prompted a happy recollection in him: 'I remember the scent of the sweet violets here... this is where the rudbeckia grew, Señorita, great drifts of them... and there an ornamental-peach where the blossom would fall like snow in the spring winds.' For the sake of full disclosure, I must admit a pang of envy, for whilst Don Paquito had regained the cherished garden of his youth, I knew mine was forever beyond my reach.

'You sound to have nothing but fond memories,' I observed.

'After my father abandoned the place, after he took to

God, he forbade any talk of it. The day of his funeral I was determined to return. The years here were the happiest of my childhood and it is here that I want to raise my own family. These are Agramonte lands.'

'What of your…' I considered how to frame my sentence.

'My brother. You can speak it aloud, Miss Kelp, the devil will not tap your shoulder. It was a terrible accident, the same as the burns Mother received, though it served me well. Las Lágrimas was meant as his: instead it is mine.'

'So you do not believe in the…'

'Curse?' A little laugh erupted from his nostrils. 'Not a word of it and, I trust, neither do you. Indeed, I'm rather grateful to have a female Head Gardener. It will give people something better to gossip about.'

Young León was growing bored of our conversation and massacring nettles. '*Papá*, where is my surprise?'

'You have been patient enough, my boy. Señorita, take us to the Picnic Lawn.'

But when we gained that particular area, the unease that Don Paquito's fervour had led me temporarily to repress, rose anew with a sudden chill. The borders remained unkempt – but the lawn was lush, perfectly flat and verdant. I had last ventured here to confront Latigez about his noise-making. Even if the sward had been scythed that same morning, if a lawnmower had been brought to it, followed by the weight of a half-tonne roller and a plentiful scattering of good seed, the grass could not have so speedily recovered. Yet we might as well have been standing on a bowling-green.

'Moyano has chosen my staff well,' said the Don. 'Farrido

has exceeded himself, and so too' – he was peering upward at the cedar – 'has the carpenter. There is your surprise, León. The treehouse. This used to be my hideaway, now it will be yours.'

The child jigged in excitement, throwing his hat high into the air before catching it, and together father and son climbed the rungs set in the trunk and disappeared from my view. A cloud passed briefly in front of the sun and that oppressive, lonely emotion that I associated with being in the confines of the black wall made itself known a little more intensely. The branches above me creaked in the wind, like a galleon at anchor.

And then León was calling and waving from the balcony of the treehouse, he in clear sight, for Latigez, in tandem with his repairs, had also removed a number of the cedar's boughs in order that the vista be opened out. I raised my hand to return the boy's greeting but he had been already distracted by his father who was pointing out the garden spread below and the surrounding forest. 'This is all our land,' I heard him say. 'Every one of the trees, so far as you can see, was planted by your grandfather.'

Shortly after, Don Paquito was by my side again.

'I couldn't but help overhear your words,' I said to him. 'I was told a different story: of the parkland being planted by one of my predecessors. A man named Tarella.'

Mention of the gardener stirred dark emotions in the Don's face. 'We do not talk of that villain! He tried to extort my father and sabotage the estate.' He rooted up a weed and threw it aside. 'Now, let us continue our tour, Señorita.'

'Where is your son?'

'He asked to remain in his new den.'

I was unable to disguise my fretfulness. 'Do you think he should not keep with us?'

'There's no need.'

'But what if he—'

The Don spoke with resolution and not a little tartly. 'I was half his age when I would spend my whole day up there. It is not your place to fuss, Señorita. I have enough of that from his mother.'

He gestured that I should lead on and, I glancing nervously backward to see the boy still on the balcony, we left the treehouse, making a bee-line to the Treasure Garden. But if I hoped this culmination of the tour would take the palm, I was proved wrong. The Don stepped through it in listless perusal, nothing of the work that had been completed giving him particular pleasure. Away in the direction of the meadow, the Wailing Wall made its melancholy song known.

'Are you not pleased?' I asked, trying to mask my disappointment. 'I have followed your instructions to the letter and expended more effort here than any other part of the garden.'

'I do not doubt it, Señorita Kelp.'

'Then what is wrong?'

He did not reply, but using the tip of his boot pushed back the foliage of the box hedging to reveal the strange, frost-like damage.

'Is it the fountain?' I asked. 'Señor Farrido is confident he can get it to work again.'

'I wish you could have seen the Treasure Garden as it was. Then you would understand.'

'These things take time. Give it a season or two. It will grow.'

'Long have I thought on it.' He closed his eyes in recollection. 'Like a piece of heaven fallen on the earth.' When he opened them anew, I saw that they were blurred with tears. 'It was for this, more than all the rest, that I wanted to come back.'

I was troubled by the rawness of his emotion and sought to distract him. 'I have more plants on order. Señor Berganza is due to deliver them within the fortnight.'

At my mention of the nurseryman, at least, the Don was cheered. 'I remember the older Berganza. Now, there was a character! He and my father were rascals together. I look forward to meeting his son again. We three were playmates, he, myself and my brother.'

There was no forewarning.

A blast of unrestrained anger struck us.

A blast of such potency as to cause me to stagger and the Don to cringe, as if some projectile had been fired against him.

Crack—

Crack—

Crack—

The sound of the axe rolled across us seemingly from all directions, taken up and answered with rancour from every part. At the exact same instant, the sun was swallowed by a cloud, not a drifting tuft, but a long, dense woolpack of the bleakest grey. The whole garden, I daresay the whole estancia, was plunged into a deep gloom as if twilight had arrived before its hour. There was a hollowing in the pit of my stomach, with it an exhausting, sagging sense of despair. And portent. From beyond the wall, I heard the snarl and bark of Vasca.

'Your son,' was all I could manage to Don Paquito.

I did not await his response, nor attempt to explain further, but instead ran, picking up my skirts with both hands, flying down the paths, between snatches of bare earth and those areas the weeds still ruled, running until my heart was fit to burst, running in the vain hope of reaching the treehouse to avert the inevitable.

Yet for all my urgency, by the time I arrived – it was already too late.

Even as I dashed across the impossibly flat lawn, the grass a dark emerald in the shadow of the clouds, I looked up and saw that the boy León was not alone. He remained on the balcony, gazing skyward as though witness to an eclipse, and emerging from the black rectangle of the doorway behind him, for there was no mistaking his bald, emaciated form, was the axeman. A hatred, a most passionate bitterness, blazed from him.

He lurched toward the boy, dragging his crippled leg, stretching out with those huge, filth-ridden hands. All at once, the boy became aware of the presence for he opened his mouth to scream, his one eye hidden beneath his pirate's patch, the other wide in fright, the very picture of terror.

The precise manner of what happened next I cannot – I will not – recall, only the outcome.

The boy withdrew in rapid retreat from the apparition, pressing himself hard against the balustrade until there was no more room for escape. The wood at his back splintered, then snapped.

And gave way.

Gave way to nothing, for there were no longer branches to break his fall.

He did not cry out but plummeted in a shocking silence – the most drawn-out silence I have ever experienced – before I heard his body impact the ground with a sickening thump.

I found myself as a woman paralysed, my breath frozen in me and legs unable to follow the command of my thoughts. I glanced upward at the treehouse. There was only the broken railing and the empty doorway… and then a rolling noise of metal against floorboards. A silver coin dropped from the balcony to land near the child's body. I was thrust out of the way as Don Paquito rushed to where León lay twisted and broken at the base of the cedar. The father fell to his knees and emitted an agonized howl before scooping his son into his arms.

At that moment, the sun broke through the clouds. I stifled a sob as Don Paquito, a man not given to a belief in curses, staggered past me, the crumpled body of his child clasped tight against him, the whole scene now bathed in rays of an intense primrose light.

Take Me with You!

THE CLOUD THAT had blocked the sun proved the harbinger of an approaching mass, driven onward by a formidable wind, and as morning wore into afternoon, the heavens knitted together into a great solidity that left the day prematurely dark. Unsure of what to do after I had helped Don Paquito carry his son back to the house, and soon pushed to the edge of the commotion around the boy, I had taken myself to my room and sat upon my bed, knees pulled to my chin, trembling all over, and waited powerlessly. The whole house felt wound tight, the long tense silences broken by an occasional shriek from the Doña and the clatter of footsteps. There was a slight medicinal odour to the air. My emotions were many – shock, fearfulness, grief, a guilt more extreme than I had experienced for Lola, anger at myself. My exigency but one:

To get as far distant from Las Lágrimas as it was possible.

So when I heard the family's motorcar brought to the front door, and peering from my window I had seen the Doña and Calista take to the backseat, the boy borne out to them on a makeshift stretcher, I made hurried preparations to pack a valise, in the hope I might depart with them.

León had not died from his fall. He was, however, most grievously wounded: his back and leg fractured; his arms and shoulders hanging with equal lifelessness; watery, pink fluid in a constant drip from his nose. Damage had been inflicted on his lungs also and, even from the height of my window, I saw that each breath was a struggle for his poor, little frame. He was deathly white and swaddled in blankets, though for some reason, perhaps fretful of causing further injury, no one had thought to remove his pirate's patch. Calista had given the child an analgesic and one of her own-brewed sedatives, nevertheless such were his injuries it was evident that he needed the skills of a professional physician. Precious time would be wasted in sending for a doctor and awaiting his return and, Buenos Aires being too distant, it had been decided the speediest course of action was to motor the boy directly through the night to the hospital at Tandil, as Moyano had predicted the family would.

In the car below, the Doña was almost out of her mind, wringing her hands and wailing, and gave the impression of being in need herself of one of Calista's sedatives. She had insisted the cook remain at her side for the journey to administer her concoctions and salves and, I suspected, for moral support. I finished stuffing those items I judged essential into my case, carried it into the corridor and was halfway down the stairs when I caught the voice of Moyano in the hallway, pleading with the Don to reconsider and not leave the estate. From my location, I could see neither man – only hear their exchange.

Don Paquito sounded husky and broken. 'What you mean to say, Señor Moyano, is that you fear being left without a post.'

'After all the work that has been done, it seems a... a waste to let the estate be abandoned again.'

'My son may die and all you can think of is yourself.'

The Don broke into a sob, the shame of which in front of a servant caused his anger to erupt. He turned on Moyano, incapable, any longer, of controlling his invective. 'It was your responsibility! The treehouse was meant to be repaired. You have shown a wilful disregard for my family.'

'I promise you—'

The estate manager was immediately cut short, there being no word of explanation or defence that could pacify the Don now. 'I offered you a chance, against my better judgement and the advice of the Doña. The advice of all others. Offered you a chance, despite what happened at your previous employer and that sordid reputation of yours—'

There was a titter from above that had me glancing to the head of the staircase where I saw two maids, girls I did not know, crouched by the banister and eavesdropping. Despite my own fraught relationship with Moyano, I felt a moment of unforeseen protectiveness toward the estate manager and, if it was not for the obvious charge of hypocrisy nor wanting my own presence given away, I would have chided the girls and ordered them back to their rooms.

The Don's implacable tirade persisted until his voice became hoarse and another sob burst forth from him. Then I heard the swift click of his boots on the floor and Moyano chasing after him, and understood that if I too wanted to escape now was my last chance. I snatched up my valise and bolted downstairs to the front door, running directly in front of the motorcar. The Don had taken up his position in the driving seat and switched on the headlamps; on the rear seat, the Doña was urging her husband to make every haste.

'Please,' I cried, shielding my eyes from the lights in the murk of the afternoon. 'Take me with you. I can help.'

'Get her out of the way,' Don Paquito ordered, and Moyano dragged me from the path of the car. There was a spit of gravel and the vehicle scorched off past us.

I had a final glimpse of the family, a final glimpse of Calista, and of them all, it was the little girl in the passenger seat next to her father, the forgotten child in all this, who left the most indelible impression. She was frightened out of her wits, a young girl who could not comprehend the events unfolding about her. What untellable damages, I thought, will this inflict on her psyche? Or, perhaps, there would come some future day when she looked back and considered it the making of her, for, as her father had pronounced mere hours earlier, *It was a terrible accident... though it served me well. Las Lágrimas was meant as his: instead it is mine*.

I watched the lamps of the car as they faded into the gloom of the trees and feared, somewhat over dramatically, for there remained a house full of staff that needed to be transported back to civilization, that I would never leave this accursed place. Moyano's grip was still hard about my arm and I snatched myself away from him.

'Will they return?' I asked.

'That was the last question I put to the Don. His wife never wants to see the estancia again. She hopes it burns to the ground.'

I felt a nuzzling breath at my fingertips and found that Vasca had joined me. 'You should have let me warn them,' I said, the guilt uprising in me. 'It was the ghost, just as I said it would be.'

'The Don saw nothing. Nothing. He said that you became quite "demented" and ran through the gardens, yelling after his son. By the time he reached the treehouse, the boy had fallen to the ground.' All this was spoken in a tone that pierced me to the heart.

I looked at the estate manager in disbelief. He said not another word — but I saw, I understood from the coldness of his eye, that he blamed me incorrectly, unjustly, irremediably.

For everything.

If ever there were frozen murder, it was on his face.

I wished not another moment in his company and, beckoning Vasca, walked to the house and up to my room, allowing the dog with me (something usually prohibited, though what did it matter now?). Once I had closed the door, I slumped to my knees and flung my arms around Vasca, she being the only companion — the only source of comfort and consolation — left now to me on the estate, and remained in that position in a mood of dejection, my fear barely suppressed, burning with the unfairness of Moyano's accusation. I also found myself exhausted, a weariness that went deep to my bones, and giving the dog a final embrace, I moved to my bed. I lay down, fully dressed and having not removed my boots, and fell into a slumber so bottomless and instant it was as if I stepped off a precipice.

Within my own private, inner darkness I may have been, but I was not alone. In my dreams, I sensed hands reaching out for me — the same heavy, filthy hands that had found Don Paquito's son.

A House in Mourning

I CAME TO with an abruptness equal to that with which I had slept. I had lost all perception of time for, although it felt as if no more than an hour had passed, outside the window there was the deep blackness of nightfall, lit randomly by blinks of lightning. The sense of those horrid hands lingered, as did a stench of rotting leaves and foul earth in my nose.

I heard also, music.

I sat up, listening intently, assuming it to be another vestige of my dreams. But no! I was quite awake and from downstairs music was unmistakably drifting up to me, mingled with laughter and girlish squeals and the occasional pop of corks.

The door to my room was slightly ajar and, whilst I slumbered, Vasca had left me. My head was thick and my body felt in need of refreshment, I having not drunk or eaten since breakfast, and so I ventured below, meeting one of the young maids who earlier had listened to Moyano's dressing-down. She had in her grasp a bottle of wine, from which she offered me a swig and, when I declined, unabashedly took a deep draught from the neck, a dark trickle of it running from her lips. I slipped past her to the hallway and was made to catch my breath at the scene before me.

Everywhere I went, doors had been flung agape and the staff newly arrived from Buenos Aires was eating and carousing with abandon, almost their entire number dressed *en fête* in clothes plainly ransacked from the Agramontes' apartments. The wine cellar and larder had been raided for the most choice items. Champagne had been taken by the case as well as legs of Iberian ham, olives and preserved artichokes from Italy, *pâté de foie gras*, fruits in liqueur, tins of Florentine biscuits. Someone had dropped a jar of candied ginger and it lay smashed on the floor, oozing its contents. An accordion was being played in the Trophy Room, that music unique to Argentina called the Tango, and when I peeped inside I saw closely entwined couples stepping to its rhythm to the cheers of those watching, an undeniable concupiscence in the air that intrigued and embarrassed me in equal parts. Yet for all my prim, rather Victorian response to the dancing, and disapproval of the stolen victuals, I was uplifted by the sight of so much liveliness after the weeks of silence. Uplifted and reassured, for, although the menace of the axeman must remain, now that the Agramontes had departed there was nothing to hold me here and, for the time being, I felt secure amongst so much company, wanting to be one of their carefree number, to 'let my hair down' as the phrase goes, even if I already foresaw the ease with which the proceedings might become riotous.

Someone plucked at my sleeve. 'I was hoping you'd join us.'

Latigez was bearing down upon me, a bottle of Cognac

in his hand. His eyes shone blearily, though he was not quite intoxicated. One side of his face was swollen and raw. His lip was split.

'What happened to you?' I asked.

'You mean this?' He leant in close so that I saw how livid was the skin of his cheek beneath his whiskers. 'Señor Moyano wanted someone to blame.' He chuckled ironically. 'Who better than a pal? Now he's looking for you. I'd make sure he didn't find me.' He took a gulp of brandy and shook his head. 'The thing is, I know for sure I repaired that railing. It was all new timber.'

He offered me the bottle, which I refused, and I realized I had been mistaken: actually, he was in a dangerous state of drunkenness.

'Great party, isn't it?' he said. 'I had the idea.'

'It's not right, not with the boy so gravely injured.'

'They've all lost jobs to-day,' he came back. 'Let them enjoy themselves.'

'It is also theft.'

'What if they're scared? Did ever you think of that, Ursula? They're already gossiping about the treehouse. Perhaps,' he sneered, 'they think your phantasm is coming to get them. Perhaps they need this to get through the night.'

'What would Calista say?'

'If I know my wife, she'd already have finished her first bottle. Would have hitched her skirts and be dancing on the tables.'

He gave me a final, queer look, his eyes running me up and down, and pushed past to join the other revellers.

From whom I took the first drink, I do not know. By-and-by, someone offered me champagne, not from the neck of a bottle but in a glass. As I had wandered through the wassailing, I had felt an increasing turmoil at my role in matters and rebuked myself that, similar to Lola, if only I had put to one side personal offence, I might have warned the Doña, and the boy yet be well. That notion became like a headache, pressing against my skull and impossible to ignore, and so the reader will forgive me for taking that proffered glass and drinking deeply. The wine was warm and not entirely pleasant, the bubbles fizzing against my throat, but I soon helped myself to another and this time poured it down my gullet, in the manner of Grandfather's trick, to prove I was the match for anyone in the room. After that, it was easy to continue. For a while I experienced a loosening of myself, the horror at the treehouse dimming, but as the alcohol took a greater effect, and the lights and walls grew hazy around me, I began to regret my decision, especially on a stomach so empty. It was thus I rambled amongst the increasingly raucous staff to the kitchen, where I devoured a plate of roast-duck and pickled peaches.

As I was finishing, Moyano entered and, expecting the worse, I stood up from the table and braced myself. He appeared somewhat dishevelled, his jaw shadowed – but cold sober. We stood appraising one another.

'Shouldn't you put a stop to all this?' I said, eventually.

'What does it matter?' he sighed, disconsolately rubbing at his wrist. 'What does any of it matter now? I have decided: the whole staff is to leave tomorrow.'

'I presume I am included.'

'You are too good to travel with the rest, Señorita. I will make sure you have your own horse and guide.'

'Thank you,' I replied, unable to contain my suspicion.

Whatever the fury that earlier had gripped him, it now seemed utterly spent and subsumed by a resignation to events. There was a blank look to his eyes that made me think of the stags in the Trophy Room or perhaps more closely, for there was nothing dignified to it, those heads on their sides that he kept in his cottage for repair.

'I am sorry,' he said after a silence, disturbed only by the noise of a bottle shattering somewhere and shouts of laughter, 'that things have ended as they have.'

'For both of us.'

'I bear you no grudge, Señorita,' he avowed, tightly.

'Nor I, you.'

'We should drink to it.'

'If you can find a glass of something chilled,' I replied, uncomfortable at the finality of his tone, for he sounded in defeat, and I thought of what Latigez had told me in the well, of Moyano taking his own life.

He went and returned in a short space, bringing with him two champagne glasses and a bottle of Pol Roger beaded with moisture. 'It's the best vintage I could find,' he said, proceeding to charge my glass. 'Myself, I can't drink it so cold.' And he reached for a bottle that had been left on one side. When his own glass was full, he clinked it against mine, and we drank, Moyano watching me briefly over the rim.

'Does it meet with your approval, Señorita?'

I nodded and took another sip before asking, rather boldly and with the encouragement of the drink in me, 'Is it true about your wife? That she took your son away from you.'

There was a pained interval. 'I told you once that Las Lágrimas is a place for those who have known loss,' he said at last. 'Yes. It's true.'

'What will happen to them?'

'I cannot say. I worry most for Alfredo and his poor lungs. Las Lágrimas was my chance to gain him back.' This gave him pause for contemplation, until he raised his glass anew. 'To families.'

Given my own history, it was a toast I had scant enthusiasm for. Nevertheless, we both drank, albeit there was very much an affected air to the ritual.

'And you, Señorita, what will you do now?'

'I do not think I will be able to find another post.'

'Berganza could help. He has many a client who I am sure would be happy to employ one of your talents.'

'Perhaps I've had my fill of gardens,' I sighed. 'I wonder if I might travel instead, see something of the continent like my grandfather did.'

'Promise me one thing. You will not return to Eduardo Gil.'

'No.'

'To travels, then.'

We drank a final toast, both draining our glasses, whereupon Moyano headed for the door.

'I do not know,' he said, 'that we will see each other in the morning. I'll make sure your horse is waiting after breakfast.'

'Señor Moyano. There was a ghost. I swear it on my life.'

'Goodbye, Señorita Kelp. Don't drink too much of the wine.'

And having spoken so, his parting words almost tender, he left me alone in the kitchen.

I remained for a long moment, feeling the estate manager's acquiescence and sadness as if I had absorbed his very emotion. Through the window, the black sky continued to flash from a storm distantly prowling the Pampas. My head felt heavy and on any other night I would have been ready for bed, but I doubted whether I could sleep with so much noise and contented myself with another glass of the excellent Pol Roger, though making the decision to indulge no more, for my brain was swirling enough already.

The centre of the bacchanalia had become the Trophy Room and it was to there I was drawn again, the space for once warm, for so many were the bodies, so energetic their activities, that the usual chill of the place had been driven from the air. The lights were piercingly bright to my eyes. Some of the staff had been playing a variation on the game of quoits, tossing Doña Javiera's hats to land on the antlers of the stags; many such remained where they had landed, at haphazard angles. Seemingly every surface – the tables, mantelpiece, bookshelves – was crowded with empty bottles and glasses. The carpet had been rolled back, the better to facilitate more dancing, for now almost everyone was whirling and staggering around, the accordion-player having abandoned the Tango to play tunes of a more urgent tempo. I weaved my way around the octagonal room, feeling the stranger amongst the crowd and hoping I might recognize at least one person, but such was the press of people that I began to feel I might suffocate, and I struggled back toward the door.

Before I had gained it, one of the stable-lads brought in Dolores. The poor girl was flushed and dizzy with drink and stood half-swamped in one of the Doña's satin dresses, the buttons at the front mostly undone. The stable-lad briefly danced with her before passing the maid on to one of his coevals, and then from man to man, they all being desperate to tread a measure with the Jezebel. She tottered and tripped often, causing the assembly to jeer at her, and I was at the point of pushing through the throng to intervene when Latigez stalked into the room and grasped hold of the maid. He hissed something into her ear and dragged her to the door – much to the caterwauls of the men – and it was at that moment, the proprietary manner in which he conducted her, that the realization came to me with little remaining doubt.

All along, I had been right! It *was* to Latigez that the girl paid her night-time visits.

I struggled through the crush of dancing bodies in an effort to reach them and put a stop to whatever Latigez planned to do to her, but even as I neared the maid, I was suddenly caught in the arms of Señor Farrido, his face ruddy, his brow sopping, who whirled me once, twice around the room before I was able to break free from his clammy grip. He shouted some drunken obscenity after me that I ignored and, to mocking laughter from the crowd, I made my escape into the hallway. I was greeted by the oil-paint eyes of Don Guido – as adventurer, courtier, gardener – and wondered how tonight's festivities compared to his parties of old. Had the staff even thought of running so wild in his day, I am sure he would have had every last one of them thrashed.

Of Dolores and Latigez there was no sign and, after searching downstairs, I clambered up the staircase and went directly to the room that had been the scene of their previous exploits. There was no indication anyone had been within all evening. I hurried back to the stairs, feeling more light-headed with each step, and up to Dolores' room in the attic. I had never before seen inside, finding it as bare as the cell of a novice, the only items of a personal nature being a small Bible on the bedstand and, lying upon the pillow of her unkemptly made bed, the toy llama I had seen her clasping the night I unmasked her in the corridor. There was a quality to the toy, something I could not entirely put my finger on, a childish, pathetic quality, that made me reach to pick it up – but instead of finding it soft and flimsy, it was heavy. I inverted it, whatever was to be found within jangling, and saw that the back was held together by a few crude stitches that took only the slightest effort to pick apart.

The toy llama spilled its contents, scores of silver pesos pouring forth on to the floor, which they hit with a noisy ringing – spinning and rolling about the room.

I waited, swaying on my feet, until every last one of them had come to a halt, trying to make sense of what I had discovered and one unpleasant explanation pushing to the fore. Two floors below, I heard the continuing sounds of the party, the shouting and accordion, though it was becoming less distinct. The door opened behind me, bringing with it a waft of ombú smoke, like old frankincense. Moyano's eyes travelled from the silver pesos scattered across the floorboards and then to me, they seeming to loom large and black. His whole bearing spoke of callousness, and reckoning, and some other, devil-sent emotion that twisted my stomach to admit.

'It made her feel special,' he said in a whisper. 'A girl no one cared about; whose parents were only too willing to send her here. I always made sure she was well recompensed. A beneficial arrangement to us all.'

'It was… you?' I had not spoken since our parting in the kitchen and was shocked to hear how slurred my words had become.

'She never complained. Her body is more resilient than ever she looks.'

'How could you… how could you hurt her like that?'

'All work and no play makes Juan a dull boy.' His voice did not sound his own. 'It was the only thing to purge my blacker moods.'

'And what of your family?'

'After the calamity of my last employer, better I was tempted by a maid than the Doña.' He was edging toward me. 'Or my English rose.'

I tried to retreat, each step requiring more effort than the last. 'You cheated her… You promised Dolores she was going to be rich… That she was going to be a lady.'

His answer was a little laugh, contemptuous and suggestive. 'She would not be the first at Las Lágrimas to be taken in by the promise of silver.'

He retrieved one of the pesos from the floor. The next moment Moyano was towering over me. He snatched up my hand, pressing the cold metal of the coin deep into my palm, and though I struggled to fight him off, I found myself too unsteady, the whole world swirling around like

[At this point a page of the journal is missing.]

Not Quite Alone

IN THE END, I suppose, it was the silence that roused me, pressing into my sunken, listing mind: a total absence of any sound, more penetrating and disturbing than any alarm. I rose slowly and thickly from the depths, blinking into the dreary light of a place that although was not unfamiliar, nor could I readily identify. As life returned to me, so did I become aware of my pounding head, my furred tongue and a thirst one could only describe as painful. I felt like I had done that noontime when I surfaced from Calista's sleeping draught, except as if I had swallowed a more potent dose. There was another sensation too, a unique soreness the details of which I shall dwell upon no further in these pages.

Springs were digging into my back and, gingerly, I pushed myself into a sitting position, coming to the realization of where I had slept with a squirm of dread. I had been in a stupor the previous night, though not totally unaware of events, yet had no recollection of staggering here. Nor what on earth would possess me to do so — for I found myself on one of the bedsteads in Tarella's cabin. Now that I was upright, a queasiness surged through my body upward into my gullet, one I knew I would be powerless to contain, and I scrambled out of the room to the front door to retch outside. My stomach heaved and convulsed several times more and, afterward, I sat miserably on my knees, panting no better than a dog, my lungs thick with mist: for a close, impenetrable fog had crept off the Pampas. I could see nothing of the lake or house and only the vague, dark substance of the woodland. All the noises of the estate had been deadened by it, even the cry of birds – indeed, for the rest of my time at Las Lágrimas, I do not recall hearing the sound of any bird ever again.

My body felt filthy, my clothes stiff with grime; more than anything, I wanted a bath. The first order of the day, however, was to slake my clawing thirst. My legs carried me stiffly to the house, past the silent, shadowed stables, entering directly into the kitchen, where I ignored the devastation from the previous night and poured myself a glass of water. A cup of *yerba mate*, or – even better – proper, English tea with milk and a teaspoon of sugar, would have been perfect, but when I placed my hand on the cooking-range it was cold. Once I had drunk my fill, I proceeded into the rest of the house, the hour earlier than I may have thought for not a soul was astir, the staff still sleeping off the effects of the party. That suited me well enough for I was in no mood for any interaction, preferring to bathe in peace. I crept to the new wing, the air of which seemed uncharacteristically crisp, and ran a bath.

The water was tepid as I slipped beneath its surface, though this did not entirely surprise for, as the house was to be vacated, I doubted Farrido would have woken himself to tend his boiler. The tap dripped noisily, echoing about the room and to the house beyond, and for the first few minutes I lay with my eyes closed, the pain at the front of my skull subsiding, before slowly, and then with rising trepidation, I came to realize *just how silent* the house was. Unnaturally so, regardless of the smothering fog.

As still and silent as a mausoleum.

I got out of the bath, towelling down myself and, as I reached for my clothes, noticed a ring of purple bruises on both my wrists, before reluctantly I dressed in my wear from yesterday, for I wanted to feel fresh, unsoiled material against my skin. Then I unlocked the door – the bolt clanging – and listened, straining to detect even the slightest of sounds. None but an immutable, awful quiet came to my ear.

I moved swiftly from room to room, seeking signs of life, and found the whole place in disarray, furniture toppled over, bedspreads pulled off anyhow and ripped, children's toys and ornaments scattered about and broken, a ubiquity of empty bottles – but not a single other person. Doña Javiera's suite had the appearance of being ransacked, clothes spilling from her drawers and wardrobes, a crumpled eiderdown lying tossed on the floor. Desperate to be free of my own attire (and not knowing if my own room had suffered a similar fate), I rummaged through the Doña's clothing, coming across a fetching plum-coloured outfit that might well fit. When I tried it for size, it could have been tailored to my shape.

Leaving my own dress where it lay, I hastened downstairs and from there to the old part of the building to continue my search, though already a terrible truth was asserting itself, for there is an undeniable mood to an empty house – and that morning Las Lágrimas was overburdened with it.

'Is anybody there?' I called out to the seething silence.

Offering a prayer that I was mistaken, I began checking every last room, my footsteps ringing out, until I came to the Trophy Room. Those animal heads not hidden by the tossed hats stared at me with baleful accusation for, if possible, this spot was in a greater disorder than the rest, littered with the detritus of the party, bottles strewn everywhere like fallen ninepieces, the charts hanging on the wall at crazy angles or frames smashed altogether, many of the books ripped from their shelves and lying broken on the floor. The false panel in the bookcase stood ajar, a filthy light flickering from the chamber within. Of all the places, it struck me as the least likely where someone might be hiding, yet such was my desperation that I stepped through the door, looking into the cell below.

The weighting junk and boards had been removed from the well and, now that there was nothing to muffle the river, it rushed noisily in the enclosed space. Perched on the brick ledge, his legs dangling recklessly over the water as if he might throw himself in at any moment, was Moyano. He was dirty and unshaven, his shirt loose and the cuffs turned up. What most caught my attention, however, was his scalp: he had shorn it clean of hair, though in the roughest manner, so that odd tufts remained alongside small cuts, some scabbed, others still trickling blood. The very sight of him made me want to vomit again – and also a little afraid; both I fought.

The estate manager rolled his face toward me, his eyes sunken and bloodshot, though they did not meet mine. 'I wondered when you'd awaken, Ursula.' His tone was deathly.

I climbed down to him and found I could not overcome a curious shrinking in his presence. 'Where is everyone?' I demanded, my voice echoing in the confines of the chamber. The ground was littered with panatela ends.

'Gone.' He had within his hand some object that he was twisting over and over, gripping then ungripping it, his forearm bulging and contracting with the motion, so that the scars upon his wrist appeared to wriggle. 'Returned to Buenos Aires or whatever slum Agramonte dragged them from.'

'You can't mean everyone.'

'Everyone.'

'What about Dolores?' I asked.

'Gone.'

'Señor Latigez? Farrido?'

'Gone. All gone.' Still he refused to meet my eye. 'Taking with them the horses and wagons and every last means to cross the Pampas.'

'Then how will I leave? How will you?'

His hands ceased their restlessness and I saw that he was holding a bloodied cut-throat razor, the type used by gentlemen for shaving, its handle monogrammed with the Don's initials. 'I said nothing of wanting to.'

'Did no one ask after me?'

'Only Latigez, and he was easy enough to convince you had already left.'

'So none knows I am here?'

He rubbed his shorn skull, giving a satisfied little shake of his head. 'No.'

'No one but you and me?' I asked.

'No one but you and me,' he replied.

'You're lying. The whole staff can't have left – there hasn't been the time. I would have heard them.'

'You have been out cold these two days. I was beginning to fret I'd given you too much of Calista's barbiturate in your champagne. Or you had drunk too freely of the bottle I left you.'

The walls seemed to fold in on themselves. Black spots swelled and burst before my eyes so that I feared I might swoon. I had to reach out to steady myself, much to the amusement of the estate manager.

'What have you done?' I said, when finally I found my voice.

'I did warn you, Little Bear.' He spoke with a vicious calmness. 'You have ruined all I had hoped for. My last chance. You are to blame—'

'I did nothing but try and help.'

'If I am not leaving Las Lágrimas. Then neither are you.'

'So we two are all alone here?'

'Yes,' he replied with a definite and terrible simplicity, before meeting my gaze for the first time, the look in his eye knowing. 'Well… perhaps not quite alone.'

Amidst the Amaranth & Moly

I REFUSED TO believe him.

I ran through the shifting, silent mist to the stables, checking each stall in turn, and was greeted by nothing but the stink of old manure. All the horses were gone. A search of the remaining outbuildings provided no other form of transport with which to cross the Pampas. My chest was tight, each breath I took shallow and increasingly an effort. I was determined to maintain as calm a mind as possible. Even if Moyano truly did wish to abandon me here – an eventuality I was unable entirely to believe – I was not convinced he intended to exile himself. I had left him in the secret chamber, twirling the razor-blade between his fingers, yet however black his present melancholy, once it had passed, he would want to return to civilization if for no other motive than for his beloved Alfredo – from which I drew the conviction he must have the means. Somewhere he had surely to have secreted a horse...

Even as the thought came to me, I experienced a flood of relief such that I might have wept.

Dahlia!

Moyano had stabled her at his cottage for this very purpose. I had persuaded myself, perhaps naïvely, that it was not his true intention to leave me alone on the estate, that rather it was a threat. He wished to punish me further for what he considered my misdemeanours but at the final stroke would not see it through. Nevertheless, such was my distrust of the man, and in shaving his head a lunacy seemed to be preying on him, that I considered it wise to reach Dahlia before he did.

I hurried in the direction of the garden, skirting the wall, and hoping I could still remember the path through the woods to the cottage. I passed by the rear of the house and into a mistiness that smelt unlike any I have ever inhaled. It clung to my nostrils, billows of the sweetest, most floral perfume one could imagine, as aromatic as commingled rose, honeysuckle and jasmine – the smell of early summer. The smell of hope and happiness. I slowed and came to a startled halt.

The door-in-the-wall, the door fastened tight for the duration of my stay at Las Lágrimas, was standing wide open.

The fragrant air wafting through the doorway was not the only invitation to step through it. From the Treasure Garden, I heard the tinkle and splash of water as it played in the fountain. There was even a fleeting moment, as though every one of my senses was being tempted, when I swore I tasted strawberries, warm and ripe with juice as if picked and immediately popped into my mouth. It was all so beguiling, bringing to me memories of carefree summer days at Grandfather's, that the possibility of any wickedness, of being forcefully drawn away from my purpose of finding the horse, did not occur to me. I stepped through the doorway as one walking in her sleep.

I found myself in another world, the garden transformed or – as might be more accurate to call it – restored to the former glory Berganza and Don Paquito had spoken of. I was on what Sir Romero had described as the 'Strolling Borders', a straight path of lustrous shingle, either side of me profusions of colour and form and scent as I have never experienced. The sheer breadth and variety of the planting challenged my knowledge: I saw poppies that lifted their heads to the sun, nepeta, acanthus, geraniums, monarda, plumbago, to name the merest few, as well as scores I was unable to identify at all. There was magic indeed in the fingers of whoever had planted this cornucopia.

Some part of my intelligence spoke than none of this was possible, and I was compelled to reach out and touch a larkspur to prove the vision before me. Its silken petals felt more warm and pulsing with life than anything I had handled in all my weeks spent at the garden. In fact, the whole climate seemed as changed as my surroundings, the chill and last of the fog having worn away from the air, which was now as balmy as a Whitsuntide afternoon, that perfect time in the year where everything is at its most vital, before high summer whose abundance and darkening colours, though beautiful, carries within the unspoken melancholy that all too soon the season will turn.

I walked on, feeling heady and unlike myself, through purple and golden beds of amaranth and moly, as in the poem of Tennyson, I thought, stopping to delight at every new wonder, lowering my nose to sample bloom after bloom. A long drift of lilies shimmered in shades of magenta, murex and a pink that evaded description. One heliotrope had an almondy scent of such intensity it was as if I were gorging on marzipan; another was like a spoonful of the cherriest of cherry pies. A pang, almost an ache in my belly, came to me for I wished to be ambling here by Grandfather's side, for only he would have appreciated the immaculate order and sensuousness of it all, I daresay joking it was wasted on the likes of Don Paquito. At the remembrance of my employer, another possibility suggested itself.

Could the curse have lifted?

For it seemed unimaginable that such a wondrous, joyful place – and I felt joy in every step I took – should exist if its power remained. Might the terrible injuries of León have sated its malevolence? I must hasten and tell Señor Moyano, I mused dreamily. Perhaps all would be well, his position secure, his family with him once more; perhaps I might remain as Head Gardener, proof at last of my abilities and my parents rightly proud of me; perhaps even, when their son was healed, the Agramontes themselves would return. I must tell Moyano, I thought to myself again…

But first, the garden beckoned me with yet further charms.

For I had surely to visit the Treasure Garden, and meandered my way to it through the various sections and areas I recognized from the Lepping plan, until I came to what was the heart of his design – only then did I understand the claims made in its name. I stood enraptured in the sweet, lulling air.

The *Jardín de tesoro* grew lush and glittering, broad and yet intimate too. At the centre, the water in the fountain tumbled musically from one tier to the next, and radiating forth from it, like verdant ripples that made one feel both protected and secluded, were the parterres, each one brimming with roses more vivid and vibrant than any others I have known, the bloomheads scattered with a myriad of other flowers, of colours within colours – scabious, asters, red and tangerine-coloured dahlias, more nepeta, alchemilla, violets, anemones – all shimmering like a hoard of gems. When at last I was able to break from this flourishing, my eye was taken to the meadow, for there was no longer any Wailing Wall, the grass gilded with tiny buttercups and, in the near distance, a dozen white stags contentedly grazed, one of their number pausing to observe me before returning to his pasture. For the first time since passing through the open door I felt a stirring of uncertainty, some muffled jot of my brain returning to the horse Dahlia and my need to find her before Moyano roused himself from the well.

Even as the notion tried to take form, the swirls of colours about me grew more intense, the air more ambrosial and languorous, scented now with ylang-ylang. I heard the happy drone of bees going about their daily harvest and from an unidentifiable place, at once close by and yet nowhere in sight, the excited cries of a child playing, a fleeting burble of laughter and japes, as once I had played in a Cambridgeshire garden.

The thought came to me as sharp as smelling-salts.

Summoning all my resolve, I set my back against that mesmerising prospect and began to walk away, the nausea and rawness I had woken with revisiting me more insistently than ever, though I disregarded it, steadily quickening my step. From behind, on the gravel, I heard another giving chase, the heavy tread of a boot followed by a dragging sound, and then I was at full pelt, running to put as great a distance between myself and that dreadful noise, gripped by a sense that, although I did not dare to look round, behind me the garden was once more sprouting tangles of weeds to strangle the flowers and that all that had briefly flourished was falling back into neglect.

I flew through the door and did not stop, continuing until I was breathless, navigating the paths through the woodland, my face slick with perspiration. I had lost all sense of time. The fog had risen, lifting to the treetops, albeit the afternoon remained dull and murky, the hour-hand having progressed remorselessly whilst the garden bewitched me; sundown would soon be upon the estate.

After a number of false turns, and then more through good luck than judgement, I gained Moyano's cottage. No smoke curled from the chimney, nor did any lamp shine from within. I went directly to the stable at the rear, feeling a lift of the heart as I saw the walnut of Dahlia's coat over the top of the door – and then a sickening horror and hatred of Moyano. Minutes earlier I had been in an ecstasy of scent and colour, now it was all I could do not to weep and gag, the pendulum swing between the two emotions so rapid as to cause my head to swim and legs to buckle.

I howled.

Moyano had taken his razor to Dahlia in the manner of a

gaucho slaughtering cattle, severing the tendons in both her hind legs to bring her down to her haunches, then thrusting the blade into her neck and working it round. A torrent of blood had poured from her, though, in the worst moment of all, I found her not yet expired, deep, awful sob-like sounds and chokings emerging from her mouth. There was nothing I could do. The knife responsible for this atrocity was not to be seen nor, even if I had recovered it, would I have possessed the courage to end Dahlia's misery.

I struggled to my feet, slipping in the straw and blood, wetting my hands as I fought to right myself, and staggered toward the cottage, finally slumping when the stable was no longer in view, a coppery taste lodged in my throat. From inside the house Moyano had built to win back his family came a clawing and whining.

'Vasca?' I called out.

The dog barked in reply and I opened the front door, the German shepherd shooting forth, her back criss-crossed in the whip marks of a savage beating. She darted through the bare garden, to the edge of the trees, where she halted to watch me, her mint-and-blue eyes seeming to warn against venturing into the cottage and whatever I might find therein.

I was trembling all over as I stepped inside.

The first thing to strike me was the acrid stench of ombú wood, as if a great fire of it had burnt for hours until nothing remained but the most bitter ashes. There was a stillness to the air and, if I had not known differently, it might have been possible to believe no living creature had stepped here for a long, long time. At the table where we had taken afternoon tea, his back toward me, sat Moyano, the baldness of his skull still a shock. Lying in random fashion about him were the unrepaired heads of stags and deers.

I stole round the table in order to see him properly and although I closed my eyes at once, the image was impressed on my mind evermore.

His face was rigid and already tinged with the faintest of blues, a shade not unlike the colour of forget-me-nots, he propped up at the table in a parody of a miser, surrounded by stacks of silver pesos. Resting between the coins was his left arm, the sleeve of his shirt rolled up and sopping, he having dragged his razor in a single stroke from wrist to elbow in the manner Latigez advised. Cradled in the estate manager's lap was the picture of a woman and child; but not that of his own family. Rather, it was an old daguerreotype – for the last faces Moyano had looked upon in this world were those of Tarella's wife and son.

A Fair Plan

I WANTED TO SING. As I sat in the kitchen with Vasca, nursing the cruel whip marks across her back, my hands continuing to tremble, I wanted to sing loudly and bright – to stir my heart. To ward off the accumulation of horror I felt. For the bruises around my wrists had grown more purple and tender, whilst those hideous things I had witnessed in Moyano's cottage kept repeating themselves in my head. Had he truly wanted to take his life, or was it the power of this place that had driven him to it? The same power putting the daguerreotype in his hand, perhaps even making him shear his head. I could think of no other explanation.

Nor could I rid myself of the estate manager's final words to me, of us being 'not quite alone'. Had he been aware of the haunting all along, only his fixation on his son compelling him to remain at Las Lágrimas when any sane man would have fled?

Was he as familiar with the axeman as I?

Yet as much as I desired to sing, the only tunes that came to mind belonged to Gilbert & Sullivan, hardly my preferred musical choice. I had to settle for scraps of 'A British Tar' and 'Monarch of the Sea', and cannot say they brought much respite.

Thus I abandoned my recital and instead tidied the mess around me, grateful to have such a humdrum, domestic distraction, and afterward made myself a supper of cold brisket, sharing the meat with Vasca. As she finished the last morsels, pushing her food-bowl across the floor, it made a loud scraping noise that, in the stillness of the house, set me further on edge. I could not speak for the dog, but for myself there was no relish in my chewing, it simply being a practical business to keep up my strength.

Once we were both done, I allowed out Vasca by the kitchen door to relieve herself and paid my own brief visit to the downstairs lavatory. Then, leaving a trail of lamps burning at the lowest flicker, to preserve their oil, the German shepherd obediently followed me upstairs to my room, where I barricaded the door, for whatever illusion of security it might offer, lighted more lamps and stoked the fire I had got going earlier. There was a glass of water on the side, a chamber-pot beneath my bed: I had no need to leave the room again until daybreak. As evening arrived, the wind had risen, and steadily increased in force as the hours progressed, squalls buffeting the corners of the house and rattling the windows. The mercury edged downward.

Given my predicament, I was as much in command of my nerves as could be expected, and though my heart continued to beat uncomfortably, I had the makings of a fair, if not altogether pleasant, plan to see me through.

When, several days earlier, I had stood at the gates of

the estancia, looking out over the illimitable plain and contemplated my flight, I had calculated there was more danger to be found in crossing the Pampas than remaining. There may have been a most extreme change in my circumstances since then, but those odds, as far as I could judge, had not much shortened. Berganza was due to arrive with his next delivery within a fortnight. All I had to do was wait for him. I had not forgotten Namuncura's parting advice for me to stay in the house, and it was my intention not to leave the confines of the building again. I planned to put the place to rights after the mess and wreck of the party, and when that was done find other ways to occupy myself, spinning out the days before my rescue. I had a library of books to read in the Trophy Room; I might even finish the Conrad. Strange the trifles one can suck comfort from!

My most troubling apprehension was that word might reach Berganza of what had befallen the Agramontes and that once more Las Lágrimas had been abandoned. There was no counter to this, I could only pray that without written instruction to the contrary, he would honour my order and return to the estancia. If not, I would give it a day or two past his expected arrival and if he had still yet to show... why then, I must trust in myself to conceive of some alternative means of salvation.

'Not to forget,' I said, giving Vasca a resounding kiss, 'that I have you for company.' I had spoken in the most hushed voice, yet still my words sounded like an intrusion.

The events of the day had left me weary in a dull, spent way, the effects of the drug I had been given, and the soreness in my lower body, still making their presence known so that, more than anything, all I wanted was to escape into slumber. I dressed for bed, wearing a shift beneath my nightgown, for the temperature had continued to decline, and when I was done, climbed beneath the sheets, having lowered the lamps, though not extinguished them. I refused to sleep in the dark. Before I left Moyano's cottage, I had been sufficiently collected to search for his torch. Now I placed it within easy reach on the nightstand, wedged securely between *Nostromo* and my gardening volumes so that there was no risk of it rolling away. I encouraged Vasca to establish herself at my side and was more reassured by her large, warm being and doggy smell than I could convey.

It would be a nerve-trying experiment – but the days would pass. Berganza would arrive.

Hideously Afraid

IT WAS THE dead of night. I awakened very suddenly from a dream: I had been at the window, staring out across the front lawn. In the centre of the grass stood a solitary, wasted figure, dressed in a black poncho. In his hand, held high, was an old-fashioned lantern that swung in the howling wind, causing his shadow to elongate and shrink... Elongate and shrink... so that when his outline was at its most monstrous it covered almost the entire area in darkness. He became suddenly aware of my presence, twisting round to glare accusingly at me. I expected no other than the axeman, though as his features resolved themselves, it was not a phantom that confronted me – but Moyano. Then I had woken.

I could not stop myself. I left the warmth of the covers – Vasca glanced up; the air was frightfully cold – and threw aside the curtains. A yellow moon was beginning to rise in a sky now stark and cloudless. The night was a wild one indeed; the lawn, however, quite empty.

I went back to bed.

A number of violent tremors coursed through my body, jolting me awake again, this time with a cry, for I was convinced I had heard a breaking and splintering as if an axe were being brought against wood. For a terrified instant in that crossing from sleep to wakefulness, every fibre of my body had turned rigid, and I looked to the door of my room and the chair wedged under the handle in fear that some force was smashing it down. It remained quite undisturbed, as did Vasca who lay gently snoring by my side. And so it was that, after a brief interval, I came to realize that what had actually roused me was not a sound, rather the cold.

The room was freezing cold. Crushingly cold.

Although the lamps continued to burn, the fire was long since ash. Every inch of my skin, and especially those exposed parts, my ears and nose, a foot that had slipped from under the covers whilst I slept, was ice. My breath escaped in thick clouds in front of my face. Such was the unnaturalness of the temperature that I could quite fancy the whole house had become as one of Mr Houghton's reefer-ships, those vessels that transport frozen beef carcasses to Britain. I rescued my foot and tugged the blankets over my head, nestling tighter to Vasca, and tried in vain to renew my interrupted slumber. More than once I had the impression of dropping off, and yet at no point was I convinced actually to have done so. It was simply too damned cold. I lay there, listening to the casements on the side of the house box and clatter in the storm, unable to control the shivering of my body.

From close by came a cracking, and with it the memory of hard winter mornings when Grandfather and I, wrapped in scarves and furs, would visit the garden pond with one of his golf clubs to break the ice.

There was another crack, Vasca pricking up an ear, and I searched the room to identify whence the sound came. Finding no obvious source, I got out of bed for the second occasion that night, letting out a sharp exhalation as my feet touched the gelid floor, and opened the curtain to make sure the window was not unwittingly open. The corners of the panes were occluded with frost. On the inside. Then the cracking sound again, this time plainly from my nightstand and, to be specific, my glass of water. It had frozen solid, fissures opening and closing in the ice.

I reached to put on my slippers and the thickest pair of woollen socks I could find and afterward, on instinct, Rivacoba's poncho, which I tugged over my nightgown. The fire I attempted to bring back to life but it refused to take, the wind blasting down the chimney forever snuffing out the flames before they had a chance to establish. I deliberated over what to do, then shook Vasca.

'Wake up, girl,' I whispered. 'We're going to the new wing.'

The boiler may have been extinguished, nevertheless the recent construction of that section of the building meant it could only be warmer, and I thought it more likely we could pass a comfortable night there huddled in Doña Javiera's counterpanes and eiderdowns.

I took Moyano's torch, not immediately turning it on, for I reasoned that I had left lamps sufficient burning in the corridor to illuminate my way and wanting to preserve the life of the battery. My first surprise was when I opened the door. The corridor was in complete darkness, a draught having snuffed out the lights. I think my nerve would have faltered there and then if it was not for Vasca unfazed at my side and the piercing cold to urge me on. I flicked the torch-switch, proceeding carefully to the stairs, where here, too, I found the lamps gone and, my free hand on the railing, began to descend into the inkiness below. I kept the beam pointed ahead and for that reason missed the wine bottle on the staircase, though I would have sworn not to having seen any littering it earlier.

It flew away from my foot, crashing and bouncing down every step, each drop jarring horribly on my nerves, until it reached the hallway where it rolled noisily across the floor before coming to a halt.

The sounds echoed through the house until they could no longer be heard over the wind.

I did not dare to breathe.

But when, after a minute came and went, nothing else happened, I let out a relieved exhalation and, with greater vigilance, continued my descent.

In the hallway, the lamps had fared better against the draughts than those upstairs, for the majority continued, their small flames fluttering in the dark so that they cast weird patterns of light upon the portraits of Don Guido. Before retiring to bed, I had made sure every door off the hallway was fastened and was reassured to see they remained so, even if they banged and juddered alarmingly in the storm. I headed toward the new wing. Vasca's attention, however, was captured by something in the opposite direction so that she broke away and scampered to the Trophy Room, where she pawed at the bottom of the doorframe. I called her to heel and, when she refused, went over to the dog in order to drag her back. Still she would have none of it. Disinclined to open the door, I placed my ear to it instead: beneath the wind there came only the ever-present subterranean rushing.

'There's nothing,' I said, as much to soothe myself as the animal.

I yanked her by the scruff and, in doing so, accidentally caught the wounds on her back, she rearing up on to her hind legs, managing to catch the handle, and causing the door to swing open. Vasca was through before there was chance to restrain her. For myself, I remained on the threshold, directing the torch after the dog as she tore around the room. It was deathly cold, the drapes drawn tight so that there was not the chance of moonbeams. Moyano had left the secret panel in the bookcase open, before making the fateful journey to his cottage, though, inexplicably, taken the effort to straighten the skewed maps and spared the indignity of the trophy-heads by removing from them the Doña's headgear. Everything else appeared as it had been: the vestiges of the party in the same disorder.

The German shepherd continued to chase circles, increasingly more frantic, growling and barking. A gamey stench hung in the air that I had never before smelt in the house.

'Vasca!' I hissed short-temperedly, for I had grown weary of her behaviour. 'Vasca!' Still she refused to obey and so, cautiously and not without misgivings, I stepped into the middle of the room to grasp hold of her.

At that moment the wind died to a whisper, the stillness more unnerving than the fury that preceded it. At first there was nothing, and then, in that eerie and ominous quiet, my ear caught a sound.

I heard breathing.

Not my own breath. Not that of the dog. Something, or someone, else. A long-drawn, rumbling snort.

I slashed my torch through the darkness, spinning in a full circle. The beam revealed not a thing in its path, which afforded some tiny relief, and yet the breathing continued. I heard it clearly and unmistakably, just to hand, somewhere very near me, a laboured respiration. I searched the room with my light, penetrating the blackness of the corners, investigating behind the furniture. There was nothing there! Yet from the rhythmic in- and exhalation, from Vasca's distress, I knew I could not be alone. My heart was pounding with such ferocity I felt giddy, my tongue cleaved dryly to the roof of my mouth. I concentrated more closely on the noise, hoping I was confused in hearing it or, if not, that I could determine exactly from where it might be coming and, in doing so, I understood it did not have a single source – but many.

I was hideously afraid.

Every strand of fur on Vasca's body was standing erect. She had stopped her chasing and stood in front of the wall of white stags, staring intently upward to the ceiling, emitting a low, anxious growl. I followed her gaze with the torch, past the jutting animal heads, and just then the beam caught the faintest shimmer of movement. I directed it back toward the highest stag and felt a prickling across my scalp that ran to the nape of my neck before plunging the length of my spine.

The white stag, its head mounted on a plaque, its eyes empty black marbles, was breathing.

The lightbeam shook uncontrollably in my hand, but I saw – and let me state it with no doubt whatsoever; not then, not now – tiny jets of steam rising from its nostrils, the same nostrils dilating and contracting with each breath. I moved the torch to the other stags in the arrangement, one after the other.

They were all breathing.

I cried out, stepping backward and stumbling and somehow in my fright the torch dropped from my hand. It died immediately, plunging the room into a darkness as can scarcely be conceived, a darkness brutal to the senses. I scrabbled around on the floorboards and with a luck beyond hope managed to find it. I pressed the switch and, to my utter relief, once more found myself with light. Then the torch's lamp blinked and died. I cursed like a dragoon and thumped it against my palm and it returned to life, though intermittently, flicking on and off thereafter. I did not shine it again in the direction of the stags. The incessant rumble of their respiration was as much as I could bear without having to see it.

I retraced my steps to the door and commanded Vasca to join me, an instruction that was soon begging when she refused. The dog was lying flat-bellied in submission beneath the stags, an endless whine escaping her throat.

Outside, there was a roar and the storm picked up anew, more ferocious than ever, a blast of wind hitting the house with such force it felt as if the building shook to its foundations.

The secret panel to the well slammed shut, startling Vasca

from her cowering position. She shot past, near knocking me over, near making me drop the torch a second time, and into the hallway, crashing down its length, veering from one side to the next, causing the lamps to overturn. It was only through blind good fortune that their founts did not spill any fuel and ignite. One by one the lamps went out, until I was left with no source of illumination except my failing, temperamental torch.

I groped my way after her, casting my thin light about me until it landed on the portrait of Don Guido as master gardener.

The canvas had been mutilated, flaps of the material hanging loosely like pieces of torn skin. There was a cut through the eyes and nose. A cut to the neck and heart. A cut to both of the hands at the point of the wrist in the custom by which Moslems punish their thieves. Running down that slashed face, glistening in the torch light, were what I first took to be tears, before realizing it was, in fact, spittle.

I became aware of a presence behind me.

I had heard neither footsteps nor a creak of the floorboards nor any other stirring, yet had the absolute, certain sense there was another close by.

My throat narrowed, making each intake of air a struggle, my heart thumping so rapidly, so fiercely, that I felt my pulse in the roots of my molar-teeth. I detected the faintest whiff of bonfires and blood, followed swiftly by an assault on my nostrils of pestilent earth and rotting leaves. Such was my dread that others of my physical functions began to decline, the strength in my limbs weakening, causing my legs to bow and the arm holding the torch to wilt, until it was no longer pointed in front of me but was directed, trembling, at the floor to leave everything above the height of the wainscoting, the mutilated features of Don Guido included, invisible in the darkness.

I felt two large, coarse hands placed heavily on my shoulders.

I could not move. I could not breathe.

The hand on my right eased my poncho to one side and traced down the length of my arm, barely touching my sleeve and yet, at the same time, as if it were under the material and against my very skin, so that I knew its roughness, the calluses and leathery fingertips. A hand, ice cold, that had endured years of labour, years of hard winds and weather.

It reached my wrist, probing those bruises I had woken with in the cabin, so that given any other circumstance I would have flinched, then down to my own hand, which was clenched in terror. One after the other my fingers were prised apart until my palm was open and exposed.

Something solid was placed in my hand and my fingers made to curl around it.

It was a length of what felt like wood: a handle worn smooth to the touch. My heart missed a beat, then seemed to stop altogether.

I was grasping the shaft of an axe.

Beneath the Ombú Trees

WHETHER I SCREAMED, whether my throat and lungs were capable of such a cry, I do not recall.

I fled, letting the axe clatter from my grip, heedless of any thought or direction, reeling and lurching along the hallway, dropping the torch, my hands flailing against the walls to keep me upright, knocking the portraits and causing them to swing madly, blundering through the front door into the roaring night with only one instinct. To get away.

Only when I gained the centre of the lawn, believing myself safer in this windtorn spot than the confines of the building, for I was able to see widely in every direction, did I feel the slightest lessening of my fear. A half-moon, huge and brimstone-yellow, hung low in a sky of dim stars. The grass had left my slippered-feet wet and numb. Glancing back, I was sure I saw a dark figure as he passed out of the house, leaving the deeper darkness of the hallway behind, and make toward me with a vanishing swiftness.

I did not wait to confirm what I had seen but took flight again, covering the rest of the distance across the lawn, reaching the Imperial Avenue, which I dashed across to the far side and then hid behind one of the ombú trees, taking what little comfort I could from the solid, shielding strength of its trunk. Its branches thrashed above me in the wind, sounding as breakers do when beaten against the shore by a tempest.

It took some time for me to peep out from my hiding place, though even then I was unable to control the tremors wracking my body.

Of the axeman, or any other horror, there was no sign.

I slumped down, trying to imagine what I should do next, the wind throwing my hair about my face, when, by degrees, the darkness began to diminish around me. I tasted suddenly blood.

Some distance from my position, at that place where the tree was missing along the avenue, a light had appeared, a single orb held at the height of man. A second light grew from the shadows to join it, then a third and fourth, until there stood a spectral retinue of perhaps some two dozen men all dressed in a black broadcloth long since out of style, all holding heavy iron-lanterns. A number also clasped carbines, whilst others were dragged forth by dogs on straining leashes, the beasts snapping and barking viciously, sounding no less than like a pack of starving wolves. There was the same wicked merriment as I had witnessed on the last occasion – of a great sport being at hand, for something held their attention – and between their laughter I heard calls for more wine, more meat, for women and song.

A man, their leader, stepped to the head of the crowd

and, with a convulsion, I recognized his face as the one I had most recently seen tattered and spat upon in canvas. Upon his head was a feathered, scarlet cap of quaint form. He was joined by the one whose voice on the previous occurrence had reminded me of Berganza, and now I understood must be his father. He spoke:

Look, he boomed. *It's the gardener.*

Tarella, responded Don Guido, his voice inexpressibly harsh.

For the first time, I became aware of what so captivated the crowd, the focus of their amusement and taunting. Sprawled before them, his shin bone bleeding and broken in the teeth of a mantrap, was a man with the appearance of a labourer and a head of raven-black hair. He writhed in pain, gasping and sobbing in an extremity of panic.

For all my own fear, the injustice of the scene blazed in me. I understood these were phantoms, yet Tarella seemed as present, as substantial, as any soul I had met since my arrival on the estate. It might have been Calista lying there, or the Mapuche boys. What would I have done if it were one of them? I did not think, but stood forth from my hiding place.

In that instant, Tarella looked up at me – no, directly through me as if I were the one not truly present – reaching out a blood-soaked hand to mine, his eyes beseeching in the sulphurous light.

Run! he urged. *Get away from this place. As far as you can go…*

I froze where I stood.

Berganza senior drank deeply from a bottle, wiping a

sleeve across his bearded-lips when he was done. *We should string him up for this*, he said, to which there was general and hearty agreement.

No, came Don Guido's reply. A dreadful smile stretched across his face. *The dogs need feeding*.

And, with the downward command of his finger, the pack was unleashed, snarling and gnashing and descending on the helpless Tarella.

Before I was conscious of my actions, I had spun on my heel and was at a dash. Running the length of the driveway, running as I have never done before and pray never need do so again for as long as I shall live. Behind me I heard ripping, tearing sounds. And screams. Screams that will be forever my nightmare. Screams that echoed through the trees, high-pitched and with the uttermost strains of agony, and which turned my heart sick at the misery of them.

I did not stop, not even when my lungs were fully out of air and ready to burst, my limbs burning at my exertion – sprinting with a speed and endeavour I did not believe my legs possessed. I was slathered in the coldest sweat. My chest heaved. Yet I did not slacken my pace for, as my body met its limits, the dark, knotted forest to my sides came to life with the bay and hot-breathed snap of hounds, the noise bearing down on me, closer and closer, until it was not behind me, or anywhere around – but somehow in my ear.

Finally, the front gates loomed. I raced through them and did not cease my flight until I must have covered another good half-mile.

Only then was I felled by exhaustion. I dropped as instantly as if a marksman had found me in his sights, and lay on the ground in a fit of terror, sick and light-headed, taking in great draughtfuls of oxygen. The wind tore overhead and there I remained, the hours without meaning, too numbed to think, mindlessly watching the constellations as they spiralled across the heavens, until little by little their distant radiance began to wane. Presently, the eastern sky was transformed from black to grey to the palest of damasks, brightening all around as if a pink lamp had been given more wick, and, as the first streak of sunrise let itself be known, so came to me the most desperate realization. I had left behind Vasca.

Once More into the House

TELL ME, WHAT other choice did I have? I doubted very much that my nerves were of a robustness to withstand another night in the house, let alone the dozen or more before Berganza was due, assuming, that is, he came at all. No, there was only one possibility.

I must attempt to make my way back to Chapaledfú.

By my reckoning the journey on foot was of at least four days. To undertake this with neither provisions nor the proper clothing was to invite failure. On my feet I wore only dainty slippers! Even if it were not for Vasca, by sheer necessity I had no alternative other than to stouten my heart and return to the house. Thus the morning found me.

I waited until the sun had risen high, though it was soon little more than a smudge of light for, as the wind continued its relentless bluster, there was a new invasion of clouds that covered the whole sky, leaving it low and colourless. As I approached the front gate, I saw that one of the bronze lions that sat atop the pillars had been toppled off and lay broken in the dirt. My heart beat at an uncommon pace as I slipped between the gates and began to march the driveway.

It seemed that no time elapsed before I reached the Imperial Avenue. In the precise situation of the missing tree was a mantrap, its metal old and rusty, its teeth snapped shut. There was no other sign of that hideous and horrible spectacle I had witnessed hours earlier. I passed the trap, giving it the widest of berths, suddenly thinking of how Moyano had taken the fallen ombú from this spot to build his cottage, the leftovers used for firewood. How much of that smoke must he have inhaled? Taking it into his lungs, the particles percolating through his bloodstream until they were deep inside him. Part of him. Possessing him. I was not sure why the thought came to me, nor its pertinence, and now was not the time to contemplate it – for I was approaching the front door, the thud of my heart becoming louder and harder. Carefully, I swung it open, half-praying that Vasca would bound out to greet me.

She did not.

I must have lingered on the threshold for a full five minutes, building up my resolve to enter only to realize what little of it I possessed. The hallway was gloomy and quiet; the great clutter of empty bottles, of wasted and strewn food had been tidied away overnight. The extremity of cold temperature – which when I dwelt upon it left me to conjecture whether it had been 'summoned' to drive me out – had passed, though a profound chill remained. There came a sharp-drawn inhalation from the depths of the house, sucking a gust of wind past me, its sound mournful and harping. The torn flaps of Don Guido's canvas, and now I saw that every last one of the portraits had been attacked, flittered briefly and settled.

I went first to the kitchen and although famished I did not dare stop to eat. From the larder I gathered armfuls of supplies: tins of corned-beef and sardines (both of which I planned to share with Vasca), lima- and butter-beans, jars of preserved peaches. Next I visited the wine cellar, hesitating as the door creaked open. Beyond the first few racks it was in complete darkness. Managing not to step inside, I lifted the nearest three bottles I could clasp, pouring the contents of two down the sink before refilling them with water and stopping their corks. The third bottle I kept intact, hoping an occasional swig of wine might fortify me on my journey.

Upstairs, my bedroom already wore an unlived in air. I hurriedly changed my clothes, discarding Doña Javiera's dress and putting on a chemise, two pairs of stockings, the one on top of the other, and the thickest, warmest outfit I possessed to which I added those items that would be the lightest to carry but might offer me the best protection from the elements – a sheepskin jerkin, my muffler-scarf, gloves, winter socks. All this I would wear beneath Rivacoba's poncho.

It was as I was freeing my fur-lined hat from its box that I thought I heard a movement in the corridor outside.

I stopped to listen, pausing my breath. The stillness of the house was awful, disturbed only by thumps of wind that rattled the windows. It was not the pad-pad of dog paws as I might have wished, rather the shimmer of material as on those nights when Dolores had slipped past my room.

I grasped the doorknob, hoping that by some twist-of-fortune the maid had also been trapped here and that we might cross the Pampas together.

Not a thing stirred in the corridor.

For the final time, I cast my eyes over my bedroom and the personal possessions I was abandoning; they were mostly too cumbersome to carry. What would become of them? I wondered. Would layers of dust gather upon them as they mouldered and fell into decay as, indeed, must the whole house? Might one day a stranger enter the wreckage of this room and speculate as to why these items had been discarded?

On the small table I had used as my desk I saw the gold fountain-pen Grandfather had given me for my twenty-first birthday. I retrieved it, placing it securely within the pocket of my dress, but leaving Sir Romero's plans and the dried, crimson irises I had pressed between its folds, and considered again some unknown individual arriving at the house in some far-off future. Would that person arrive wary and alert, as well they should, or full of naïve optimism as had I?

Was it my obligation to leave a word of warning?

I spent no more than ten minutes searching the house for Vasca, sneaking from room to room as might a burglar; such was the steady accumulation of dread in me, I was unable to face a longer period and even in that short time it felt like eternities came and went. There was no sign of the dog. When it came to the Trophy Room I pressed my ear to the closed door. No sound, of any description, broke the silence – but I did not dare to open it.

I retrieved my Ayres & Lee boots and revisited the kitchen, where I packed the food (not forgetting a tin-opener) and bottles inside my knapsack, then laid both it and my poncho on the table, afterward exiting the house by the backdoor and resuming my hunt for Vasca.

Being free of the dismal, oppressive confinement of the house did not lessen the tension in my chest, nor did I breathe more easily, for as I slunk about outside I had the increasing sensation of being observed and of the patience of that observer running thin. I felt as if at any moment some terrible happening might befall me.

I hurried around the garden, under the shadow of the black, pagan wall, visiting as many of the dog's favourite spots as I knew and, afterward, ran to the stables and then the meadow and back again, keeping as far distant from Tarella's cabin as possible. Should the slightest memory of his mauling enter my head, I at once dismissed it; I neither understood what I had seen last night nor wanted to dwell on its meaning. Beneath the vast, featureless sky, every location I visited had the feeling of long abandonment, a sort of emptiness of human endeavour, so that the recent comings-and-goings of the house might never have happened. But if the ghost had succeeded in driving out the living, there was no sense of exultation, or even residual anger.

Instead, an atmosphere of loss, mingled with injustice and aching despair, pervaded the whole place.

In the end, and as I grew evermore desperate, I began to

call Vasca's name aloud, shouting for her to come to me, my voice echoing eerily around the grounds, though to do so felt incomparably reckless, like lighting a beacon deep within enemy territory. When the German shepherd still did not appear, my agitation grew worse. I wanted to cry tears of frustration. For I had placed much of my determination to cross the Pampas, the courage and resilience to do so, in the assumption we would travel together.

But the sun had already reached its zenith and, as each minute passed, I was acutely aware that soon the afternoon would commence its inevitable surrender to the darkness. I wanted not just to be away from the estancia but to have put a good many miles between myself and it before nightfall. There remained the chance that Vasca had returned to the familiarity of Moyano's cottage but – regardless of how dear the animal was to me, regardless of how I yearned to have another beating heart by my side on the journey ahead – I could not have ventured to that place had I been offered all the treasures of the world.

'Vasca!' I yelled, no longer caring how my quavering voice disturbed the hush. 'Where are you, girl? Vasca, please! *Vasca!*'

It was futile. The estate was too large and sprawling if she did not respond to her name and my courage to persist had already been stretched to its furthest limit.

And so reluctantly, with the bleakest of hearts, I accepted I must leave alone.

I felt numbed as I made my path back to the house via the front lawn, following a circuitous loop, past places I had not yet searched. Waiting by the front door were the knapsack and poncho I had left on the kitchen table. The most hateful hands had flung them out, a number of the tins having fallen free and lying scattered and dented. Once I had gathered them, I wrapped the poncho around me and eased the knapsack on to my shoulders. It was more awkward than I had imagined and punishingly heavy, yet I was aware that all too soon its lightness would be the cause of my concern, not its burden. Upon my head I crammed my hat, lowering the brim to shield my eyes from the wind. The time to leave was overdue.

There came a final moment of hope when I trudged past the gates that led to the ruined mansion. That was the place where first I had seen Vasca and her daughter, joyful pilots as they had been. Might I find her there again? I ran to the house, my knapsack clinking with cans, and found it more forlorn than ever. I called the dog's name with renewed vigour.

Silence was my only answer.

After that, I retraced my earlier steps, maintaining a brisk, steady pace, but whereas the inward journey seemed to take no time, in reverse it was the opposite, the minutes dragging frightfully with no sense I was closer to the exit. I feared the malevolent force of this place had been toying with me, allowing simple admittance to the house, and now preparing to deny me egress. The gloom of the trees on either side grew thicker, the wind sharper. I scanned every inch of ground for mantraps.

The gates, when eventually they came into sight, had been opened wide. It was then that my nerve failed me and I broke into a run, not quite the flight of terror I had experienced the previous night but a dash, nevertheless, fretting that those rusty gates would clang shut before I should pass through them. I did not pause until they were at my rear, once again covering a fair stretch before I felt secure enough to rest – and, though I did not want to look back, some inexplicable compulsion made me reverse my view.

I expected him to be watching me, as a prisoner might do, through the bars of the gate. For me to face, one final time, that emaciated form and rotting, black poncho, that hairless head. To see those brutal, gnarled hands, one of which would be grasped around an axe.

No dark figure stood there.

And yet, if there was no one to observe my departure nor did I feel entirely alone, being unable to shake the sensation of some scrutinizing eye. I did not linger but turned from the estate to confront the perilous journey before me.

Thus was how I left Las Lágrimas, my last vision of it showing me the circumstance in which it would lie from this day forth: separated from the world-of-the-living by that wall of forest, the wind rushing through the trees like an angry sea. A dark place, an abandoned place, a place – I cannot bring myself to write it in English – *maldita por siempre jamás.**

* Cursed forever more.

The Endless Way Ahead

I HAD ESCAPED the house. In the matter of provisions, I had adequate for a week's travel and, for the moment, I remained determined, even valiant. On the deficit my nerves were shredded; I had neither compass nor map and only a vague notion in which direction to head, I taking a rudimentary bearing from the position of the sun. Perhaps my greatest trepidation came from recollecting the morning I had ridden out of Chapaledfú and how swiftly all sense of the settlement had fallen away. I might walk directly past the town, no more than a mile or two off course, and be none the wiser, trudging on thereafter until either my supplies or spirit were exhausted.

If I had allowed myself to consider it, even as I set out the odds on my perishing were high, no matter the frequency with which I encouraged myself to 'Stiffen the sinews, summon up the blood'.

That first night, I pushed on until the ground and sky merged into an immense darkness, and to maintain my flight was to risk stumbling and twisting my ankle. Some time earlier, I had reached the boundary of the estate – that line where the charred maize fields gave way to uncultivated land and the wastes began – and could say at last I was truly free of Las Lágrimas. I experienced no sense of release, if anything I grew more prone to anxiety, glancing repeatedly over my shoulder as the gloaming took hold, in high fear of some pursuing figure. Once, upon the wind, I thought I heard the howl and snap of dogs.

I found a slight depression and there laid up, eating a whole can of corned-beef, each mouthful accompanied by a pang for Vasca. Then I nestled into the tightest ball my body could manage against the weather and tried to sleep, the night so shockingly black that if my eyelids were opened or closed it made no difference.

I awakened stiffly and cold the next morning to find I had lain through the night in a patch of those rare crimson irises, the ones I had made a collection of at the quarry and that Rivacoba called *las flores del diablo*. I had no memory of seeing them – and so abundantly – when I had chosen my sleeping place, though supposed this oversight due to the darkness of the hour.

I chose a jar of peaches from my knapsack and made my breakfast but, as I chewed, a consternation took hold of me for, on closer observation, I had not slept in the midst of the flowers, rather I had curled up in an area of bare grass encircled by them. Encircled in a red ring of perfect circumference, with myself at the centre, as if the irises had been sown around me whilst I slumbered. If the notion were an improbable one, it proved stubborn to shift, adding to the burden of my anxieties as I trekked my long, windtorn path across the Pampas that day, I making sure to finish my march whilst there was light enough to choose a rest-place untouched by flowers of any kind.

The following dawn, a peculiar rattling and clinking startled me awake, the sound being of metal against metal. Even as I sat up, I saw that I was again the bullseye in a crimson circle, though it was not the irises that caused me the most immediate alarm – rather, the child crouched over my knapsack and rooting through its contents.

At first I thought myself to be dreaming, for it was the boy from the quarry. During our previous encounter his face had been in silhouette, now I saw him clearly: he had unwholesome-white skin drawn over pinched features, his hair mucky and black, and was dressed in the threadbarest of clothes, wearing neither coat nor any covering on his feet. He gave the impression of one half-starved and fully feral. I went to demand what he was doing, yet before the words could pass my lips a cold horror sluiced through me, the hairs on the nape of my neck bristling.

I knew this boy.

I had seen him before, posed next to his mother in the old daguerreotype that had hung in Tarella's cabin and lately been cradled in Moyano's lap.

Sensing that I had stirred, he turned to look at me, his eyes sunken and bright as with a fever, burning with an intense malice.

The next instant he was away, cursing me as he ran, his arms laden with my precious food. For all my fright I gave chase, for I was nothing without my supplies, demanding the thief stop and hand over what was mine. Tins fell and scattered from his grip.

And then he was gone, vanished as into thin air – though somehow I did not witness the actual moment – and all around me, in every direction, mile upon mile of empty grassland stretching to the far horizon, the only proof I had not imagined the whole episode being the trail of cans and jars.

Everywhere the child had stepped, new irises were erupting from the earth.

I salvaged the strewn items and did not even consider breakfast, wanting to be away with all haste, so that it was already the afternoon before the grumbles from my stomach compelled me to the rest. During that time, I kept a wary vigilance for the boy, ready to bolt if he appeared. Never again did I see him in body, though our encounter left me as fearful as any of those other happenings I had borne witness to. It was a dread that I was unable to shake for several days, by when the more pressing need for food came to consume my mind for, as I was about to discover, he had visited a most cruel wickedness upon me.

I found a spot for my lunch, my nerves not entirely quieted, and chose a jar of butter-beans. From the moment I twisted off the lid, and the foul smell that was released, I knew that they were inedible. Given the paucity of my rations that was a disappointment, yet worse was to come when the next proved also rancid and the corned-beef thereafter was furred with mould. I began to sort through the bag, that small stock of hope, with an overwhelming distress, nearly every item I opened being in a similar condition of putrefaction. The bottle of wine had turned to vinegar. In the end, I salvaged only a can of fish and few of beans, these items being at the very bottom of the knapsack and undisturbed by the boy; my water was about drinkable but unpleasantly brackish.

The last of these meagre resources I finished on my fifth day since leaving Las Lágrimas. If, thankfully, I did not see the malicious child again, nor awakened in any other circles of iris, during those intervening, eternal days I did stumble across great drifts of the flower, some seeming to stretch for miles like immense brushstrokes of blood daubed across the landscape. I refused to walk through them, taking instead prolonged detours that caused havoc with my route. At night, always at that moment before crossing into sleep, I was tormented by a child's anguished cries, begging for food, or else a low, mean whispering close at hand, I jerking awake and in alarm to both, the pattern recurring throughout the hours of darkness, so that I dozed only in snatches, compounding my exhaustion further. And all the while, the wind blew and blew: in squalls that lasted one or two minutes, then fell silent before the next came; to air blowing up from the south, Antarctic floes in its breath that cut to the bone; to roaring funnels that forced me to proceed bent double.

By the seventh or eighth day (I was losing count), I had begun less to walk than plod, like a pack-animal, each step being a greater effort than the one previous, an intolerable ache in every limb and joint, most especially my swollen feet. My lips became brittle and cracked from the remorseless wind. Worse than these physical complaints were the gathering whispers in my head that by now I should have reached Chapaledfú and that, in truth, I had altogether missed the station-town, thrown off course by the elaborate paths I had pursued to avoid the irises. The way ahead seemed endless, and only the most impossible of fantasies sustained me: that I might cross paths with a gaucho; that in this immeasurable land I would chance to meet Rivacoba who took me to the cosy shack he called home, where we dined on thick steaks, potatoes, pudding and wine. Unless I was vigilant, my mind turned constantly to food.

Later that night, as I lay on the ground, a gale about me and too ravenous for sleep – too ravenous even to be afraid any more – I experienced a loneliness of the most absolute kind. It was not only my present isolation that grieved me, but the awareness that no one else knew of my predicament, that there sat no person by the homefire, awake and anxious, fretting over my safe return. I grew savagely bitter at having made it through everything at Las Lágrimas, only to expire in this unconcerned emptiness, my body left for carrion, the remains perhaps never discovered. The Pampas would make a curious last resting place, I mused, for a woman born in London and raised in Cambridgeshire, whose true home existed only as a place of memory.

Where, exactly, would my soul wander?

I trod through another day, increasingly and painfully aware that my ailing physicality would not allow me to continue for much longer, telling myself 'just one more step, Little Bear, one more step' (and later, as if my mind were regressing, 'just one more step, Deborah'), putting one foot in front of the other, minute after minute, hour after hour, toward the distant horizon, and then, as dusk touched the landscape and the heavens became an enormous, mauve cupola sown with the first stars, I saw...

I saw a miracle!

Shimmering in the distance, their number accumulating in response to the hour, was a huddle of lights.

My first instinct was to abandon all caution and tear toward them, but the distance was indeterminable – several miles at least – and the darkness already thickening. In my reckless haste, I might yet cause myself an injury so severe as to render the final stage of my odyssey impossible. As much as I craved company, hot food and a bed, reason endorsed me to settle down for one last night in that great emptiness.

But now that salvation was within reach, those laments that kept me from sleeping through the dark hours visited anew, grown outraged and more determined. I heard the boy howling with hunger, begging for the least scrap of sustenance, pleading not to be left alone in the wilderness, his voice echoing at an infinite distance one moment... then near enough that I caught a taint of sour breath... then out away on the plains again. All through that black night the wretched cries continued, chiding me, imploring me, filling me with the utmost despair, until I could suffer them no more. The temptation to flee toward the town-lights was great, excepting that some intuition warned me that this was, in fact, the child's ploy. Instead, I hung my head and covered my ears, loudly entreating the voice to let me alone, not in the hope of my instruction being obeyed – rather to block out the dreadful noise.

It was in this position that, from no direction and yet all around, I felt small, cold fingers rake through my hair, tentatively at first and – when I was too stricken to respond – with a mounting viciousness, pulling and tugging at my locks, then snatching up a great bunch and yanking with all their force. I toppled backward in a state of terror, and in that instant knew for a certainty that those little hands wanted to drag me away into the darkness where never again would I be found.

I fought and scrabbled, for the hands possessed a force beyond their size, exerting all that remained of my strength, before managing to break loose, feeling a clump of my hair ripped free and fly to the wind. Already the fingers were grasping for me again, my scalp shrivelling at their icy touch, and with a courage born of desperation, I spun round with a roar to face my assailant.

None was there. I heard a final plea of need and longing – fleeting and far away – after which came only silence. And a crushing sense of desolation.

It was at the extremes of fatigue and hunger that I tramped into town the next morning, not Chapaledfú as had been my purpose (for the streets were asphalted, the buildings more numerous and of brick) but, as later I learnt, Las Flores, where several weeks prior I had changed trains to catch the branch-line. How that felt a lifetime ago; how I felt another woman. It was market day, the place lively with gauchos and cattle, though as I passed by people would cease in their activity to gawp at me and whisper.

I made my way to the town's one hotel, where I took a room and immediately ordered the hot water service, so that I might bathe, and a huge breakfast. Before either could be fetched, I had slumped on to my bed, descending into a fathomless sleep that lasted the length of the day through to the next. A sleep full of nightmares and delirium. For now that I was back to safety, to the comings-and-goings of everyday life, the floodgates of my recent experiences were set to open. At night, my screams woke the entire establishment, so that the following morning the proprietor was obliged to visit and anxiously enquire whether I had any relations or associates he might contact to aid me. I could think of no one other than the Houghtons to whom a message was dispatched, Mrs Houghton and Bernadice arriving in short time with the family's physician. All three were unmistakably shaken at what they found, at my limp, emaciated appearance and, most especially, terrorized countenance, for I did not need a mirror to know how wild I must appear.

The doctor made an examination of me and, though I shared none of the details with him save for my long trek, he said it was evident that my system had suffered a considerable shock. Malnutrition, he diagnosed, combined with the worst case of 'mental turmoil' he had ever attended, he going on to suggest that his preferred course for my recuperation would be for me to return home, to Britain. When I declined, he ordered at the very least an extended period of rest and that I required feeding-up.

'I think, too,' he added, 'you've had more than your share of the Pampas. A change of environment is what you need, Señorita. Some place to clear the mind.'

'Perhaps a dose of good sea air,' suggested Mrs Houghton, to solemn agreement all round.

And so I travelled to Mar del Plata and my room, here, at the Hotel Bristol. The rest the reader knows.

For five days I have sat at my bureau, breaking not once, reliving those terrible experiences, every word of them the truth. Now my fingers are stiff and stained with ink; my head is heavy and, I hope, ready to drop. For the first time since I arrived at the Bristol my bed looks inviting.

There is nothing else to write. I feel weary beyond belief. Emptied out. Wanting but one thing. To let my eyes close and drift dreamlessly away.

My story is told.

Please, God, let me sleep.

OCTOBER 1913

Postscript

WRITE IT ALL down, I had imagined Grandfather saying, and *it will trouble you no further.*

If, however, I hoped the words committed to this journal would see a lessening of my anguish, I was bitterly disappointed.

In the small hours, nightmares continued to haunt me: visions of a limping, dark figure; of forest paths lethal with traps; of the mouths of dogs, beslobbered with blood. Many a night I startled awake to the echo of an axe. During the insomniac stretch that followed, as I waited for daybreak, I subjected myself to rigorous introspection. Amidst all the horrors I had endured, I could not free my thoughts of Moyano's gouged wrist and how, in his death throes, he had wanted to grasp the picture of Tarella's family; the stench of ombú smoke seemed lodged in my nose.

In examining my tumultuous psyche, I came to understand that I still had so many unanswered questions from Las

Lágrimas (elements unexplained, pieces that seemed part of a whole yet which remained inchoate), my conclusion being that as much as I wanted to discard the whole experience, only the truth had the power to change my prospects and set me free. Or so I trusted. There was but one I could think of who might be able to help and I sent a pleading telegram to his offices:

> HAVE LEFT L LÁGRIMAS STOP AGRAMONTES'
> SON LIKELY DEAD STOP MYSELF LUCKY TO
> BE ALIVE STOP PLEASE I MUST TALK TO
> YOU STOP

Berganza replied post-haste, informing me that he would catch the first train from Tandil to arrive by the day-after-next.

Hearsay & Speculation

'I'VE HAD YOU on my mind, Ursula,' said Berganza as he greeted me, taking my hand to his lips. 'The more so since the Agramontes arrived at the hospital.'

I had taken advantage of one of the Bristol's private dining rooms and arranged a luncheon for us, ordering a generous spread (I had not forgotten the nurseryman's appetite), kept hot in chaffing dishes so we might serve ourselves and not be disturbed by waiting staff – albeit, in the end, he only picked at the food and I ate not at all. The decanter of port on the table between us was a different matter, Berganza swallowing copious glasses throughout. His voice was less booming than I remembered, his appearance haggard, as if he were recovering from a nasty bout of grippe or his recent sleep little better than mine. Grey strands veined his black beard. We settled into our chairs, his eyes assessing my face.

'I feared for you, my dear,' he confided.

'Do you know what happened to their son?'

'It has been the talk of Tandil, and none of it good. I'm afraid to tell you the boy died.'

I received this news sorrowfully, though I cannot say it came as the greatest shock. 'Do you still believe it to be coincidence?' I challenged him. 'Or will you admit there was a curse? Perhaps, you suspected it all along.'

When no response was forthcoming, other than an aversion of his gaze to study his port wine, I told him all that had happened since last we made our leave, not those matters concerning Moyano or Dolores (nor especially the subsequent incident in the maid's room) – but the lights in the trees, the axeman and the lake, the mantrap, my glimpse of Tarella and those dreadful, dreadful events I had borne witness to on the final night, my voice increasingly shrill and unrecognizable as the words spilled forth. When I described Moyano's end, something told darkly upon Berganza's expression; that aside, he listened mostly without reaction.

'I do not believe you told me the whole truth, Señor,' I said after I had come to the end of my story and received still no answer. He had opened his cigar-box in that time: the air around him swirled, thick and acrid.

'No,' he conceded at last and with more than a hint of self-reproach. 'No, I did not. I promise you, Ursula, I thought none of it to do with you. I never thought you would come to harm. You seemed so proud of your new position; I did not want to be the one to frighten you away.'

'Will you tell me now?'

There was another extended silence, which Berganza seemed determined not to break. Underneath the table I was aware of him drumming his fingers against his leg.

'Please, Señor,' I demanded, in obvious agitation.

'I would rather not – but fear I must.' He drained the last of his port with resolution and rose. 'Come, let us take some air, to clear the cobwebs from my head. My wife and I had our *viaje de novios* here' – I had acquired a new Tauchnitz dictionary: honeymoon – 'the oceanside was always our favourite spot.'

He spoke no more until we were walking along the water's edge. To an observer, catching us from a distance, we may have appeared as father and daughter on the point of confiding grave news in the other: his incurable illness, her broken engagement. Despite the barometer in the lobby of the Bristol set at 'Fair', the Atlantic was a seething grey mass that churned and boomed against the shore, a dilute and watery sun struggling through the clouds. Seagulls reeled above, their cries high and piercing. As the waves reached their highest point on the sand, to be roughly dragged back, I thought of poorest Lola.

'What I am to tell you,' began the nurseryman, lowering his voice for all that the beach was sparsely populated, 'I did not see myself. My father shared some, when he was dying and fearful of the priest, when perhaps he had reason not to be the most reliable, but much is hearsay and speculation. To a point everything I recounted before was true: the Don dismissing Romero Lepping, tasking Tarella with the garden instead, leaving for the Old World…'

'And then?'

'To encourage his labour, Don Guido struck a bargain with Tarella, promising him a peso, a silver peso, for every tree he laid down. Whether the Don was sincere in his offer, whether he conceived of how many trees Tarella might plant,

I do not know. What is certain is that Tarella undertook his task with astounding industry. He was a simple fellow with no means other than the toil of his hands, and though happy enough, he wanted more for his family. A little land to call their own, perhaps a garden for himself: something to pass on to his son. And now Tarella found himself with an opportunity few men ever get. A peso a tree, begod! Can you imagine the reward? So he slaved away, year after year, planting a forest as he had been instructed to until, at last, Don Guido returned home.'

Now that the truth was at hand I felt my mouth dry and, though I could not be harmed by whatever came next, still my heart kicked against my ribcage like a trapped animal. Berganza saw my expression: I nodded at him to go on.

'My father told me the scene took place in that octagonal room Don Guido demanded be built to display the souvenirs of his European trip; it was yet half-finished. Amidst the trestles and builder's mess, Tarella presented his employer with a bill for tens of thousands, the very fee that had been agreed by the two men years earlier. A fee to the value of – if not greater than – the entire estancia! The Don would rather have razed Las Lágrimas to the ground than hand it over to any man, least of all a servant. He refused to pay or consider any settlement, no matter how meagre, accusing Tarella of extortion and, when he dared to protest, had the gardener flogged. Flogged in front of the whole staff before hounding him and his family from the estate.'

'What of their contract?' I said, aghast. 'When last we spoke you said Tarella's wife had insisted upon one. What of all the receipts I showed you? They must have proven something.'

Berganza shrugged uneasily, one might go so far as to say, guiltily. 'There was a trial – not at the local magistrates but the courthouse in Buenos Aires. Tarella, of course, lost. What chance ever did he have? A simple labourer against one of the wealthiest, most powerful men in all the country.'

'Is there any wonder he cursed Agramonte?'

'That was yet to come for, in the meantime, the Tarella family were left with no choice but the slums. It pains me to think, Ursula, how a man born of the Pampas, of wide spaces and greenery, suffered in the squalor of the city. He took whatever navvy work he could, his wife found employ in one of the meat-factories. Then, as if Fortune had chosen to hate these people, there was an accident at the factory – a fire – though it was to be many months before Señora Tarella succumbed to her injuries. It was during that time, I think, that thoughts of revenge took hold of her husband's mind. If he had been cheated of his silver, then so would Don Guido be of his trees. Thereafter, Tarella returned to Las Lágrimas to begin a campaign of poisoning the roots and, when this did not satisfy the violence of the injustice Tarella felt, he took an axe to the trunks.'

'Rather a futile gesture, I would say, given their number.'

'A declaration, nevertheless. It was when he felled one of those magnificent ombús on the approach to the house that Don Guido acted. He put down traps, waited with men and dogs to capture Tarella – the climax of which you know more vividly than I.'

It was a memory I had fought to hold sway, kept at the fringes of my mind, but at that moment the images rushed upon me in all their unmitigated horror. 'To die in such a manner,' I said. 'To be torn apart by dogs.'

'But Tarella did not die – even if his disfiguring does not bear consideration. Perhaps from mercy the Don spared him and called off the pack, perhaps he wanted him alive to prolong the gardener's suffering. He had Tarella banished to the monastery near Chigüido,* at the edge of the Pampas, and there the wretched gardener spent his final days, consumed by a misery and hatred so intense that the Jesuits who tended him came to quake at their duty, he raving in anguish for himself and his son.'

'His son?'

'They had been together on that fateful night, and when the child could not release his father from the mantrap, Tarella urged him to flee.'

'*Run*,' I murmured. '*Get away from this place. As far as you can go…*'

'The boy escaped on to the Pampas, and though Agramonte's men pursued, no sign of him was seen ever again. He must have perished out in the wilds, lost and starved to death, crying for his father. Tarella must have known it also. You are too young to appreciate it, Ursula, but there is no more unbearable sorrow than knowledge you have failed to protect your offspring. It was said that, in his torment, Tarella wrung

---

* Most likely the Monasteiro de San Ignacio though I have been unable to verify this since the original building was destroyed in a landslide in 1883 and all records lost.

his hands till they were raw. Picked endlessly at his crippled ankle. Tore from his head every last shred of hair.

'Finally, he died, cursing Don Guido to the last, vowing vengeance for everything that had been taken from him. Vowing that as he had lost his son, so too would the Don – and every other Agramonte that followed.' The nurseryman's whole attitude answered my own, expressive of pity and revulsion. 'The Jesuits sent word that they had given him a Christian burial. As soon as Tarella was returned to the earth, an axeman was seen to walk the grounds of the estate. The Don's prize stags were slaughtered, the throat of every last animal cut in a single night. The guest mansion caught fire and the Doña hideously scarred. His son drowned. Thereafter, Las Lágrimas was abandoned.'

'Until the estate came to the present Don.'

Berganza nodded gravely.

'What of this story does he know?'

'That, Señorita Kelp, you would have to enquire of him yourself.'

'Did you visit him in Tandil?'

'Doña Javiera is from Montevideo. The family have gone there and will see no one.'

After that we spoke no more, us both brooding over our own unquiet thoughts, reversing the route we had taken along the beach. I was working myself up to the final question I had surely to ask. When we reached that set of footprints that first had brought us from the Bristol to the margin of the waves I sensed that Berganza, his business now told, desired only to be away. I did not try to dissuade him, wanting to be alone to churn over all that had been disclosed to me.

For his candour, I thanked the nurseryman.

'I do not think we'll see each other again,' was his reply, he solemnly taking my hand and clasping it until, all at once, I blurted out:

'There is one last thing I must know, Señor.'

He sighed bleakly, as if in expectation of this. 'Yes.'

'You were a friend of Moyano?'

'We knew each other from before. It was I who proposed him to Don Paquito.'

'How did he appear to you on the day of your visit?'

The nurseryman pondered my question. 'If I am honest, not quite right.'

'By which you mean?'

'He seemed distracted, or else absorbed by some private matter. He was not himself.'

'Do you think…' I pictured him again at his last with his shaved, razor-nicked scalp. 'Do you think he might have been possessed by whatever power haunted Las Lágrimas?'

'I am not sure such things are possible.'

'But some thought troubles you.'

'When I said Tarella died, I did not tell you the cause. In his cell, he was permitted nothing by which he might harm himself or others. But the day of his death, he appeared less demented of mind and begged the Jesuits for a flower to look upon. Not a cutting. A living flower, in soil. Thinking no harm could be done by it, and that it might signal a change in the gardener, the priests obliged, bringing Tarella a pot with a bloom in it. When later he was discovered, he had broken that pot into pieces, taken the most jagged shard and with it opened his wrists so that none could stem the flow of blood.'

I felt sickened to my heart.

'I shall say a prayer for his soul tonight,' I said, when at last I found the words. 'For his son and wife also.'

'Praying will not help. See what little it achieved for Guido Agramonte.'

'Then what?' I begged.

'Let us simply hope that Don Paquito's daughter is never with child. And most certainly not a boy. Now I must hurry, if I'm to catch the three o'clock train.'

I watched him hasten away across the dull, damp sand and, for a long time after, made no attempt to follow, I simply standing there, trying to imagine what comforts Grandfather would have offered in response to these revelations. Struggle as I might, I could not summon his voice, the only sound to fill my thoughts being the unceasing beat of the ocean. And so I remained, unaware of the world except for the wind tugging at my hair, until, eventually, dusk closed over me. One by one the lights along the rambla came to life, their brightness serving only to deepen the darkness. Then, as if in a trance, I made my way toward them.

Before the week was out, I had left Argentina for good.

W.M. Cleese is the pen name of a bestselling thriller writer. He studied literature at London University before moving to Brazil from where he travelled widely across South America, including Argentina. At an estancia in the Pampas he was told a curious tale about the planting of a forest that he never forgot and which became the basis for *The Haunting of Las Lágrimas*.

He currently lives in rural East Anglia, near Anningley Hall, setting of 'The Mezzotint', his favourite M.R. James ghost story.

@wm_cleese

For more fantastic fiction, author events,
exclusive excerpts, competitions, limited editions and more

VISIT OUR WEBSITE
titanbooks.com

LIKE US ON FACEBOOK
facebook.com/titanbooks

FOLLOW US ON TWITTER AND INSTAGRAM
@TitanBooks

EMAIL US
readerfeedback@titanemail.com